MW00412593

CONUNDRUM

C. S. Lakin

Boulder Creek, CA

CONUNDRUM by C. S. Lakin

Copyright ©2012 by C. S. Lakin
All Rights Reserved

This book is a work of fiction. The names, characters, places, and incidents are products of the writer's imagination or have been used fictitiously and are not to be construed as real. Any resemblance to persons living or dead, or actual events, locales, or organizations is entirely coincidental.

ISBN-13: 978-0615687629
ISBN-10: 0615687628
LCCN: 2001012345

Cover designed by Jessica Bell
Interior designed by Ellie Searl, Publishista®

Morgan Hill, CA

Novels by C. S. Lakin

CONTEMPORARY SUSPENSE / MYSTERY

Someone to Blame
Innocent Little Crimes
A Thin Film of Lies
Intended for Harm

FANTASY

The Gates of Heaven Series
The Wolf of Tebron
The Map across Time
The Land of Darkness
The Unraveling of Wentwater
The Crystal Scepter (2013)
The Sands of Ethryn (2013)

SCI-FI

Time Sniffers

To my mother
If only . . .

CHAPTER 1

June 1986

THE CONUNDRUM WENT LIKE THIS:

A man walks into a nondescript restaurant tucked away in an alley. It's taken him years to find such a place, and his agitation is palpable. He orders albatross—broiled. With trembling hands, he picks up his fork and knife and slices off a piece of the seared white flesh. Juices drip onto his plate as he brings the morsel to his mouth. The aroma nauseates him as he squeezes his eyes shut and bites down.

The man's weathered face relaxes. He sighs, sets the knife and fork down on the starched linen tablecloth, and places a hand over his heart, as if to calm its beating.

He smiles at the waiter, who bows politely and attends to the other diners. Relief washes in absolution. He raises his eyes to heaven and whispers, but no one hears him.

"Thank God, I'm free."

OF ALL THE WACKY CONUNDRUMS Raff piled on us over the years, that was the hardest—if I discounted the convoluted tale of the surgeon who performed a highly skilled operation, yet was supposed to be missing an arm. It took Neal and me three days of battering

Raff with desperate yes-or-no questions to arrive at the answer. I remembered him gloating, sporting that sixties' Beatles haircut so popular back then, his black straggly bangs falling into his brooding pubescent eyes. He never relinquished hints—even when we begged out of frustration. Even when we beat him with pillows and punched his arms as hard as we could. Raff loved to wield his secret knowledge over us measly peons of his intellectual kingdom, a king with the power to wave his scepter and send dissenters to the gallows of humiliation—something he often did.

And the answer was so simple, as most of those conundrums were.

A group of starving shipwrecked soldiers during World War II resorted to cannibalism before an unexpected rescue. But to alleviate guilt, one group ate human flesh, and the other, albatross—the only meat they could find on their deserted island. No one knew which they were served; thus, they could assuage their consciences, live in blissful ignorance. But the man in our conundrum had spent his life in anguish, needing to know. Until that question was answered, he would have no peace. He somehow had to find a way to taste albatross before he died. The truth—so late in coming—set him free.

I wondered—as I tromped up the fourth flight of stairs—what would have happened if he had taken that bite and didn't recognize the albatross, recoiling in the realization he had eaten various body parts of his friends? Would he still have felt free? The gist of the conundrum implied no, but that fabricated story begged the question: does freedom lie in the absolving of guilt . . . or in the liberating wings of truth?

Was discovering truth what really set him free?

That's what I needed to know, random musings as I marched up the stairwell of Hillcrest Hospital and Mental Health Clinic on the drab, foggy morning of June sixteenth.

The sixth floor. It could have been worse.

One time I'd had a podiatrist appointment in the city and forgot to ask. Already out of breath from finding a parking spot seven long blocks away, my heart berated me when I checked in at the lobby reception desk and learned my doctor's office was situated on the seventeenth floor. I nearly turned and headed back out the beckoning glass revolving doors—my right foot coaxing me with unrelenting pain. No way was I going to make it up seventeen flights of stairs in my Hopalong Cassidy gait.

I allowed myself only a token glance at the elevator doors. How smoothly they opened, their shushing sound so inviting. But I knew their deceptive appearance wouldn't fool my gut. I'd be clawing the slick metal walls of the elevator by the third floor—it didn't matter how big and roomy the space. I asked the receptionist to let my doctor know I'd be late, then found the stairs and hoofed it to her lofty office that boasted a sweeping view of the Golden Gate Bridge half buried in a shroud of fog. I had arrived sweaty and disheveled, with my foot on fire. I never made that mistake again.

I stopped at the landing of the hospital's fifth floor and caught my breath. Nausea racked my body, and a wave of dizziness made me grab the railing. I consciously slowed my breathing and clamped down on all the fears battering the door to my heart, insistent on breaking in and trampling me down. Why, in the midst of my own maelstrom, did Raff have to do this? I had neither the time nor the energy to face him and his demons, when my own were a clamoring mob at the edges of my sanity.

I couldn't get that T. S. Eliot poem out of my head. *Prufrock*. Raff used to recite it, among hundreds of others. When he wasn't rattling off pi to the hundredth digit—just because he could. Or Edward Lear's "The Owl and the Pussycat,"—in French, no less. I still can recall the first few lines from, what, sixth grade? *"Hibou et Minou allèrent à la mer, dans une barque peinte en jaune-canari . . ."* That was during his French phase in junior high school, when he thought the girls would find him hopelessly attractive, fashioned after some nineteenth-century Don Juan, with a swath of hair falling into his mooning eyes, spouting poetry from the Romantic era.

Neal and I never thought to ask why. Why in the world memorize everything under the sun?

So, as I pounded one step after another, the phrases tumbled into my brain effortlessly. *"And indeed there will be time to wonder, 'Do*

I dare?' and 'Do I dare?' Time to turn back and descend the stair . . . with a bald spot in the middle of my hair . . ."

The poem lent itself to a nice cadence as I arrived, finally, to the sixth floor stairwell door, a bit out of breath from my recitation.

"Do I dare disturb the universe? In a minute there is time for decisions and revisions which a minute will reverse."

Now was the moment of decision. Like I had a choice? No one else in our family dared talk Raff out of his slouch toward destruction. I snorted as I pushed the heavy metal door open to a shiny bright corridor with glossy linoleum floors—so spotlessly clean I saw my scowling face looking up at me in all clarity. What made me think I could help him, when a half dozen doctors and psychiatrists couldn't?

"Streets that follow like a tedious argument of insidious intent. To lead you to an overwhelming question . . . Oh, do not ask, 'What is it?' Let us go and make our visit."

That was all the prompting I needed.

Raff had checked himself into this facility two days ago amid protests from both his wife and therapist. "They tell me it's all in my head," he said from a pay phone near his office, before he drove toward North Beach that morning. "You think? Styron calls it a brainstorm. Of course it's in my friggin' head! Like suicidal depression rages in your big toe?" All I could think of while he ranted in his manic passion was: Could he make it to the hospital without smashing his beautiful lipstick orange Ferrari 412? Kendra would throw a hissy fit over that.

He didn't want visitors, but tough, he would see me. I'd play the only role I was good at in this family—caretaker and nurturer. What a joke, I thought, with my life unraveling like a sweater thread caught in a blender.

My mother told me in her typical cryptic manner not to indulge Raff in his misery. That he was only having a temporary breakdown; give him a few days and he'd be back home with his wife and kids, making loads of money at the bank so he could keep up the payments on his palatial estate in Tiburon. Keep it all hush-hush, no one needed to know. Give him forty-eight hours, a drug cocktail, and this too shall pass.

I could just see my mother restraining her seething with a tight smile. "Get a grip, Raff," she probably said. *For the children's sake.* More like for her sake. Nothing like a little drama to put a crimp in her schedule. I mean, those jaunts from Marin into the city to the hospital were such inconveniences.

But forgive my embellishing. I thought nothing of the kind that day. My whole mind wrapped around only Raff and his pain. Ungrounded, unprovoked, and entirely unacceptable pain.

I heard how he fell apart at work the week before. Kendra had to come get him, between dropping the twins off at ballet and picking up Kevin from baseball practice. Raff had locked himself in his office and was trying to crawl out the transom window of his ninth-story office, yearning for the ledge and oblivion below. Good thing he was a hefty six foot two and the window was a bit too narrow for his bulk. Good thing Raff had a problem with broken glass—the way I had a problem with balloons. I couldn't even stand in the same room at birthday parties with a clown twisting those skinny balloons into wiener dogs and rubber crowns without going into simulated cardiac arrest. Besides, I imagined those glass panes in Raff's fancy banking center were shatterproof, and possibly even bulletproof. He hadn't gotten very far by the time security had hacksawed through the dead bolt and pried him away from the window, where he collapsed in a weepy mess into a guard's arms.

So my mother had told me—although Kendra would have denied it. In the thirteen years they'd been married, I'd never seen my brother's wife lift more than an eyebrow in ire. Not an elevated pitch in tone, not a single curse word under her breath. She could win the award for stalwart and unruffled under adversity. What adversity? You couldn't tell me living with my brother was a walk in the park. Or did Raff only dump his histrionics on his blood relatives? Well, he knew how to keep up appearances too.

I found Raff sitting on the edge of his neatly made bed in what could have passed for a rundown Motel 6 room, albeit without windows. The nurse at the entrance station had pointed me down an echoing hallway, where I marched to the end, trying not to glance at the other patients populating the ward. But they sure noticed me. Eyes locked so tightly, my breath squeezed from my ribcage. *"I should have been a pair of ragged claws scuttling across the floors of silent seas . . ."*

Raff's face was pasty and lined. Bits of skin flaked across his forehead and his hands trembled in his lap, as if he had palsy. He looked fifty, not thirty-three. I awkwardly waited for him to stand and embrace me, but he only sat there and lifted his face, his slippered feet dangling slightly off the side of the high bed, making him look even more lost and little. He forced a smile, but I could see in that simple gesture how much it cost him.

"Hey, welcome to the Hotel California. You can check out anytime you like . . ."

"But you can never leave." I grinned like a gawky high school girl trying to make conversation with the cute boy at the lockers. "Well," I said, taking in the pukey green walls and drab furniture. "Not five-star accommodations, but . . ." I shrugged. My brother, swimming in wealth, who traveled first class and ordered only the most expensive wines—the cost of one bottle more than Jeremy brought home in a week. I wondered if Kendra had visited yet. If she would.

"For twelve hundred a day, they could at least give us better food. If you aren't sure you want to die before you check in, the green Jell-O and powdered mashed potatoes remove all doubt." A chuckle escaped his chapped lips, but it was empty of joy. I could tell he shaved, but with the taboo on razors in this place, I guessed he used an electric shaver. I caught him looking longingly at my purse.

"Sorry," I said. "They went through it at the nurse's station. Took my gun, switchblade, and my bottle of prescription pills." Raff's eyes radiated hunger and disappointment.

He stood and walked over to the doorway and looked toward a lounge area. "I tried to scrounge some plastic bags out of the trash. They're thorough here. Years of experience. Hard to suffocate on a Baggie or a candy bar wrapper. Ever try it?"

A few patients sat in front of a TV mounted on the wall, looking fairly drugged. But maybe that's how everyone looked when they watched the soaps for endless hours a day.

"All the windows have bars. No bathtubs. No stoppers in the sinks. You don't even get plastic knives with dinner. They cut up your food."

I pictured green Jell-O in little cubes. Tough, overcooked, and unidentifiable meat in small bite-size squares. Twelve hundred a day.

Raff continued. "This is like going through your second childhood—in case you missed your first. Except this one's more warped, like something out of Kakfa." He shifted into a dramatic voice. " 'As Gregor Samsa awoke one morning from uneasy dreams, he found himself transformed in his bed into a gigantic vermin.' You know, most translators used the word *insect*, but the German word implies an unclean animal. Fitting for this place, wouldn't you say? One day you're a normal human being, the next . . . vermin." His voice sounded hoarse, his throat dry.

"Will they let me bring in Chinese?" I shook the image of Raff as a giant cockroach out of my head.

"And take a chance you'd laced it with arsenic, to speed me on my merry way? Deprive them of their joy in handing me my plastic tray full of slop three times a day? Not gonna happen." Raff started shuffling down the hallway and I followed. "Let me give you the five-cent tour." His voice carried and bounced off the scrubbed and shiny walls. No one noticed.

As Raff ambled, he pointed out the drug station where they handed him a paper cup of water and his meds three times a day. He named the patients we passed, who loitered around or sat with pained expressions on their faces. Pain filled every space of this place, thick and contagious.

"That's Gladys," he said, nodding at an older woman in a shabby housedress. "She's been here for years. Slicing wrists her forte. Whereas Josh over there"—I looked over at a young guy, nearly emaciated, flipping a deck of cards in his hand—"loves pills. Any shape, any color. The more the merrier. Pops M&Ms just to keep in practice."

My mind wandered as Raff droned on, evidently growing pleased with his crass humor. And perhaps glad to have a riveted audience giving him undivided attention. Here, he would be listened to. Not like in the real world, where his antics for help fell unnoticed. Or, rather, were squelched in embarrassment. When you made tons of money, had a beautiful wife and three adorable kids—when you were the envy of your community and coworkers—you had no right to behave badly. Stop whining, chin up, take Prozac, and pretend your pain isn't ravaging your soul. Millions of Americans suffered from depression—and they took pills and were fine, just fine. Except for the ones that did manage to off themselves. But, that's not polite conversation in upscale circles. Designer drugs, yes. Suicidal mania, no.

My heart literally wrenched in pain. Like someone had grabbed it and squeezed hard, forcing tears out my eyes. "Hey," I said, when we had returned to his room. I sat in the only seat—a stained, heavily upholstered armchair that looked like the ones adorning those old downtown hotel lobbies. Something from a bygone era. "Remember those conundrums you used to tell?"

His eyes brightened. "Yeah, all of them. That was a while back. Let's see. You remember the guy who takes the elevator down from his apartment to the first floor? By the time the doors open, he knows his wife is dead."

Oh, that one. Something about a wife hooked up to an iron lung and the power going out. I threw one out that came to mind. "What about the one where the guy gets ready for bed, turns out the light, and in the morning hears something on the radio—then kills himself?"

I immediately cringed. Should I have been talking about people committing suicide?

Raff smiled. "Yeah, the lighthouse keeper. An ocean liner crashes because he turned out the wrong light." He grunted. "Come to think of it, most of those conundrums are about death."

That cheery thought actually seemed to lighten his mood. His brain started spinning in familiar fashion. My brilliant brother—who had named every plastic dinosaur and army man—even his houseplants and the rocks he collected from Glass Beach. Boxes and albums full of coins and stamps with not a one missing, even if it meant spending six month's allowance to get that rare mint coin. His an ordered mind and an even more ordered world.

Everything accounted for, nothing missing, no unsolved puzzles. That, as far back as I could remember.

Raff expounded a litany. "There's the one about the guy lying facedown in the desert with an unopened package. The guy hanging dead in an empty locked room, next to a puddle of water. The guy found drowned in the ocean with a drinking straw clutched in his hand."

They all came barging back into my head: the parachute, the block of ice, the third man who couldn't fit into the lifeboat and drew the short straw.

There was always a simple answer, once you figured it out.

Raff stopped talking and tears filled his eyes. The moment hung in the silence, like a sheet flapping on a clothesline in a vast, empty field. He had run out of steam. I couldn't begin to imagine the effort it took him to present a normal face to the rest of the world. *"There will be time to prepare a face to meet the face that you meet . . ."*

He collapsed on the bed and lay prone, staring at the ceiling.

"All I want to do is die, Lis. And all I keep thinking is how Kevin and Ashley and Brittany will hate me for leaving them—just as I hated Dad for doing this to me."

My breath caught in my throat. His words were filled with venom. Our father had died of leukemia at thirty-three, leaving behind three small children and a bereaved wife. My brother hated him for copping out on life—the coward! We had heard the story throughout our lives: how Dad suffered from depression. How he had later found his real father, a shlub who had abandoned him during the Great Depression. How this shock made him feel unworthy and dirty. He had bad blood, and so gave himself a blood disease—leukemia. So the fairy tale went. Raff was eight when our dad died. I was only four and didn't remember him at all.

But Raff remembered. He remembered everything. I cursed his perfect memory.

"I know this sounds stupid and irrational, but I can't help it. I can't outlive my father. How can I do this to my children, cause them this pain—" Raff moaned with agony. Tears filled his eyes and spilled onto his cheeks, as if oozing out of his very being.

How could I help him? How could anyone help him? Manic depression was not something you could cure with reason. Raff knew he had a great life, that he was supposed to be happy. No one would willingly inflict bereavement on their own children. No doubt, the guilt over his impending appointment with death was almost as debilitating as the pain.

"The doctors will find you the right meds. Something will work . . ." I knew I shouldn't have said that. *"I am no prophet—and here's no great matter; I have seen the moment of my greatness flicker, and I have seen the eternal Footman hold my coat, and snicker, and, in short, I was afraid . . ."*

Raff rumbled in fury. "The drugs take weeks to kick in, if they work at all. If they don't, you start all over and you wait. Do you have a clue what this pain is like? How every damn second is a knife in your heart? You have no idea!"

No, I didn't. I clamped my mouth shut. I had to believe in our age of miracle medicine that a drug was out there, one that would give Raff some semblance of a normal life. If he could hang on that long.

But would that solve everything? Erase the anger and resentment? Wash away the disappointment and feelings of abandonment he'd carried like an albatross around his neck his whole life?

My mind flashed to that conundrum—where the guy in the restaurant ordered albatross. The truth set him free. Was there a truth to be found out there to solve the most perplexing conundrum of all?

The one that went like this:

A man, with a happy marriage and three wonderful children, a great job as a mathematician and physicist for an aerospace company, decides one day he does not want to keep living. He wills himself to die and develops leukemia. Nine months later, he is dead.

I suddenly understood Raff's lifetime obsession with categorizing everything neatly in its place. All to make up for the one glaring element that didn't fit in anywhere—our father's inexplicable death.

Was that all there was to the puzzle? *Or was there more?*

I sucked in a breath. In all my thirty years of life I had never stopped to ask that question. That was the pat answer we were given and so we believed it. Our mother's words played like a broken record in my head: "You're too young to understand. When you grow up, it'll make sense."

But I'd grown up and it didn't make sense.

For the first time in my life, that explanation rang false. Could I write my father's death off as simple manic depression, an illness that obviously ran in the family? A death wish born from a chemical imbalance in the brain?

But really—could people *will* themselves into developing leukemia? I knew practically nothing about the disease other than it had to do with blood and bone marrow and white cells. That it wasn't contagious or genetic, so we kids didn't need to worry we'd get it. New Age philosophy and holistic medicine might claim you could contract a disease psychosomatically. And I understood that—to a point. You could make yourself sick from stress. But give yourself cancer? My mother always spoke as if it were established medical fact. Want to die? Give yourself the corresponding disease. Feel unworthy as a woman? Give yourself breast cancer. And so the line of reasoning went.

What if Raff's real problem was not manic depression? What if it stemmed from the years of pain and anger roiling under the surface of his self-esteem? What if abandonment mixed with misunderstanding had created a poison just as debilitating as depression? What if the truth could be uncovered?

I dared to imagine . . . what if there was some truth out there that could set him free? Was the freedom in the absolution? Or in knowing the truth? Could I single-handedly solve this one conundrum—the only one that really mattered?

Our father's expertise was in something called Boolean algebra. It sounded like some Middle Eastern dance to me. That form of mathematics was a precursor to the developing of computers, something my father worked on in the fifties. A system of logic operators where a question could be answered in one of three ways: *and, or, not.* Only recently, I had been thumbing through a book of brain teasers and startled at finding a Boolean algebra conundrum, of all things.

Two guards each stand before a door. Only one is the door leading to enlightenment. One of the guards always lies; the other always tells the truth. You want to open the door to enlightenment, yet you can only ask one question, and only of one guard. What is the only question you can ask that will tell you, with certainty, which door you must choose?

Well, without going into a lengthy discourse to explain how the algebra figures in, the answer was this: Ask either guard this question: "Will the *other* guard say he is posted at the door that leads to enlightenment?" If the guard you asked answered yes, the door behind him was the correct door. If he said no, it was the other door. It's simple, once you saw how the parts all broke down. Boolean algebra reverted to simplicity. In any problem, there was only AND, OR, or NOT. Either "this answer AND that answer are both correct," or "This answer OR that answer is correct," or "NOT any of the answers are correct."

As I hugged Raff good-bye, leaving him floundering in his pain, venting his anger at me, I thought about finding that door to enlightenment. I thought about the answers we'd been given for our father dying. Maybe we never asked the right questions that led to the right door.

I grunted as I started back down the stairs. We never asked *any* questions, did we? So how did we know whether or not the guard was telling the truth or lying?

My mother's face came to mind. Every time we had tried to ask her questions about Dad, she changed the subject. Never once in my entire childhood had she talked about him, or her marriage. The facts I had about my father would barely fill half a page.

He grew up in New York. Spent years in one foster home after another until that nice couple took him in and raised him. Had a brother who was adopted with him into the Sitteroff family.

Married our mother, joined the Merchant Marines near the end of the war, came back to work in LA for the Penwell Corporation. Spoke seven languages, accepted some award in Belgium for physics, took our mother to Paris for their honeymoon. Twelve gloriously happy years of marriage until the day he decided to die—the truth according to Ruth Sitteroff.

I'd only seen two photographs of him—that's all our mother had. One of him in his Merchant Marine uniform and the other a family portrait right after Neal was born. Eight months before our father died. A lot of blanks to fill in. And just what happened to that brother of his—my uncle? Was he still alive, and why had we never seen him while growing up?

Suddenly, I had way too many questions. They overflowed, like lava spewing from a volcano, burning my insides. I rushed out of the hospital into the foggy street, thinking obtusely how the gray swallowing up the streets of San Francisco reflected my mental state. I knew just where to go first to look for answers, but I doubted they would be readily forthcoming. *"And should I then presume? And how should I begin?"*

My mind brewed with ideas, and I felt a headache coming on from lack of sleep. After a volatile argument that had dragged on past midnight, I hadn't been able to konk out until after three a.m. Thinking of finding Jeremy waiting at home flared the ache in my sinuses. But where else was I to go? I had a barnyard of orphans waiting to be fed, and a doe about to kid.

"Should I, after tea and cakes and ices, have the strength to force the moment to its crisis?"

I couldn't get the image of the man in the restaurant out of my head.

I'm free, he said.

Did the truth really set you free? Or was that too simple? Maybe there were no answers at all. *And, or*, or *not*?

I loved the last lines of Eliot's brilliant poem. *"We have lingered in the chambers of the sea . . . by sea-girls wreathed with seaweed red and brown . . ."*

Those lines tickled my consciousness the whole drive home, over the Golden Gate Bridge, up the corridor through Marin

County, even as I bounced along the long rutted dirt road with the brown rolling hills languishing in early summer's heat a backdrop to my small farmhouse in Petaluma. I pulled up in the circular drive and cut the engine. Buster and Angel, my two rescued mutts, galloped from around the side of the house and panted with excitement at my arrival.

My mind fell suddenly quiet.

Jeremy stood by his truck, a bundle of clothes draped over his arm. My eyes took in the load of U-Haul packing boxes neatly stacked in the truck bed. I opened my car door and got out.

"Lisa . . ." His voice sounded as if it drifted up from the depths of the sea. Faraway, muted. "I wasn't expecting you back so soon. I thought it would be less painful if—"

He gestured apologetically to the cowardly scene I had stumbled upon. My nausea returned with a vengeance as I looked with confusion at my husband of ten years, Jeremy, the only man I ever loved, oh, so loved.

Like waves breaking against a rocky shore, his words slapped me awake from some sleepy stupor I had been lingering in—for the better part of my adult life.

"Till human voices wake us, and we drown."

CHAPTER 2

"IT'S JUST FOR A WHILE—to give me time to clear my head," Jeremy said. I noticed the tremble in his throat. Shreds of cloud skittered overhead and threw strange patterns on his freckled face as he searched my eyes. "I'll only be down the way, at Daniel's place."

His store manager's house. Daniel was in his early twenties, single. I pictured a small spare bed in a cluttered den. A couch with some blankets and a lumpy foam pillow thrown over ratty upholstery. Jeremy, six foot six and hefty, could barely sleep comfortably in our California King. An expensive bed he had picked out and paid for.

"Don't do this, Jer, please." Even though I meant the words, part of me hoped he would get into his truck and drive away. For now. I was too exhausted to go another round. But maybe Jeremy felt the same way. Our marriage was like a gracefully spinning gyroscope, so steady and almost perfect in its spin until decay set in, and with friction, threw our shining relationship off balance into a wobble and decline. Toppling was inevitable.

He offered his hand to me in a conciliatory manner and I took it as the breeze blew through my hair and cooled my face. His skin was warm and soft, his grip meant to be reassuring.

"I can't take any more fighting. It's making me sick. I can't concentrate at work." The edge had left his voice.

I nodded. My queasiness subsided as he spoke. Buster, a chunky yellow Lab with some Chow in him, licked my hand, demanding attention. I mindlessly scratched the top of his head until he had his fill and trotted over to the front stoop to plop down beside Angel, a border collie mix that couldn't resist herding all the goats in the pasture at every opportunity.

"And I can't take your mother's ranting. Coming over here and running our lives." His voice sounded more tired than angry. He squeezed my hand, then let it drop. "I mean it, Lis."

I had no answer for him. We'd been over this a thousand times. I understood how frustrated he was. We had spent the last ten years building this house, putting in gardens, adding a deck, Keystone fencing around the pasture, split-rail fencing along the drive, a complex water system with two one-thousand-gallon tanks, over a hundred old roses, reclaiming an orchard back from brambles of blackberry bushes, had even dug a huge pond, landscaped like something out of *House and Garden* magazine. All our savings, hours of manual labor, all our disposable income, but owning none of it.

My mother had bought this property for us when we first married. Just as she had supplied the down payment on Raff's fancy home overlooking the Bay before he got his promotion at the bank. She had only wanted to help us get started, get on our feet when the feed store first opened and we didn't have any savings. I saw it as an act of love, but Jeremy read it as a noose. Something she could use to lead him around with, make him do her bidding, make him beholden to her. His upbringing in rural Montana—coming from a traditional two-parent home—dictated that men provided for their families. It irked him that I had gone to my mother and asked for help. She even offered to loan us money as starting capital for the store, but that's where Jeremy drew the line. He buckled, though, when I found this five-acre parcel for sale, reduced in price, the property of my dreams, complete with a babbling creek hugging the foothills. Now Jeremy cursed the day he said yes, letting my mother buy it for us. Keeping the title in her name.

Jeremy slammed his cab door shut and nodded to the house. "I still have a few more things inside to . . . put in the truck."

I couldn't help myself. A sob tore out of my chest without warning, and tears flooded down my cheeks. Jeremy only hesitated for a second before coming over and gathering me up in his comforting arms. Arms that only last night longed to lash out and smash something.

Rafferty's voice poked the back of my mind. *"Things fall apart; the center cannot hold."* Which poem was that from?

"Hey, shh, now. It'll be okay." He let me cry for a minute, then lifted my chin and wiped my face with his cuff sleeve. He was wearing the green plaid flannel shirt I bought him for Christmas. The colors made his rusty hair look redder than usual. With his jaw clenched, his smoky eyes caught mine and I saw my pain reflected back.

Everything felt skewed, even the way he held me. So right and so wrong at the same time. I ached for his comfort, but I had to resist the urge to push him away and wiggle out of his arms.

I let him hold me like that for what I deemed the proper length of time, swatting away the memories of his acerbic attack of last night. The screaming, fist-pounding fury he had unleashed at me made me roil with anger. Why did I find those arguments so hard to let go of? Did I suffer some sick addiction, needing to mull over each hurtful word, relive the sharp barbs until bleeding began all over? Like picking at scabs and poking at wounds. Maybe I thought if I replayed those words over and over, they'd come out differently.

"The blood-dimmed tide is loosed, and everywhere the ceremony of innocence is drowned."

Yeats. How could I forget—the famous "Second Coming"? I could hear every word in Raff's dramatic Shakespearean actor lilt. *"The best lack all conviction, while the worst are full of passionate intensity."* In Raff's estimation, the former disdained group Yeat's referred to included most everyone in the world. The latter—most notably himself, and maybe a handful of others. Pitiful, intense, hopeless romantics. The world needed more like him, or so he protested in defiance of Yeats's declaration.

"Come, I'll make you some tea before I head out." Jeremy started for the front door when I heard a screeching cry from the barn. "What in blazes is that?" he asked.

My heart skipped a beat. "Sassy. Maybe she's kidding." I did a quick review in my mind. She wasn't due for another week—at least by my estimation. But goats never kept to a tight schedule when it came to giving birth. At least I had her in the kidding pen with fresh straw and plenty of water—away from the motley menagerie of rescued animals fenced in the pasture.

"I'll come with you," Jeremy said.

He mostly left tending the animals to me. It was my passion—rescuing farm animals that were abused and abandoned. Over the years I'd gained a reputation. The vets and animal shelter directed people to me who called all hours of the night, or sometimes just dropped lost ducks or sheep on my doorstep. Right now I had sixteen assorted animals, some in bad shape, some pregnant, like Sassy. Jeremy was raised on a ranch—horses and cattle—and with his knowledge of feed and medicines, he never got squeamish when I asked him to hold a struggling animal that needed wounds cleaned and bound, horns disbudded with a hot iron, even castrating with a sharp razor. I sighed and a lump of melancholy sat heavy in my gut. We made a great team—or used to.

My eyes adjusted to the dim light in the barn as I made for the back stall. Sassy bellowed again, clearly in distress. Goats rarely made that kind of clamor when delivering their kids. Usually, they just popped them out with ease. But Sassy was a pygmy goat with a narrow pelvis, and by her massive girth, no doubt carried triplets. I had plenty of experience pulling out kids. The vets, with their big hands, went for the C-section every time. Until they learned I was willing to go out on calls and try to extricate the stuck kids. They gave out my phone number and I became known as the "goat lady." I never accepted money for my house calls, for I had reward enough in seeing a doe relieved of her stress and delighting in her kids.

I found Sassy rolling on her side, her head pointing at the barn roof and her tongue lolling out the side of her mouth. Great.

"Jer, fill that bucket with hot water," I said, pointing at the sink. "I need the iodine, some towels from that shelf." I stroked Sassy and spoke to her in a soothing voice as I repositioned her so I could get a good look. Sunlight streamed through a small dirt-encrusted, cobwebbed window, giving me enough illumination to see a dark nose encased in membrane protruding out the goat's backside. A strong scent of ammonia and straw wafted around me.

"First one's coming out," Jeremy hurried back and set down the basin and towels. He leaned close enough to see but didn't get in my way. I fished around with my finger until I felt the tip of a hoof in the canal. "Found a leg," I said.

We both grew quiet as I concentrated. Sassy's heavy panting sounded like a small tractor revving. Every once in a while she let out a little bleat of discomfort, but I talked softly and kept her calm. I managed to cup my hand over the small emerging head and loop a finger around the hoof. I tugged firmly and felt the small body move an inch. Then it hitched up. I muttered under my breath.

"What?" Jeremy asked. "Can I help?" I repositioned both my arm and the goat, which caused Sassy to wail again.

"Help me get her to standing."

My leg was cramping under me, and my stomach knotted up. The rancid smell of the barn and the amniotic fluids from the goat made bile rise to my throat. I fought another urge to throw up. Maybe the combination of stress, lack of sleep, Raff's urge to die, and the sting of my failing marriage was stewing inside me, merging into one sickening putrefying mass in my gut. I took deep breaths, caught Jeremy studying me in puzzlement. I avoided his eyes.

I hefted Sassy to all fours and tried with my left hand for better positioning in the birth canal. That proved to be a better stance. I withdrew my hand from the slippery space and yanked off my wedding ring. I handed the simple gold band covered in slime to Jeremy, who looked at it and flinched. The significance hit me, although I didn't have time to ponder it.

"I'll lose it in there. Please, just keep it for me—for a few minutes."

My words seemed to shake Jeremy out of his reverie. I never took off my wedding ring—ever.

"I got the document from the lawyer. The devise." Jeremy's tone was hard. Like he'd practiced saying that in the mirror.

When I didn't respond, he added, not masking his anger, "I'm going to insist she sign it. If she won't put the property in our name now, she's going to have to make good her promise that this house, this property, will be left for us in her will."

I spun to face him. "Look, she already has it for us in her trust. You *know* this!"

"And she can remove it anytime she damn well pleases. This way she has to put her money where her mouth is. Sign something to prove she means it."

"Jer, she's my *mother,* for God's sake! Family means everything to her. Please, let's not do this. Not now." I gestured at the distressed goat that stood panting hard and shaking from head to hoof. I exhaled hard, wanting to be done with this argument already—the argument that had gone on for hours the night before.

"Fine!" I added. "Give her the paper and let her sign it. Then you'll see. All this fuss over nothing. You know it has something to do with her taxes—"

"A flimsy excuse. She owns your brother too. Her name's on his deed. And Neal—she made him *sell* his house so she could have more ready cash. Dammit, Lisa, why can't you see this?"

I pinched my lips together in frustration. "She's my mother. Don't I know her better than you? You're just talking out of your paranoia." I turned my back on Jeremy and concentrated on Sassy. I closed my ears to everything but her labored breathing.

Time moved slowly and I hated seeing Sassy in such distress. Her groans and grunts tore at my heart, so I worked as quickly as I could, getting my hand around the head again.

"Why won't she push it out?" Jeremy asked.

'Because . . ." I grunted, "that leg goes to a different kid." I closed my eyes and with my mind followed my hand along as I traced the front hoof up to the stifle in that confining space, feeling the first bend forward, the second, backward at the hock. Hind leg, not front. I pushed that leg back into the uterus as far as I could and fished around for a front leg. I only needed one front leg that corresponded with the appropriate head and I would be in the clear.

Finally, I found one that connected to the neck of the goat sticking partway out of the birth canal.

"Got it!"

Sassy screamed as I pulled gently, foot and head, then waited until she got back to pushing. Along with her efforts, I cleared the shoulder over the cervix, the head and legs sliding out with the rest of the small wet body following. Jeremy handed me a towel and I placed the small doe baby on it, under Sassy's nose, so she could sniff and lick it. I heard Jeremy chuckle and a warm feeling rose to my heart, followed by a pang of despair that I hid in my attending to the next new arrival plopping out onto straw.

How simple it seemed to give birth to new life, and how very impossible. Something right here in my grasp was completely out of my grasp, denied me.

I choked up over all the years of frustration, heartache, and disappointment and dried off the next kid, a little gray buck with a white blaze on his forehead. Both kids were already standing on wobbly legs and baaing in cute warbly voices. Sassy spoke back to her babies between frantic licks. I always found it humorous watching does attend to their newborns. A third kid came with one more Sassy squawk—another buck, this one a runt. He fit in the palm of my hand. While Jeremy petted the other two, I rubbed that tiny guy with a towel, but got little response. Once I iodined the umbilical areas and made sure Sassy was done, had food and water, passed her placenta, I stood. My legs shook from squatting so long and my head spun hard until I got my balance.

I picked up the runt, still wrapped in a towel. "This one needs warming." I unlatched the gate, where Buster and Angel stood, alert, sniffing at my little bundle.

"Do you need me to stay here and keep on eye on these guys?" Jeremy asked.

"Only if you want to. But, they're doing fine." Better than I was. I just wanted to get in the bath tub and soak, lock the door, wallow in my misery. Instead of lifting my spirits, these three new lives only sank me deeper. I gritted my teeth so hard my jaw began to ache.

One child. That's all I wanted. Was that too damn much to ask for?

Jeremy closed the pen gate behind him and followed me back into the house. Two boxes sat on the counter, partway full of kitchen items. I heard Jeremy suck in a breath as the reality of our situation came careening at him. He stood by the counter while I filled two empty plastic soda bottles full of hot water and laid them against the flanks of the baby buck. I wrapped the towel back around the kid and, within seconds, the heat brought his attention around. His eyes lost their glaze and his face grew alert and animated. Within two minutes, he began mewling for milk, sniffing my hand for a teat.

"That's amazing," Jeremy said. "The way he perked up so fast. No oven this time?" He'd seen me put babies in towels on the open oven door, with the heat blasting out at them, like a mini sauna. It disconcerted the dogs to see the kids placed in the same contraption that produced tasty food. They'd give me distressed glances, wondering if I really intended to cook the kids for dinner, lingering close by and giving the bundles a face washing from time to time.

"He seems to be coming around just fine. I need to take him back to the barn so he can nurse." I gave his little dark head a scratch, and he pushed up against it in pleasure. I looked into his eager eyes and my own longing grew unbearable. I turned to Jeremy.

"Why don't you finish what you were doing here?" My voice sounded flat and unemotional to me. Jeremy seemed to flounder for words. Before he had the chance to say anything else, anything that might make me beg him to stay and not throw away ten shared years, I hurried out the door with my charge in my arms. I cradled the little bundle and let the tears stream down my face as I hurried to the barn. Maybe Yeats was right. Maybe once things fell apart, the center couldn't hold, no matter how tightly you hung onto it.

In the soft light, I placed the buck on the straw, still wrapped in his towel and flanked with his hot water bottles. Sassy sniffed him, then started with her licking and baaing. His little voice responded back each time she spoke to him, a staccato duet. Eventually, he wriggled free of his swaddling and got to his feet. He pushed over to where his brother and sister were sucking noisily, and I pulled his sister off to get him situated on a teat. He nosed around for a moment until he got the warm nipple in his mouth and sucked. Sassy stood content, chewing her cud, and making sporadic little noises at her triplets.

I picked up the placenta that lay on the straw and threw it away in a plastic bag. Already the babies had fluffed up, their coats damp and steaming in the air. The barn was warm, so I decided not to run the propane heater. I slid to the straw and tucked my knees under my chin, willing my stomach to stop cramping. Only then did I see a stain of blood seeping through the crotch of my jeans.

I heard Jeremy's truck engine start up, then heard tires crunching the gravel road and down the driveway. I listened until the noise faded, leaving me to the quiet of the barn and the sounds of a new family luxuriating in their joy and contentment.

Jeremy didn't know I was three months pregnant. I had hoped beyond hope that this time would be different. That maybe our luck had changed, that we could put all the pain and sorrow behind us, a chance to start again. I emptied my mind by sheer will and let a calm detachment grow as I stumbled back into the house, doubled-over, heading to the bathroom. On the small table against the wall, I spotted the application forms from the adoption agency. The forms Jeremy had brought home last week. Which triggered last night's argument. Among other things.

I clenched my teeth and forced it all out of my mind—every bitter memory that begged for acknowledgment. Every thread of hope, every hollow reassurance. Everything. A bitter laugh burst out of my mouth. Who was I kidding, thinking I could save Raff? Help him recover, heal, bounce back to a normal life. *Really.*

But if I didn't try, who would? What did I have to lose?

I'd already lost so much. And, it was clear at that moment, as my stomach cramps turned into serious pains, as blood dripped from my body like spirit leaking from my soul, that I was about to lose this baby as well. My third miscarriage in three years.

"The blood-dimmed tide is loosed, and everywhere the ceremony of innocence is drowned."

I looked at my ring finger as I sat on the toilet. It felt naked and stripped bare without the gold band, the way my life felt when I thought about Jeremy sleeping on some neighbor's couch. Jeremy had forgotten to give the ring back. Or maybe not.

CHAPTER 3

WHEN I WAS FIVE AND Neal only two, my mother, busy unpacking boxes, told me to canvass the neighborhood and find a friend for my little brother. What was she thinking? Granted, my father had just died and my mother was distraught, relocating from Los Angeles to a new town, burdened with three small children. And I was a hyper bundle of energy, always needy, always underfoot.

We had moved to Mill Valley only days earlier, halfway up a steep road that ended at the base of Mount Tamalpais—or Mount Tam, as the locals called it. Just north of San Francisco Bay, the sleepy community of Mill Valley featured a tiny downtown neighborhood of dark wood-sided shops surrounded by towering redwood trees and punctuated by wisps of fog that drifted like ghosts through the streets. Aside from the main flat thoroughfare, most of the residential areas spread up into the hills by way of single lane potholed roads, replete with blind curves. Cars whipped around the sharp bends, their drivers always in a hurry, and the houses all sat at the base of rutted narrow driveways, buried in trees and giant shrubs that proliferated in the abundant rainfall.

Not that I noticed. I was on a mission to find Neal a playmate.

Dutifully, I made myself scarce, and taking Neal's chubby hand in mine, went door-to-door, knocking until some stunned neighbor opened up and listened to my cheerful inquiry. Did they have any little kids that Neal could play with?

Fortunately, I hadn't had to dodge traffic for long. For less than a block away, Anne's mother, Sarah, no doubt horrified by the thought of two small unaccompanied children gallivanting around the neighborhood, ushered us into her plushly carpeted living room. I don't remember the scolding she gave to my mother over the phone, but when I brought it up that Wednesday, Anne seemed to remember every word.

"Oh yeah," she said, munching on an apple as she got her shoes out of her car. "I remember Mom clenching her fists while asking you to recite your new phone number. She did a great job keeping her cool. I think she was ready to hand you and Neal over to child protective services, right then and there. You looked like two little waifs, to her. But I was glad you showed up. It was meant to be."

We had a standing date each Wednesday at noon, there in that parking lot on the south end of Mill Valley. Although jogging was still the big craze, Anne would not deign to humiliate herself by wearing coordinated jogging outfits and expensive Adidas sneakers. A few inches shorter than me and at least fifty pounds heavier, Anne's exercise regiment excluded anything that worked up too much of a sweat. Unless it involved chasing after deadbeat dads or pedophiles. Then watch Anne run.

Anne slipped out of her heels and into her walking shoes. The paved road we pounded each week to the beach was part of the Golden Gate Recreation Area—and cars filled every space in the lot. A one-mile walk each way. Physically, I felt much better that day. The nausea had vanished along with my budding new life. Hormones were returning to normal not even a week later, even if the rest of my life wasn't. Every muscle in my body felt stiff, as if I had been beat up in my sleep. Emotionally, I was in denial—about everything.

The air was cool and moist, with a hint of salt spray. It tingled my face as I waited next to the car. The coastal range wrapped around us and the blue sky shimmered. Rolls of clouds oozed over the tops of hills and spilled in slow motion to pool in the fields hugging the hills. The fog that frequented Marin seemed to have personality, reminding me of T. S. Eliot's fog that rubbed its back and muzzle on windowpanes and curled up around houses and fell asleep. I drew in a long breath. I would make myself enjoy the beautiful Marin County summer day.

Anne set the pace, determined and focused—as she was in all aspects of her life. She looked straight ahead at her goal and never wavered. I valued her clear head, her analytical mind. She often supplied the voice of reason my own brain so sadly lacked. I had come to depend on her over this lifetime of friendship to be honest and forthcoming with me. Although, today, that was the last thing I wanted.

Anne's birthday was exactly a month before mine, but she always seemed years older and wiser. I didn't find a playmate for Neal that day her mother invited us in, but I'd made a fast friend. And Raff ended up best friends with Anne's brother, Kyle—another serious intellectual. Nerds, the both of them—before nerds were ever cool or respected. While Anne and I wiled away hours playing jacks in the smooth linoleum hallway, Raff and Kyle were writing some satire of Dante's *Inferno* or coming up with trick questions for their next car rally. The door to Kyle's room stayed shut and we girls were threatened on penalty of hamstringing not to enter—ever. We did spend some giggling hours peeking through the window slats at their antics, hidden in the bushes outside, but after a while we invariably grew bored.

Anne panted as she walked. Joggers passed us on both sides, going to and from the beach. Bicyclists pedaled, weaving through the current of bodies. Anne breathed hard, pushing herself, but I knew she wouldn't slow down. I had a hard time keeping up with her.

"So, what's the latest with Rafferty?" Her voice oozed compassion. She had watched the gradual descent of my brother's sanity into madness in stages at her very own house. "He still in the hospital?"

"I think he plans to stay there until they get his meds right. His psychiatrist wants him to go home. Kendra wants him home. No doubt my mother has put in her two cents."

"Ha, no wonder he wants to stay put. A lot safer in there—on all fronts." She slowed to a less frantic walk. "And Jeremy?" She turned to meet my eyes, knowing my tendency to hedge.

"He's moved out. Temporarily, he says. To clear his head."

"Hmm."

I knew that look of hers. The professional assessment of a social worker. Weighing what to say, what advice to give, knowing most of it would be ignored. But gearing up to say it, anyway.

"Sassy had triplets this week . . ."

"Lisa, you know I don't give a damn about the goats or ducks or sheep." She halted in her tracks. Joggers whizzed by; their slipstreams whipped my ponytail whereas Anne's frizzy thick hair lay pinned to her head, dotted with beads of perspiration across her forehead. Flashes of colorful fabric caught my attention, but Anne brought my attention back around.

"He'll come home, Lis. He loves you. It's your mother he can't stand."

"I know that. But I can't take sides—"

Anne grabbed my arm and pulled me off the path and out of traffic. "Yes, you have to. He's your husband—"

"And she's my mother. She came first."

"It doesn't work that way," Anne said with some disgust. "Your mother is trying to destroy your marriage. Look what she did to Raff and Kendra. They'll be divorced after this whole thing shakes down."

"Anne! How can you say that?"

She grunted and scowled in my face. The same expression she'd display when I used to beat her at gin rummy. "Because it's true. Lis, you know it's true."

I scowled back. "Is not."

Anne clamped her mouth shut and resumed walking the path. We slipped into the flow just like merging on the freeway. I could hear the ocean soughing mingling with the slapping of shoes on asphalt.

I thought about Sarah, Anne's diminutive and always smiling mother, dressed in her Hawaiian muumuus and never far from the kitchen, where glorious aromas drifted into all the rooms of the house, an ambiance quite absent from my childhood home, which had housed a lone parent who could cook a passable meatloaf and little more. My memories of Anne's house all centered on those tantalizing scents, which included the weird cooking experiments I'd be invited to participate in. We'd bake Aunt Rose's crescent almond cookies, and some obscenely sweet concoction we called "Anne's Decadence"—nine layers of chocolate and butterscotch chips, flaked coconut, condensed milk, pecans, raisins, and a few more ingredients I couldn't recall. No wonder we'd stay up late after midnight watching old black-and-white movies on her little TV set, unable to fall asleep. Hundreds of hours I spent on their living room floor, playing endless card games with Anne, lounging by their big stone fireplace, reading books together, playacting scenes from Jane Austen. Sarah, to me, was the consummate doting mother. Every time I stayed overnight, they always had roasted chicken and mashed potatoes for dinner. Big warm oatmeal cookies for dessert.

Sarah had never failed to give me bear hugs, something I craved and was denied by my mother. I tried hard, as I walked fast to keep up with Anne's short but speedy legs, to recall any instance when my mother had hugged or kissed me when I was a child. All I could dredge up was an occasional touch of my hair, a slap on my face, a belt smacking the seat of my pants.

"Why would my mother want to destroy my marriage? She loves Jeremy."

Anne sighed and picked up her pace. I went back to half jogging to keep up. We were nearly over the final rise with the stretch of sand in view when she answered softly, "Lisa, just don't see it. You have blinders on. You want to believe your mother is some kind of saint, but she's far from it. You're too close to the trees."

"So, explain it to me." I tried to keep the anger out of my voice, but all those arguments with Jeremy had frazzled my finesse. Her argument was dismantling me.

Anne huffed while she spoke. "Your mother is almost sixty, right? She's alone, no husband, no one to take care of her. All she has is you three kids. And money. She knows no other way to ensure your loyalty and devotion than with bribery and threats. Give you money, make you her slave. She's done it to Neal, to Raff, and to Jeremy. She *owns* the lot of you. And I'd hate to see the day when any of you double-crosses her."

I stopped abruptly and two joggers almost ran me down. One mumbled some profanity. "I thought you liked my mom. What's gotten into you?"

Anne led me over to one of the picnic tables positioned askew on the sand. The ocean thrashed and rallied against the shoreline a hundred yards away. We sat and she scrunched her face. "I know you don't want to hear this. You never do. You're fiercely protective of your mother. And I understand that. But, your brother's trying to kill himself, and your husband's just walked out. Neal floats from job to job, watching baseball from your mother's couch. And in the midst of all the chaos is Ruth, orchestrating this, to her delight."

"What? You think she's happy Raff wants to die? Please, get real!"

"No, of course not. But it's all about control. Controlling her empire and all the players in it. The world's a stage, Lis, and your mother the director. You take all your cues from her. Try to see it from Jeremy's side for once. Try to distance yourself a little and stop playing the part of the loyal, dutiful daughter."

"I'm just trying to keep the peace. Hold us together. Help Raff . . ."

"Lisa, forget trying to save Raff. You gotta save yourself first."

"Look, I know you have more insight into my family than anyone else, but it doesn't give you the right to pontificate."

Anne shrugged, and that one gesture carried layers of meaning. She would acquiesce—for now. But that little twitch of her shoulders was also a subtle brush-off and insult. It said, *Lisa, you are so dense. Just wait. You'll see . . .* My gut began its familiar knotting. I'd had enough of this topic.

"I have this strange idea," I said. Anne spotted my strategy right away and sighed in exasperation. We'd pick up where we left off on some other day, of that I had no doubt. Anne always scored. And I loved that bull-doggedness about her. If I ever needed an advocate on my side, she'd be my first pick. I felt sorry for the poor slobs that had to sit in a courtroom and listen to her diatribes. Just the thought of watching her in action gave me chills.

"I've been thinking about my father—who died when I was four." I told her about my father's death and the mysterious and suspicious circumstances coloring my early years, years she'd never heard about. Being so close throughout our childhood, it might have seemed strange that I'd never broached the subject. But that just showed how my father had been so neatly erased from my life after he'd died. I wove what bits and pieces I had into an incomplete and unsatisfying picture, and gave that to her to pick apart.

"Wow, pretty weird," she said. "But fascinating."

"So, what do I do now?"

"Well, it seems to me, the person who'd best know the truth about your dad would be his brother. Do you have any idea where he could be? Maybe you could talk with him."

The thought had never occurred to me. My uncle. "Maybe still in New York? That's where my dad grew up. I don't even know my uncle's name. Or if he's even alive."

"Did your mom ever mention him?"

"For some reason I remember he was a doctor, or something medical."

"So, that wouldn't be hard to look up. Sitteroff's not that common a name, is it? Check the library. Medical journals. Call the AMA. If he's practicing medicine, he'd be registered or licensed somewhere. It's a place to start." Anne put a hand on my shoulder. "I think it's a good idea, digging into your past. You should learn more about your dad—it's a big giant puzzle piece missing from your life. And maybe you'll uncover something that will help Raff. You never know. The truth can sometimes set you free."

"So I've heard."

Although, truth sometimes wielded a sharp two-edge sword. But what could it hurt to look for my long-lost uncle? I suddenly had a strong need to find him. I could look up references to my father too. Maybe he'd written articles, abstracts in physics quarterlies or other academic publications. I stood and wiped sand off the seat of my jeans.

On the way back to our cars, Anne was quiet. I tromped at her side, my mind wheeling with plans and ideas. The Marin County Library would have limited resources, but I could go into the city. I had nothing to do the rest of the afternoon. Two gardening jobs, big estates, but I could start on those tomorrow.

"My mom once told me about the time she went to the public pool with your mother." Anne said, the words coming out in a rhythm with her pace. "You and I must have been five or so."

"Hey, I remember that pool. Didn't they bulldoze it at some point?"

"Yeah. To build that subdivision—over in Corte Madera."

I recalled a gigantic rectangular pool with low and high diving boards. Tons of kids yelling. A lifeguard with a bullhorn, blasting "no running allowed." I used to love swimming at that pool during summer vacation.

Anne continued. "Raff and Kyle were splashing around with the bigger boys, playing Marco Polo. We were playing on the wide steps with our mothers sitting on the ledge, dangling their legs in the warm water. Mom said you slipped and floated down to the bottom of the shallow end. But the bottom of the pool was slanted, remember? By the time my mom and your mom stopped chatting and looked back over, you had disappeared."

Instantly, I conjured up a memory. Lying on my back, feeling the rough concrete grazing my shoulder blades as they scraped along, looking up at the wavering images through the surface of the water, blotches of color, distorted faces. The sudden quiet and the alluring weightlessness. The memory jarred me with its sharp sensations, but I didn't recall being afraid.

"I remember . . ."

"You do?' Anne asked.

"But I mustn't have been underwater that long. Someone jumped into the pool and rescued me. All the adults gathered around me and I remember their concerned faces and shouts of relief. That's weird," I said, exploring the textures that memory brought back—the hefty smell of chlorine, the hot sun on my face as I lay on the pool's ledge, the cacophony of voices as women in rubber bathing caps and cotton one-piece swimsuits fussed over me.

"That was my mom," Anne said. "She's the one who jumped in."

I slowed down and looked at Anne. I tried to conjure up the face of my rescuer, but I drew a blank. She continued, but her voice was measured. "Before Mom died, she told me how she spotted you gliding down into the deep end, underneath all the myriad of kicking legs and paddling arms. She hollered and shook your mother's shoulder, pointing at you. She could see your eyes wide open in surprise, your limbs unmoving. When she turned and caught the expression on your mother's face, she was so shocked, she couldn't move a muscle. A moment later, after shaking off her surprise, she threw her sunhat to the ground and dove into the deep end. She wasn't the best swimmer, but that fact never entered her mind. She managed to bring you to the surface and pull you over to the side of the pool, where a dozen hands yanked you up and out."

I stopped at the end of the pathway, where our cars baked in the noonday summer sun. I strained to remember but only recalled a whoosh of motion, someone pulling me to the surface, my head emerging into a sea of air, sucking in and filling my lungs.

Anne gave me a big hug, her arms familiar around my waist. "Funny, you remember that day, and I don't recall it at all. I probably never even noticed you disappeared." She unlocked her car door, then turned back to me. "Let me know if you find anything at the library. You've piqued my curiosity."

"Anne," I said, pulling keys from my pocket. "Why did my mother's expression cause your mom such distress? What did she see?"

Anne shrugged noncommittally but I made her look at me. "Something that frightened her. Like your mom didn't want to listen, didn't want to acknowledge the danger you were in."

"Maybe my mom thought she was joking." I added, "That was a long time ago, and I'm sure the incident happened so fast, all those impressions were a blur."

Anne nodded, but it was clear she didn't agree with my assessment. If she had more to say on the subject, she kept it to herself. Just why had she brought that up anyway?

I watched Anne get into her car and drive away. Suddenly, another memory came out of nowhere—the time I accidently set the house on fire.

I was about ten, and Raff was sleeping over at Kyle's. Neal was in the den watching TV. That night was my first stint as babysitter. Neal and I had finished dinner and the dishes were loaded in the dishwasher. I went to my room to do some homework and had lit a taper on the nightstand next to my bed, but didn't think to move the large box of matches away from the candleholder. I had forgotten all about it when I went to join Neal to watch my favorite show—*Time Tunnel.* By the time I smelled smoke, half my room was up in flames. My mother was at her business manager's house, going over investments and taxes. My mother made a lot of money buying and selling commercial real estate, on the advice of her manager. That was how she supported us after my father died.

I rushed into the kitchen and dialed the phone number she left for emergencies. Harv Blake put her on the line, and when I told her about the fire, she told me to get bowls of water and put the fire out. Then I was to run into the street and yell "fire." That was in the days long before 911. I did as she said, and by the time the fire trucks had come screeching up to our house, I had the fire put out, but smoke filled every room in a thick hovering cloud.

I called my mother back, as instructed, and told her everything was fine and under control. I sobbed into the phone as the shock of the incident sent a delayed wave of fear through my heart. My entire body shook in fits and starts. Neal hugged my leg and wouldn't let go. I had tried to be so grown up and was proud I had put the fire out. I asked my mother how soon she'd get home. Soon wasn't soon enough for me.

She said she was sorry, but she couldn't leave. Her manager insisted she stay and finish what they were doing. Hours went by. I opened all the windows as the quiet dark of night blanketed the neighborhood, trying to make the smoke seep out. All the walls in the house were blackened for two feet below the ceiling. After I tucked Neal in bed and waited until he was asleep, I sat on the front porch, huddled in a blanket in the chill air, and watched for my mom's car.

Finally, late into the night, she drove up. I don't remember what she said, but her anger spilled out of her mouth as she walked from room to room, assessing the damage. She bedded me down on the living room couch without a kind word. My bedroom was charred and my bed uninhabitable, but I'd been able to find a pair of pajamas in my partially scorched dresser by the door.

The next day, she kept me home from school and demanded I write one hundred times on lined paper: "The next time I decide to do something stupid like that, I will ask permission first." She made me get up on a ladder and scrub the smoke residue off all the walls, something that took the better part of a week. I never could abide the smell of Lysol after that incident. She must have gotten over her anger, because I recall thumbing through books of wallpaper patterns, and her letting me choose a design for my bedroom walls.

I had no idea why that memory rushed back at me as I stood next to my car, my keys gripped in my hand. But twenty years after the fact, the obvious question came to mind.

Why didn't my mother rush out of her manager's house and hurry home? How could she have stayed away all those hours? I always blamed it on Harv Blake. *He wouldn't let me leave*, my mother had said. *I had to stay*. It was his fault.

All those years, I'd never questioned her excuse. Wasn't something very wrong with that picture? If I had been the parent and my daughter called to tell me the house was on fire, I would have been out the door with tires squealing before my business manager could say a word in protest. Just what had she been doing with Harv that night? I began to doubt it had anything to do with investments.

As I drove over the bridge into the city, through the crowded, traffic-ridden streets heading for the massive gray brick library building on Powell, I replayed my conversation with Anne. Those two disparate images stuck in my mind—Anne's mother pulling me from a watery grave and my mother turning her back on her children engulfed in flames. The images felt heavy, imposing, significant. But they were isolated moments, only small pieces of the whole tapestry of my life. And had nothing to do with my current purpose—uncovering the truth of my father's death.

I shoved those lingering images to the back of my mind and let my father's name roll over my tongue. *Nathan Sitteroff.*

Hard as I tried, not one memory surfaced. His name drew a blank. And, for some reason, that distressed me even more than the recent revelations of the afternoon.

CHAPTER 4

THE LIBRARIAN LEFT ME ALONE with the microfiche machine, after explaining how to access the different periodicals by date and keyword. I had used those machines on occasion in college when working on term papers, maybe eight years ago, and I never liked them. I spent an hour putting in one rectangular film after another under the small warm bulb, searching for the name Sitteroff in medical and scientific journals. I found a half dozen references to people whom I couldn't imagine would be related to me, but it wasn't until I started in on the newspapers that I came across something odd.

A contributed article in *The Washington Post*, dated only eight months earlier, mentioned the name Nathan Sitteroff. I skimmed through the piece and nearly discarded it—something to do with mothers and abusive husbands and custody battles. A woman named Mandy Glessman wrote it, apparently an attorney who was going through a bitter divorce offering practical advice for abused wives. My eyes were tired from the strain of reading small type in bad lighting, and my recent fitful sleeping combined with the stuffy room made it difficult to concentrate. In my excitement to get to the library, I had skipped lunch, and my stomach, now free of nausea, cried out for food. Yet, a secondary glance at the author's byline showed her to be from New York, so that made me stop and reread.

I woke from my ennui when I found the sentence with my father's name.

"I named my son after an uncle I'd never met—Nathan Sitteroff. My father used to tell me stories of how he and his protective older brother were moved from one foster home to another during the Great Depression. How they survived starvation and poverty and cruelty. Often the agency would try to place them in separate homes, because no one wanted to take on two children at once. Yet, my uncle Nathan refused to let his little brother Samuel—"

I drew in a breath. Sam Sitteroff. I knew that was my uncle's name. And there was the bit about the foster homes.

"—be taken away from him. How he'd cry and cling to my father, until the agency relented. Finally, one kind couple, with two sons of their own, agreed to take them in. Those sweet people were the grandparents I knew growing up. They raised Sam and Nathan as their own, putting them through school and eventually adopting them."

The article went on to discuss how Mandy had married a violent man and the legal steps she'd had to go through to gain custody and protect her son, Nathan, from his father. The article filled three columns, and nothing more was said about Nathan Sitteroff. But that was enough proof for me.

The whole time I sat hunched over in that room, Lewis Carroll's "Jabberwocky" ran through my head. Raff had always been enamored with *Alice in Wonderland* and *Through the Looking Glass*. He had spent a hefty sum on a large, illustrated and annotated edition of the book that featured richly colored drawings alongside commentary and text. I kept picturing Raff, the brave but foolhardy champion, stalking the fearsome Jabberwocky with the jaws that bite and the claws that catch. He and Neal used to act out the poem, replete with foppish costumes made from sheets belted around the waist and tied around his neck for a cape, old Halloween attire, and illustrative cardboard embellishments, such as chest armor and a woeful dragon-type mask that sported bright red eyes drawn in our mother's lipstick.

Surely, Raff's current mental nemesis was not unlike this colorful fabrication of Carroll's mind, a phantasm of evil with eyes of flame, something unsettling and horrifying that whiffled through the tulgey wood of Raff's brain to haunt and torment him in his darkest hours, burbling as it came. What Raff needed was a true vorpal blade to fight the Jabberwocky, a blade that, according to the poem, went snicker-snack as the fearless hero fought the beast. "*One two! One two! And through and through . . . He left it dead, and with its head, he went galumphing back.*"

I printed out the article and moved on to the AMA Journals. It didn't take long for me to find contact information for Samuel Sitteroff MD, with a license to practice in the state of New York. As I sat in the hardback wooden chair, a sudden memory came to mind—of a small apartment inside a dark building that smelled musty, of dust and exhaust. A dank and creaking elevator with an iron grate that slid closed over the opening, entrapping me like a prison gate—and I could still hear the deep whirring sound the elevator made as it slugged upward, passing pale yellow metal doors with large black numbers for each floor.

Whenever I thought of New York, those were the images and smells I associated it with, but why? I strained to recall that apartment, a room that made occasional appearance in my dreams, with heavily upholstered couches covered with clear plastic. Plastic runners over the carpet. A tall glass cabinet filled with ceramic figurines. The smell of chicken soup? Stale cigar smoke. Two short, rotund people. The man hacking with a deep chest cough, sitting in an armchair and staring at a TV with the sound way up. The woman with tight white curls pinned to her head, in a pale blue floral housedress and clunky brown orthopedic shoes on her feet. European accents, hard to understand. Reserved smiles, polite, but no sense of feeling comfortable or welcome.

Those were my grandparents, I now understood. West Gunhill Road. Bronx. Where had that bit of trivia come from? I couldn't dredge up any other impressions, except for a strange New York skyline, one that had something like two spaceships hovering in the air next to a giant metal globe along the side of a busy throughway. Something incongruent, but so identifiable as New York in my child-mind's eye. I don't remember ever having been there, but perhaps I had.

Maybe Raff would remember; he was four years older. Had he even been with me there, at the time? I looked up the number for the New York Bar Association, figuring maybe I could call tomorrow, since it was too late Eastern Time to do more that day. Maybe I could find Mandy, my cousin.

I rolled the word *cousin* around in my mouth. Unlike most people I knew—who had so many family members they couldn't keep track of all the names—I had just my little arena of close relatives. My mother was an only child. She had aunts and uncles and cousins back east, but for some reason we never saw them while growing up. No one ever came out to California to visit us. Mandy Glessman would be my only true first cousin on my father's side. Maybe there were more cousins I didn't know about. Like little Nathan Sitteroff, five years old, named after my father.

A strange affection entered my heart for this long-lost cousin who thought to honor my own father by naming her son after him—something even my brother hadn't cared to do. No doubt the thought had crossed Raff's mind. But maybe by dismissing it, he meant it as a slap in our father's face.

A tinge of annoyance stirred within me. Mandy Glessman had been told more about my own father than I had. I felt deprived of something due me, and hoped that my uncle and cousin would have stories to tell me, those keepers and caretakers of my father's past. Even if they only had a little light to shed on the person of my father, I wanted to hear it.

Sometimes we walk into a restaurant and smell food cooking, and only then do we realize how starving we are, that we'd gone all day without eating. Every olfactory sense wakes up and sends an alarm. That's how I felt, holding the phone number of my uncle's medical practice in my hand. I had gone through my whole life never once thinking about my father. For how could I miss someone I didn't remember? I was always the odd kid at school, the aberration with only one parent attending PTA night or the

Christmas show—back then in the days before divorce was the norm. The principal of our elementary school had sat next to me at sixth grade graduation as a surrogate father, trying to make up for my lack. Kids who came over to play would remark on how strange it was our mother worked full-time and that we had Mexican maids living in our house and making us dinner.

But in that moment at the library, standing there in the microfiche cubicle, I sensed a fresh loss, like I'd lost a limb I never knew I'd had. I ached for a father I'd never had the opportunity to know. Maybe my tumultuous emotions could be credited to my displaced grief due to my miscarrying. That was the likely culprit. And then I considered: what if my mother, in her grief, felt she had to shut every door that opened to a memory of my father? Why she never talked about him. Why we stopped seeing relatives. Maybe that was the only way she could cope and get on with life, raising three children on her own. Who could blame her for that?

Maybe enough time had gone by, and perhaps, once I spoke to my uncle and heard his story, I could offer something back to my mother, to my brothers, some gift of knowledge that would heal us and shed some light on the unspoken tragedy that defined and bound our family together, for ill or good. Here, perhaps, would be my vorpal sword.

I walked through the solemn halls of the library, imagining swinging my sword against myth and misconception. *One two! One two!* My sword would sing out with truth and revelation, banishing the dark and scary things hiding in the woods of the past.

I pondered how in "Jabberwocky" the reader is given a warning by an unidentified character *"(Beware the Jabberwock, my son!)"* and later: *"Come to my arms, my beamish boy! O frabjous day! Calloh! Callay! He chortled in his joy."* It never occurred to me before, but surely that voice belonged to the young champion's father, who issued warning, and yet followed up with joyful praise over his son's conquering of the loathsome beast with eyes of flame.

I had no doubt that Raff heard that pointed warning and quaked in fear as he faced down his foe. But he carried no vorpal blade, nor any weapon that he could fashion against his faceless assailant. And why did the young hero's father issue such a warning? Could it have been framed by his own disheartening experience of defeat?

I pictured our father, dying in a hospital bed, racked with disease, the monster's flaming eyes pursuing him through his cold-sweat nightmares. My father, impotent in rage and valor, wallowing in failure, and my brother standing at his bedside, smelling camphor and death, seeing firsthand the horror of the beast and his own ineluctable fate rushing toward him out of the tulgey wood.

My father's voice called out from the grave in challenge and warning: *"Has thou slain the Jabberwock?"* But Raff's answer of *"not yet, perhaps never"* gave no guarantee he'd be welcomed into anyone's joyful arms. Or so Raff believed?

I drove home in the dusk, my mind full of imaginings, full of dialogue between me and my cousin, as I pictured a wellspring of information that could fill in the blanks of my life. I pulled up to the house and opened the car door, the invitation for Buster and Angel to leap on me, their faces overwrought with the nuances of anxiety characteristic of dogs that sense a shift in the security of their home. Usually, Jeremy would be there by this time of evening. My menagerie at the barn bellowed and baaed and neighed, a dozen stomach alarms ringing in distress—as if I ever forgot to feed them.

With the dogs at my heels, I made my rounds, filled feeders with hay and scattered grain on the dirt. I checked on Sassy and watched her triplets push each other off the makeshift teeter-totter Jeremy had built out of a two-by-six plank and a piece of split firewood. The kids looked robust and energetic, and Sassy seemed settled happily in motherhood, lying with her hooves tucked under her and chewing her cud.

I set my purse down in the kitchen and flipped on lights, trying to discount the ominous silence that filled the house like a thick fluid. Why was silence so much louder than sound? The small noises—the clock ticking, the hum of the refrigerator—seemed magnified by Jeremy's absence, the house a cavernous echo chamber that hungered for vibration. This would be my third night apart from my husband. We'd taken trips in the past that separated us, but that loneliness was always tempered by the assurance of reuniting.

I noticed the red dot flashing on the answering machine and pressed the play button, my eyes catching on the phone number Jeremy had scribbled on the notepad for me, in case I needed to reach him at Daniel's house. Hearing Jeremy's voice choked me up, but I bit my lip and listened as I spooned dog food into two bowls. His tone sounded tired and harried. I heard people talking in the background. Customers in the store. He wanted to let me know he had swung by at noon and dropped off my ring. He didn't want to risk putting it somewhere and forgetting.

Forgetting what? The ring, or our relationship?

I pressed Stop, walked over to the sink, and took the ring off the window sill, where it lay next to the soap dish. I slipped it on my finger as I walked over to the TV in the living room, where I flipped channels until I found something innocuous on the Turner Classics station. I recognized Marilyn Monroe and Richard Widmark, talking in hushed voices in a hotel room. I turned the sound up, then settled onto the couch, open invitation for my dogs to flank me. They hopped onto the comfy cushions, smelling like Alpo Beef, and made sure my arms received lots of slobbery licks before they squirmed around and settled with sighs by my side.

Marilyn Monroe grew dreamy, lost in memory over her fiancé, who had disappeared in a plane over the ocean. Apparently, she was a bit confused, thinking Richard Widmark—a total stranger she had invited into her room—was her lost love. I watched the rest of the movie, which involved some nosy, suspicious neighbors; a little girl bound and tied in the next room; and a smarmy house detective. In the end, though, Marilyn's mental state had deteriorated such that the police had to cart her off to the loony bin. The apparent result of living in denial. If only she had just accepted the truth—that she would never see her lover again—then she wouldn't have lost her marbles. I decided I really disliked that movie, whatever it was called.

Fortunately, *The African Queen* was on next. At least Humphrey Bogart took fate in both hands, albeit in the shape of a bottle, drinking whiskey until he passed out. And this movie had a happy ending, despite his ship blowing up. In the wreckage and flotsam, he had at least found love. I liked to believe he and Kate lived happily ever after, now that the Germans had been thwarted.

See, I told myself, giving a nod to Bogey, love can survive untold tribulation—even Nazis. Surely, Jeremy and I would work all this out.

Surely.

CHAPTER 5

I SET MY ALARM TO wake up early, so as the sun streaked dawn across the dew-laced pasture out my kitchen window and my water boiled for tea, I called New York. My uncle's service picked up and said they'd relay my message, that he was busy with a patient. After a few directed calls, I located someone with the Bar Association who gave me an office number for Mandy Glessman. I was surprised when she picked up on the first ring.

I don't know whom I expected—someone lawyerlike, with a detached manner and a cool East Coast accent, perhaps. But as soon as I introduced myself and briefly explained the reason I called, she gushed with excitement and colorful expletives. Mandy pummeled me with question after question: where did I live, what line of work was I in, did I have a family, what did I look like. Her enthusiasm ignited my own and soon we were chatting like friends who hadn't seen each other in years. I told her I had called to reconnect, that I didn't have much family, but I decided to avoid elaborating on the topic of suicidal depression and related issues this early in the game.

"Man, my dad will be so thrilled to hear you've called. I think he's always been a bit sad that he didn't get to watch his niece and nephews grow up."

"He knew about us? My brothers and me?"

"Sure. For heaven's sake! He's even got pictures in the photo album. A cute one of Neal—boy, was he a butterball. And your dad playing catch with Rafferty."

Pictures. I thought of the two lone photos I'd seen of my father. Mandy continued. "Let's see, I'm the same age as Rafferty, and the last time we were out in California was for your dad's funeral." Her voice dropped in energy and I sensed her take a long breath. "So, I was about eight. And you were, what, five?"

"Four," I said, trying hard to recall a visit from her family. "I don't remember."

"Sure, you probably were too young. I remember flying over the huge groves of orange trees as the plane came down to land. I even saw the Matterhorn—you know, the mountain at Disneyland—outside my little round window. That was a kick. I thought the snow was real and was amazed it didn't melt in the sun. Funny, huh? The things we remember."

My memory was a fishing net that snagged on odd unwanted bits of information, but had huge holes where the important events of my life slipped through. For instance, why on earth would I remember the license plate of my mother's blue Corvair from twenty years ago—JLW 671? Or our first phone number back in Mill Valley pre–area codes: 789-9541? In fact, if I dredged hard enough, I could recite every phone number from every place I'd ever lived. Maybe Raff and I got those uncanny skills from our mathematician father. We were both weird with numbers that way.

Neal never shared our fanatical interest in numbers and had almost failed math, where Raff and I excelled. Maybe Neal couldn't take the heat of competition, for Raff and I faced off plenty of times in contests of numeric prowess. Even though I was four years behind Raff in school, I sometimes had the advantage of speed in my recollection of utterly useless bits of information. We must have driven Neal crazy, for he manifested the only sane response to our behavior—mediocrity. Rather than wither beneath our towering shadows, he'd glued himself to the TV, watching mind-numbing episodes of *Speed Racer* and *Gumby*. He sailed through school with average grades, attracting no attention, getting in no trouble. No one expected much from him, and he seemed content with invisibility. Except for baseball, his passion. He wanted more than anything to be a pitcher on his Little League team, but couldn't make the cut. Settling for second baseman was the nadir of his life's disappointments. What I would have given to trade his miseries for mine.

Mandy's voice brought me out of my wayward mental straying. "So, you just *have* to come out and visit. What do you say? I'd love to go back to California, but Nate is in school and I have my practice. Plus, I don't think I could get Dad on a plane again. You won't believe this, but years ago he was flying to Chicago for a medical conference and the plane had to make an emergency landing on the runway. The wheels broke off and the plane caught fire. No one got hurt, but he swore he'd never fly again, that God was giving him a clear warning—can you believe it?"

Go to New York? The idea took me by surprise, but just the thought of getting off the plane in the Big Apple tantalized my imagination. Mandy talked on about all the things she would show me, oh the places we would go—Rockefeller Center, Radio City Music Hall, The Metropolitan Museum of Art. Culture, food, Broadway. Sounded like the diversion I needed right then. Escape the drama that was my life and go see a musical where the performers sang and danced their way to a happy ending. I knew Jeremy would be glad to stay at the house and care for the animals—and sleep in his own bed, even though I hoped it would feel as empty to him as it did to me.

"Let me see what I can arrange. I have a pasture full of animals that need tending, but it sounds great. I really want to talk to your dad. Is your mom there too?" Mandy hadn't spoken of her and I was hesitant to ask.

"Oh, Mom and Dad divorced years ago. My sister lives in London with her husband, so you won't get to see Becka, but Mom lives just outside the city. We can take the train over and visit her.

I'll call my dad and tell him about our conversation. I know he'll want to call you. This is a trip!"

"Please do that. I should be home later today. I'd really love to speak with him."

After I hung up, I grew aware of a stirring in my soul. I was Rip Van Winkle awakening after twenty years of sleep. The world looked similar but different. How would that awakening alter my perception of my life, my family?

I should have remembered that my mother moved faster than the speed of sound. That is, after my speaking briefly to Raff at the hospital (they limited calls to five minutes) and sharing the highlights of my conversation with Mandy, my mother appeared on my doorstep as if she had folded time and space to get to Petaluma. I knew at least an hour had passed, for I'd managed to get both bathrooms scrubbed and put a second load in the dryer when she walked through my front door. I already had my gardening truck loaded with five yards of compost. I had to run by the nursery first thing and pick up some five-gallon shrubs I had on hold. I was eager to start my gardening day.

But, the look on my mother's face told me I wouldn't be getting out the door that fast. I guessed her unexpected visit had everything to do with my brief conversation with Raff. Why? I had no idea. Raff had only mumbled and grunted at my news. Didn't seem at all interested in New York or long-lost relatives. The fact that my mother didn't first call before making the hour drive, taking a chance on finding me here, implied the seriousness of her mission. Frankly, I was not in the mood to talk with her at all.

Only eight a.m. and her attire was impeccable. A smart linen pantsuit, tailored to hide her extra weight. Gorgeous Italian leather loafers. Her hair a new shade of blonde—so unflattering to her olive skin tone, but she loved sporting a California look and grew horror-stricken at the sight of a single gray hair. My mother loathed exercise of any kind and had a particular distaste for her flabby arms, so always wore long-sleeved blouses, regardless of the weather. At fifty-six, her face was etched with tired lines that she masked artfully with makeup. Her breath reeked of coffee as she walked past me on her way to my freezer. She took out the loaf of rye bread and pried off a frozen slice to pop in the toaster.

"No coffee left?" she asked, eyeing the clean coffeemaker with suspicion. Jeremy always had two cups before he headed out for work in the morning, but I couldn't drink the stuff—gave me stomach cramps and migraines, and my mother knew that. I avoided catching her gaze as I filled the carafe with water at the sink.

"I'll make you some. What's with the early visit? I have to get to work, you know."

"It can wait," she said, her tone bitter enough to make me nearly drop the glass pot as I slid it in the coffeemaker. I took out the French roast beans from the freezer that I kept in a glass jar and ground up enough for a half pot. My mother buttered her toast and took it over to the dining table and sat down.

As the coffee percolated and filled the kitchen with aroma, I wiped the crumbs off the counter that my mother left in her wake. I'd never known anyone who could make such mess in so short a time. Wherever she went, disorder followed. She never thought to clean up after herself. Maybe all those years of having housekeepers in our home made her that way. She could pour herself a cup of coffee and that singular event would result in a full kitchen cleanup.

"You upset Raff with that phone call this morning. Just what did you say to him?"

I had planned to sit at the table with her but thought better of it. I kept my distance, hovering by the coffeepot. "I really need to get to work—"

"Lisa."

She had a way of saying my name that made my heart sink in my chest. Her disappointment and chastisement was calculated, as always. "What is this I hear about you calling your uncle?" Her scowl changed into a tight smile. "Whatever made you think of getting in touch with him?"

"Well . . . I ran across an article in *The Washington Post*—"

"*The Washington Post*?"

I ignored her accusatory tone. "—And saw it was written by my cousin, Mandy."

"Miranda. Is that what she calls herself, Mandy? Rather childish name, don't you think?" My mother pointed at the coffeepot as its gurgling stopped. I poured her a cup and added one spoonful of sugar. I set it in front of her and watched her drink and finish her toast. She sloshed the cup and spilled some on the table, but just scooted over so she didn't get any on her sleeve. Toast crumbs fell on the chair and floor as she ate. I set a napkin next to her but she ignored it.

She turned and stared at me. "Just what did you think your little phone call would accomplish? Raff said you planned to talk to Samuel, ask him questions about your father."

I steeled my nerve. "Well, I have this idea. I thought if I could learn more about dad and his life, his childhood, maybe it could help Raff. He always seems so angry at our dad and—"

"Oh, get real, Lisa. How can stories from thirty years ago make any difference? It's all brain chemistry, you know that. Depression runs in families and nothing you learn will change that. You're giving him false hopes, and you'll only dredge up facts that will make Raff more upset. Your father was a brilliant man and a good father. He loved you all very much."

My mother began to get a little teary-eyed. Even after all these years. Was she right—was I venturing down a path that would cause more hurt than help? "Well, it's also really nice to connect with a part of my family I don't know. We don't have very much family."

"And there's a reason we don't talk to your uncle."

"And why is that? Why haven't we stayed in touch all these years?"

My mother stood and brushed crumbs off her clothes. She pursed her lips and looked out the large dining room window at the rose garden. "They're bad people. Your aunt and uncle did things that were shameful. They mistreated your grandparents and spoke badly of your father. I didn't want you to hear the hurtful things they said, so I cut off contact with them."

"Well, it's been over twenty years. Maybe they've changed. My cousin sounds really nice. She's an attorney."

"Spoiled, both those girls were." She seemed to choose her words carefully. "Lisa, I don't want you talking to them. Your uncle will only tell you things you will regret hearing."

"Why? What will he say?" Her line of reasoning confused me. What could my uncle tell me these many years later that would cause me grief?

"Just believe me. Let dead dogs lie and leave well enough alone. Please, for Raff's sake. If you care anything about your brother, you'll drop this." End of discussion. "And where's Jeremy?""Mom, he always leaves early for work." Even as I said the words, I knew my mother didn't believe my ruse. My voice came out unexpectedly querulous.

"He's moved out, hasn't he?" Just like her. She had some arcane sixth sense about everything. Well, if she wouldn't elaborate on my uncle, I surely wasn't going to go down that path.

I mustered up nerve to look her in the eyes. "Did you get the papers Jeremy sent to your lawyer?"

She waved her hand in dismissal and emitted an exaggerated sigh. "Lisa, we've been through this so many times. Why doesn't Jeremy understand? There's nothing I can do; my hands are tied. My tax accountant says I have to keep the title in my name. You get to live here for free—isn't that enough? Why, after ten years, doesn't your husband trust me?" Her face looked pained.

"He's a guy, Mom. He's built this house and put years of labor and income into the property—we both have. He just wants to know he owns something."

She strode over to the door and looked at her watch. "Well, he owns the feed store, doesn't he? And that expensive new truck. What does a silly name on a stupid piece of paper mean, anyway?"

"I know, Mom." I exhaled and my stomach clenched. I hated having to be the go-between and the peacemaker. Like talking to two walls. Jeremy never believed my reassurances, and my mother never budged. "Well, then just sign the devise. That will ease his mind, convince him you have our best interests in mind."

"Really, Lisa." Her tone turned abrupt and snappy. "This is getting out of hand. You have the letters from the trust stating this property will go to you when I die. You get to keep your house,

Raff has his, and Neal will get mine. It's all legal, now; *drop it* already. I'm not going to live forever."

I dutifully shut my mouth at her acrimony. But something knotted in my gut and needed voicing. "How come you never talked about our dad? Not a single word, the whole time growing up. It's like you erased him from our lives, like he never existed."

My mother's face showed how taken aback she was by my comments. A ripple of emotions crossed her face, but when she spoke, her voice was even, almost apologetic. "Back in those days, people didn't discuss death. We didn't have all the pop psychology that recommended talking about pain, bringing things out in the open. Doctors and friends said the best thing I could do for you children was put the past behind me. Move on. Don't dwell on the hurt. What did I know? I had three small children to feed and clothe. I didn't have time to even think about fallout from your father's death. I worked long hours at my job, and if it hadn't been for VA money, we would have lost the house. So, I didn't have the luxury to weigh what to say and what to ignore."

"But years later, still, you never talked about him, never gave us a clue about Dad's life or personality."

"You kids never asked."

I almost scowled at her remark. "Well, maybe it would do this family some good to sit down together and talk about it."

My mother grunted and shook her head. "Lisa, it's been, what, twenty-five years? Just what on earth will that accomplish? You haven't been listening to me. Dredging up bits of the past will do nothing to help Raff—it will only make him angrier and obsessive. The best thing you can do for your brother is trust the doctors. They're the professionals and will see to it Raff gets better." She pulled a compact out of her purse and reapplied her lipstick.

Frustration rumbled through my body like a passing train. Why was she so resistant? I resented her unwillingness to talk about my father. Not just because I felt she owed it to us kids to tell us about him. But, more pointedly, she seemed not to care about my father, and her tone spoke defiance and disrespect to his memory. And that prompted me to blurt out my plans without thinking.

"I'm going to take a trip to New York. To see Mandy and her dad."

My mother stopped in the threshold and turned to face me. Her words came out slowly and enunciated. "That's a bad idea." She scowled but kept her voice quiet and controlled. "But, you'll do as you wish, always running foolishly into decisions and regretting them later. Don't think about anyone else but yourself, what heartache it may cause Raff."

I called out to her as she walked down the steps to the driveway. "I would never say anything to hurt him. I'm not stupid."

She shook her head and got into her car without a wave or good-bye. I hadn't seen her that pissed off in a long time. As I watched her Mercedes coupe head down the road, Buster and Angel trotted past me into the house. By the time I had grabbed a rag to wipe the table, the dogs had snuffed up all the crumbs from the floor. I gave them each a biscuit and herded them out the kitchen door, closing it behind me.

I'd hoped my uncle would have called by now. I was more eager than ever to talk with him, and considered what questions I would ask. Would he answer me truthfully? Maybe I would wait to delve into the sensitive issues until I saw him. Talking over the phone was awkward, and I wouldn't be able to see his expressions.

That decided it for me. I would stop at the travel agency on my way to my landscape job and book a flight. I called Jeremy at work and informed him about my sudden trip to New York. He was polite and didn't ask questions. I told him I wanted to see my cousin after all these years and he agreed to house-sit. He suggested a vacation would be good for me, help me clear my head. I didn't tell him that was the last thing I wanted to do—clear my head. I had high hopes this trip would fill my head to the brim with facts about my family. Whatever my mother feared I'd find out didn't worry me. I was a big girl now, and I could take it. I wanted to see for myself why my mother thought my uncle was a horrible man. Hear his side of the story.

I got in my work truck and started up the engine. Stevie Nicks was singing on the radio: "Talk to Me." It seemed an appropriate theme song for my day. A wave of weariness washed over me. I was already exhausted and the day had just begun. But the sky shone bright with a few soft clouds sailing overhead. The air buzzed with insects and promised to turn warm and chase the chill away. I looked forward to digging in the earth, getting my hands dirty, smelling the rich compost, and putting plants into the ground. Gardening was all about encouraging life and growth, and adding beauty to the planet. Turning a drab section of untamed ground into a work of art. Bringing order to chaos.

I flashed on the recent Challenger disaster, the film clip of the space shuttle exploding silently against the backdrop of a beautiful, calm day in Florida. How shocked I was—everyone was—by the unexpected and unthinkable turn of events. The image of the trail of white smoke seemed imprinted on my brain, reminding me again how suddenly things can change—hope to despair, calm to chaos.

I grunted. My mission—bringing order to chaos. Finding the door to enlightenment. I hoped that when the door finally swung open, a host of heavenly angels arrayed in brilliant garments would sing hallelujah and healing would flow like milk and honey. But what I feared was that I'd just find another door, one locked and barricaded.

I thought of Raff's hopelessness, the way it had travelled through the phone lines, his desperate impatience over his impotent medications. How much longer would he have to stay in that hospital? How much longer could he tenuously hold on to his life? How much longer could he face down the Jabberwock before he fell to his knees and let the beast ravage him?

That last question was one I didn't want answered.

CHAPTER 6

HOW WAS IT POSSIBLE MY father's handwriting matched my own? That, more than anything else, startled me as I reread the two-page letter my uncle had faxed to me via the local Kinko's in Petaluma. Was handwriting somehow genetically passed on?

After the plane took off and leveled out at a cruising altitude, I let my eyes drift over the rolling sentences filling the pages. Why my uncle wanted to send me this letter in advance puzzled me. We'd had a short congenial conversation, but I got the clear impression Samuel Sitteroff was one of those people who hated to talk on phones. His sentences were choppy and awkward, but he did express a warm invitation for me to come to New York and visit. He'd arranged a room for me in a clean nearby hotel, and Mandy would come to the airport to pick me up.

How could I even begin to relate the emotions I felt as I read that letter? Two pages, written by my father a few months before he died. Oozing with pain, shame, and remorse. I'd read the letter a dozen times, but it kept drawing me. I was a thirsty wanderer in a desert searching for spiritual water between the sparse enigmatic lines written by my father's hand. I tried to picture him with a pen in his grip, scrawling out the words from his bed of pain. Rather than provide answers, his secretive allusions to scandal and impropriety stirred up more questions. But, most importantly, my mother's picture of a happy marriage beset by tragedy had been shattered.

I read slowly, wishing I could make the words sing their deeper meaning instead of mumble incoherent hints of anarchy.

Dear Samuel,

When I read your letter this morning, I cried like I hadn't in years. There is so much to say, but it's not possible to fit it all on a piece of paper. The years have somehow forced a hard crust of fear over all the true nature that I have. There is so much I've hidden from you because of shame that I don't know where to begin. Someday I want to tell you the real story of my marriage, which is so important in this picture of mine. You're right—I did intentionally withdraw from you, but you represent all there is in the world to me—love, affection, understanding, father, mother, brother, family, life. And you are right, the crap has to stop piling up. Still, what can I say in a letter? When you hear my story, when you listen to what may appear to you so bizarre, so strange, and in some ways so alien to every last thing you believe in, I pray with all my heart that you will have the compassion to still love me.

I've sinned so much, my life has been such a mess, especially these last seven months. I'm afraid to say any more in this letter, because I don't know how you'll take it. I'll simply say that, while I have the most wonderful children in the world whom I love very deeply, for nearly ten years it's been an ever increasingly difficult married life, exceedingly difficult to endure. There is no point in trying to fix blame. It hardly matters anymore. Guilt on my part was great—I wanted out. But I felt to overcome the guilt that I needed to commit suicide (not very pleasant) through pernicious anemia, drinking, and finally, emotionally induced leukemia. I have done something so horrible, I know it will bring grief to my children. There is so much more, but I'm afraid to go on.

Great guns, I think I could go on for hours but I'll finish here. If I don't get to see you, I'm afraid I'll have to drop another bombshell in your lap, which frankly I feel would upset you too much now. But as you see, I'm beginning to open up. Write me soon. Love to you from the bottom of my heart.

Nathan

That one sentence stuck in my craw: "*I have done something so horrible, I know it will bring grief to my children.*" What was he referring to? Would my uncle have a clue? I thought of Macbeth asking the witches, *"How now you secret, black, and midnight hags? What is't you do?"* Their reply so branded my mind that I mulled it over for hours as I dozed on and off during the plane ride: *"a deed without a name."* What unnamable deed had my father done—something that brought on the ensuing penalty of death?

Now I had an inkling of why my mother opposed my trip. Fortunately, I had avoided further encounters with her before heading to the airport. Jeremy'd even offered to give me a lift, but I declined. My mind was too preoccupied with my father's words, words that had infiltrated my heart and mind like a penetrating dye. I couldn't handle the distraction of trying to make small talk with Jeremy, and certainly was not up to wading into deep, treacherous waters of topics that centered around either my marriage or my mother. Instead, I caught a Super Shuttle and, half aware of my surroundings, checked in my bag and found my gate.

Now that I was gaining literal distance from my mother, I pressed myself to reflect on the emotional distance that seemed to be lengthening daily. Just who was this woman who had raised me? Did I really know her at all?

The intrepid and stalwart champion of her family, the hapless victim of unexpected tragedy—these were the personas my mother wore and which she wielded to gain pity, employment, admiration, and favor. All done with a quiet and self-effacing grace that drew people to her over the years of our life in Mill Valley. I'm not sure when things shifted, but at some point, perhaps as we kids grew older and appeared less pitiable, my mother stopped evoking compassion and began her more complicated wranglings to gain unwavering loyalty from her peers and coworkers. Her commercial property portfolio grew and she socialized within the richer entrepreneurial circles of Marin County, attending parties and "functions"—fundraisers where she made sure her name appeared on programs as sponsor or donator, and charity events that reflected her concerns for a host of causes—homelessness, education, pollution, and dozens more. She served on the board of the Chamber of Commerce from 1967–1970 and occasionally hosted chamber mixers at her office.

The swinging sixties swept into Marin, and from time to time I'd go to sleep after doing homework and hear noises coming from my mother's room down the hall. More than once I heard giggles and whispering as I lay in bed at dawn; my mother was either naive or unconcerned that her clandestine affairs got picked up on our radar. My brothers and I never talked about it, but on occasion we'd make faces at each other across the dinner table, when our mother "hosted" a male friend. She never did remarry, but clearly blamed that all on me.

The only time I ever saw my mother cry was when I turned fourteen. She had been dating a man named Elliott Blass, someone she met at one of her parties. Elliott made a regular appearance in our home for a time, even took us out to play miniature golf and see movies. Of all the men she dated, Elliott was the only one who stuck it out long enough. They had even talked about marriage.

But I made the mistake of walking into my mother's room one morning—why, I don't recall. There was Elliott, standing naked next to the window, facing me in all his alarming nudity. I recall my mother turning over in bed and looking at me, her eyes widened in horror. I rushed out of the room without saying a word, and she never brought it up.

But sometime soon after, I found her sobbing in the small upstairs office in our house. The sight shook me to my core. My mother was my rock and fortress. Strong, unwavering, nothing ruffled her. Seeing her broken and in despair caused me great fear. As grown up as I thought I was, I turned into a sniveling toddler at the sight.

Yet, my panic turned to horror when she dropped her hands from her face and gave me a look that chilled my heart to ice.

"You have sabotaged every single relationship I've ever had. Every chance I had to remarry, you ruined it. You, with your big mouth and hyper personality. Drove every decent man away, as soon as they met you." And on and on her ranting went.

I was struck with the truth of her words. I had been a difficult, demanding child. My brothers endured humiliation from my fierce competitiveness. An aggressive tomboy, I could bat a ball farther, climb a tree higher, beat them in a race any day. I never once considered how it made them feel, and I was a sore loser. We used to go bowling every Saturday, but I was grounded for a whole year when I threw a temper tantrum at the bowling alley because I lost a game. I went through my early childhood obnoxious and vocal. I spent most of kindergarten and first grade in the corner, for excessive talking. My nickname was "blabbermouth."

By age twelve, I had mellowed considerably, yet had lived with the label "hyperactive" all my life. How my mother lamented that she hadn't put me on drugs to control my behavior. That no one ever told her about sugar and what it did to kids. When I think of all the boxes of Chips Ahoy I ate, the cartons of ice cream we kids devoured while watching TV, the bowls of cereal that began our day—sickeningly sweet Captain Crunch and Lucky Charms—it's amazing all my teeth hadn't rotted and fallen out of my mouth by age ten.

I never thought about the shrapnel damage from my hyperactivity until that moment when my mother blamed me for her ruined life. I had never associated what I considered was my uncontrollable medical condition with a blatant attempt at destroying every chance of happiness for my mother. Seeing my mother cry due to my heartlessness struck a stake through my heart.

The resultant flood of guilt changed me that day, started me on the path as loyal and fawning daughter. I sought to expiate my guilt over the years, but knew, somehow deep inside, that I was not, nor would ever be, forgiven. That day stood out as some kind of red-letter day, changing the dynamics of out relationship.

That day, I had somehow lost my mother. I realized while flying thirty-five thousand feet over the landscape of my life, seeing out of hawk's eyes the landmarks of my childhood, that I had been trying for the last fifteen years to get her back.

As I stared out the airplane window at the flat patchwork farm landscape, it hit me that maybe the reason I had been so obnoxious was I craved attention from a mother who had rarely been home. Up until I was four, my mother was my life. She was a homemaker, as most wives were back in the 'sixties before women's liberation. My father's sudden death ripped her away from me. I was shuffled off to day care, left with maids who couldn't speak English, and had to drop out of ballet and piano classes because we couldn't afford them. No wonder I rallied all my energy to one end—to find ways of getting my mother's attention, of getting her back.

Not long after my father's death, I went on a stealing binge. I rode my bicycle around the neighborhood and took recyclable bottles and cans from neighbors' garages. I pilfered change out of friend's change jars and piggy banks, even pocketed Barbie clothing and Tonka trucks from my playmates' toy bins. I wandered behind houses, strolled through walkways between homes, looking for what I could take. My success at going undetected made me brazen, which led me to start stealing candy from the local liquor store at the bottom of Molino Drive. Only when I was spotted by the pimply college student running the cash register—which caused me to run a mile uphill, then hide for the better part of an hour—did I question my behavior and stop stealing. Psychiatrists would probably have said my stealing was a cry for attention. I'm sure that was part of it.

Years later, with Raff away at college, my mother busy with her social calendar, and Neal playing baseball and other sports nearly every day after school, I was set adrift. Raff had been a gel that kept us together. His magnetism and authority wove a spell over Neal and me when he was around. Once he left home, my sense of family disintegrated, but against the backdrop of my mind, Raff was larger than life, infallible, awe-inspiring.

Until the night he suddenly appeared at our house, a week before school let out for summer.

I had been given no notice. I don't even recall how Raff had gotten home from the airport. Although I strained my memory, trying to fill in the missing details, I couldn't place Raff anywhere other than on the edge of my mother's bed, his face buried in his hands, my mother's hand resting on his shoulder as he cried in convulsing jags. I knew he had been driving home in his light blue Datsun—all the way from Colorado, for summer vacation. So where was his car?

Then it struck me. He had told me on the phone before finals were over that he was bringing his best friend with him. That Steve had never seen the ocean, imagine that? They would take a road trip, visit the Grand Canyon, check out Death Valley, then weave up through Yosemite and arrive home by the end of the month. It was only mid-June. Where was Steve? Had Raff's plans changed?

My mother had noticed me standing in the doorway of her bedroom late that night, speechlessly watching this disturbing display of anguish. I couldn't help myself—seeing Raff losing it had the same effect as seeing my mother cry only months earlier. Tears flooded down my face and I started to speak, but my mother held up her hand and stopped me.

"Raff was in an accident. But it wasn't his fault."

She turned to Raff and hardened her voice. "You have to tell yourself this, Raff. Because it's true. It wasn't your fault. Whatever you say on the phone, don't let those words out. I know you feel to blame. But if you tell them it was your fault, they will sue me for every penny I've got. Tell them how sorry you are, but make sure you say it was an accident. You did nothing wrong."

My mind frantically chased after my mother's words. What accident? What happened? I didn't dare utter a sound as my mother handed Raff the phone receiver.

I could still see that scene so clearly in my mind. The old black dial-up phone sitting on my mother's lap. The rumpled bedcovers, Raff's argyle socks—tan and navy—on his feet, resting on the pale gold long-shag wall-to-wall carpeting. Passing car lights spattering through the blinds. I had watched in horror as my brother cleared his throat and wiped his eyes, listening to my mother dialing a number she read off a piece of scrap paper, and waiting for a voice on the other end.

From where I stood I could only hear Raff's choppy sentences, phrased between sobs. My mother kept one hand on Raff's shoulder to steady him, but even as Raff broke the news to Steve's parents and recited the words as instructed, I saw little compassion in her eyes. Her intense focus was on the content of Raff's speech, and after he hung up, she nodded and told him he did well, as if he had just pulled off a stunning performance on stage. Raff hardly heard anything she said; he was drowning in his guilt.

I only learned what happened the next morning, as my mother rushed to get ready for a day's work at the office and Raff hid in his bedroom. I don't remember where Neal was.

Raff and Steve had just switched driving. They were traveling through New Mexico when it started to rain. The road, oily and dry, became slick as the first spatterings of water wet down the asphalt. Steve was asleep in the backseat and Raff took a curve a little too fast. The car spun out, hitched as a tire caught when Raff tried to correct the skid, and the car tumbled and flipped twice before landing upside down. Steve was somehow thrown out of the car and onto the highway. Three of the four roof supports were crushed. The windshield was smashed, the glass shattered. But Raff, strapped into his seat, his section of the roof still intact, came through the tumble unscathed. Apart from the bump on his head from smacking the windshield, he didn't have a cut or bruise.

By the time he unbuckled and worked his way out through the broken windshield, the rain pelleted steadily. He looked inside the car and found Steve gone. Moments later he found his friend unconscious a few yards behind the car. Steve died in his arms.

The officer who took Raff's statement wrote in the report how that particular stretch of highway was known for fatalities. That as soon as it started to rain, people often skidded out and crashed on the curves. He told Raff they needed more warning signs, and that maybe they'd put some up now. I remember listening to my mother's detached report of the accident. And her instructions to me to make Raff some breakfast.

After she left, silenced smothered the house. I stood in the kitchen, the smell of coffee and fried eggs strangling the air, wondering how my mother had found an appetite to eat breakfast. Or to leave for work, abandoning Raff to his anguish. How could she have done that? The charred bacon smell nauseated me.

I kept picturing Raff holding his friend in his arms, crouched on the side of the road, in the dark, in the rain, in an unfamiliar place, alone and afraid. At some point someone drove along and stopped, went and got help, called the police, an ambulance. Who knew how long that took, but I was sure an eternity passed for Raff. Surely, Raff felt Steve's death was his fault. I pictured them talking excitedly in the car, Raff telling him how beautiful the ocean looked, how they would drive up the coast along the San Andreas Fault, stop in Bodega Bay for fish and chips. Then I pictured the vague face of a woman with her ear to the phone receiver late in the night, wondering who was sobbing on the line, trying to make out some young man's words that made no sense, no sense at all.

Even though Raff's accident occurred sixteen years ago, as I stared out the plane window, tears dropped hot onto my cheeks. I couldn't imagine a more devastating end to childhood innocence than what Raff had experienced. His first year away at college. His life as an adult opening up to him with all its promises and potential. The heavy burden of guilt he would now carry around with him for the rest of his life, regardless of my mother's assurances of his blamelessness.

The fun, adventurous summer I had eagerly awaited was replaced by Raff carrying Steve's death in his arms everywhere he went, an invisible weight that bent him over and made him sluggish and enveloped in ennui.

That summer, Raff had crawled into himself, like a snail retreating into a shell. No one questioned his two months of depression or his unwillingness to join in our activities. We gave him a wide berth, spoke in quiet voices around him, the hushed tone you hear in hospital corridors. And then the dreary, oppressive summer ended and Raff returned to college, sending me into my melancholy and music, the horizon of my own future now tainted dark and foreboding.

CHAPTER 7

I HAD NO TROUBLE PICKING Mandy out of the crowd loitering by the cars along the curb at JFK Airport. Her bright face, her dancer's body—petite yet muscular—gave her away. With an enthusiastic wave, she beckoned me over to her car and gave me a vigorous hug. She wore khaki shorts and a gray tank top, and her thick dark hair wrapped around her face and tickled her shoulders. I searched to see some family resemblance but found none. Maybe she favored her mother.

"How was your flight? Got all your stuff?" she asked.

I nodded as she grabbed my suitcase and tossed it into the trunk.

"Great, then we're off to Dad's. Do you need to stop, get something to eat?"

"I had a meal on the plane—if you could call it that. But, I can hold out until dinner." I had left San Francisco at seven a.m., and it was now nearly four in the afternoon, New York time. The air smelled like every other airport, but felt thicker, muggier. Heavy clouds filled the sky.

"They're predicting rain, but it won't be more than a brief thundershower," Mandy said, getting in behind the wheel. I sat in the front seat and took in the city sights as we drove along the throughway, the traffic heavy but unimpeding. Mandy gave a rambling, enthusiastic monologue—my personal tour guide—pointing out buildings and relating trivia facts that started fleshing in my surroundings for me.

I had to ask. "I have this odd memory of a giant globe alongside the highway. Does that make sense?"

Mandy laughed. "The Unisphere—from the World's Fair. It's still there. In Flushing, Queens. My folks took you kids there, with me and Becka. You ate this giant lollypop, you know, those rainbow spirals on a stick? You threw up in the car on the way home." Mandy laughed as I shook my head.

"You'd think I'd remember that," I said.

"My mother had a fit, because it was their new car—a Lincoln something. Dad pulled over, off the road, while Mom tried to clean the floorboards. I remember being grossed out by the smell." She smiled and patted my arm. "Don't worry, no one holds that against you. Do you remember the little cedar boxes Dad bought us there, at the fair? I still have mine."

That little jewelry box sat on my dresser, among a few other mementos from my childhood. I had no memory of where I got that box, but as soon as Mandy mentioned it, the gift shop appeared in my mind in minute detail. Shelves filled with small statuettes of the Statue of Liberty, snow globes of Rockefeller Center, miniature versions of the colossal Unisphere of various sizes, some that functioned as piggy banks. Models of various planes and space capsules hanging from wires overhead, illuminated by bright spotlights.

The rush of memory startled me, coming from some strange cache in my brain. I could see my uncle Samuel at the counter, in a dark green tailored shirt, with gold cufflinks, buying the varnished cedar boxes while Mandy and I clamored excitedly at his side. How many times had I been to New York? Maybe many of my memories got tangled with others so that the places I daydreamed of, locales from my childhood, were miscatalogued in my brain as Los Angeles and Marin County.

"I still have my box too. Who else was there with us? Was my mother there?"

"I don't think so. Not sure."

We talked about shows currently playing on Broadway, kicking around ideas of how to spend the next few days. Mandy had bought tickets for the ballet, hoping I was game. I told her I was up for anything.

"Where's Nathan?" I asked, suddenly remembering her son.

"At Dad's. We'll be there soon."

I recognized Central Park as we drove alongside it—the green lawns and pathways. We drove up the Westside, Mandy giving me a roundabout tour of Manhattan, passing theaters and the Lincoln Center, until we turned onto Seventy-sixth Street and parked. The brownstone buildings crowded together and people filled the streets, hurrying, shopping, waiting for buses. A small Greek restaurant took up the corner, with patrons sitting on small café tables under a drooping awning. Street markets dotted almost every block, with fruit perched against the buildings in crates and displays, barely allowing room for foot traffic to squeeze by. I wondered if New York had its own distinct aroma, for the smells of the traffic and the streets and the trash bagged up in piles along the sidewalks triggered recognition in me. San Francisco, with its briny air and ocean breezes, had a different redolence, fresher, cleaner. But even though the air in New York felt stale and damp, it still invigorated me.

I followed Mandy into a posh, well-preserved older apartment building, hefting my suitcase along. To my relief, Mandy passed the elevators and opened the door to the stairwell. She stopped abruptly.

"Oops, forgot about your suitcase. My folks are on the next floor, so I always take the stairs. Do you want to use the elevator?"

"No, I'm good. Elevators and I don't agree."

Mandy studied my face and nodded. "Well, I guess we'll pass on the visit to the top of the Trade Towers, then. Although, a lot of people like walking up the stairs at the Statue of Liberty. We can do that, if you want. And the Staten Island Ferry is fun."

I followed Mandy up to the second floor and down the hallway to apartment 2A. She opened the door and within seconds I was bowled over by a small person with a head full of black hair. Two big round eyes looked up at me and shrieked in delight. Nathan's little arms wrapped around my knees and I worked to balance myself.

"Hey, sport," Mandy said to her son, "don't tackle her."

"Hi, cousin Lisa!"

"He's very excited you're here," Mandy said, disengaging Nathan's arms from my legs. "Go get your sketch book. I'm sure Lisa would love to see your drawings."

"Okay!"

Nathan flew out of the room and Mandy called out. "Hey, we're here. Pop, where are you?"

A tall, lean man came in from a back room. I instantly recognized his oval face and kind eyes, and his resemblance to Rafferty was uncanny. His thinning hair on the top of his head was gray and not the chestnut brown I seemed to remember, but his manner and the way he walked toward me was more than familiar. Samuel Sitteroff was lodged in my memory, and although I couldn't bring to mind any specific moments of my childhood with him, I knew I had spent time with him, had sat on his couch and watched TV at his house, eaten at his table, and gone to the zoo with him. How had I erased him entirely?

I now realized I had spent many childhood summers over here, in this apartment, and my lack of memory agitated me. Head trauma, or some horrific pain—I had nothing to blame for the blank pages in my past. Was something wrong with me? Did anyone else have these lapses of memory? It seemed so incongruous to me that I could recall dozens of verses of random rhyme and entire scenes from plays but couldn't call to mind things that really mattered. Maybe I had been so wound up as a child, I hadn't paid any attention to my surroundings. Or was there another reason?

While my mind ruminated over this perplexing problem, Mandy had gone into the kitchen and brought out a tray with a pitcher of lemonade and glasses. The apartment was a little too cold for my liking, with the air conditioner running—an appliance I never had need of in the temperate climate of Marin. My uncle gave me a hug and gestured me to sit in an upholstered chair beside the couch. Nathan was soon back at my side, tugging on my sleeve.

"Look! Look!"

He showed me all the pages he'd colored in his Superman coloring book and I made the appropriate noises of being astounded by his artistic prowess. My uncle and cousin chuckled as they watched on, Mandy sidling up to her father on the couch. The apartment was tastefully appointed, with some artwork and family photos adorning the walls. The colors were a bit dark and the stained wood molding around the doorways and windows were elegantly milled, from an earlier time, perhaps. A charming and welcoming apartment, with big windows.

After Mandy got Nathan set up with his crayons, he retired to the dining room table to draw. Once Samuel was assured I didn't need to eat yet and we finalized our dinner plans, we spent the next hour catching up. I tried not to let show all the emotions that had been ravaging my heart over the last two weeks, but I'd never been good at concealing my feelings. Perhaps my uncle's soft bedside manner, his gentle questions that didn't feel like prodding, lulled me into a feeling of safety.

Soon, I was in tears, despite my best efforts, detailing everything from my miscarriage, my fears over my marriage, and my mother's attempts at sabotaging my happiness for the sake of "family unity," to the reason why I had come. We had a long discussion about leukemia and its pathology. My uncle had always wondered why my father was told his leukemia was "emotionally induced." Samuel had spoken to my father's doctor when he visited Nathan in the hospital before his death. The doctors, as expected, had no answers or postulations as to how anyone acquired leukemia. It was the mysterious disease of the decade, and even twenty-five years later, medical researchers were still flummoxed.

Samuel discounted the idea that a person could *will* himself such a disease. He had doubts about my father's depression, though, and that surprised me. My mother had painted a grim picture of my father's mental state, his death wish, his feelings of bad blood. Samuel dispelled all that with a description of a young man who was exuberant over life. Sure, my father'd had a tough early childhood, but Samuel remembered Nathan as happy, easy-going, and even-keeled for most of his adult life. That is, until years into his marriage with my mother. That's when Samuel noticed a change in my father's temperament. But, he admitted, it was possible Nathan was bipolar. Often the symptoms didn't manifest until a person was well into their twenties. Samuel just wasn't around Nathan during those years—a whole continent of land had separated them.

Mandy and Samuel behaved graciously in the face of my mother's cruel accusations about "their" side of the family. Mandy came to the defense of her parents when I told them what my mother had said about them—that they had neglected my grandparents, among other acts of familial treason.

"That's so not true!" Mandy said, with her father patting her arm, urging her to calm down. "Pop, you and Mom were the only ones who cared for them before they died." She turned to me. "My folks came over daily, made sure they had around-the-clock care, food in the fridge. My other uncles couldn't give a hoot. At one point Pop hired a wonderful nurse—what was her name, Pop?"

"Trina," he said. "She stayed with them the last year—on their pull-out sofa. A big heart, that woman."

"Trina. That's right." Mandy's attorney voice took front stage. She was presenting evidence to her jury of one—me. "Where in the world did your mother come up with such bullshit?—excuse my French."

I waved my hand in dismissal. "That's okay." I could tell Mandy was a person that, once she got going, was probably hard to stop. Good litigator material, no doubt. "My mother's like that. Quick to find fault."

"But she turned you kids against us—why?"

I shrugged. "I think she didn't want us finding out the truth about her marriage. That she and my dad weren't as happy as she wanted us to believe."

Samuel added. "I remember Nina and your mother had some words. The two of them didn't get along well."

Mandy jumped in to elaborate. "My mom didn't like yours. Thought she was manipulative, pushy. There was a fight, right, Pop?"

"A minor thing," he said with a frown, studying Mandy. "Arguing over childrearing. Ruth thought Nina was spoiling you and Becka, letting you stay up as late as you wanted, watching old reruns on TV. Something like that."

"Seems kind of petty," Mandy said.

Samuel shrugged, bowing out of taking sides. "But maybe Lisa's right. When I came to visit your dad when he was first diagnosed," he said to me, "your parents put on a pretense of living together. But, your dad took me aside and told me. They'd been living apart for many months."

"Really? Did he tell you he'd had an affair?"

My uncle thought for a moment. "Not in so many words. But he said he was living in an apartment in Hollywood, that he couldn't take living in the house with Ruth, with the way he was feeling. At that point, he was just starting his chemo and radiation, and spending more time in the hospital than out. Your mother acted as if everything was fine and put on quite a show for Nina and me. But I could see the pain in Nate's eyes—not just from the cancer. His whole world was crashing down on him. It broke my heart."

When Samuel's voice choked up, I looked closer and saw his eyes fill with tears.

"We don't have to talk about this, if you don't want to," I said. "When are our dinner reservations?"

Mandy looked up at the wall clock. "Pop, we should get ready. Lisa, aren't you starving?"

"Yeah, I'm getting hungry."

Samuel stood and Nathan jumped up from the table.

"Are we going to Gino's? Pleeease?" Nathan tugged on Mandy's arm so hard she nearly toppled.

"Nate! Not so hard. Yes, we're going to Gino's. Now, let's get you washed up." She took her son by the hand and led him to the bathroom. Samuel turned to me and his voice was kind and sincere.

"I'm so happy you've come to visit us. It's been too long."

I nodded. "Yes, it has." I gave him a hug and we gathered up sweaters and purses and toys for the restaurant.

On the way down the stairs, Samuel turned to me. "I remember when your folks were dating. Your dad was looking to join the Merchant Marines, and your mother would come over every weekend and help my mother out in the kitchen. Ruth wanted to get married to your father, more than anything. Who could blame her? Your dad was handsome, smart, gentle. But he wanted to go to college and couldn't afford it. Your mother kept promising him that if he'd marry her, her folks would help pay. She put a lot of pressure on Nate, and my mother thought Ruth was an opportunist, trying to bribe Nate into marrying her."

"Your mother didn't like her."

"No. And she thought it suspicious that Ruth would make such promises of financial assistance when her own father was a plumber and didn't earn all that much. How would they be able to help?"

"What did you think?" I asked as we went out the lobby doors to the street and the balmy New York evening.

Samuel measured his words. "Your dad joined the Merchant Marines to get away from her, from the pressure. He could earn money for college without asking for handouts. Then, right before your dad was ready to ship out, after his training, she told him she was pregnant."

"What?" I stopped on the sidewalk and my family stopped too. "With Raff?"

Mandy had been walking in front of us, with Nathan pulling her along, eager to get to the restaurant. "What are you two talking about? What am I missing?"

Samuel waved her on with a gesture that said "I'll fill you in later." Mandy shrugged and resumed her lead. I saw the sign for the restaurant on the corner of the next block.

I repeated my question with a lowered voice as we continued walking. "Was she pregnant with Raff?"

"This was two years before Raff was born. But it backed Nate into a corner. Back then, you got a girl pregnant, you married her. Your father wouldn't dare shame her or her family."

"So, they got married?"

"Right away. They had talked of marriage, but your dad had been undecided. Wanted to wait until his stint in the service ended, to see if their relationship had lasting power. Now, he had no choice. They couldn't get the large hall they wanted for the reception, but they did have a nice wedding, with dozens of relatives from both sides. Your mother looked stunning and Nate actually seemed happy."

"You guys coming in?" Mandy asked, while little Nathan yanked on the heavy door to the restaurant.

"We'll be just a minute. Go on ahead," Samuel said. He drew closer to me and I leaned in to hear his soft voice. We moved away from the door so other patrons could enter. Samuel's face grew serious. "After your dad left overseas, he found out the pregnancy was a false alarm."

"Imagine that," I said with some sarcasm before I could catch myself.

Samuel nodded in understanding. "She claimed she miscarried after the eighth week, which is quite common, you know. But your dad always wondered if that's what really happened. Frankly, I think your mother wanted to make sure Nate married him before he left, in case he had a mind to forget her during his travels."

"So, not a great way to start a marriage."

"No," Samuel said. "But we shouldn't make Mandy wait. We'll talk some more later.

And talk we did. For the next few days, while eating, taking in the city and the sights, and more eating, I learned everything I could about Nathan Sitteroff. The story my uncle painted of my father's childhood was grim and revealing, but he kindly told all in an honest and sincere voice, conjuring up a story in my head that tugged at my heart.

CHAPTER 8

NATHAN IS FIVE YEARS OLD when his father dumps him off at the local child services. The Depression, in full rage in 1931, causes Mel Schumacher to lose his job as a tailor in a haberdashery shop on Westchester Avenue in the Bronx. Having two older children—Judith and Aaron—whom he can barely feed, he convinces his wife, whom he refers to as a useless lazy bitch, that the youngest has to go.

By the time he has been shuffled around from place to place, Nathan remembers little about his parents and siblings. The orphanages and adoption agencies have their hands full, and placement and adoption records are poorly kept. Worse, the stipend issued to foster parents, although meager, is enough to tempt the dregs of humanity to offer a spare room—which, in Nathan's case, often proves to be a mattress on a floor, or a pile of flea-infested blankets in the corner of a room, which he shares with three or four other mishandled children.

Nathan remembers his father as a lanky man with thick bushy eyebrows and a continual scowl. But, he pushes from his young mind Mel Schumacher's other unpleasant characteristics. Not until he relocates his father nearly thirty years later does he encounter a man so repulsive and vulgar that Nathan refuses to believe this was the same man that used to buy him Hershey's chocolate bars every Friday evening after dinner at the local soda shop. The horror of those four years of being dumped in one crowded, filthy apartment after another never leaves Nathan. Samuel, five years younger, only spends two years in the foster home system with Nathan—joining him later—and has no memories at all of being shuffled from family to family.

The first time Nathan lays eyes on his younger brother is when the two-year-old is dropped off at the apartment Nathan shares with a Romanian family that doesn't speak any English. He doesn't know he has a younger brother until the agency worker tells him to take Samuel's hand and watch over him. The agency, committed to keeping siblings together, finds it hard to place both boys as a unit and so takes whatever accommodations are available. And that usually means the worst places on their lists. But what choice do they have in such dire conditions? They can't allow a two-year-old and a seven-year-old to wander the streets, searching trash cans for food, as the many squatters and vagrants do.

Over the next two years, Nathan and Samuel are placed and removed from various homes, where the foster parents frequently scream at each other, at the children, succumb to alcoholism, illness, depression, and—on occasion—death. Without any warning or explanation, Nathan and Sam are plucked from an apartment and dragged across neighborhoods, only to stand at the looming door of yet another fearful foster home.

Each apartment seems worse than the previous. Nathan's pervading awareness is of hunger. He is nearly starved in each home, as food is scarce and rationed. Foster parents often use ration coupons to buy their own food and deprive the children in their care. Nathan takes to rummaging out of the trash for scraps, even eating cockroaches he catches as they scurry across floorboards and up walls.

His father's promise is his only thread of hope—that he will return for him soon, and bring a Hershey bar. Nathan spends endless hours looking out windows to the sidewalks below, searching for his father's shape, his coat, in the crowds on the streets. Every time a front door opens, Nathan rushes toward it, hoping against hope that Mel Schumacher has come to save him from this horrific existence, has rushed to whisk him home, where he will be safe and where his own bed awaits. He knows his being pawned off on other families had been a grave mistake, and the error would be rectified, the trauma put behind them all. Oh, how his parents miss him and did all they could to arrange to get him back. It had been a terrible thing they had done out of necessity, but Nathan forgives them.

But as the months grow into years, Nathan's expectation blooms into anger, and then hate. And it may not have ended so badly had his emotions remained locked there. Instead, Nathan grows melancholy with self-doubt and self-condemnation. Surely, the reason his father never returns is he, Nathan, is unworthy of love. His sister, Judith, and brother Aaron are never handed off, thrown out like trash. Nathan knows he must have done something terribly wrong to earn his parents' disgust, for them to forget him so readily. He is despicable and detestable, unworthy of regard.

So, Nathan grows listless and depressed, wasting away with little notice until the placement agency representative comes to call at the foster home where Nathan and Samuel stay. Nathan sleeps in a narrow bed with Samuel, who wets the mattress each night as he sleeps. When Nathan refuses to tell his foster mother who did such a heinous deed, she takes out a belt and beats both children raw. Nathan can't bear to see Samuel so mistreated, so he admits to the offense and takes the daily beating upon himself.

By now, New York City is inundated with casualties from the Great Depression. Children are often the ones that suffered most—from neglect and abuse. One look at my father's unwashed, wasting body is all it takes for the woman from the agency to pull Nathan and Samuel out of their current home and into an orphanage where they will at least get bathed and eat real food.

Despite all the efforts of the workers at the orphanage, Nathan will not pull out of his depression, and he has to be force-fed. He slowly hardens into stone, and shoves the memories of his father, his mother, his siblings far, far back where they can't haunt him ever again. Through persistence, those at the orphanage are able to get Nathan stronger; he gains some weight, color comes back to his face, and after a time, he joins in with the other children in games and reading. A young woman volunteer notices Nathan's keen interest in books and teaches him to read, which he latches onto with a hunger not unlike his physical one.

Weeks later, the woman who runs the orphanage interrupts Nate as he sits on the floor, against the wall, reading a book.

"Nathan, I want you to meet someone."

Nate looks up into the face of two small smiling people—a man and a woman who approach with their arms linked together. He feels their eyes assess him, and a stab of panic races through him as he imagines these two strangers taking him away from the only place he's ever felt safe and cared for. He drops his gaze back to his book and scowls, hoping his fierce expression will scare the couple away.

The director speaks again, in a soft voice that makes Nathan dare lift his head. "These lovely people want to take you and Sammy home. They have two other sons, one your age. And you and Sammy would have your own room—and bathroom."

Nathan looks up and scrutinizes the faces bearing down on him. They smile in a friendly way, but he knows they can't be trusted; no one can.

He mumbles and looks at the floor. "Why can't we stay here?"

"Because, this is no life for a child. You know that, Nathan. You and Sammy need a real home, a family."

"I already had one of those."

Nathan hears the director sigh, resignation in her voice. Nathan is doing what he can to make those people disappear. They are just like all those other foster parents, smiling at first, assuring the placement agency they are great parents, just love kids. And then, once they'd get him and Sammy alone, it would start. The yelling, the starvation, the filth, the beatings. He lets his mind harden up and tightens his muscles. He will not budge. There is no way they will make him go. No way.

Nathan lifts his eyes at the sound of his brother running over and laughing. He watches in surprise and fear as Sammy grabs the lady's leg and hugs it in a fit of giggles. Nathan jumps to his feet to pull Sammy away, but stops as he watches the woman look down and stroke Sammy's head. There is something so natural and comforting in her gesture that Nathan freezes up and watches in fascination. Sammy is naturally affectionate and happy-go-lucky, but what does he know? He is only about three years old. Life at the orphanage, for Sammy, is an adventure and full of games and puzzles and snacks. He'd walk off with anyone, and that's why it is Nathan's job to look out for him, to protect him from the evil in the world—evil that lurks just steps outside the door to the orphanage.

But something melts in Nathan at that moment, as the director stands watching him, as Samuel plays catch-me, circling the woman's legs and the couple laughing at his antics and tousling his red hair. Some fierce need takes hold of Nathan, like a thirsty wanderer spying an oasis in the desert, compounding his need, making him hurry. The sight of simple affection and careless laughter prods in him the courage to take a hesitant step forward.

Samuel, breathless from his antics, drops laughing to the floor, but the woman lifts her head and meets Nathan's eyes, and without reservation, opens her arms to him. Before he can think, forcing away chastisements and warnings erupting in his heart, he falls into her arms and lets their warmth and comfort enfold him. He feels a manly pat on his shoulder and looks into the encouraging eyes of Arthur Sitteroff.

The kindly old orphanage director speaks. "Just try it for a few weeks. If you don't feel comfortable there, you can come back here, okay, sugar? Would you like that?"

Nathan's throat closes up so tightly the words can't come out. He nods and presses tears back. He can't let them see him cry. Crying is for sissies, and only results in a beating. He kneels and looks at Sammy's wide sparkling eyes and speaks in a whisper.

"What do you think? Do you want to go home with these people?"

Sammy nods and throws his arms around Nathan. Little soft arms that musses up his shirt and hair.

"Okay," Nathan tells him, feeling a great weight lift from his heart. "Then let's get your stuff."

My uncle told me many stories while I visited with him and Mandy. What it was like for him and my father growing up in the West Bronx, that my dad was well liked. I was surprised to hear he loved musical theater, and when in high school, starred in some school plays and actually sang in front of an audience. Somehow those images didn't jibe with my picture of the serious scientist. My dad—singing Gilbert and Sullivan? But I was glad to hear my father had a happy life growing up with the Sitteroffs. That at least he had some years unencumbered by anger, guilt, or misery.

My uncle also told me what happened to Judith and Aaron—their older brother and sister who had been privileged to remain at home—although that phrase could only be used sardonically. Aaron became profoundly schizophrenic and spent most of his adult life in an institution. My uncle was contacted many years later, after he had finished medical school, by a governmental agency that had tracked Samuel down. How they found him was a mystery. But my uncle told me stories of the years of visits he had made upstate to visit Aaron and how mentally and emotionally incapacitated his older brother was. Somehow, he had learned that Judith had moved to Europe and eventually committed suicide. Surely, mental illness did run rampant in my family.

My mind and heart filled to overflowing with stories until I couldn't process anymore. Mandy and I spent one day visiting my aunt Nina, whose no-nonsense, austere demeanor also triggered an avalanche of memories. We had a lovely visit and, before I knew it, the day of my departure arrived. With gratitude, I hugged my family good-bye as they saw me off at JFK.

As I stood on the curb watching them drive off, I was struck by the stark realization that I felt more simple affection for my uncle and cousin than I did for my own mother and brothers.

CHAPTER 9

WHEN I ARRIVED HOME, EXHAUSTED and jet-lagged, Jeremy was at the house, throwing the ball for Angel on the driveway, with Buster barking up his usual storm in protest. As much as his Lab genes pressed him after the tennis ball, Buster kept his distance from Angel's snapping jaws. No one came between Angel and her fetching target—be it ball, sock, or rope. But both dogs rushed over to the Super Shuttle, yipping and prancing when they saw me emerge from the van—Angel with the ball tight between her jaws, her welcoming barks muffled but enthusiastic.

Jeremy stood on the flagstone walkway and gave me a lackluster hug when I approached. "Kendra called a little while ago. Your brother's home from the hospital. I thought, if you weren't too tired, we could go over and visit."

I assessed Jeremy's demeanor. He seemed relaxed, happy to see me. I pondered his words. Did this mean Raff was better? Or did it only indicate Raff couldn't take those ugly green walls a day longer? I luxuriated in the cool evening clime, absent of the clinging humidity so oppressive in New York. The scent of honeysuckles and roses filled the air like a mist, adding to the more pungent smell of mowed grass—the heady aroma I always associated with the start of summer. Across the pasture, the pond glistened in the dusky light and a few frogs chortled, loud enough for me to hear from this distance. My heart grew melancholy at the pristine surroundings—this Eden Jeremy and I had created. Despite all outward appearances, there was trouble in paradise.

When we had first set up camp in our small trailer, nature engulfed us with its tall grasses and brambles. Trees dropped ungainly limbs on our roof at the wind's meager rustlings. We cut a swath with the ride-along mower from our door to the gravel drive, slowly taming the wild beauty into submission. With help from a contractor friend, the piles of lumber, brick, rock, flagstone, and concrete sand all morphed into a simple but stunning ranch home, where the wildness was now kept at bay behind the half circle of Bigleaf maples. Deer often strolled across our back lawn, and migrating Canada geese lighted on the pond in season. Occasionally, a snowy egret or blue heron perched on the pond's edge, searching for fish. Bears, raccoons, skunks, even the rare mountain lion roamed over those oak-studded hills, making us forget that urban plight and traffic jams were just a few scant miles away.

Jeremy came alongside me. His quietness bespoke a drinking in of the life proliferating around us. The property was more than ground, more than a compilation of hours spent in physical exertion. We had sunk more than love and roots into this place; our very souls were enmeshed and pulsed with the seasons that ebbed and flowed here. I worried that the threads that tied us together were inevitably sewn up with this land, that if either of us walked away from it, it would tear the fiber of our relationship apart, with no hope of repair.

After a while, I broke the spell. "How is Raff? Better?"

Jeremy only shrugged, the man of few words. Often he said more in his silences than in his speech, a language at times fluent with nuances words failed to address. Either he didn't know Raff's status or he wasn't telling. My trepidation grew as I walked into the house. Would Jeremy's things be back in place, or would he be returning to his rented couch down the way? With my mind so preoccupied with the discoveries from my trip, I hadn't given much thought to my life with Jeremy. Now I realized I had shuffled it into that drawer in the back of my head labeled "denial."

A quick glance told me things were as I left them. I guessed one week's separation was not enough to make Jeremy realize he needed me as much as I needed him. A throb started in at my temples and I squinted in the bright kitchen lighting. I poured myself a glass of water at the sink. "Do you want to go see him?" I asked.

A pause. "If you want me along."

His was a face I read easily, from years of careful study. That crooked smile belied his reticence. I didn't blame him for wanting to avoid the melodrama of my family. His parents couldn't pose a greater contrast—quiet, reserved, polite. Visiting Jeremy's folks in Montana was like stepping into an episode of *Little House on the Prairie*. Conversations were simple, topics nonvolatile. Life in their home felt uncomplicated. Problems needed only practical, timeworn solutions. If the well pump stopped working, you went out a bought a new part and fixed it. That was the approach the Boltons took to all problems, great and small, external or internal. I tried to imagine how they would react to the kind of flamboyant emotionalism that characterized any gathering of my family. No doubt, they would look on in disbelief and confusion. The way I often reacted, as well—needing subtitles for the ponderous subtext.

"Maybe I should go alone," I said, offering him reprieve. A flicker of relief flashed in his eyes. "If Raff isn't doing well, things could get ugly."

Jeremy nodded. "I fed the gang." He gestured to the barn. "The kids are getting big and are a kick to watch. Shayla injured her leg somehow and I've been treating the wound. It's not deep."

Shayla was a small, lame white Arabian horse I acquired last year. Her owner had moved away and left her to fend for herself in a rundown corral. Fortunately, a PG&E repairman spotted her languishing and called the rescue organization. Shayla had a sweet but fiery disposition. No one would ever ride her again, but she enjoyed her status in my pasture as the top dog. Sometimes she got ornery and chased the sheep and goats, kicking up her legs and snorting the way Arabs do. But as much as she tried to appear aloof, invariably I'd find her sleeping at night flanked by the goats, who'd sidle up against her legs and rest their heads on her hooves.

"Well, I think I'll take a quick shower and then head over." The kitchen started closing in on me just a little. Jeremy must have sensed my discomfort. He walked over and gave me a quick kiss, pulling away before I could react.

"I'll bring by a load of hay after work tomorrow." He added with a look that I read as apologetic, "Glad you're home. I hope your visit with your relatives went well."

"It did, thanks. Why don't you stay for dinner when you bring the hay? I'll tell you all about it."

"Okay."

In that brief moment I knew he had more to tell me, unpleasant things that I dreaded to hear. I was struck by the tone of sadness in his manner. I noticed it not just in his voice; a blanket of unhappiness draped his whole being.

I felt suddenly guilty for his condition, as if I had wrapped him up in this net of misery and trapped him there. That had never been my intention in this relationship of ours. The morass we were floundering in seemed to have arrived like a sudden storm, catching us unaware. Before we had time to shore up the doors and windows of our love, something dark and brooding had battered us. Maybe the squall had been coming for a long time and I just didn't see it. Maybe I had ignored all the warning signs that Jeremy kept pointing out to me.

I thought about Anne's words, her stating so confidently that my mother was the cause of our meltdown. Sure, Jeremy was often at odds with my mother, but a lot of people didn't get along with their in-laws. My mother could be rude and demanding, but for most of the last ten years Jeremy put up with her demands without complaint. Yet, she also complimented him, and showed her appreciation when he fixed things at her house or worked in her yard. Jeremy had enough self-esteem to take her occasional bashing and never had a problem telling my mother to back down when she pushed too hard. So why had things escalated to this level of tension? Had something happened between my mother and

Jeremy? Something I didn't know about, some conversation or confrontation I was not privy to?

I realized Jeremy was still there, waiting by the door, studying me. He caught my eyes and every great fear within me became confirmed in that look of his. His face held untold pain.

Something *had* transpired while I was away.

I wanted to tell him I loved him, but the words refused to form in my mouth. I knew, in my heart, they would sound feeble, an attempt to ameliorate the weightiness of our predicament. Even the air around us changed and grew heavy, almost tactile. I sighed as Jeremy gave a little wave with his hand and walked away. I was left standing there, on some dividing line, with my past behind me and my future clouded.

An obscure lyric of Joni Mitchell's drifted into my head. *"Out on some borderline, some mark of in-between, I lay down golden in time, and woke up vanishing."* She sung of a bird, mocking us as we grasped for ideals and power and beauty—things that faded in everyone's hand. *"Behind our eyes, calendars of our lives, circled with compromise. Sweet bird of time and change you must be laughing."* I could almost hear that bird laughing at me.

I felt like climbing under my covers and going to bed, but it was only seven o'clock. Instead, I called Kendra and told her I was on my way. Knowing they would have already eaten dinner with the kids hours ago, I threw together a tuna sandwich and ate it while the shower got hot.

I was surprised when Neal answered the door. I hadn't seen my younger brother in about a month. He'd just gotten a haircut and his dirt brown hair barely tickled his ears. And he sported a moustache, which was a new look for him. I constrained a giggle. He scraped about six feet tall, a little shorter than Raff but a lot heftier, although every bit of poundage was muscle. When he wasn't bartending—at least I thought that was his latest occupation—he was at his health club working out, lifting weights, playing pickup basketball.

"Hey, good to see you," I said, giving him the once-over. His eyes, a stunning emerald shade, always captivated me. I touched his moustache and he pulled back. "What's with the new look?"

"I hear women love facial hair." He gestured me into the house. I recognized one of the Brandenburg Concertos playing through the speakers in the living room. The kids were probably all in bed, or Kendra was tending to them.

I turned back to Neal. "Where'd you hear that?"

"A poll in Cosmo. Hey, don't laugh!"

I couldn't help myself. Neal—always looking for the secret to finding the perfect woman—just didn't get it. Commitment scared him so much that one whiff sent him running. He talked about settling down, raising a family, but I'd never seen him last more than a month with one woman. There was always something wrong with his latest acquisition—physically, emotionally, behaviorally. At some point the perfect date revealed a fatal flaw, at which moment Neal dropped them like the proverbial hot potato. He didn't break many hearts because he never allowed those women to get close enough, but he sure pissed off quite a few. He wasn't the type to stay friends with the women he ditched. I chalked it up to shame. I'd long ago given up chastising him on the way he treated them; it never accomplished anything and fomented an argument every time.

I strolled into the ornate living room that oozed wealth from the simple antique furnishings and Oriental rugs. Gorgeous oil paintings adorned the cherrywood paneled walls—local artists' work that Kendra purchased. Sweeping landscapes of Sonoma and the Bay. Supporting and touting upcoming talent was a hobby of hers. She had many hobbies but no real job. Why bother? Raff made a fortune and kept her in a lifestyle I would find awkward. In response to my mother's growing wealth during my teenage years, I resisted indulging in a lifestyle of affluence on the basis of principle. The sixties, barely behind us, had left its mark on me. I had embraced hippiedom with fervor and only bought my clothes from thrift shops and the Salvation Army store. My recycling habits drove my mother nuts, as did my strict vegetarian diet. I think I even accused her of letting children in India starve while buying expensive clothes and cars, money that should have been donated to orphanages.

I let my eyes wander over the tops of the glass cabinets, which displayed an array of family photos, mostly of Kevin and the twins with their bright blue eyes and soft skin, taken at beaches, Disneyland, the Grand Canyon. All three kids favored Kendra, but Kevin had the dark thick eyebrows characteristic of the Sitteroffs. Gorgeous children.

Neal followed me in and sat on the camel-colored divan. He picked up a nearly full bottle of beer and drank. Raff came in from the kitchen, looking little better than I had last seen him. I gave him a hug and felt his arms shake slightly in my embrace.

"Hey," I said, keeping my voice light. "I'm so glad you're home and can eat real food again. I bet you had your fill of Jell-O." That brightened his eyes a little. "The kids must be glad to have you here."

He nodded but it seemed an automatic gesture. Pain still flared behind his eyes. I didn't want to ask him about meds or treatments or progress. If he wanted to broach those topics, then I'd listen. "So, anyone want to hear about my trip to New York?" I plopped down in a burgundy upholstered armchair beside the grand piano.

Kendra wandered into the room about halfway through my tale, giving me a friendly wave and taking a seat close to Raff, but I sensed a chasm between them. Kendra looked tired, but only trained eyes would pick that up. Her bronze straightened hair caressed her cheeks, and her makeup was subtle but right out of a magazine. I wondered how long it took her each morning to put on her face. And, with the tight schedule she ran with the three kids, plus grocery shopping, preparing dinner, carpooling to lessons and sports practice, how did she manage to look so unruffled at the end of a day?

Neal fidgeted as I spoke, no doubt working up to a speech. I didn't dare mention my secret theory, my hope that uncovering the truth of Nathan Sitteroff's death would save Raff—or at least open a door to healing. I also held back the information that might lead me to doctors and colleagues with answers to our father's mysterious onset of leukemia. Instead of garnering a positive response to my dazzling and enthusiastic tale of our father's upbringing, the heretofore unknown siblings, and the portrait of childhood I painted against the backdrop of 1930s New York, Raff grew more morose with the telling. True to form, Neal put his hand out and stopped me midsentence.

"Enough, Lis. Can't you see how this is upsetting Raff? You just blab on, totally unaware of anyone else in the room."

Kendra shifted in her seat. This would be her cue to go make tea or claim she heard the twins wake up. After my initial shock dissipated, I looked hard at Neal. Kendra left the room without a word.

"Just what is your problem? Is it my rambling, or the fact that I'm trying to keep things light and cheerful? Like Raff really needs a heavy serious discussion right now." I noticed my fists clenched against my legs and consciously tried to relax them. "At least I'm trying to help Raff, by learning more about our family and our father's past."

"Didn't Mom already tell you to lay off?"

"Excuse me, but last time I checked, I was all grown up and able to make my own decisions. Whereas you . . ." I said too much, and it was too late.

Neal jumped to his feet. "You never think; you just act. And you only think about yourself. Maybe Raff doesn't care about our father's miserable childhood. Maybe he—"

Raff nearly screeched, trying to shove a sentence in between our verbal volleying. "Why are you two talking about me like I'm not in the room!"

Neal and I both looked over at Raff. His face was flushed and his forehead dotted with perspiration. I waited and didn't move, and then he spoke again, this time a hoarse whisper.

"I really appreciate the sentiment, Lis. I do. But we all know that Dad suffered from depression. It doesn't matter if he ate bugs or caviar when he was a child. It's genetic, a chemical deficiency. You can't blame circumstances or upbringing or—"

"I know that," I said as gently as I could. Neal stood with his arms wrapped around his chest, scowling. "But I thought if you learned more about what he was like, you might stop hating him. You might . . ."

I wanted to say "forgive him" but I couldn't get the words out. What if Raff interpreted my intention wrongly, thinking I was judging him harshly?

Raff hung his head. He looked utterly exhausted. "I hate him for abandoning me. Even if he hadn't meant to do it, tried everything he could to face his demons and keep living, I still resent it. In the end, he quit on me. That's just damned unacceptable!" A sour chuckle escaped his lips. "Do you know about the curse he put on me?"

"What? What curse?" *Come on, Raff, get real.* The only curse I knew about was the one my mother had cast on me from time to time throughout my childhood. It went like this: "Someday I hope you have a daughter just like you. Then you'll understand the heartache you've put me through." I shook my head. If only her curse had come to pass. How grateful I would be . . .

Kendra came back in with a cup of tea in her hands. The room grew still. She looked at Raff while he spoke.

"The last words Dad said to me, the last time I saw him in the hospital before he died. He told me, 'Son, you're the man in the house now." Raff's voice took on a harsh, authoritarian tone. "You have to be grown up, take care of your mother and sister and Neal. Stop crying and be a man.' He robbed me of my childhood, then and there. I never got to just be a kid, get in trouble, act reckless. Always that curse of responsibility hung over me like the sword of Damocles, chastising me whenever I slipped. It wasn't fair for him to say that to me. I was only eight . . ."

"Maybe you took him too seriously. Surely, he didn't want you to feel burdened. To miss out on the fun of being a child." It struck me how quickly I always jumped in, making excuses, pitting logic against irrationality. I kept forgetting that Raff now played by different rules, ones that spurned logic and embraced emotionalism. The contest no longer revolved around which argument made the most sense or who could rally the strongest facts but which explanation felt the most painfully true. I couldn't play by rules I didn't understand.

Even though I'd only been there about an hour, Kendra stood and placed a motherly hand on Raff's shoulder. His eyes glazed over and he stared out in space, at nothing. Her voice hid the exasperation I knew lurked under the surface.

"I think it's time to call it a night. Raff needs his rest and . . ." Her sentence trailed off, but it was easy for me to finish her thought. *Biting off each other's heads is a bit counterproductive to Raff's need for peace and quiet.* But she was right.

I watched Neal put on his coat and grunted. Lately, he'd been parroting our mother more and more, like he was her spokesman. Maybe, living in her house and listening to her complaints was brainwashing him. She had a knack for persuasion. Somehow every argument always got twisted to her point of view in the end.

Over the years we kids learned to nod our heads to bring her tirades to an end, something Jeremy just didn't understand. It wasn't that he was confrontational; something within him, some ethical principle, forbade him from tolerating her passive-aggressive attempts at stirring guilt and manipulating him into doing her bidding. Just as he couldn't abide Neal's constant complaining—whining, Jeremy called it. Jeremy chalked up Neal's wishy-washy life to the lack of a male role model in his upbringing. He was a momma's boy, Jeremy claimed, and couldn't even change a washer in a faucet. *Useless*, he often said about both my brothers, inept and useless. Although he always treated them kindly and with respect, keeping his opinions confined behind the closed doors of our home. He didn't understand why Raff and Neal didn't stand up to Ruth and tell her to go take a hike when the occasion merited it. But Jeremy'd had a father who taught him to be handy, to tackle challenges with confidence and inventiveness. Jeremy was the consummate problem solver. No matter what needed fixing, he'd figure something out, no matter how long it took. I frowned, wondering if he'd take the same tack when it came to our floundering marriage.

I sighed as I grabbed my sweater and gave Raff and Kendra hugs. I mumbled some apology to Raff but he brushed it off. Neal had already rushed out the door without a word. I made sure his car was gone before I walked outside, not wanting to go head to head with him at this late hour, hear him lecture me in my mother's tone. By my New York clock, it was well past midnight.

As I closed the door behind me, the strains of Bach seeped out from the window and T. S. Eliot revisited me. *"I have known the evenings, mornings, afternoons. I have measured out my life with coffee spoons. I know the voices dying with a dying fall beneath the music from a farther room. So how should I presume?"*

I knew just how. First thing in the morning, I would try to find Ed Hutchinson, my father's former boss. Perhaps he still lived in Los Angeles, still worked at Penwell. If Information didn't have his number, maybe I could pay an investigator to find him. Whatever it took.

I thought about my father's mathematical slant on life. Was it that easy to reduce all problems into three possible answers—and, or, or not? Did it matter what answer I arrived at? What if, after I found out everything I could, there was no way to tell if my answers were all correct or if only one explanation held the truth? What if nothing I discovered could be proven true? Even if my father could arise from the dead at this moment and tell me what really happened to him, would it make a difference? Could anything he'd have to say undo the damage twenty-five years had wrought? Extricate Raff from his depression?

Eliot's poem rallied back at me as I stood at the curb listening to the crickets whirring under the bright streetlamps' light. *"Would it have been worthwhile, to have bitten off the matter with a smile, to have squeezed the universe into a ball to roll it toward some overwhelming question, to say 'I am Lazarus, come from the dead, come back to tell you all.' If one, settling a pillow by her head should say, 'that is not what I meant at all. That is not it, at all.' "*

CHAPTER 10

ED HUTCHINSON HAD LUNG CANCER. In between his incessant hacking and short gasps for breath, he managed to tell me he didn't have long to live. Smoked three packs a day since he was twenty—Camels, no filters. When I called Penwell Corporation in Los Angeles, they told me he had taken early retirement, but the last division he had run was at their Mountain View branch, near San Jose. That put him only a two hours' drive away, at most. I told him who I was—Nathan Sitteroff's daughter—and it took a moment to register.

"Ah, Nathan, a good man, great mind." His attempt at sounding cheerful set off another bout of coughing. The sound came from some deep, raw place in his chest and made me cringe to hear it. He sucked in air greedily. "One of my best boys. But you, what did you say your name was, honey?"

"Lisa."

"Lisa, right. The last time I saw you, why, you must have been three or four. And you have a brother, right?"

"Two. Rafferty is four years older and Neal is three years younger."

"Well, how about that? All grown up, you kids. How old are you now, honey?" More coughing. I pulled the phone away from my ear till the noise lessened.

"I'll be thirty this year."

He made a clucking sound with his tongue. "So fast. You kids grow up too fast. Where did the time go? So," he said in short gasps, "how's your lovely mother?"

"Fine. We live in Marin, not that far away."

"Your mother's living here too?" I sensed the hard strain in his words, which made me think I should end the conversation soon. The small talk seemed to debilitate him. But even through the cheerful tone, something about Ed Hutchinson's voice irritated me. Something obsequious and phony.

"Well," he said with some finality, "be sure to give her my regards. Such a shame, what she went through. But she was a tough one. Raised you kids up right, I imagine. She ever remarry?"

"No."

The line went quiet. Had Hutchinson keeled over? I waited a minute, then spoke. "Mr. Hutchinson, I was hoping you could tell me more about my father. About the work he did."

I heard a loud intake of air. "Sorry," he said. "Had to get some oxygen. Got a contraption I wheel around with me. Portable air. Started with emphysema. I had to get out of the smog in LA. That's why they transferred me here. Long story."

I doubted he could take much more talking on the phone. "Do you think I could come over, speak with you?"

"Well, sure, honey. But do it sometime before the century runs out. I'm on borrowed time, or so the doctors say."

I thanked him and got his address. His coughing had quieted down, so I ventured one more question. "You know my father died of leukemia, right? I have a letter he wrote my uncle, saying the doctors claimed it was emotionally induced, that he willed himself to die. Did he seem, well, self-destructive to you? Depressed?" I didn't know if this man would have noticed such things about my father. How close had they been? Had they worked in the same office? Shared confidences? I thought about the letter, the mention of shame and terrible things my father did. Would he have confided in Ed Hutchinson? Maybe Ed could tell me who my father's closest friends had been. Maybe I could track them down. I hoped I could get answers when I visited him.

The line went silent for a long moment. "That could have been a factor. Why he volunteered for that experiment—"

"Wait." A shiver raced across my neck. "What experiment?"

"Well, maybe my memory is failing me, sorry. A bunch of the fellows had volunteered to go to San Diego, around the time Penwell was working on a number of top-secret government projects. This was shortly after the war, and all the aerospace companies were vying for government contracts and dealing with Russia and the Cold War threat." The coughing resumed, the barks deeper and drier.

He gasped again and spoke in short spurts. "Thought your dad went too. Let's see, around 'fifty-nine. Some talk of exposure to radiation. I figured that's why he got sick after he came back."

My mind went numb. I couldn't get questions to form. An experiment? Something dangerous? Why had I never heard about this? I listened to Ed Hutchinson cough and knew I had to let him off the phone—as much as I wanted to learn more.

I would just go see him. As soon as possible.

"I'm sorry I've caused you such distress, talking to me for so long. Can I come over, for a short visit? Tomorrow morning?"

He choked out the words. "Tomorrow? Yeah, sure, honey. Anytime. I'm not going anywhere. Well, except the great beyond." He tried to laugh and that set off another bout.

After getting his address and directions, I said good-bye and hung up the receiver. I stared at the phone, as if willing it to pour out the secrets I sought. Surely, if my father had gone on some secret mission, my mother would have known about it. Wouldn't she? If the experiment took place in San Diego, he would have been away from home for a time. It's not like she wouldn't have noticed his absence.

Before heading out the door to pay my mother a visit, I made a quick call to my uncle and luckily got him instead of his service.

"An experiment? Nate never mentioned anything about that," Samuel said. "I told you he was elusive and ashamed about something, but I'm guessing he had an affair. As far as I know, though, he worked at his office in Burbank until he got sick."

"If the assignment had been top-secret, maybe he was sworn not to tell," I said.

"Well, I still think he would have told me. Especially once he knew he was dying. I'm a doctor; I think he would have wanted me to understand the cause of his disease, if he knew what it was. He would have described the experiment or how he had been exposed—something." He sounded frustrated. "We were close, Lisa. What point would there have been in keeping that a secret on his deathbed? Some sense of loyalty?"

"Maybe if he exposed the experiment, his survivor benefits would have been forfeited. Life insurance cancelled or something. Maybe the participants had been threatened somehow, sworn to secrecy. I mean, if the government really was using citizens to experiment on, putting them in danger, do you think they'd want that to leak out to the public or the press?"

My uncle grew quiet. He loosed a long breath. "I don't know. It doesn't sound right. I can see him doing something self-destructive, even suicidal, if he really had been bipolar. But I just don't buy the idea that the United States government would go to a private corporation and look for volunteers to expose themselves to radiation."

"And it's not like I could look this up in a news article. Although, it's been twenty-five years. Someone may have spilled the beans."

"It's possible."

"Well, I'll check, although I doubt I'll find anything. Seems if a bunch of people all died of leukemia—people who worked for the same company at the same time—someone would notice. Don't you think?"

"Lisa, I don't know. And I'm not sure by following this lead you'll find an answer. And if you do, what then? What does it prove? That your dad, maybe because of his supposed death wish, jumped at the chance to end his life in glory and service to his country? Or perhaps there were other circumstances you couldn't know about, that maybe the experiment went wrong, there'd been an accident. Or maybe depression had nothing to do with it, and he just volunteered in ignorance along with a bunch of other unsuspecting employees."

There was the whole scenario just as my father would have laid it out: and, or, not. His mathematical logic seemed to saturate every corner of my life. Was truth solely subjective and not something wholly apart from human perspective? Would I ever feel certain about anything ever again?

I thanked my uncle and hung up. It was late morning, a Thursday. My mother was probably at her office. As much as I dreaded seeing her, this topic was not one I wished to discuss with her over the phone. I called to see if she was free for lunch and she said to swing by and pick her up. She'd found a new restaurant to die for. I just had to experience it.

We made small talk in the car and I tried to relax, but the tension between us was electric. I needed to broach the topic about the legal papers and find out what had transpired between her and Jeremy while I was in New York. Yet, all I wanted to discuss was this secret experiment and learn if she had known about it.

The restaurant sat up against the bay, in Sausalito. We were led to a window table with a stunning view of the sailboats and ferries plying the water. Dozens of seagulls squawked and dove for fish in the blustery wind, but we were sheltered by thick glass, which muted the bird cries. Soft piano music played in the background, which I realized came from a pianist in the far corner. I rarely ate at such a posh restaurant, and certainly not for lunch. I felt conspicuous in my jeans and tank top, when everyone around me sported business suits and expensive attire. The place was filled with young upwardly mobiles, many with their briefcases opened and scribbling on notepads. A vase of beautifully cut flowers—roses, carnations, and bearded irises—sat on our starched white tablecloth, and the silverware was so shiny the reflected sunlight hitting my eye made me squint.

I let my mother order for me, and once that business was finished, my mother assessed me—and found me wanting, no doubt.

"So, Lisa. What's on your mind?" A gorgeous, slender waitress brought my mother a cup of coffee. Looking around, I gathered that only thin, attractive people were hired to work here. I stirred my iced tea, wondering where to start.

"And please," my mother said as I opened my mouth to talk, "don't start in about the past and your father's childhood. I think we've spoken enough on that topic."

Despite my mother's pleasant smile, her tone of finality was enough to embolden me. "What can you tell me about a secret experiment Dad participated in? In San Diego, before he died?"

My mother nearly dropped her teaspoon into her coffee. "Who told—" She snorted. I'm sure she assumed it was my uncle who had provided that information, but I had no intention of telling her about my conversation with Ed Hutchinson. She would go ballistic if she knew I was pursuing this further. And I surely was not going to mention my planned visit to Mountain View. What struck me was the flicker of emotion that crossed her face in that short second. I knew without a doubt that my father had been involved in that project. And my mother knew I knew.

"Well, I don't see why it matters at all. I never told you kids about it. Why should I have? It only would have driven home your father's wish for self-destruction and cast him in a bad light. I didn't want you to think badly of him."

"So, it's true, then? That he volunteered for some experiment, something dangerous."

My mother sipped her coffee and splashed some on her crepe tan blouse. She deftly dipped her napkin in her water glass and attacked the stain before it had a chance to set. I wondered why she didn't just bring a bib with her whenever she went out to eat.

For some bizarre reason my mind leapt to Macbeth's wife, sleepwalking and muttering about the blood on her hands. *"Out, damned spot! Out, I say!"* There was something about the brusqueness with which she rubbed, and with a mindlessness that reminded me of Lady Macbeth—unaware, disturbed, confused. *"Here's the smell of the blood still: all the perfumes of Arabia will not sweeten this little hand. Oh! oh! oh! . . . What's done cannot be undone."*

I reined in my imagination, but thoughts of conspiracy and concealment marshaled forces against my attempt to postpone judgment. Yet, the words pounded at me: *cover-up*.

"Lisa, I know this fact is shocking and unacceptable, but your father wanted to die. Like many bipolar people, he yearned to end his life, but was too afraid to kill himself. They had none of the antidepressants we have today. When he heard about the program in San Diego, heard it was dangerous, well, there was his opportunity. His ticket out. I begged him not to go."

My mother exhaled with finality. She reached for a warm roll in the basket positioned between us and sliced it open with her knife. I watched her slather whipped butter on it and bring it to her mouth, mesmerized by the butter dripping unnoticed onto her lap. At least her linen napkin had been returned to its place there and would catch the drips.

"How long was he gone, to San Diego?" I asked, careful not to emote.

"Something like three months." She polished off the roll and dabbed at her mouth with her napkin. "He came home shortly before Neal was born, but it took a couple months to show signs of the poisoning." *What's done cannot be undone.*

"Why didn't you protest about this? Wasn't it illegal, exposing people to high levels of radiation. Even if they did volunteer?"

The napkin dropped like a stone into her lap. "Heavens, Lisa. What kind of stupid person do you take me for? Once I learned your father had contracted leukemia, I went on a rampage. I investigated every angle—spoke to authorities, the heads of Penwell, even called the newspaper to see if they could uncover something, anything, that would expose this heinous project. Sure, they admitted they'd advertised a volunteer assignment in San Diego, but it had nothing to do with radiation. Nothing at all. Or so they said. I had no proof."

My face flushed from my mother's elevated voice, as nearby patrons cast us curious stares. Our food arrived. Sautéed sea bass with capers, rice pilaf, steamed asparagus. My mouth watered at the aroma and sight of such artfully prepared food on my plate. We ate in silence for a while, and then my mother continued in a measured and dulcet tone. "At the time, I couldn't get the names of anyone else who had participated in the program, or even learn what it was called. But my hunches were all confirmed many years later when I ran into your father's best friend."

"Who?" I asked nonchalantly, between bites of fish that nearly melted on my tongue.

"Dave Lerner. He and your father had offices next door to each other. They often worked on projects together. Dave was an engineer, and your dad would get called in to help with the math. They designed machines for aircraft; I remember a riveting machine in particular, for airplane wings. He also worked on fuel components for the upcoming Gemini spacecraft."

"So, what did he say? When you ran into him?"

My mother seemed to pull her attention back and dug into her rice. "He told me there were others that had contracted the disease and died shortly after Nathan had. I never did get any names, but it had been so many years, water under the bridge. Things clearly hushed up, records purged, whatever. It didn't make any sense to sniff after cold leads. You children were growing up, I had my career, life went on." End of story.

I chewed and let my mind wander. My mother finished everything on her plate and ordered dessert for both of us, despite my protest. I'd already eaten way too much and knew I'd be fighting lethargy all afternoon as I dug holes and planted shrubs. I replayed in my head the scene with Lady Macbeth. The doctor and the lady-in-waiting, watching Macbeth's evil wife as she sleepwalked—with her eyes open but her senses shut, as Shakespeare so nicely put it. Listening to her mumble about her bloodied hands, and then, off she went to bed.

The doctor's ominous words that followed struck a chord within me. *"Foul whisperings are abroad. Unnatural deeds do breed unnatural troubles; infected minds to their deaf pillows will discharge their secrets."* What an unnatural deed my father had engaged in—that deed without a name—submitting himself to danger, despite having three small children who depended upon him—not to mention his wife. But what secrets did my father carry to his pillow? A secret my mother had known about, that his letter hinted at? Did he despise my mother so much that he grabbed any chance to get away from her? Had she learned of an affair and sent him away?

Maybe my uncle was right. Maybe my father had no idea the project was dangerous. Maybe he saw the temporary reassignment as an opportunity to get away from my mother and their suffocating marriage, even if for just a few months.

I stole a glance at my mother as she signaled the waitress for more coffee. How much was my mother hiding from me? I could understand her wanting her children to believe theirs had been a happy, trouble-free marriage. Parents needn't unnecessarily burden their kids with details of unrest and disharmony in an adult relationship. My mother's claim that my father went headlong into danger to satisfy his death wish rested on the assumption that he knew the experiment was risky, hence the call for volunteers. Maybe he had embraced the danger, not wishing to die, but merely wishing to escape his marriage. Either way, it looked as if he cared less for his physical safety than for his emotional relief. He needed distance and he took it.

I felt suddenly sad for my father, so pressed to escape, unable to stay with us kids and revel in his role as father and husband. I pictured Raff, at home with his three children, unable to delight in their company, unable to feel the simplest joy, to muster a genuine smile. How frustrating for Kendra, wondering why Raff couldn't be happy with all he had. Such was the nature of manic depression—it was a heartless thief, stealing every wonder, every beauty found in this world, and leaving an empty, lifeless tomb. *"Out, out brief candle! Life's but a walking shadow, a poor player that struts and frets his hour upon the stage, and then is heard no more."*

This stark contemplation of my father's wasted, too-short life brought on a hollow feeling inside me. My parents had been married about ten years at that point—the length of time Jeremy and I had now been married. Was Jeremy secretly as miserable with me, but, like my father, unable to confess his feelings? Would I someday learn of a letter he had written his brother, telling how unhappy he was, how—to put it in my father's words—*for over ten years it's been an ever increasingly difficult married life, exceedingly difficult to endure. There is no point in trying to fix blame.*

The horror of that thought came out in an audible sound, causing my mother to turn to me.

"What is it?" she asked.I gulped some water and avoided my mother's scrutiny. Was Anne right? Was my mother trying to sabotage my marriage, driving a wedge between me and Jeremy? Maybe Anne saw the obvious while I buried my head in the sand.

Snippets of conversation came to my mind. My mother berating Kendra to Raff, harping on her failings, her lack of intelligence and compassion, her sternness with their children. My mother, so congenial and appreciative toward Kendra when she was in the room, but tearing her apart behind her back. Casting aspersions—is that what it was called?—like drops of acid that slowly ate their way through the fabric of their relationship. Were her actions calculated or perhaps unconscious? Maybe she meant well; did that absolve her, though?

I thought of her countless rants about Jeremy over the years: he was insensitive, treated my brothers with contempt, whined about money, was never satisfied—and so much more. But her words were always sweetened with honey; her loving attempt to point out his faults was for my own good, the good of our family. We Sitteroffs needed to band together and protect the inner circle from attack and invasion. I saw how she had done this with my aunt and uncle, shutting them out. Protecting us—she said. Yet, after meeting my uncle and hearing his side, Sam Sitteroff hardly seemed a bad person who mistreated others. But, I hadn't been privy to their conversations twenty-five years ago. Maybe my uncle had exchanged harsh words with my mother. Maybe, back then, he had been a different man, one guilty of the attitudes and manner my mother claimed defined my uncle.

Well, I needed to protect my inner circle from attack too. I loved Jeremy too much to let my marriage become a spoil of war, even if my mother hadn't intended to engage me as the enemy.

"What's going on between you and Jeremy?" I steeled my nerve and looked my mother in the eyes. "Did you have a fight while I was gone?"

As if by divine revelation, in confirmation of my fears, my mother began her automated litany. I listened, still as stone, as she listed Jeremy's faults, not so much in scathing but with a sprinkling of pity and condescension. When oh when was I ever going to see that Jeremy was a loser? That he had emotional problems, that he was so ungrateful for all she had done for us. Yes, she and Jeremy had exchanged "words" while I was gone, but my mother preferred spouting generalizations rather than elaborate on specifics.

I let her toxic words crash against the seawall I built around my heart, and although over time the force of water wears down even the hardest concrete, I determined at that moment to shut the sea gates and keep her out. I had listened too long over too many years to her lulling statements, catching myself often in agreement and ignoring the raging in my heart that yelled "traitor."

There was Lady Macbeth, through logical argument and persuasive wiles, convincing her husband to murder Duncan, in his sleep no less. They would perpetrate a ruse, setting up Duncan's guards for the fall, and taking no blame themselves. *"Away, and mock the time with fairest show: false face must hide what the false heart doth know."* Was that a false face I was looking at across the beautifully laid-out table—hiding a false heart? I couldn't be sure, but could I chance discounting the possibility?

After my mother let slip out, "I'm surprised your marriage has lasted this long," I placed my napkin on the table and stood. My mother had already paid for lunch and finished off my half-eaten slice of raspberry cheesecake. When I made no comment, she tried a different tack to rattle me somehow. Clearly, she wasn't getting the response she'd hoped for.

"I've been putting this off, Lisa, but cash flow is tight. I'm going to have to ask you and Jeremy to start making house payments."

My jaw dropped enough for a sound to escape. I kept my voice low as we walked toward the front of the restaurant, the friendly wait staff and hostess nodding good-bye as we passed. "We pay the property tax. And we're still paying on our construction loan. Those are our house payments."

"Well, yes, of sorts. But they're not payments to me. I paid for your property in cash, ten years ago—"

"I know that!" My words came out snappier than I'd have liked, and the tone only served to amp up my mother's ire.

"And all this time, you've never made any attempt at paying me back—"

"How, pay you back? You own the property—and our house. If you would turn the title over to us, we'd be glad to set up a payment schedule, so you'd get all your investment back." I sounded just like Jeremy.

My mother spun around as we exited the restaurant. The warm sea-drenched wind slapped me, as did my mother's words. "How dare you?" She shook her head in consternation. "You've been letting Jeremy's pathetic arguments brainwash you. Can't you see what he's doing—turning you against me, against our family—"

"Jeremy is my family."

"No he's not. He's just someone you married. Someone you bumped into at the county fair and decided to live with. You don't have a family. He hasn't even given you any children—"

My heart clenched in pain and bile rose like molten lava in my throat. I literally stamped my foot on the sidewalk where we stood waiting for the valet parking attendant to return with my car.

"That's enough! I don't want to hear another word."

From the corner of my eye, I noticed a taxi at the curb three cars back. I strode over to the car and asked the driver if she was available to take my mother home. I rummaged through my purse for my wallet, my hands fumbling, and handed her a twenty, knowing that would more than cover the scant few miles to my mother's house. As the taxi pulled up to the loading zone, I gestured to my mother.

"There's your ride home. I've already paid. Thank you for the lunch, but I'm late for work. And I better not miss out, seeing as I now have to come up with money to keep you in the lifestyle to which you've grown accustomed."

For once, I didn't regret the words that blurted from my mouth. I meant every one of them.

I turned my back while my mother huffed and got into the taxi and shut her door. As the car drove off and mine appeared at the curb, my body shook, every inch of it. Tears poured down my cheeks, but I wiped them away as I tipped the attendant. An ominous feeling came over me, as if I'd crossed some invisible line.

I was switching camps. The loyal daughter was now the adversary. I hadn't even known there were sides until that moment. But it was too late for regrets or apologies. *Here's the smell of blood. What's done cannot be undone.*

CHAPTER 11

I HAD JUST GOTTEN HOME, weary, my clothes caked with dirt, when Jeremy drove up with the flatbed. He backed partway into the barn and started unloading the half ton of hay while I went inside and washed up. My shower could wait. I'd spent the afternoon attacking the ground, digging holes with fury, planted a couple dozen large shrubs and trees in record time. I hadn't let my mind lapse into that state of peace and rhythm as I usually did when planting. I sought no healing or refreshment from my task; instead, I mulled over and over my recent conversations with my mother, my uncle, thinking of what questions to ask Ed Hutchinson when I saw him tomorrow. My head hurt from all my mental musings, but I kept my heart in check.

I'd had plenty of collisions with my mother over the years. We always worked through it. Perhaps my mother, feeling stressed over her current financial straits, was taking out her anxiety on me. She'd had such a run of success over the years, buying and selling commercial real estate while the economy boomed, that she allowed her spending habits free rein. Trips to Europe, weekly visits to her spa and masseuse, eating out nearly every day, buying clothing from expensive designer boutiques. Having to watch her bottom line was foreign to Ruth Sitteroff.

I didn't know what shape her portfolio was in, but forcing Neal to sell his house in Novato to get back her investment seemed to indicate more than a minor passing problem. Why hadn't she just taken out an equity line of credit and let him stay there? Would the payments have been too high? No doubt it had something to do with her taxes and cash flow. I never asked.

I had wanted to make Jeremy a nice dinner, but with the day's aggravations, I had no energy left. I threw together some burritos, which he always loved, and popped open two Coronas. I heard him on the front porch, pulling off his boots, as I put food on plates. A smile rose on my face, listening to him mess with the dogs, roughing them up and talking silly to them. Buster and Angel were his babies too. What would happen if Jeremy decided to divorce me? Would he fight over custody of our dogs? The thought sent an ache straight to my stomach and I pushed the whole mound of fear back behind a concrete dam I erected in my heart. I would not go there.

"Do you want to eat on the back deck?" I asked. "The bugs aren't bad yet."

Jeremy nodded and took his plate from my hand. He opened the French doors and I followed him out. His manner was unusually tense, a contrast from the day before, when he had seemed pliant.

We ate in silence until I just couldn't take the strain. "Jer, I want to apologize."

"For what? What did you do?"

"Well, I'm always stuck in the middle between you and my mother. And I'm always siding with her. You know how I feel about that. But, I realize now I haven't been very compassionate about your side of things. Seen it from your point of view."

Jeremy made a little sound. His face turned thoughtful. I could almost hear him think the words, *about time.*

When he didn't respond, I continued. "I'm at a loss right now. The more I try to make things better with my mother and my brothers, the more I seem to feed the fire. Everyone's so worked up."

"Yeah, well. With Raff dealing with his issues, it's affecting everyone."

"It's not just that. I . . ." My words lodged like a clod in my throat. It hurt to get them out. "I love you so much, Jer. I hate what's happening with us. I feel powerless to stop our relationship from disintegrating, but I don't know what to do—"

Now Jeremy snorted. "I know just what to do. Get your mother off our backs. Draw the line."

"You've already done that, sending her those legal papers. She just brushed them away as of no account. I've tried to talk to her—"

"Talking to her doesn't work. Like talking to a brick wall. You always let her win. She bowls you over every time. We have to do something, be firm."

I bit my lip. What? How? Frustration shifted into annoyance. "Well, what do you propose we do? You've already insisted she sign the devise. She said no. We've tried to set up a payment plan to pay her back for the property, but she won't budge. Refuses to change the title."

"You're just now realizing this?"

I cringed at his chastisement. "So, what's your new plan? How do we draw the line?"

Jeremy tipped his beer back and finished it off. The dogs chased each other over by the pond and the farm animals watched the antics from the pasture in between taking bites of hay from the feeders. A flock of songbirds warbled in the tall fir next to the house. I yearned for the peacefulness of our home to descend and coat our conversation, but it seemed to scream in dissonance at me.

"I've been talking to a lawyer friend of mine. He says we can file a lawsuit and take legal action against her—"

"What!"

Jeremy threw his hand up and his tone grew harsh. "Just hear me out, Lis. We have ten years of letters, papers from her trust, stating this property is essentially ours. We have folders of receipts, showing the amount of money we've invested here. There's something called promissory estoppel, where we can press the issue for ownership based on the assurances and promises your mother has given us over the years. We can prove we poured our money and labor into this place based on her promises, and she has to concede to us."

"Jeremy, there's no way I'm going to file a lawsuit against my own mother."

"Then I'll do it without you."

Heat flushed my face and I held back a strong urge to scream. "Why? I don't understand what you're doing. We've lived here all these years, without my mother making any demands on us—"

"Until now." He slammed his hand on the patio table and startled me. "Or don't you know about her latest scheme?"

"You mean, about us making payments on the property?" At that moment I felt about three inches tall, like a mouse about to be squashed under a mighty boot.

Jeremy's glare bored a hole through me. "Well, at least she had the decency to tell you. I got this in the mail, delivered to my store." He pulled a folded sheet of paper out of his back jeans pocket and threw it at me. He started pacing the deck behind my back as I read. It was a letter from my mother's attorney, stating that, in order for us to remain on the property, we were required to begin making monthly payments of twelve hundred dollars beginning on July 1. My breath hitched when I read the next paragraph.

"What? She's expecting us to pay back rent?" That was unbelievable. She wanted what her lawyer called "a reasonable compromise," considering the work we'd put into the place—four payments of twenty-five thousand dollars each, over the next four years. At that point a negotiation could be ensured to transfer the property into our names.

"And not one legal guarantee that, after all those payments, we'd even get clear title of the land. Not one."

I didn't want to look in Jeremy's face. I just listened to him pound the Trex decking with his boots while I calmed my breathing. My voice came out papery thin. "Where in the world could we get that kind of cash? We can't afford to take out another loan."

"And I sure as hell am not going to borrow against the store. No way."

"I'll talk to her, Jer," I said, trying to let him know I meant business.

"Yeah. What good will that do?"

I pictured what would happen if we brought in lawyers. The costs would destroy us; we barely got by each month. But not only that, the dynamics with my mother would shift irreversibly. There would be no turning back once we started down that path.

"At least let me try." I sighed in resignation. "And if doesn't work, then maybe we should meet with your lawyer friend and let him outline all our options." I took a chance and looked at Jeremy. Anger roiled over his features. He stopped pacing and glared at me.

"One chance, Lis. And I don't want hollow assurances. I want something in writing from her lawyer by next week. Something that says if we start paying her for the property, then she signs over the title *now*."

"Okay."

I knew I would have to do the only thing I hadn't yet done. I would beg. Beg my mother—for the sake of my marriage, and for the sake of our entire family. Shower her with gratitude, expose my utter need, my dependency on her, my desperation. And I wouldn't have to exaggerate, for my desperation at that moment was very real. If I failed, the consequences were unthinkable. I would either lose Jeremy, or I would lose my family. No two ways about it.

Jeremy picked up his plate and the empty bottle of beer. He tipped his head and studied me. "I've been very patient, Lis. All these years. I'm not one to complain and you know it. I've put up with more crap than most men would tolerate. A lot of guys I know would do some damage to a mother like yours. I've never said an unkind word, threatened her, treated her unfairly. I've put a clamp on my mouth time and time again. Well, she's pushed me far enough. And I'm not budging, not anymore." He narrowed his eyes. "If it means I have to walk out and never look back, then . . . that's what I'll do."

Lines from my father's letter ran through my mind. He had hung on so long to a bad marriage, ran off to do shameful things that ate him up with guilt. What had my mother done to make my father so miserable, to make him want to leave—to want to die? How could a woman wield such power over a man?

I looked into Jeremy's angry, pained eyes and realization struck me. Without a doubt, I knew. It had nothing to do with manic depression, with feelings of unworthiness or bad blood or horrible childhoods. It stemmed from something more essential, more basic. The very character and core of a man could only take so much. When men acquiesced and compromised over and over, they were like logs tumbling in turbulent water. The bark eventually wore thin and stripped away, their confidence and personality smoothed into compliance, leaving a drab piece of driftwood. Every day, they lost a little more of what defined them. That's how Jeremy looked to me, at that moment.

I thought then of another famous poem, by Shelley, one Raff had especially liked to recite, due to its strong emotional content—and because he couldn't resist enacting the ocean vomiting up the scores of pirate ships that the deep kept trapped in its holds.

"Unfathomable sea! whose waves are years. Ocean of time, whose waters of deep woe are brackish with the salt of human tears! Thou shoreless flood, which in thy ebb and flow claspest the limits of mortality! And sick of prey, yet howling on for more, vomitest thy wrecks on its inhospitable shore. Treacherous in calm and terrible in storm, who shall put forth on thee, Unfathomable sea?"

I pictured some future day, Jeremy and me as survivors, scavenging through the wreckage of our lives vomited up by the sea onto the shore, searching for broken scraps to reclaim from the throes of my mother's insouciant tossing. In the end, stripped of memory, years, strength, health, we would both become bare bones, bleached by salt and sun, our objections erased by the unforgiving, relentless elements. I saw us picking at the tidbits of memory, the color and flavor leeched away, bland and unnourishing. They would be all we would have to fare on. Not enough pieces left to build a shelter, to harbor a hope, to stave off fear. Only splinters small enough to lodge under the skin, small but still able to cause festering and infection. I would only be able to gather what memories I could hold in my hands, finding the pieces light, weightless, without substance. How easy it would be, then, to throw them into the wind and let the brisk ocean breeze catch and carry them back into the sea, leaving my hands bereft of any memory worth clutching.

At that moment, I imagined I could cry an ocean of salty tears. Yes, my mother was both treacherous in calm and terrible in storm. And undeniably, an unfathomable sea. Her demands never ceased, her hunger never abated. Jeremy was right. We had to draw a line and stand firm on it, a borderline, as Joni Mitchell called it. Some mark of in between. Regardless of the outcome. We would just have to salvage whatever we could and hope it would be enough.

I felt as if I had momentarily blinked and my world disintegrated in that instant I wasn't looking.

"I lay down golden in time, and woke up vanishing."

CHAPTER 12

WHEN I ARRIVED AT ED Hutchinson's home at eight a.m., he met me at the door in a ratty flannel bathrobe and wearing brown corduroy slippers. I suppose I expected him to be old, the way he sounded on the phone, but his face surprised me. Despite being ravaged by disease, his was a handsome face, with few lines, and with strong cheekbones and chin. His stature suggested he once carried more weight, that he had been muscular and dashing, in a Rock Hudson kind of way. Two bronze eyes looked me over and I couldn't help but sense an overt lechery in his welcoming grin. He carried himself erect and poised, about six foot two, and his hair was thick, ruddy brown. He gestured me in, coughing all the while, and told me to find a chair and wait while he dressed.

I entered his den and took in the dark mahogany furnishings, the heavy drapes and thick carpeting, the many framed certificates and awards on the walls. Those slips of paper testified to a man devoted to scientific advancements, dedication to his company, and faithful service in the military. In contrast to the abundant number of academic accolades was the glaring absence of any personal or family mementos. Only one small framed photo sat on his desk, showing a young and dashing Hutchinson with his arm around a girl, perhaps twelve, smiling for the camera. Did he have a wife? Was this a photo of his daughter?

I heard his footsteps and sat in a wide leather chair across from his desk.

"Come, you can help make some coffee while I show you something," he said, picking up a stack of periodicals off his desk. He had put on a pair of Levis (that apparently used to fit him but now sagged below his waist) and a plain white T-shirt, but remained in his slippers.

I followed him into the kitchen as he alternately coughed and wheezed. He reached for a can of Folgers on the counter and pointed at the coffeemaker. "You do know how to make coffee, don't you, honey?"

"Sure. How strong do you want it?" He waved at me while trying to calm another attack, giving me a go-ahead to make it however I wanted. I didn't have the heart to tell him I didn't drink the stuff, but I could handle a neighborly cup. Even so, I kept the brew a little on the weak side.

He looked me over before collapsing into one of the dining chairs. "You sure look like your dad, you know that? Same dark eyes and hair, same nose. Not much of your mother in you, from what I can tell."

I guessed the husbands that had worked together at Penwell in my father's department had all known each other. Maybe they had barbecues or company picnics. Talked about their wives and children, shared photos. I found mugs in the cupboard and filled two with coffee. I brought them to the table and sat across from Ed.

"You want some nondairy creamer? There's some on the counter. Sugar's over there too."

"Black's fine," I said. "I appreciate you letting me come over."

"Nice to have company. Especially someone as pretty as you." He smiled again and let his eyes roam over my body. If he hadn't been ill, I would have considered making excuses and backing toward the door. His gaze was just plain rude. "Who wants to sit and visit with someone at death's door? It's no fun, I can tell you." He sipped his coffee and that seemed to soothe the raspiness out of his voice. "So, you have questions about your dad. Ask, and I'll tell you what I can."

I decided to get to the point. I didn't know how long he'd last before a coughing episode would make talking difficult. He seemed much less distressed than he was on the phone the day before. "You mentioned something about an experiment, in San Diego. I asked my mother and she said my dad had volunteered, and that the experiment was dangerous. Do you remember anything about it? Who else may have participated?"

"You know, I thought about that after we hung up. And I looked through my newsletters and bulletins. Nothing. I know there was a project going on down there. I can't recall who headed it, what it involved."

"Was that common—asking people to volunteer for assignments outside their normal jobs? Was Penwell connected with the government or the military?"

"We handled a lot of government contracts, but the employees were all hired by Penwell, a private corporation. Your dad too."

"Well, how did that experiment in San Diego get advertised? Would they have posted a notice on a wall, or sent a memo?" If it had been top secret, how would they recruit? Take each man aside privately and lay out the details? If my mother was right, and the whole thing had been covered up, surely they wouldn't have publically posted this mission for all to see.

Ed Hutchinson sucked in air and his throat rattled. He shook his head. "Sorry, honey, I just don't remember."

"Do you know anyone else who participated and came back sick? Did anyone else in the company get leukemia or die soon afterward?"

Again, he shook his head, but his eyes avoided mine. There was clearly something he wasn't telling me. I thought about my conversation with my uncle and the question of secrecy. Had Hutchinson sworn not to tell? What did it matter if he told, now that he was dying? Now that twenty-five years had passed?

"Hey, I thought you'd like to look through some of these annual reports. Some stuff about your dad in there." A deliberate change of direction. I made a note to get back on topic once I heard him out. He flipped open one magazine-sized brochure to a page with rows of photos, arranged like a school yearbook.

"Here's your dad. Handsome fella. Always had to push the girls away." I looked at Ed's strange expression. What did he mean by that remark? What girls? I turned back to the page and studied my father's face. He was handsome, smiling for the camera. I thought it strange that I would always envision my father at thirty. Unlike my mother, whose aging face erased my memory of her younger self. When I looked through photo albums and saw pictures of her with us kids, when we were in elementary school, I barely recognized her. But my father would never grow old in my mind.

He would have been about my age, in this photo. That realization gave me a start. He would be my contemporary, my classmate. And someday in the not-too-distant future, I would be old enough to be his mother. He suddenly seemed way too young to have died, and too young to have fathered three small children. I could barely picture myself with the maturity to handle that much responsibility.

Ed placed another opened magazine before me. A large black-and-white photo showed my father standing next to a young Ed Hutchinson and two other men. They posed in an airplane hangar, with a half dozen giant aircraft in the background. But next to them stood some cylindrical dark objects, about two feet wide and six feet tall. I read the caption. "Penwell scientists display the new sleek design of the SNAP 3."

"What's SNAP?" I asked, studying Ed's face in the photo. There was something strangely familiar about him. Had I seen a photo of him and my father somewhere else, maybe long ago? I surely had seen him before. I pulled over the first brochure he had shown me and found his photo two rows above my father's. Maybe it was his resemblance to Rock Hudson that clicked—the lingering movie star aura about him. Talk about a hunk. Most of the other men in the pictures looked like your typical college nerd—glasses, goofy haircuts. Like they were too wrapped up in their research to ever look in a mirror or comb their hair. But Ed Hutchinson could have been a poster boy for the all-American heartthrob.

"SNAP? That was a big project we all worked on in the late 'fifties. Your dad was instrumental in its development. Stands for Systems Nuclear Auxiliary Power. Generators that created electricity from radioactive decay. The first one launched into space in 1961, aboard a Navy transit spacecraft. They used the RTGs—radioisotope thermoelectric generators—on most all the spacecraft: the Apollo missions, the probes, Viking, Pioneer, Nimbus. They were especially useful for craft that traveled too far from the sun to employ solar panels. But the RTGs had other uses: powering lighthouses, remote sensing stations. Even though the thermocouples were reliable and long-lasting, the RTGs turned out to be inefficient, and after a while, the SNAP program was dismantled. You can still find defunct RTGs in old lighthouses in Russia, although there are some rotting in the sea. Like the one aboard Apollo 13. It's lying somewhere in the Tonga trench, in the Pacific Ocean. Who knows how much radiation could be leaking into the water from these things right now."

"Wait, so these RTGs are radioactive?"

"Well, the plutonium 238 only had a half-life of about eighty-seven years. But you don't just get exposed that easily. It doesn't penetrate the skin like exposure to a nuclear bomb. You'd have to ingest the radiation somehow, to get into your internal organs." Ed looked at me and must have seen where I was going with this line of reasoning.

"Look, we didn't build the things—we designed them, honey. Your dad worked on a chalkboard; he didn't handle radioactive material. That was done in a different location, nowhere near our facility. Once they were built and the radioactive material housed and encased, they were perfectly safe to handle. Penwell built loads of these things, without incident. They're still used by the Navy and Air Force, with no problem."

The phone rang and I sipped my coffee, forcing it down, while Ed spoke to someone for a couple of minutes. I heard him say, "Okay come on over, if you must." He didn't seem very happy when he hung up.

"Maybe I should go. I've taken up enough of your time and you've been gracious to show me these photos."

"Oh, don't rush off. That was my daughter. Says she has to bring me something. Can't imagine what that'd be. I hardly ever see her."

His voice reeked of bitterness. I thumbed through more of his journals while he tried to contain his coughing. It seemed to escalate as I sat there, looking at pictures of various airplanes and machinery I couldn't identify. I tired to imagine my father working in an office, writing equations on his chalkboard, throwing ideas around with his coworkers. I looked at Ed.

"Would you mind if I borrowed this?" I held up the one magazine that featured all the Penwell employees in my father's department.

"No, sure, honey. Take it."

"Do you remember someone named Dave Lerner?"

Ed nodded as he tried to calm his chest. He plodded into the other room and pulled out an oxygen tank that rolled on a platform with wheels. He put the mask over his mouth and breathed steadily for a moment. When he lowered the mask, his voice was hoarse. "Sure. Dave worked at Penwell for a long time. Till he retired, I think. But he was still in LA when I relocated up here. Probably still down there."

"Did he know my father well?"

"I guess so. They worked together on just about everything."

The doorbell rang. I decided to broach the topic of the experiment one more time. "My mother said she ran into Dave Lerner years later," I said, following Ed to the door. "That he told her he knew of others from their department who had been exposed to radiation and who had died. Other men who had gone to San Diego."

Ed's hand stopped halfway to the doorknob. He gave me a stern look. "Honey, why belabor this? Who knows what really happened? You're never going to get answers. And all those years—it was so long ago."

He sounded just like my mother. And just as cagey. Was I overly suspicious of everyone, or was there a reason why Ed Hutchinson seemed to be hiding something? I stepped back as he opened the door.

"Well, look at you, all dolled-up," Ed said acerbically to the tall, blond woman standing on the threshold. "Come on in." He gestured to me. "Julie, this is Lisa Sitteroff. This is my one and only child—Julie."

I smiled. "Well, my last name is now Bolton. Nice to meet you." I shook her hand and met her friendly eyes. She looked like a model from Cosmo, dressed in a slinky top and tight jeans, her hair styled to perfection. I never looked that good any time of day, let alone nine o'clock in the morning. I guessed Julie to be about my age. "But, I'm just leaving . . ."

Julie rested a hand on my arm as Ed marched toward the kitchen. "Please," she said in a stern whisper, "stay for just a minute more."

I caught an urgent expression in her eyes. What in the world was that about?

"All right. But I should be getting to work."

Ed called out from the kitchen. His voice was thick with irritation. "So, what did you bring me, that you had to come right over?"

Julie held her perfectly manicured hand up to me, asking me to wait. She went into the kitchen and hushed whispers followed. The tension in their relationship drifted to my ears. I kept standing by the door, fiddling with my purse, clutching the Penwell brochures. A few minutes passed, some coughing ensued, and I grew more uncomfortable, hearing the rising tone in their voices. Julie strode back to the door, her face flushed. She seemed angry and struggling to contain her feelings.

"I really should go . . ." I said.

Julie pressed something into my hand. A business card. She lowered her voice and leaned close to me. I heard Ed lapse into a coughing frenzy in the kitchen. "Lisa, I have to talk to you. It's terribly important. Please call me at noon, at my office number. I'll come see you."

I studied her face, puzzled by her intensity. What could she possibly have to say to me, a complete stranger? Had she mistaken me for someone else?

She didn't give me a chance to ask any questions. Her father walked toward us, dragging his oxygen tank. Julie pasted on a smile and turned to her father.

"Dad, Lisa needs to leave." She opened the door for me and the warm morning breeze drifted in. The bright sun hurt my eyes and I reached in my purse for my sunglasses.

Julie stood between me and her father, so all I could do was give a little wave. "Thank you, Ed, for seeing me. I really appreciate it. I hope—well, I hope you feel better." My words sounded stupid. What do you say to someone who is dying—get well soon? I nodded at Julie who mouthed words to me as her father came up behind her. *Call me. Noon.* I nodded again.

"Thanks, honey," Ed said to me, "Come visit anytime. Just make it this year, okay?"

"Sure thing."

Julie stepped back inside. I heard the door close briskly behind me, and I felt disoriented and befuddled. I looked at the card Julie gave me. She worked at a realty office in Cupertino, and went by the last name Hutchinson. I assumed that meant she wasn't married. There was nothing written on the back, nothing to shed any light on this odd encounter or her urgent request to speak with me. For the life of me, I couldn't figure out what in the world she could possibly need to say to me. I supposed I would just have to wait three hours to find out.

As I got in my car, I looked back at the door to Ed's house. I pictured the guard standing in front of the door to enlightenment, waiting for me to ask the only correct question that would grant me entrance. Everywhere I went, I saw doors. I heard the witch in Macbeth chant. *"By the pricking of my thumbs, something wicked this way comes. Open, locks, whoever knocks."* Ed Hutchinson had been guarded, hiding something. I brought to mind the small photo of him in his dashing younger days, standing next to my father beside the SNAP generator.

My hand stopped in the air as I lifted the key to the ignition. My breath caught as I shook an outrageous thought from my head. I chastised myself for my wild imagination and started the engine. I didn't believe in coincidences, but I did trust my intuition. And in that moment my intuition told me Julie Hutchinson had something earth-shattering to tell me.

CHAPTER 13

I FELT ABOUT TO CRAWL out of my skin.

With two hours to kill before calling Julie, I needed to do something. My visit with Ed Hutchinson had left me irritable and tense. Scraps of conversation with my mother at the restaurant kept nipping at my thoughts like annoying mosquitoes. I fought the urge to pull my car over on some shady suburban street and sleep. When stressed, my brain often went numb and my thoughts drifted, unfocused, leaving me in a stupor. Maybe that was my survival instinct kicking in. Go find a dark place to hide and wait out the danger.

I stopped by Raff's house after I crossed the Golden Gate Bridge. I rang the bell and listened for footsteps, thinking of my mother just a few miles away. My stomach clenched, imagining her puttering around her house, Neal cleaning up after her, her grumbling about me and Jeremy. What went on behind those closed doors? Conspiracy? Did my brothers even know what she was up to, trying to squeeze money from us, trying to beat us into submission? Did they even care?

Kendra opened the door. She was dressed in a casual top and jeans, her hair a little out of place. She looked like she hadn't slept well in a long while. Her voice lacked welcome, although she managed a smile.

"Hi Lisa, what brings you here?"

I waited, but she didn't invite me in. I backed up a step. Kendra never liked surprises. Or people randomly dropping in without notice. I could never call her last minute and ask her to meet me for lunch. It had to be planned weeks ahead and reconfirmed at least three times. Her eyes told me in a subtle flicker that I had broken protocol.

"Just thought I'd see how Raff was doing. Is he home?"

"Well, no." She shut her mouth as if worried some other words might leak out.

"So, he's back at work? That's great—"

Kendra shook her head. "He's at the doctor's. Trying to rework his meds."

Meaning, the drugs weren't keeping his monsters at bay. I let out a breath. "I'm sorry. This has got to be tough on you, on the kids."

Kendra's face drew tighter. My attempt to commiserate with her was backfiring. I had crossed over the neutral zone and was igniting hostilities. I changed tacks. "Well, he's got the best psychopharmacologist in the Bay Area. I know something will work. And Raff is strong and determined. He won't give up."

Her look told me she didn't agree. And then I thought that maybe it wasn't Raff who wanted to quit. I'd heard my brother gripe about his marriage, how if it weren't for his kids, he and Kendra would have split up years ago. I knew she swore to stand by Raff, for better or for worse, but the current "worse" was not conducive to healing their troubled relationship.

I shuddered at the thought of Kendra walking out on Raff, taking the kids back to Ohio to live with her parents. That would send my brother over the edge. And surely, Kendra knew that. The pressure was on her to keep the home environment as stable as possible, but I wondered how long she was willing to give it a go. That calm, controlled exterior was beginning to crack.

Raff had told me he had been misdiagnosed for years. That his episodes of bipolar depression didn't match the usual patterns.

Even his psychiatrist had pooh-poohed his insistence on admitting himself into the hospital. Told him he was suffering from stress, too much overtime at the bank. Unlike most afflicted with his illness, Raff's up-and-down cycles spread across years, not months or weeks. He'd have a whole year where he leaned toward a manic high-flying exuberance, followed by a year of spiraling downward to a crash.

His senior year in high school was marked by outrageous risk-taking and laissez-faire—to use the French term he liked to throw around. He had gone to Paris with his Honors French class that summer after graduation and ended up nearly arrested and thrown in prison. I recall my mother listening in horror as Raff bragged how he climbed a flagpole in front of the French Embassy and detached the flag from its clips, then scooted to the ground and proceeded to do a victory dance across the lawn, waving the flag in, what he learned later, was blatant disrespect. The gendarme came at him with pistols drawn and handcuffed him. In his perfectly mastered French he weaseled his way out, explaining how, in America, students studying French kept a tradition on Bastille Day—in honor of the storming of the Bastille in 1789—that involved jimmying up flagpoles and retrieving such flags in the manner in which he had performed. Somehow the police found his enthusiastic tale heartwarming, and they let him go with a warning that such patriotic proclivities, although appreciated, were not legal in France.

At summer's end, Raff went off to college in Colorado, giddy with the promise of adventures and intellectual challenges and Rocky Mountain air. His initial letters and phone calls bragged of all the clubs he had joined, his newly acquired skills (skiing and Thai cooking), and his academic achievements. By Thanksgiving, the calls and letters had dwindled. And by Christmas break, it took all our urging to get him on a plane to come home. His lackluster countenance and short, choppy answers left us all worried and confused. We had no idea we were witnessing the first of Raff's many downward tumbles into depression. I'd tried to get Raff to go Christmas shopping with me, bowling, visiting Kyle and Anne, even ice skating up in Santa Rosa (which had been one of his favorite holiday pastimes despite his lack of coordination), but he wouldn't leave his room. He wrote poetry—dark and enigmatic—and sometimes lapsed into French when mumbling to me while lying on his bed, staring at the ceiling. I'd thought something had happened to him at school—a girl had dumped him or he got a B on a test for once in his life. I knew nothing of the storm raging in his mind, and he didn't let on. When break ended, we saw him off at the airport, looking despondent and reluctant to leave. I remember my mother's face as she watched him trudge down the ramp to board the plane. A mixture of worry and trepidation. Perhaps she had seen something of my father in Raff at that moment—the resignation in his walk? The past replaying to haunt her?

Kendra started making some excuses about needing to finish cleaning the house before she picked the girls up from school. Still standing on her front porch, I fumbled for something to say, but only asked if I could use her restroom before heading out. When I came into the hall, she politely offered me a cup of tea, but I knew I was supposed to say thank you but no. Which I did.

We exchanged good-byes and some empty promises of getting together soon. I really wanted to get Raff alone, to try talking with him without Kendra or Neal around. I asked Kendra to have Raff call me later, but I doubted she'd tell him. Or that he'd call me back.

Anne's office was on my way home, a mile off the freeway in San Rafael. Maybe I didn't want to go home to an empty house, although a brisk walk with the dogs across the hills sounded appealing. I needed to do something with this restless energy. I had plenty of work waiting for me, and the weather was ideal for planting, but I had to talk with Ed's daughter at noon. What if she insisted on meeting with me today? Clearly, what she had to tell me couldn't be said over the phone. I pondered the mystery of her urgency as I walked up the stairs to Anne's second floor office of the drab county building for Health and Human Services.

Anne's door was open, and as usual, her miniscule office looked like a whirlwind had just blown through. The file folders that wouldn't fit on her desk spilled out onto piles on the floor. A large appointment book buried the phone, and since the bookshelves and filing cabinets were burgeoning, mountainous stacks of papers rose from the tops of surfaces, taller than I could reach. Anne's most important piece of furniture in her office was her foldable stepladder.

I knew there was a chair underneath some of those piles, but while I was considering clearing a space on the floor to sit down to wait, Anne popped her head in the room.

"Oh, it's you." She looked at her watch and brushed some unruly curly hair from off her forehead. The old building lacked air conditioning, and the room was close to sweltering. "Sorry, I'm due in court as an advocate, like, in ten minutes. I wish we had time to chat, but I can't. Now, where's the file on Morales? Lisa, look over there."

She pointed at a teetering stack of folders in the center of her desk while she shuffled through her bulging shoulder bag. "I could have sworn I stuck it in here . . ." She stomped her foot and I stopped and looked at her. "Aha! Here it is—right under my nose." Anne laughed with gusto and reorganized her bag—pulling out extraneous folders out and dropping them to the ground. "I feel like I'm bouncing off the walls—the way you used to act when you didn't take those damned drugs your mother fed you. With the budget cut, I lost my best assistant. There, that'll lighten my load considera—"

"Wait," I said, rewinding her string of words back until I got to the line I nearly missed. I came over to her and took her arm to stop her frenetic movement. "My mother never put me on drugs. What are you talking about?"

"No, Lisa, but she did." She narrowed her eyes at me. "What, you don't remember?"

I shook my head. "She told me she consulted a doctor once about giving me something for my hyperactivity. But she claimed the pills only made me worse, that I reacted funny to them. Where did you hear that?"

"I didn't so much hear as saw. You remember how you'd come sleep over? Your mom would pack a bottle in your overnight bag and instruct my mother to make sure you took your medicine. Now, my mom was no nurse, but she knew what Seconal was. She was horrified your mother had you on addictive barbiturates and scolded Ruth about it, refusing to give you the damn pills. By ten p.m., you went from mellow yellow to hell on wheels. Oh, don't look at me like that! Pill popping was all the rage in the sixties. Although at that time, parents didn't give downers to their kids, like they do now. Do you know how many cases we get of parents drugging their kids to keep them quiet? I even read of a case where a daycare provider was spiking the toddlers' bottles with allergy medication to make them take their naps. One two-year-old even died—"

"Anne!" I nearly yelled to get her to stop. She was almost out the door when she swung back around at me, exasperation on her face.

"What?" She tapped her watch and raised her eyebrows, telling me she was more than late. I searched my mind, trying to recall my stint of pill-popping, but nothing surfaced. I hated taking pills. It wasn't likely I'd down them without a fight. Wouldn't I have some memory of that?

I waved Anne on. "Go. I'll catch up with you later. But we need to talk about this, okay?"

"Sure, call me. Tonight, whenever."

I watched her tromp down the hallway, fussing with her skirt. When I exited the building, a breeze dried the sweat on my neck and sent a chill down my spine. I decided to walk over to a coffee shop I liked on C Street. I could relax, read the paper, then call Julie at noon from the pay phone outside.

I ordered an iced tea and a bagel with cream cheese, then sat in a booth looking out on Fourth Street. San Rafael bustled with shoppers and the occasional guide dog in training draped with a green blanket. For some reason, talking to Anne had upset me. Maybe I was reacting defensively, primed by my mother opposing me on one hand, and Jeremy on the other. Anne was a big sister and confidant. As often as we argued or disagreed, I had never before felt this sense of alienation or judgment. I couldn't tell if it originated from her or my imagination, but her tone had seemed harsh and condemning. Was I stupid? Naïve? That's how her words made me feel. Did everyone else see me one way—Anne, Jeremy, my mother, Neal—a way radically different than how I saw myself? How had I fallen into this sudden identity crisis? And how in the world had I forgotten about those pills?

I stared vacantly out the window, mulling over my childhood memories. As I thought about my father's face, I remembered a dream I had last night. I was three or four, standing next to my mother and father. Neal was a baby in my mother's lap and Raff stood behind me. While sipping my tea, a sense of great agitation came over me as I realized the image was the photograph my mother kept in a drawer, the last—and perhaps only—family portrait taken, in black and white, before my father died. But in my dream, we were riding in an elevator and it was freefalling fast. I knew we were about to crash and I wanted to scream. No one else seemed concerned. I pounded on the sealed doors until my knuckles bled. A strain of muzak filtered in over staticky speakers—the Beatles' tune "Helter Skelter." *"When I get to the bottom I go back to the top of the slide, where I stop and I turn and I go for a ride, till I get to the bottom and I see you agaaaiinnnn . . ."* Their faces stayed frozen, their smiles in place, their eyes fixated and vacant. Only I knew what awaited us, the horror we faced, the impending crash. I tried to open my mouth, but my lips remained glued together. Before the elevator reached the bottom, I had startled awake. I was Cassandra, powerless to warn my family of what was to come, knowing they wouldn't believe me, anyway. Why did I even bother? Disaster was inevitable.

A few minutes before noon, I called Julie. She refused to tell me what was so urgent, only saying it involved my father. I nearly dropped the receiver.

"What about my father?"

I waited and listened for a reply. Julie's voice came out in a hush. "Lisa, I have so much to tell you. I never thought I would connect to you, but I've been looking for you—or rather, for someone in your family—for three years now. I only had one name: Nathan. I had no idea he was someone who worked at Penwell, with my father, or I could have pieced that together right away. My mom never gave me particulars, but I have to know. Know if it's your father."

"Know what about him?"

Julie hesitated. "Please, can I come to you, so we can talk in person? It's a long story and I'm hoping maybe you can tell me more."

From her tone, I knew I wouldn't get any more information out of her. Just what could be so important that she'd been looking for my family for three years—twenty-odd years after my father died? Did she know something about his death? The timing was too uncanny. I had so many questions, but I restrained myself. We agreed to meet in Sausalito, at a small park not far off 101. That would cut down her drive time.

In the hour or so it took for Julie to arrive, I came up with plenty of scenarios. I reflected on the tension between Julie and her father and the little love between them. How Ed Hutchinson had only one photo on his desk. How he had leered at me with such aplomb.

I watched cars pass by as I sat on a sun-drenched bench. Julie pulled into a spot and walked over to me as I waved. The sun lit up her gorgeous blond hair and caused her silky teal blouse to shimmer. I stood and said hello, and she took both my hands in hers, smiling as if reuniting with a long-lost friend. Something in her face seemed familiar—the shape of her eyes, the Milky Way of freckles dotting her nose. Maybe, like her father, her movie-star looks created some unconscious connection with someone famous. She could surely be Doris Day to his Rock Hudson.

"Thanks for meeting with me. I'm sorry for all the mystery. I just couldn't talk this morning with my dad around."

"That's okay."

She sat on the bench and turned to face me. "You probably noticed my dad and I don't get along. But, I had to come over when I heard him mention your name on the phone. Well, when he said Nathan's daughter. And then how you were the daughter of someone who used to work for him at Penwell in Los Angeles. I about fell over. It's too strange to be a coincidence."

I waited, afraid to move, wanting her to keep talking. "Go on."

She blew out a breath and shook her head. "Okay, this may sound crazy to you, but I'll just jump in. My mother died three years ago, but before she did, she confided in me. About a lot of things—some of which I knew and others, well, those came as quite a shock. I was very close to my mother—I'm an only child. My dad married her when she was barely eighteen. She was an aspiring magazine model, someone he met at a party. My dad was in his thirties at the time, much older than she was. He basically swept her off her feet and married her. He used to be pretty good-looking, my dad."

I nodded. "I saw some of his photos. Of him and my father."

"Well, the marriage didn't last long. My dad was quite the swinger, and had affairs right out in the open, didn't care how much it hurt my mother. Her name was Shirley. I was born a couple of years after they married, and two or three years later, my mother divorced him. It was a bitter fight, because my dad couldn't bear to have her walk out on him. He was violent and abusive, and I thank God my mother had the good sense to get away from him while I was young."

"So, did she raise you alone?"

Julie nodded. "I saw my dad on some weekends and holidays after they divorced, but he didn't care about me. Which suited my mom just fine. She did a good job with me but she never remarried." Julie took a deep breath that shuddered as she exhaled. "I loved her deeply and I miss her very much. When she got breast cancer, she wanted to fill in the blanks of her life for me. She never would talk about her past while I was growing up, but she wanted me to know some things before she passed away."

Julie stopped abruptly and looked at me. "Just why did you come to see my father, if you don't mind my asking?"

"My father died when he was thirty-three. He had contracted leukemia and I think it had something to do with an experiment he volunteered for while working at Penwell."

Julie leaned closer and narrowed her eyes. "An experiment?"

"Something involving radiation."

"But why now? Why are you looking into this so many years later?"

"Curiosity, I guess. I never knew my father, and my mother hardly ever spoke of him. I'm just trying to put some pieces together."

I got quiet while Julie mulled over this. "Lisa, your father had an affair with my mother. He lived with her the last few months before he died."

My breath caught. "Are you sure?"

"Here's what I know. She met someone named Nathan. Someone very smart and gentle. She never told me where he worked or how they had met. He was married and unhappy with his life. My mom, miserable and humiliated by my dad's affairs and his blatant cruelty toward her, wanted someone to show her some kindness, some affection. I think at first she had an affair to get back at my dad, but the way she spoke about Nathan—well, she seemed quite fond of him. They moved in together for a short while—months at most. My mother said this man died tragically. It shook my mom up, but rather than go back to my dad, she filed for divorce and never returned home."

"Well, where were you at the time? You must have been, what, two or three?"

"My mom said she took me with her, so I must have lived with her and your father for a time. I don't remember at all."

"Did she say anything about going to San Diego? Or where they lived when they moved in together?"

Julie paused. "San Diego? That sounds familiar. Why San Diego?"

"That's where the experiment took place. I asked your dad, and he thought my father participated in that experiment. But he couldn't name anyone else involved. Or what the experiment was about. There was nothing written up about it. But, supposedly it was top secret, maybe covered up." I stopped talking as a thought formed. "Wait, did your father know about their affair?"

I watched a flush come across her face. She dropped her gaze to her feet, then looked back up at me. "He did. But would he have known if my mom went with your dad to San Diego? I don't know. My mother didn't elaborate, just said my dad was furious she walked out on him."

"Maybe they went there to get away. Away from . . ." Maybe not just Ed, but also my mother. And us kids. Away from all of it. Maybe my dad didn't participate in that experiment, but lied and used it as a cover. An excuse. My head spun at all the possibilities. Or had my mother claimed Nathan volunteered for the experiment to cover her husband's obvious absence? But, if that were true, and my father hadn't been exposed to radiation, just how did he contract leukemia so suddenly? A fate of nature? Bad timing? I was back to and, or, or not.

"Interesting," Julie said, interrupting my thoughts. She smoothed out her hair as a breeze kicked up. A flock of seagulls wheeling overhead and squawking made her look up. The birds resembled my disparate thoughts, each vying for attention. "I really don't know anything about that. It's possible your father went to San Diego for this experiment, and took my mom and me along."

My father mentioned in that letter to his brother how he suffered from shame and guilt. Maybe this was what he had been intimating about. This affair. I tried to envision him getting up the nerve to leave my mother, to leave behind three small children. How horrible he must have felt, racked with guilt yet unable to stay a minute longer in his own home.

"It's not like they were in love," Julie said. "My mother knew that. They were both seeking something, some solace from their pain and unhappy marriages. If our fathers worked together, I can see how my mother would have met him somewhere—at a party or company picnic. Maybe they started talking and realized they shared a common misery."

As Julie spoke about her mother, I pictured my father back then and imagined what transpired. I could see him at a company picnic—the men smoking under the oak trees at a park with the branches casting shadows over them. The wives filling the tables with food carried in Tupperware containers, laying out paper plates and cups, containers of Kool-Aid, Rice Crispy Treats cut in ragged squares for dessert. Children squealing and playing on the jungle gym and the monkey bars in the large sandbox. Spinning each other on the metal carousel. My father ambling away, frustrated, fed up. Wanting to feel the familial joy the others seemed to so easily experience, delighting in the antics of their children, the men teasing their wives in a carefree manner. My father feeling trapped, claustrophobic, wanting out. Pretending to be like everyone else, but silently suffering.

Then he happens upon Shirley Hutchinson. Young, tall, gorgeous. Deep blue eyes that hold secrets and pain. She moves with grace and a model's poise and stature. Elegant for her young years, but every gesture cries out for attention. My father picks up her need in the sway of her hips, the flash of her eyes. They make small talk by the water fountain, reminding each other they've met before, my father pointing to his two children playing on the swings. Shirley nodding in polite acknowledgement, oozing her unhappiness. She speaks of her marriage in couched terms, in generalities and pleasantries, but my father is not fooled or stupid. Yet, Shirley does not come on to him, not deliberately. The words move from hinted misery to outspoken anguish. Perhaps my father shares his beer with her. The day is hot, suffocating. Their thirst is considerable, and not just for liquid to soothe their throats.

After a while, as neither my mother nor Ed Hutchinson notice their partners have wandered off, my father walks with Shirley, and at one point in their conversation, their eyes catch on the other's, lingering a little longer than is customary. What do they have to lose? Shirley has already lost her husband to more women than she can count. Ed all but ignores her, except when he wants her in bed. And my father has long since felt any stirring at all—in his heart or his loins. Shirley absently brushes against his hand, maybe even touches his arm in kindness, in commiseration, as they speak of things not considered proper. But my father is at his wit's end. And he is beyond caring what consequences may now erupt from his desperate need to flee his marriage. Shirley mentions they should head back, before someone notices.

But before they part from each other, to return to the picnic from different directions, they have already joined in conspiracy. If not verbally, then by some other means of communication, shared pain that is palpably felt and exchanged. Maybe, in a fleeting moment of madness, my father grabs Shirley's arm as they pass behind the baseball bleachers. Maybe he swings her around and before either of them have time to think, he kisses her in a passion he never experienced with Ruth before. But he is not fooled. He knows he is not in love, or even succumbing to lust. He just needs to feel—something, anything, again. Feel life flowing through his limbs. Shirley, perhaps, wants something altogether different. She just wants to be noticed and admired. And listened to. And maybe, beneath her awareness, she wants to hurt Ed, to repay him for the continual humiliation and betrayal. Maybe she toys with the idea of having an affair to get back at him. Or if she's not that vengeful, just yearns for a chance to feel some stimulation—to taste the forbidden pleasure her husband indulges in without remorse or concern for consequences. Fairs fair, she thinks.

When Julie finished talking, I let her words linger in the air. She turned to me and I thought she had more to say. But the expression on her face shifted.

"I'm sorry I took up so much time," she said. "Do you want to get some coffee?"

I looked at my watch. Nearly an hour had passed and I felt sleepy and needing a nap. It was too late in the day to start any projects or run by any of my jobs. But I had plenty to do in the barn. The goats' hooves needed trimming and all the animals were overdue on their shots and worming. I hadn't worked Shayla since her leg wound had healed. I needed take her on a walk with the dogs. I swept my mind of the lingering image of my father's lips on a stunning young blonde's mouth.

"I should get home. I have animals to tend to. Thanks for seeing me, and talking to me. I hope I was able to fill in some of the blanks for you. About my father."

Julie looked sorry for telling me about the affair. She nodded and I walked her over to her car. I dug in my purse, wrote my phone number on a piece of scrap paper, then handed it to her. "If you want to call me . . . to talk."

Julie took the paper from my hand, then stopped. "Are you also an only child?"

Her question hung on the air. She had blurted it out and then smiled, as if to cover some embarrassment.

"No, I have two brothers. One older and one younger."

"Oh," she said, nodding. "What are their names?"

I wondered why she brought this up all of a sudden. "Rafferty is four years older, and Neal is three years younger." I waited to see if she wanted more information. Maybe she was trying to remember something her mother told her.

"Oh, okay." She looked at the scrap of paper with my phone number on it. As she said good-bye and started to get into her car, she seemed to avoid meeting my eyes. Had I said something that offended her? Disappointed her?

I mulled over the things she had told me as I watched her drive away. I thought of how tenderly she'd spoken about her mother. How this mystery man, Nathan, had intrigued Shirley, caused her to search for some connection to him.

Then Julie's visit struck me as odd. Her mother had an affair for a few months—so what? Julie admitted Shirley and Nathan were never in love, that theirs had been an affair of mutual consolation and solace. But why would that brief encounter make Julie express such an urgent need to talk with me? Just to meet the daughter of a man her mother slept with for a few months twenty-five years ago? It didn't make sense.

I recalled the way Julie's gaze had turned from me when we spoke, and how she avoided my eyes when she left. What had Shirley Hutchinson said to her daughter three years ago, before she passed away, that filled Julie with such a need? *"I have to know. Know if it's your father,"* she said.

I looked up. The seagulls were gone, leaving a hole in the sky—a sky so bright it almost shimmered. The sun beating down on me seemed to illuminate Julie's words that still hung in the air, spotlighting an obvious detail I was missing. There was more to the story. Something unsaid, something important.

Something Julie Hutchinson was hiding from me, and perhaps even her father. Something Julie was afraid to tell me.

And, in that moment as I stood alone in the park, I knew I was afraid to hear it.

CHAPTER 14

NEAL OPENED MY MOTHER'S FRONT door before I rang the bell. I had considered running back to my car and driving off before being seen, but he thwarted my plan before I chickened out. My stomach churned in acid, thinking of confronting my mother, of the begging I would soon do. When had our relationship turned so caustic? Not that long ago, it seemed, I would drive over to see my mother with anticipation and joy. Spending time with her had always been pleasant—we'd go shopping, walk along the path that meandered around the Bay, go out to lunch, talk about books and movies. For the life of me, I couldn't fathom how all this hostility had erupted. I was determined to find some compromise, magic words to say that would clear the air and restore the balance of harmony we had before.

But when I looked in Neal's stern eyes and caught his grip on the threshold of the door, what shred of optimism I had fled with my voice.

"What are you doing here?" he asked, suspicion in his tone.

"What do you mean? I come over and visit Mom all the time. She's here, isn't she? Her car's parked in the driveway." I wanted to ask him what he was doing home on a late Tuesday morning.

Why he wasn't out looking for work, seeing as he was again presently unemployed and apparently mooching off our mother. Tuesdays were when my mother worked at home.

Neal backed into the house as I heard my mother's heels click on the tile floor. Her newly purchased two-story house on the water had Spanish tile throughout the downstairs, and the tall ceilings made the sound echo as she approached.

"Well, come in already," she said, overhearing my voice. "You're letting in all the heat."

I went inside and cool air-conditioned air dried the perspiration on my forehead, sending a chill down my back. I watched Neal retreat to the large rolltop desk in the far end of the living room, where he sat and went through papers. I had hoped Neal would be out; I really didn't want an audience and certainly didn't need the two of them teaming up against me.

"Can we sit outside?" I asked as my mother got a can of Diet Dr. Pepper out of the fridge in the kitchen. I noticed she didn't offer me one. After she closed the refrigerator door and headed for the patio, I got out a can for myself. I glanced back to make sure Neal wasn't following us outside and was relieved to see his back still turned to me.

My mother popped open her can and sipped as she took a seat in one of her patio chairs. The hot air was so still that the water on the Bay shone like glass, making me put my sunglasses back on. I sat down with trepidation, gathering humility around me, telling myself to do whatever it took to appease my mother and make her back down. I pictured Jeremy's anguished face and my head started throbbing.

"Mom, I'm sorry about the other day, at lunch." My throat clogged up. Tears filled my eyes but I wiped my face. I was suddenly overcome with emotion. I was a little lost girl, wanting to feel my mother's arms embrace me, and aching to realize that it wasn't going to happen. I felt bereft of all the many times I had needed those arms to comfort me—all through years of scrapes and hurts and disappointments. Instead, I had been chastised, criticized, pushed away.

I stymied the unwanted anger rising in my heart and batted it away with all my resolve. This was not the time. I was on a mission. Anger would not serve me now.

I allowed my eyes to meet hers and my heart sank. Where was the compassion I so desperately needed? All I found glaring back at me were two icy orbs of glass, like a hawk's gaze upon its prey. I knew then my mother wasn't going to make this easy. And that she knew exactly what my game plan was. I was sunk before I even began. I rested my head in my hands and tried to still my frantic heartbeat.

"Lisa, what am I to do with you? Still the whirlwind, stirring everyone up, running roughshod over your brothers. Don't you see what you're doing? How Jeremy is twisting your thinking, turning you away from us? How can you not see it?"

I bit my tongue. I would not rise to her baiting. Instead, I softened my voice. "What do you want from me, Mom? Just tell me."

My mother snorted. I guessed I surprised her with that question. "Want from you? Lisa, I don't want anything from you—I just want you to be happy. And you've been so unhappy recently. I know it's hard when your marriage is falling apart—"

"My marriage is not falling apart. Jeremy and I have problems, sure. But so does everyone. Look at Raff and Kendra."

"Well, of course they have problems—Raff's illness is untenable and Kendra is a saint, the way she holds up under his erratic behavior." My eyebrows lifted at her unexpected praise for my sister-in-law. But, comparisons must be made at some concession.

"I'm just saying that what Jeremy and I are going through is fixable. We love each other, and we're good together—despite what you might think."

My mother shook her head in her trademark expression of pity and disappointment. "I know Jeremy has moved out. You can try to hide it all you want, but—"

"But that's none of your business. If we need some space, some time apart to clear our heads, what's wrong with that?" I heard the defensiveness rising in my voice and clamped my lips shut. I brought Jeremy's anguished face back to mind and willed myself to calm down.

"Mom, we can't do this—pay you a monthly rent on the property. There's no way we can afford it."

"There are ways to cut back. Stop eating out. Grow your own food—"

"Oh, come on, Mom, get real. How can we save twelve hundred a month by growing a few tomatoes? And Jeremy and I rarely eat out. Or go shopping for clothes or frivolous things. Most of the money we've earned we've put into the house and property."

"Well, you spend a fortune on feed for those animals. Why do you have to have so many? They don't do anything. And you just took that extravagant trip to New York. What did that cost you?"

"Extravagant? The plane ticket was under a hundred. Maybe if you didn't eat out all the time, and buy expensive Italian suits and shoes and million-dollar homes . . ." I made a sweeping gesture with my hand and knocked my soda can over. Black fizzy liquid poured out on the flagstone patio, like acid. The fizzing seemed oddly symbolic of my relationship with my mother. I knew I shouldn't have finished that sentence, but I did, anyway. ". . . then you wouldn't have to ask us for money. Jeremy and I work damn hard to be responsible and frugal. We pay all our bills on time, don't have credit card debt, make sure we keep everything up on your property, which has increased value many times over, as if I didn't have to remind you."

I stomped my feet as I went into the kitchen to get a wet rag to clean up the mess I'd made. I wished there was a rag I could use to sop up this bigger mess. I knew I had put my foot in my mouth, despite all my effort to remain in control. My mother knew every button I had and she pushed them all with delight.

I felt her glare at me as I wiped up the spilled soda. I set the soaked dish towel on the glass side table and turned to look at her. Her voice came out even and unemotional.

"What I spend my money on is none of your business. And beside the point. I earn my money, and I have the right to spend it as I choose. When are you going to stand on your own two feet and stop taking handouts? If you were leasing that property from anyone else, you'd have to pay rent. You're not a child anymore; how long do you think I'm going to support you?"

"Support me? Jeremy and I work hard. You don't support us." My words came out in fits and starts. I had trouble catching my breath, as if I had just run a mile. I pointed into the house. "If you're so gung-ho about having your children stand on their own two feet, what's Neal doing here—eating your food and lounging on your couch? Why don't you kick him out and make him get a life?"

My mother cocked her head and stared at me as if I were speaking Latin. "This is not about Neal. This is about fulfilling your obligations and carrying your own weight."

"No, mother." I dragged out those words. "This is about you and Jeremy. You just can't tolerate anyone who won't grovel, who isn't ready to rush to do your bidding at your slightest command. You've tried to train him to be a faithful puppy dog but it didn't work. It's not enough you have two sons that slobber at your feet, you had to do everything you could to break Jeremy's back. To break his spirit. You can't stand to have any man say no to you—or put you in your place."

My mother's eyes glazed with raging fire. "You're walking a dangerous line here, young lady—"

"Is that what happened with Dad? With your marriage? Did you threaten him too? Is that why he walked out on—"

Before I knew it, my mother was on her feet and I felt a sharp sting on my cheek. I lifted my hand to my face and realized my mother had slapped me. I started to laugh. I don't know why, but that seemed the only response I could muster from her action.

"I knew that visit to your uncle would fill your head with lies. Just what did he tell you?"

"Oh, my uncle told me plenty. But he didn't have to enlighten me about your failing marriage. I read Dad's own words—in a letter he wrote Uncle Samuel before he died. How your marriage was a sham, how unbearable it was for him to endure you any longer." I grew giddy with the power I conjured up with my secret knowledge. My mother had no clue about the letter—that was evident in her stricken expression. I boldly went on, although I knew I was adeptly sealing my fate. "I know all about the affair—"

My mother tried to put words together, but all she got out was, "what . . . affair . . ." She backpedaled so hard I could almost see her legs pumping. She spoke through clenched teeth. "You're making this all up."

"I most certainly am not." My tone changed into a syrupy cynicism. "I'd be glad to make you a copy of that letter. In fact, I think I should give everyone in the family a copy. It's quite enlightening, you know. All about—"

My mother slapped her hands on the frame of her chair as she stood behind it. She fumbled as if trying to set up a barricade against me, against my barrage of words, but floundered in the attempt. I toyed with telling her about Julie Hutchinson, my visit to Ed. Instead, I fed her more bait, knowing I was marching foolhardily to the gallows. Yet, the satisfaction of seeing her like this was worth my demise. I would go down in a screaming blaze—a sight that would take her breath away.

Neal, finally aware of the commotion on the patio, came rushing out, his face flushed. I cast him only a brief glance, then turned back to my mother.

"Does the name Shirley Hutchinson ring a bell?"

I watched my mother's face go pale and her hands clench into fists. The moment hung in a silence pregnant with every foul and bitter emotion possible. I felt the wind go out of my sails as my entire body started to shake. I exhaled a big breath and said quietly, "So, don't talk to me about how my marriage is falling apart and what I'm doing wrong. You're not in a position to give me any advice at all on that topic. But, hey, you're great at destroying marriages. Maybe if your real estate empire topples, you could find a new career utilizing that skill."

Every nerve in my body screamed at me to leave and to shut up. I knew the damage was done. I also knew that I couldn't keep up the confident front of attack any longer; I was seriously spent. Before either my mother or Neal could think of a clever retort, I had swooped up my purse and marched out the front door. I rushed to get into my car and fumbled with my keys. I couldn't think of anything other than the need to make a hasty getaway before they came after me, although I assumed they were still in shock and hadn't moved a muscle.

I drove a few blocks, turned down a side street, went around the corner, then parked the car. I was in no condition to drive, but needed to be safely out of my mother's purview. What on earth had I done? How had I veered off course like that? Tears started pouring down my face—not tears of relief, but of chastisement. I knew what I'd just done would have consequences, severe consequences. What would Jeremy say? I had promised him I would try to appease my mother and instead had opened a Pandora's Box of disaster.

I sat there, in my hot stuffy car, for ages. I cried, not so much for my stupidity and lack of control but in self-pity. Why had I been stuck with the mother I had? Why couldn't I have a mother like Sarah, Anne's mother—someone sweet and kind, supportive and understanding? Someone who gave hugs without reserve and thought nothing of doling out praise. Someone willing to dive into the deep end of a pool without a second thought to rescue a helpless, floundering child. I felt like a starved waif, like Oliver Twist in Charles Dickens's novel, begging with a bowl in his outstretched hands, "Please, sir, I want some more." Only, I was starved for approval instead of sustenance.

And how had I ended up with two brothers who hung onto my mother's skirts, who didn't have one ounce of courage to defy her—ever? I thought about my father lasting ten years under that kind of oppression. No wonder he had a death wish. My mother's pat theory about his having "bad blood" and giving himself leukemia was a joke. No, it was a cover-up. What disturbed me even more than my mother's tyranny was her egregious denial of it. Surely she knew her culpability in the failure of her marriage, and of forcing my father to look elsewhere for comfort and attention.

What did any of this matter, now? I would just have to go home and talk to Jeremy. I pictured Jeremy's reaction, his "I told you so." Meeting with a lawyer, paying exorbitant legal fees. The litigious battle that would follow, the sides of support drawn. I knew I had made an untenable situation worse, that bad times were ahead.

But I had no clue how bad. I underestimated the reach of my mother's arm. And her need to win at all costs. As I sat there in my sweltering car, I thought I could imagine every possible outcome to this situation, every worst-case scenario. We could weather it out, survive, if Jeremy and I banded together. Our love could pull us through.

Or so I thought.

CHAPTER 15

I MET ANNE THE NEXT day at our usual hiking spot. She immediately noticed how distraught I was, and rather than hike, we ended up in a small park in Sausalito overlooking the harbor and talked. I told her everything that had transpired in the last few days and she listened with rapt attention and a face laced with compassion. She had seen this coming; she had warned me. She really didn't have much advice for me, and I wasn't looking for advice as much as for a boost of courage. I had no choice but to go through the firestorm I had unleashed. She assured me this wasn't my fault, despite my many protests to that effect. Despite her condolences and reassurances, I was racked with guilt and a sense of culpability. Nothing she could say would ease those heavy weights of judgment I'd hung around my neck.

She muttered condolences and hugged me good-bye. At the gas station down the street, I dropped in a couple of quarters. I knew I was asking for trouble by calling Raff. He had managed to return half-time to work and I hoped to rally his support before my mother turned him against me. What was I thinking? Even if I could get him to talk to me, I knew he would give me his pat line: "Lisa, I can't deal with the stress. Don't talk to me about your problems; I have enough of my own." His secretary answered, but when she tried to connect me, she came back on the line and told me in a polite but dismissing tone that Raff was busy at the moment. She would pass on the message that I called, with no promises that he would get back to me.

I drove home, deciding to immerse myself in work. I had to do something with all this anger and hurt. Fueled by frenetic energy, I mucked out the barn, took the sodden straw out in wheelbarrows to the rose garden, and worked it in as mulch around the bushes. I trimmed hooves, gave shots and worming medicine, cleaned out the two water troughs, tightened the loose latch on the goat pen gate, and swept out the barn. It was nearly dark out by the time I walked down the gravel drive to the mailbox, Buster and Angel bouncing along at my side, the air redolent of lilac. When I sifted through the pile of papers, I almost missed the small brown postal notice tucked in between the bills and the local market specials flyer. A registered letter that had to be signed for, from my mother's business manager.

The moment my eyes locked onto the name on the notice, my knees turned to jelly. My heart pounded hard in my chest and I struggled for breath. A sweeping sensation of doom fell hard on my body, crushing me in fear. "I can't do this," I muttered aloud.

I fell in a heap next to the mailbox. The air, warm and still, felt portentous, the harbinger of a storm coming on the horizon. My hands shook so hard I dropped the mail in a heap to the dirt and stared down the empty road. The smell of gravel dust and sagebrush surrounded me, a heady aroma. Dizzy, I steadied myself and stood, then turned to look at my property in the fading light—the rough-sided barn; my beautiful ranch home draped with perennials in bloom—roses, penstemon, hydrangeas, and dozens of others crowding the windows and sides of the house; the pond off in the distance, where the frogs were kicking off their evening chortling. I stood there until darkness sucked away every last shred of light, erasing my world as if it had only been a fanciful illusion.

I felt a warm tongue on my wrist. Buster looked up at me, wondering if we were going for a walk. His tail swung in hopeful anticipation. I gave him a perfunctory pat and stumbled my way back to the house. I tossed the market flyer in the recycling bin and hesitated, considering throwing the postal notice for that registered letter in there too. But, I knew that would only delay the inevitable. Whatever my mother had set in motion, whatever legal procedures, they would not be sidetracked by any resistance on my part.

I dropped into the chair by the kitchen phone. I was numb, void of emotion. As if that little piece of paper had drained the life out of me, every drop. I found the sticky note on which Jeremy had jotted his phone number. It took all my nerve to punch in the numbers.

Jeremy's employee, Daniel, answered the phone and said Jeremy had run down to the store but would be back soon. Maybe the disconsolate tone of my voice alerted him to my distress, because rather than call back, within the hour Jeremy showed up at the door. I hadn't heard him drive up, as I had been in the shower, letting hot water pound my shoulders. But, from my bedroom, I heard Angel yipping in the yard, so I threw on some clothes and found Jeremy standing on the stoop, waiting for an invitation to come in.

Without a thought, I threw my arms around him and broke down. He muttered words of comfort as I soaked his flannel shirt with my hot tears and wiped my running nose with the back of my hand. His arms hung loosely around me in an awkward embrace. I dared look up to meet his gaze, and rather than see a victorious "I told you so," I was taken aback by something foreign and much more disturbing.

Fear.

CHAPTER 16

AT SOME POINT DURING THE night I had fallen asleep. Without any discussion, Jeremy chose to stay over—whether for his comfort or mine, I couldn't tell. Neither of us ate any dinner and we immersed ourselves in silent domestic chores, coordinating a polite dance around one another as we straightened the house, swept floors, vacuumed the upstairs carpeting. Whatever solace we hoped to find in these mundane, familiar activities didn't manifest. My body moved, but I felt like a hollow shell, the life within me withered and turning to dust. Neither of us bothered with niceties or made attempt at conversation. And when we finally worked our way into the bedroom, undressed, and slipped under the covers, I reached for Jeremy, not with any expectation of passion, but to soak up physical warmth, responding to some basic primal need that equated warmth with safety; yet, that safety eluded me as well.

Jeremy lay on his back—the way he always slept—and stared out the window that faced the hills, without speaking. Curled on my side, I draped my arm and leg over him, wanting to spill out the details of my fight with my mother. But we'd had too many arguments in this bed, and in recent months this sanctuary of our love had morphed into a battlefield, contaminated with our barbed words that detonated hurtful accusations. I wondered, as I held him there, if the contagion would ever dissipate or if it would taint us the rest of our lives, casting a shroud of discomfort every time we made love—if we ever would again.

Through my hand on his chest, Jeremy's heartbeat thumped so quietly I could barely feel it. His breathing was shallow; he seemed hardly alive—as if his entire biological system was winding down in entropy. I thought of how some scientists believed that once the universe stopped expanding, it would reverse course and collapse in on itself, imploding in an instant of time—the converse of the Big Bang. Jeremy's stillness belied something just as portentous, his manner duplicitous and masked. My fear grew as the hours passed; I closed my eyes and pretended to be asleep, but I don't think I fooled Jeremy, and I don't think he cared.

In the morning haze, when I uncurled my body amid the tangled covers, I touched Jeremy's side of the bed. The sheet was cool and the house ominously quiet. I found the bedside clock and was surprised it read nine fifteen. How had I slept so deeply? I hardly felt rested. I made my way to the window and looked down at the driveway. Jeremy's truck was gone. I had no idea if he'd be back. Being Thursday, I assumed he had headed to the feed store to work. My back muscles ached from my frenetic activity around the barn yesterday, so I took a scalding hot shower, then forced myself to eat a piece of toast and two fried eggs. Eating did little to calm my fluttery stomach. I kept my distance from the counter where the postal notice lay beside the phone, but I dared glance over to test my nerve, knowing I'd have to make the trip to the post office at some point and sign for the letter. To my chagrin, the small slip of brown paper was gone.

Before I could run through the meaning of the paper's disappearance—I had misplaced it, Jeremy had thrown it out, Buster had knocked it to the floor with his curious nose—Jeremy's truck came barreling up the driveway, sliding to a stop with such abruptness that gravel flew in all directions under a cloud of dust.

Jeremy moved with so much fury that I flung the front door open, afraid he would splinter it with the force of his anger. I instinctively cowered, curling into myself, not knowing what to expect. I was thoroughly acquainted with the magnitude of his sheer energy; just his size alone gave his emotions weight and clout. One look told me he wasn't angry at me at all, but that did little to relieve my terror.

In a brisk gesture, he slapped a priority mail envelope on the kitchen island counter. He shook his head, at a loss for words. I could tell he'd been railing in his truck, something he told me he did from time to time—screamed at his windshield as he drove, where no one could hear him. His hair was damp, his face beaded with perspiration, even though the morning was cool and foggy. He looked as if he had used up all his words and now nothing would come out of his mouth. I knew he was waiting for me to open the envelope and read what my mother's business manager had sent us.

I moved cautiously to the counter. Jeremy's breath came out in spurts through his nostrils, but he stood there, stiff and unmoving. It was apparent we had received more than just a rent notice. I didn't dare look in his eyes.

I pulled the letter from its sheath. A single sheet of paper. The kitchen silence enwrapped me. Outside, the dogs were roughhousing; the goats clamored for breakfast. The sounds of a normal morning went on beyond the walls of my house, muted, distant, as if the rest of my existence was blocked by some invisible force field. I was underwater again, in that pool, drifting down the concrete slope, staring up at the world through the rippling surface, knowing I was sliding to my doom without anyone noticing. If you scream underwater, can anyone up above hear you?

My hand shook as I held the paper to read it. Just the imposing letterhead with its official businesslike appearance set my gut wrenching. I had to read the scant three paragraphs four times before the words strung together in some sort of coherence. Nouns linked to verbs, triggering the synapses in my brain, but I grasped for some sense of it as if I were translating Latin. Yet, the words were simple and void of legalese. They stated quite plainly that Ruth Sitteroff, out of financial necessity, had sold the property located at 328 Rural Route C to Blake Enterprises. The occupants were to consider this document their thirty-day notice to vacate the premises.

Blake Enterprises. Harv Blake—my mother's business manager. The occupants were listed by name: Jeremy and Lisa Bolton. They sounded like strangers to me. Thirty days—how long was that?

Vacate. Leave. Move.

My head reeled in denial. This was a joke, right? My mother's attempt to rattle us into submission, to one-up me for trumping her two days ago. My eyes asked these questions, but when I directed them unspoken to Jeremy, his expression gave me the answer I dreaded. I shook my head almost spastically.

"No. This is wrong. She would never—she can't do this, can she?" My voice cracked, coming out in broken pieces from a broken heart. I never expected anything like this—never in a million years. There had to a mistake. The letter was sent to the wrong people. The property listed was in error.

Thirty days? To leave?

My mind flashed over the years of labor we had put into our home—the hours compiled beyond my ability to guess. I thought about my dozen residents in the barn. Where would we go? Would I have to find homes for my animals? Visions of packing up boxes and hauling furniture into a big U-Haul truck barraged my mind. I batted each image away as it attacked. They flew at me from all directions, these horrible fractals of my home, my haven and retreat, being dismantled. And then I pictured some people—faceless, shapeless—being handed the key to my front door, a handshake, a smile. A voice saying, "Oh, look, honey, what beautiful roses, and a pond! And I hear frogs—isn't that quaint?"

I wanted to scream and shatter the pictures, but my voice was gone. Some sudden illness had ripped it from my throat—the same malady that had struck Jeremy. We were in a nightmare, that moment when you have to cry out but can't. Where you need to flee, but your feet are frozen to the ground. Where you are naked and exposed and everyone can see you and they laugh and you can't do a damned thing about it.

I heard my mother's laughter and I covered my ears. I squeezed my eyes shut and found myself falling, falling off a cliff, my feet pedaling for purchase but finding none. I collapsed to the kitchen floor, needing Jeremy to hold me, to gather me up, to tell me he had a plan, had worked it all out. Would make it go away, this madness.

Jeremy's voice made its way through my gloom. His tone was even. I expected to hear much more—defeat, anger, panic. The sound of his voice chilled my heart, its lack of emotion, something beyond resignation.

"I spoke with that lawyer. Dropped by his office after getting the letter at the post office." Jeremy paused and looked out the window toward the rose garden. His eyes were vacant, as if he had already put this place, our home, behind him. What I saw frightened me to my core. "He said, at this point, there's absolutely nothing we can do. We could try . . . in time, to . . ." He gulped in a breath of air and cleared his throat. "Push for some legal action, some remuneration. That, maybe in months or years, we could be reimbursed—"

"But what about this notice, that we have to move? Can't we refuse? Can't we—"

"No. We could stall. Wait until we're evicted. That would buy us a little time." He turned and faced me, but it seemed he looked past me, to something distant. I almost wanted to follow his gaze, try to see what he was staring at, but I was afraid I'd see what he saw. "Lisa, it doesn't matter. Your mother won. I give up."

"What do you mean, you give up? You're going to just, what, walk away? Hand her our house on a—"

"Dammit, Lisa! It's not our house any longer. It never was! This was her plan all along. Why she never let us buy the place, put our names on the title. You just don't get it, do you?"

I tried to get up from the floor but had no strength. I looked up at my husband, who seemed to tower over me. "Jer, please. We've got to try. There has to be something . . ." My throat clamped shut, preventing anything else from coming out. A rock the size of a grapefruit lodged in my throat. I rubbed it to try to ease the pain.

I watched Jeremy take a long look around him. His gaze traveled across the kitchen, out the window, over to the front door. The calm that draped over him alarmed me. I shook uncontrollably, but not a muscle twitched on Jeremy's body. He was like the living dead from some horror movie.

"That's it, then. I'm done. I'm outta here."

Before I had a chance to respond, get my voice working again and force words past the lump in my throat, he was out the front door and in his truck. I yelled at my legs to move, but they didn't hear me. No one heard me, no one listened. I was screaming at the bottom of the pool, desperate for air, for rescue, and everyone in the world above was going on their merry way, oblivious to the danger I was in, to the few seconds I had left before I drowned. After some time I got to my feet and stumbled out the front door. Buster and Angel trotted back through the settling dust on the driveway, their faces animated and exuberant after chasing Jeremy's truck to the street. How could they know that they were soon to be ripped away from their home?

Thirty days? Where would I go? That wasn't enough time. Jeremy was wrong. My mother would change her mind, back down. Give in. We would refuse to leave. Harv Blake could try to evict us, but we wouldn't budge. We'd get a lawyer to put together some sort of stop order—something to prevent the eviction until the legal matters were settled. Maybe Jeremy's lawyer was wrong, unfamiliar with this type of situation. Maybe he specialized in water rights or something irrelevant.

I pictured Harv Blake's smug face. His beady eyes and bulbous nose. I thought back to the day my mother had been "working" at his place, the night I set the house on fire and my mother didn't come home for hours. *"Harv wouldn't let me leave,"* she said. As if any man could restrain my mother from doing what she wanted.

The word collusion came to mind. *What's done can't be undone.* Macbeth and his wife, whispering plans, murdering one innocent after another. I would be added to the list of vanquished—alongside my father, my brother, my husband. I pictured my mother carving another notch on her belt with a blunt knife and smiling.

I went inside and left a message on Anne's home answering machine. I needed to talk to someone, but not over the phone. Anne would be at work until five. I asked her to please come right over, as soon as she was able. Anne would be my voice of logic, my clear head. She would have advice, know what I could and couldn't do. How to proceed. *"And should I then presume? And how should I begin?"*

I moped the entire day. I could do nothing but wander through my house, letting my hand light on the walls and furniture, but nothing felt solid or familiar. I took the dogs for a walk over the hills, unaware of the temperature, unable to tell if I was cold or hot, uncertain how many miles I walked before I wended my way home with my feet blistered and aching. I fed all the animals and took the little doe, Sassy's baby, into my lap. She balanced on my legs and butted my hand as I scratched her head. I couldn't even cry as I thought about finding homes for my charges. Maybe I could get a place to rent with a fenced yard and some shelter. I snorted. How likely was that? It would be hard enough to find a place that would allow dogs, let alone sheep, goats, and a lame horse.

As evening descended, I wondered about Jeremy. Would he come back here or return to Daniel's? Did I dare call him at work? Had he even gone to work? I pictured him driving, screaming in the car, pounding the dash with his fist, the way he had pounded the wall those few weeks ago, before he moved out. That argument now seemed so long ago—years. I tried to imagine how he felt, what he would do now. Would he sell the store and move back to Montana, leaving me behind? What did he mean by "I'm done. I'm outta here"? Done with me, our marriage? Did he mean here, as in our home, or did his words imply some larger concept that I just couldn't grasp?

I went into the house. The message light blinked on the answering machine. The first message was from Anne. She was on her way. She noted the time in her message, which meant she'd be arriving shortly. The second message was from Daniel, wondering what was up with Jeremy. My husband had come into work, locked himself in his office briefly, then left the store without a word.

Daniel needed to find him, to ask about a purchase order, and did I know how to reach him.

Did I? Apparently, I didn't. I had no clue how to reach Jeremy—literally or emotionally. I figured Jeremy needed time alone, to sort this all out, if it could be sorted.

I had a sudden image of Raff and Kyle, over at Anne's house, working on their play adaption of Dante's Inferno. The two boys would try out scenes on Anne and me, their captive audience. Raff would tell us to hush, that this was serious stuff, but how could we keep straight faces when Raff, dressed in a ridiculous costume made of sheets, spouted lines from The Divine Comedy, the stilted translation reworked into modern slang? And what was with that title, anyway? What was so comedic about nine circles of hell, where all manner of horrors awaited those in the underworld—beatings, burnings, being buried in ice up to your neck, buried headfirst in the ground while your feet roasted in flames? I heard Raff's voice, but this time the words haunted rather than amused me.

"All hope abandon, ye who enter in." No problem—done.

Dante was in a crisis. He had strayed from his path and found himself lost in a dark wood. "Death could hardly be more severe," he noted. After straying down a hill, he realized he had just survived a night of sorrow, that he had endured the pass that never had let any man survive. I pictured Jeremy as Dante, facing the bearded ferryman Charon at the riverbank. The ferryman told Dante and Virgil they would not be permitted to cross—that only dead people were allowed to enter his boat and travel to the other side. And then I heard Jeremy say, "I'm already dead. You must let me cross."

I shook my head, dispelling these rancid thoughts. My brain was wandering crazy paths in order to avoid reality. I called Daniel's number and he answered. He told me he hadn't seen or heard from Jeremy. I asked him to call me if he got word. And then I heard a rumble on the driveway. Anne's car materialized in the twilight.

Anne pushed Buster down as she got out of her car. For someone with great compassion for mistreated children, she had zero affection for animals. That made no sense to me. But maybe it wasn't a motherly instinct that made her protective of her State charges. Maybe it was her love of justice and equity that impassioned her. I realized I had never heard her speak longingly for a family of her own. Maybe she had no interest in getting married and having kids. Funny that I didn't really know how she felt about that.

I could tell from her clothing that she had rushed out of her house to come over. Usually, she never wasted a minute changing out of her work clothes and into comfortable jeans and sneakers. That simple act of loyalty touched my hurting heart.

"What gives?" she asked, studying my face as she approached the front door, where I stood.

All I could do was shake my head. We hugged for a long moment. "Thanks for coming, Anne. I know this is a long way for you to drive—"

She scolded me with her snarl, but I knew it was an attempt to lighten my heavy mood. "Like I have some hot, heavy date on the horizon? Well, even if I did, you know I'd cancel. You look a mess. Where's Jeremy?"

I sighed and gestured her to come in. While I put some water in the kettle to boil for tea, she made herself at home, rummaging through my fridge and finding a carton of yogurt. I'd never thought anything of it—the way we freely feed ourselves at each other's homes, but we'd been doing it since kindergarten. It struck me that she seemed more at ease in my house at that moment than I did.

I showed her the letter and she whistled and smoothed back her hair from her forehead. She collapsed into one of the dining chairs and devoured the carton of yogurt while making disapproving grunting noises. The letter had a similar effect on Anne—stole away her words. I waited in desperate anticipation for her to say something, anything, that might give me a shred of hope. She wasn't a lawyer, but she knew lawyers—plenty of them. And she knew how the court system worked, knew every municipal and superior court judge.

I told her I couldn't count on Jeremy to battle alongside me, but I was not ready to call it quits. Not without a fight—whatever the cost. What did I have to lose now, at this point? I'd already lost my family's love—if I ever really had it at all. I grunted in self-condemnation. So much for my altruist endeavor to solve my father's death—in the hope of bringing my family closer, of rescuing Raff from the clutches of his Jabberwock. I saw now the futility and naivety of my mission.

We spoke in subdued tones for about an hour. Anne looked weary and exhausted as she kicked around ideas with me. She stood to leave a little after nine, assuring me she would bring to bear all the resources at her disposal, and call in favors from friends and coworkers. She tried to sound hopeful and positive, but I knew she was just as befuddled as I. We had just been broadsided by a car coming out of nowhere and were stumbling, dazed and injured, across a highway, trying to get our bearings. She held me a long time in a bear hug, then wiped her face and drove off. Not a minute had passed when the phone rang.

I tensed, resisting answering. What if it was my mother—or Harv Blake? Then again, it could be Jeremy. I let it ring two more times, thinking the machine would pick up. I stared at the phone, then watched the recording light come on. I heard my pat instructions to leave a message after the beep.

I didn't recognize the male voice. "Hello, I'm trying to reach Lisa Bolton. This is Officer Sean Wilson with the Marin County Sheriff's—"

I grabbed the receiver and clicked off the machine. "I'm Lisa Bolton. Who are—what are you calling about?" I had images of a sheriff's car zooming up my driveway, telling me I had to get out of my house, that I didn't live there anymore and had no business being there. I then figured out it was probably another one of those calls for donations—to help fund the extraneous events the local sheriff's department sponsored. I was in no mood to sit through a pitch about buying tickets for some corny country-western concert. "I'm sorry, could you call back another time? I'm not—"

The voice cut through my speech. "Mrs. Bolton? I need to speak with you about your husband, Jeremy Bolton. Mrs. Bolton?"

I pulled the receiver away and shook my head as if I had water in my ear. I could hear the officer's voice as I stared at the receiver in my hand. "Mrs. Bolton, are you there? Your husband's been in an accident—"

CHAPTER 17

I SLOWLY BROUGHT THE PHONE back up to my ear. "Accident? I don't understand." What accident? How? Jeremy didn't have accidents. I narrowed my eyes and tried to focus. "Where? How? I mean, what—"

"He's alive, but he sustained some bad injuries. An ambulance is on its way to Marin General. He flipped his truck taking the curve too fast around the Nicasio Reservoir . . . went over the guardrail . . ."

The Point Reyes road out of Petaluma. We'd taken that drive dozens of times out to the coast, to the wildlife refuge and lighthouse. Had picnics on the beach, hiked the trails. A repository of some of our best times together.

I traveled the road in my mind and stopped at the bend before Willow Road. I knew just where Jeremy had flipped his truck. The low metal guardrail wrapped around the narrow two lanes, with a shoulder of loose gravel and a steep long plunge off the other side to a creek below. I tried to guess how far his truck must have fallen. Fifty feet? One hundred feet? Would the truck have flipped and landed on its roof? Would it have crushed Jeremy as it smacked into the rock face of the cliff as it tumbled? Had Jeremy worn his seatbelt?

The officer said accident. It had to have been an accident. Or did Jeremy gauge just how fast he'd need to go to crash over the railing and spill over the edge? Was his body only following where his spirit had already gone? I couldn't fathom the thought of Jeremy purposely crashing his truck.

I thought of him deliberating as he took the straightaway to the reservoir, blankly pressing his foot all the way down on the gas pedal. The image took my breath away. I could see him stare down the railing a half mile off, it beckoning him, his eyes squeezing tears away as he gripped the wheel, determined not to lose focus, lose his nerve.

An audible whimper came from my mouth.

"Mrs. Bolton, are you okay, still there?"

"Yes . . ." I found it hard to listen, to focus. His voice was lulling me, like a soporific. "I'm sorry. You said he's okay."

I heard a sigh. "You need to come to the hospital. Can you drive?" Meaning, was I in any condition to drive? I wasn't even in any condition to breathe, let alone drive.

"But, how is he—I mean, what can you tell me so far?"

"He's unconscious, some broken ribs. They don't know yet the extent—punctured lung, and internal bleeding. He'll be in Emergency in a few minutes."

I went numb. I tried to stir up some emotion but nothing registered. I was made of stone. Maybe I was in shock. I heard the officer clear his throat. "Mrs. Bolton, there's something else. A note on the floor of the cab—to you."

A note? What did that mean? I thought I asked this in my head, but I must have spoken the words aloud.

"I think you should wait to read it. You need to come to the hospital. Is there someone you can call, to take you over there?"

I replaced the phone on its cradle and heard the line click. I thought of how Jeremy's eyes looked when he spoke those last words to me—the gray smokiness clouding over, the way a fog bank settles into the crevices of the hills, blotting out the sun, obscuring vision.

His eyes were what captured me ten years ago. A hot September Indian-summer day at the county fair. Raff and Kendra sitting on the bleachers in the tent, listening to Steppenwolf. Neal off wandering the crafts booths, looking for the perfect gift for his girlfriend flavor of the month. The heat had made me woozy, and the closest food trailer was the lemonade slush—which, in sizzling temperatures topping one hundred, was the nectar of the gods, as far as I was concerned. Even inside the open-air performance tent, the heat sweltered and drained—and the music was too loud, compounding my growing headache.

I got in line for my slush and fingered the change in my pocket. I had stuffed coins and bills in there as I rushed out of my apartment in the city, having heard Raff's insistent honking below my window. I knew he'd never find a parking spot.

Maybe it was the heat that put me in a fumbling stupor. I struggled to pull money from my shorts pocket to pay for my drink and it all tumbled out onto the beaten-down grass. I didn't notice that the man in line behind me had stooped to help until I raised my head, annoyed at myself for my clumsiness, and found myself gazing into Jeremy's eyes. You could laugh all you want at those corny sayings, but I felt a jolt of electricity, and yes, it was love at first sight. His face was so . . . beautiful, comforting. The kind of face I would carve out of marble, were I a sculptor. Angelic, innocent, gentle—I read it all in less than a second, and the reading smacked me hard, like a blow to the head.

Before I could turn into a blathering idiot, I clamped my mouth shut and nodded thanks as he handed me the random change he had gathered from the ground. Bits of grass tangled with the coins and, with a careful touch, he pulled the withered strands from my handful of money and then smiled at me. I rallied my concentration and paid for my slush, eager to run back to hear the tail end of "Born to be Wild," but reluctant to end a moment that seemed marked with a bright yellow highlighter pen.

Jeremy made the decision for me. "Hey," he said in a voice that suited his face and stature. "Don't you just love that classic?" He tipped his head, inviting me to walk with him. We listened to the last verse of the song while standing in the rear of the tent, peering over the heads of the cheering crowd.

I don't remember what we talked about for the next hour as we strolled the rows of arts and crafts booths. I drank in his voice, mostly looking around, careful not to let myself fall into those smoky eyes too often. I was afraid I would never find my way back out. Finally, we sat at a table, under a stand of oaks, face-to-face. Jeremy talked of his family in Montana, his plans to open a feed store in Petaluma. I told him about college life and the classes slated for my senior year at SF State. When he asked me about my dreams, my plans after graduation, I didn't know how to answer. For years, the words would come out by rote: grad school, emphasis in studio art, a minor in botany. The more I spoke, the less certain I was of this clear path I had delineated for my life. I found myself asking questions, and as Jeremy answered, my future shifted and erased lines I had drawn in indelible ink.

By the time Raff and Kendra found me, stating they were tired and wanted to head out, even my final school year loomed nebulous and puzzling. Panic rose as I stood to leave, as my brother introduced himself, as Jeremy rested a hand on my shoulder, such a light touch, but so potent and charged. I spun to meet his eyes a last time, almost painful, anticipating parting from him, feeling something tear inside. I already envisioned him giving a slight wave of his hand, a warm smile, and turning his head and forgetting me, forgetting we ever sat and talked—while I would mull over what I must have said to make him lose his interest, as I rode in silence in Raff's car back to his house for dinner. Those predictable scenes that clicked into place shattered as Jeremy slid his hand from my shoulder to my forearm and stopped me—stopped my self-deprecating thoughts, stopped my heart.

"Let me take you to dinner Saturday. It'll give me a chance to come into the city, put on some nice clothes." He pulled a pen out of his short-sleeved shirt pocket and, to my amusement, poised to write on the back of his hand—something I hadn't seen since my elementary school days. He raised his eyebrows in a sweet concession. "I clean up pretty nice—for a hick."

Raff and Kendra had politely backed away, engaging in polite quiet conversation to allow me this moment. No doubt, they had seen the march of emotions so readable on my face—the disappointment followed by surprise, then the self-conscious blush I knew was heating my cheeks. I couldn't bear to disturb this moment by reaching in my purse for a scrap of paper; his actions were just too precious. I rattled off my phone number, repeated it to be sure I still had all my marbles in tact. Jeremy shook the ballpoint pen, no doubt having trouble with the ink on his sweaty skin. I worried that he would accidently rub it off before the day was over, before he had a chance to copy it down on something more durable. But, he managed to get it written, although I suspected at that moment he put it to memory, envisioning the same scenario of the numbers rubbing off.

We said our good-byes and he watched me walk away. Even after I reached the far end of the fairgrounds, I looked back and he was still there, standing with one foot on the bench, making sure I knew he had his eye on me. I felt discovered, like some unknown country happened upon by an intrepid explorer out to find adventure and something magnificent, something no one had ever seen before.

That's what I read in those smoky eyes that day. Nothing like what I saw only this morning when those words, those unbearable words, had spilled from his mouth: I'm done . . . I'm outta here. A dying flash, an ember flickering out.

Jeremy had written me a note before he crashed his truck. Something he was going to mail to me as he skipped town? Or leave for me to find in the wreckage? I pressed my lips together and forced back tears. He wouldn't have been headed west if he was leaving town. I knew instinctively what that note said, but I didn't want to face it.

For a moment, as I stood at the kitchen counter, I saw my father with the same resignation in his eyes, turning to my mother, and voicing those identical sentiments. What had my mother felt when those words hit her and he walked out the door? Had she hurt? Had she even cared?

A growl grew in my chest—something animal and maternal. Jeremy was hurt. This was my mother's doing, her work, her symphony of betrayal. She was like a madwoman on a rampage, mowing down one victim after another, the fathomless sea that vomited out all who dared ply her waters with too heavy a hull. She had to be stopped.

Anger rose in me like an errant wave, lifted me and carried me to the door to my car. Anger fueled me across roads, onto the freeway, down to Sir Francis Drake Boulevard, and into the parking lot of Marin General Hospital. Time lost cohesion; I stormed through it as if a vapor that parted in my ire. I marched in to the reception desk and learned my husband was barely alive. He'd been taken to surgery on the eighth floor. I could wait up there, in the waiting room. The nurse said she would tell the doctor I had arrived.

Oh, yes. I had arrived. Like Sir Francis Drake himself, commanding the English fleet against the Spanish armada. I would make no concessions, take no prisoners. I didn't dare think about Jeremy lying in an operating room, hooked up to tubes and sensors, fluids dripping into his arm, scalpels cutting into his flesh. Instead, I strode toward the stairwell, then stopped.

I caught the gleam of metal in the corner of my eye. I turned my head and looked over at the elevator. I watched the silver doors open and close, watched people step in and out without a thought, without breaking a sweat. I loosed a deep breath.

In that instant, I remembered my dream—of being in the elevator with my frozen family. Of the freefall as the elevator car sped unattached, about to crash at the bottom. No one else aware of the danger, no one else feeling trapped. My pounding the doors, pulling with bloodied fingers to pry them open, but to no avail.

I closed my eyes and saw my small fists pounding on another door. I was hunched over, squatting in the dark, hemmed in, panicky. I was yelling, crying out, but I couldn't make out my words. Something brushed against my head, my hair, making me scream more. I tried to see, but it was too dark. I couldn't breathe well—the air was thick, hot, stifling. I had no room to stand. I batted at the clothes hanging over my head. I fell back against a hard wall, jumped forward against the door, tripped over shoes. There was no handle inside, only narrow slats that let in slivers of light.

My eyes jerked opened. I knew exactly where I was—in my bedroom closet, back at the house I grew up in. My breath came out in quick pants. I tried to slow my pounding heart as I stood in the foyer of the hospital. People hurried by me without a glance. I felt invisible in a swirl of revealing memory.

The slats were the gaps in the louvers on the door. This wasn't a nightmare I was recalling. This had actually happened—and more than once. My being trapped in my closet had been no accident on my part. I knew just how I got there—and who put me there.

With a big exhale, I faced down the elevator doors. I pressed the up arrow and watched the red numbers on the wall count down to one. No one else waited beside me to go up. Every human being on the face of the earth vanished. I was alone. My skin tingled and my stomach lurched. Bile rose in my throat and I fought it down. I refused to let my mother have any victory—not even this one. Not anymore.

The elevator pinged and the doors slid open with a soft whoosh. Every muscle in my body shook as I stepped over the threshold into the brightly lit, spacious elevator car, a line of demarcation. I pressed the button for the eighth floor and braced my legs. I knew in that moment that if the elevator cables snapped and I fell to my death, I wouldn't care. Not one bit.

With that truth planted in my mind, all the terror and anxiety fled—in an instant. A calmness washed over me as the elevator ascended. The gentle whirring of the motor soothed me.

I grunted wryly, remembering the conundrum. I'm free, the man said, as he bit into his albatross. I watched the doors open and stepped out into the corridor. I felt oddly giddy. I had opened a door—a closet door—and freed myself.

But, with one look around me at the nurses in blue scrubs communicating in hushed whisperings, it struck me. A knife pierced my heart and stole away my singular victory. Somewhere down that hall, Jeremy lay on a bed, wishing he would die.

I had escaped a cage only to find myself trapped in a bigger one. And I didn't know if this cage even had a door.

CHAPTER 18

A GENTLE HAND ON MY shoulder startled me awake. I opened my eyes and squinted under the strange glow of fluorescent lighting. The clock on the wall read 3:25, but it took me a moment to realize it was the middle of the night and that I was slumped in a metal chair outside the ICU. The sterilizing smells and soft whirring sounds of monitors brought me forcefully back to the hospital, and that awareness brought with it a rush of distress. Jeremy lay close by, separated by only a few feet of wall, but it could have been a gaping chasm, by the way my heart berated me.

"Mrs. Bolton," Jeremy's surgeon said, "your husband will pull though."

I looked in the woman's face—her kind Asian features reassured me. As she explained to me the extent of Jeremy's injuries—two broken ribs, a punctured lung they were about to reinflate, trauma to his liver that had caused internal bleeding but was not punctured, assorted broken bones with Latin names I couldn't place anywhere on my body, and a fracture in his left forearm—I thought of another conundrum, probably the oldest in the book.

A man and his son are driving in a car. They get into a car wreck and the father dies. The son is rushed to the hospital and into surgery. But the doctor stops at the sight of the child and says, "Wait, I can't operate on him—he's my son!" Back in the sixties, this puzzle stumped everyone. If the father was dead, how could the doctor say this child was his son? Was he the boy's stepfather? Godfather? Once women's liberation entered the scene, the conundrum was moot. The answer was obvious—the doctor was the child's mother. But in that era, no one would have guessed the doctor to be a woman.

I chased after my wandering mind and brought it back on a leash to focus on the doctor. I had managed a few hours' sleep on the uncomfortable chair, occasionally getting up and stretching, pacing the hallway, checking in at the nurse's station for news. Initially, the doctors worried about the internal bleeding and the extent of the trauma to his organs. I knew I should have been relieved that he was out of danger, but I couldn't rally any emotion. My head was thick and groggy and my heart was a concrete block in my chest. Everything about that place appeared surreal and intangible. I had to touch my leg to be sure I was really there.

"Is he still unconscious? When can I see him?"

"He'll be coming out of anesthesia soon. Once he's alert enough, we'll let you know. It may be another hour." She rested a hand on my arm. "Your husband made it through surgery, but he's not in the clear just yet. His spleen was damaged, and we nearly had to remove it because of ongoing bleeding and a drop in blood pressure. But we were able to avoid that necessity. He has a chest tube in for his punctured lung and will be on a mechanical ventilator for a few days. Tomorrow, if he's strong enough, we can begin to wean him from that. The laparotomy packs for his liver injury need to remain for another twenty-four hours or so. Fortunately, his pancreas is fine and his spine intact."

I nodded and thanked the doctor. She suggested I go downstairs to the cafeteria and get some coffee and something to eat. But I couldn't bear the thought of straying that far from Jeremy's side. A great need to see him seized me. I thought of his arms around me, my head pressed against his chest, his big gentle hands running through my hair. We were connected by some tenuous strand that threatened to snap if I stretched it over too great a distance.

A sob broke out of my chest and startled me. I collapsed into the chair and cried, a great gush of tears accompanied by heavy heaves that felt like waves of pain washing over me. My Jeremy—broken, hurt, bleeding. A man so capable, so competent, so confident. How could this have happened to him? And what could I do to help him? How could I make it better, make this nightmare go away?

A hush draped the hallway. A nurse sat at the desk near the elevator. No one else loitered near the ICU. I could feel the seconds passing as if in slow motion. I walked over to the payphone attached to the wall by the restrooms. I dug into my purse and found three quarters, then dialed my mother's number. She was a heavy sleeper, so I knew to let it ring, trusting that Neal would have no inclination to pick up her phone at four in the morning.

My hand shook with restrained anger and my heart began to thump my chest so hard it hurt. I heard the click as my mother answered. My breath hitched.

"What? Who's calling this early?"

Sudden terror overtook me. I nearly dropped the phone. But I managed to force the words out, drenched in acid. They burned my throat as they traveled out my mouth.

"I hope you're happy now. Jeremy drove his truck off the road. He's in Intensive Care." Phrases tumbled through my mind in a disconnect with my mouth. I stood there, trembling, waiting to hear what my mother would say, toying with the temptation to slam the receiver down. But I really wanted to get a reaction from her.

"Lisa?" I could almost hear the wheels turning in her brain, trying to formulate just the right thing to say. Surely, she wouldn't try to console me. And heaven forbid she apologize for anything. Ever.

"Lisa, I don't understand—"

Oh, it would be the play at innocence and naivety. I knew how that line of argument went. "What's to understand, mother? You're taking everything away from us and destroying our lives. Jeremy couldn't take it anymore—just like Dad. How many more men do you plan to add to your list of victims, huh, mother?"

"Calm down. I know you're upset, but this has nothing—"

"Oh, I beg to differ. I take that back—I will never beg anything from you, ever again. You think you've won, forcing us out of our home. You have no clue. You're the loser. You destroyed your marriage, and now you've destroyed this family—irreparably. Take our house! Take it all! I don't care anymore; I just want to get away from you. Whatever it takes."

"Lisa, I—"

"And I don't want to speak to you or hear your voice ever again. You have anything to say, send it to my lawyer through your lawyer. We're done."

I slammed the receiver down and slipped to the floor as if someone had delivered a hard punch to my gut. I had done what I had to. I knew in that moment the only way Jeremy would get better, would have a chance, was by my severing all ties to my family. Like a flight or fight response, I could sense danger and my only thought was to flee. Protect what precious left I had in the world. Jeremy.

Maybe we could move to Montana, start over, leave our memories behind us. Maybe in time we would heal—emotionally and physically. Even if, by some miracle, my mother had a change of heart and rescinded her decision to force us out, how could we stay? As long as we remained under my mother's control, we were prisoners. And Jeremy would die—one way or another. Quickly or slowly. Inevitably.

I buried my head in my hands and sat there, on the cold linoleum floor, until I saw two black shoes through the cracks between my fingers. I looked up and saw the nurse.

"Your husband's awake." She offered me a hand and helped me stand. I followed her down the hall and around the corner to a door. She opened it and I spotted Jeremy in the dim lighting, on an elevated bed, with an IV drip going into his arm. The nurse gestured me in, then walked away. Strangely, the sight did not distress me; rather, I had a sense of déjà vu, as if I knew all along this is where we'd end up—him in a hospital bed and me helplessly looking on.

This, I thought as I studied him surrounded by machines with blinking lights and all the attendant hospital paraphernalia, *is the real door to enlightenment.* This door opened to truth, to understanding, to stark, unmasked reality. I had wanted to be enlightened. To be set free. I had sought out a different door, but this was the one that opened to me. And, strangely enough—I realized as I walked over to Jeremy—I had found enlightenment. Not what I expected or wanted. But, apparently, what I needed right then. The answer to all my searching, the solution to all my problems: I needed Jeremy and he needed me. Nothing else mattered.

When I came beside him, he stirred and opened his eyes. A lump lodged in my throat at the sight of him hooked up to tubes and monitors—my nightmare made solid and tangible.

"Hey," I said, taking his hand. His gaze drifted, but he found my face.

"Lis . . . you're here . . ."

"Shh, Jer. You don't have to talk. You're going to be fine."

Jeremy squeezed his eyes and grimaced. "Sorry . . . so sorry. I wasn't thinking, I was . . . so mad."

I stroked his face, noticed one eye was swollen and his cheek bruised. I was careful not to touch that side of his face. I looked at the machinery and devices easing his pain and realized they were doing the job I should have done. My heart ached painfully. "Hush, it's okay. Just get some sleep. I'm here, not going anywhere."

He let his eyelids close. *Hush-a-bye.* A little tune went through my head. I sat on the edge of Jeremy's bed and watched his breathing deepen. From somewhere deep inside me, I heard words and a melody sung in an oddly familiar voice. I let the sounds come through my lips, almost a whisper.

"Too-loo-loo-loo-loo, hush-a-bye. Dream of the angels in the sky." The melody had a haunting, sad lilt, an old lullaby. It sounded Russian to my ears. More words came, but from where?

"Too-loo-loo-loo-loo, don't you cry. Daddy won't go away . . ."

I held my breath. I saw a face, my father's face. His eyes were muddy brown and his skin pale. His chestnut brown hair was thinning and receded off his forehead. His head seemed big as he loomed over me, as his hand brushed hair from my cheek.

"Sleep in my arms as time goes by. Childhood is but a day . . ."

I was in my crib—a light pine wood, up against a wall with nursery rhyme characters in bright colors. I saw the three blind mice, and Little Bo Peep with her sheep. There were words in rainbow block letters, and although I was too young to read, I knew what they said, because my father had often pointed to them and recited them to me: "Hickory Dickory Dock, the mouse ran up the clock."

"Even when you're a great big girl . . . Daddy won't go away."

I closed my eyes on cue as my father repeated the last line, his voice growing quieter as he lulled me to sleep: "Hush-a-bye, hush-a-bye . . ."

I could see my father's face so clearly—the love in his expression, the way the skin around his eyes crinkled as he smiled at me. The sight took my breath away. This memory was like a treasure washed up upon a barren shore—unexpected, but priceless. It infused me with something I couldn't name, imparting to me comfort and a faith of sorts. Faith that I could go on, that I could prevail.

Had my father sung that to me at night when he was ready to give up? Were his words "Daddy won't go away" a promise or a hopeful wish? Or was he lying to me, or to himself, when he sang that? Had he meant it in some ethereal way—that even though he planned to abandon me, he would never leave me, in spirit?

I watched Jeremy sleep. The drugs relaxed his face and I realized how long it had been since I saw such peacefulness attend his features. I sang that song to him, but put my name in place of "Daddy." I might never know what my father's thoughts were when he sang that lullaby to me, but I knew my intentions. I would never leave Jeremy. Even when he recovered and was again "a great big boy," I would stay by his side—if he'd have me.

The nurse came by and suggested I go home and get a shower, get some sleep. Exhaustion about knocked me over at the mention of sleep. I knew I smelled rank, and my stomach churned in acid. At home, I could make a decent breakfast and not subject my gut to hospital fare. Jeremy needed rest and I could come back in a few hours. It was all I could do to get to my feet and walk down the stairs to the parking lot. I wasn't up to confronting the elevator again, not knowing if I had it in me for another test of my nerve. I was spent.

At the hospital entrance, a nurse hurried over to me. She handed me an unmarked envelope and said it was from the officer who had found Jeremy in his truck by the Nicasio Reservoir. I stopped outside the front doors, in the early morning chill, and pulled a small piece of white paper from the envelope. I saw my name written in Jeremy's wobbly handwriting.

Without a further glance, I crumbled up the note and the envelope and threw them in the trash bin on the curb. I didn't want to read what he had written in his darkest despair. I knew the words would haunt and berate me. I already felt guilty enough.

In a daze, I drove home, below the speed limit, with cars on my tail, angrily racing around me on the freeway. I was Humpty Dumpty, shattered in pieces, with all the king's men standing around, puzzling how to put me together again. It's no use, I told them, too many pieces. The ribbon of nursery rhyme characters appeared in my mind—including Humpty Dumpty perched on the wall—before his tumble. No doubt, whoever created that whimsical wall décor wanted to spare children the darker side of those merry songs—displaying only what came before—not after: Jack, tumbling down the hill and breaking his crown, the spider that sat beside Little Miss Muffet and frightened her away, the cradle rocking in the treetop that fell—cradle, baby, and all. And what about the Black Plague sung about in "Ring around the Rosy"? I remember hearing that the lyrics referred to a symptom of the plague—a red rash in the shape of a ring, posies in the pocket to ward off the disease.

Ashes, ashes, we all fall down. Dead.

Didn't that sum up life? Hopes and promises, so high-flying, only to be suddenly dashed in a moment's reversal.

I pulled up my driveway and fed all the animals before I went inside. I felt oddly unhinged. I walked through the living room to the kitchen with a sense of trespassing. Already I was unmoored and drifting away from this place I had called home the last ten years. I gave Buster and Angels their kibbles and Alpo, then took a deep breath. First, I had to call the feed store and talk to Daniel. He could take care of everything, no problem. I wasn't sure what to tell him. I doubted Jeremy would want his manager to know about his accident. I could be vague and say something came up, that Jeremy wouldn't be in for a few days. Not to worry.

The message light blinked but I didn't have the heart to listen. What if my mother had worked out a snappy speech, designed to wreak more havoc on my emotions? Would she dare? And then I considered that maybe the hospital had called. I couldn't take a chance on missing any news from the doctor. All I wanted was to take a hot shower and crawl under the covers. I wished I had someone there to care for me, damaged as I was.

I pressed Play and heard Raff's voice, which startled me. Perhaps Kendra had given him my message, after all. But, as I listened to his strained voice, I chided myself for entertaining such a thought. My mother owned him—every strand of hair, every cell in his body. How could I hope he'd try to stand up to our mother? The effort would surely send him over the edge. Only once had I witnessed Raff upset enough to turn on her. I didn't recall the circumstance, but Neal, Raff, and I were all over at her house, and he had shaken a finger in her face.

"It's all your fault I'm sick. You did this to me. I blame you for everything!"

At the time, I remember reacting in shock at such mean words. My mom had recoiled in hurt and dismay. She uttered phrases of consolation and love, calming him down and diffusing his anger, a look of pity in her eyes. He never said anything like that again, at least to my knowledge. It's possible Ruth Sitteroff made sure he never did, with some kind of veiled threat.

I realized I had played Raff's entire message and hadn't heard a word. I pressed the Play button again.

"Lisa. I don't know what's going on with you and Mom, but this has to stop. All this bickering and fighting—I just can't take it. And no one thinks about me and how this is affecting me. Doesn't anyone care how sick I am, how I can't take this kind of battle? I'm the one suffering here. Or have you forgotten—"

I looked at the time display for the message. He'd called at least a half hour after I left the hospital. I had no doubt that my mother had stirred him this morning, rallying him to her side, shoring up her defenses with my brothers as her battlement. Had my mother even told Raff about Jeremy's accident? Maybe she had, and maybe Raff didn't care.

I suddenly felt annoyed beyond measure at my brother's trump card. Yes, he was sick and suffering. I knew that. But I sure as hell wasn't going to sue for peace with our mother just to spare him some pain. My mother was making Raff suffer more, by dragging him into our war and using him as a pawn. It was not my responsibility to spare him by sacrificing my own sanity and my marriage. I would not pay that price to save him—mainly because I knew that wouldn't cover the bill.

Raff's message ended and a chuckle escaped my mouth at his feckless whining, and that chuckle grew into uncontrollable laughter. Surely, I was losing it. But I found something ironic in the situation. Here was my husband, battered, bleeding internally, with a punctured lung and injured spleen and liver. So depressed he tried to kill himself. Does anyone in my family call to console me? To offer help? To commiserate? How many times had I heard my mother spout how important family was, how we all had to stick together and support one another—through thick and thin? Family was paramount.

My life, my home, everything we had built over the last ten years, was about to be stolen from me, and I was helpless to do a damned thing. I should have known the fairy tale would have a reversal in the end—just like all those other nursery rhymes. You break in pieces when you fall off a wall. You crack your head, when all you're doing is fetching a pail of water. You never see it coming.

Ashes, ashes, we all fall down. Not some of us. All. No one gets away unscathed.

Another message started to play on the answering machine. I stopped laughing and wiped my eyes. I recognized the voice, but it took me a moment to realize Julie Hutchinson was speaking. She sounded tense and uncertain. Almost as if she'd been crying.

"Lisa, I'm sorry to bother you. I should have told you everything when I saw you. It's just—you seemed upset about something, and I didn't want to drop a bomb on your head. But, well—this may not be such a big deal to you, I mean, you have a family, your brothers. I don't have anyone, not anymore." There was a pause as Julie calmed her breathing. My first thought was that her father had died. Maybe she was grieving, despite her estranged relationship with him.

"Please, I have to see you again. I'll drive to your house—I don't want to put you out. But, call me. You have my number."

Her words sounded vaguely similar to the words my father had written to my uncle those many years ago. *"I'm afraid I'll have to drop another bombshell in your lap, which frankly I feel would upset you too much now."* Maybe it was my weird sense of twisted fate, but the idea came to mind that Julie's bombshell was related to my father's bombshell. The image triggered another spastic chuckle. It was raining bombs on my head, and my umbrella was just too flimsy to protect me. Holes were forming at an alarming rate.

Julie could wait. Whatever surprise she had for me would wait. A shower and some sleep would not.

I rubbed my weary eyes and trudged up the stairs, hoping the hot pounding water would melt all the anguish away.

Whom was I fooling?

CHAPTER 19

I HADN'T MEANT TO SLEEP so long. When I rolled over, the afternoon sun had baked my face into a clammy sweat. It took a few minutes to orient myself as images—like frames in a movie reel—of the accident, Jeremy in the hospital, the letter notifying us of our eviction besieged my mind in a cacophonous roar. I forced myself to sit up, the bedcovers tangled around me. I threw them onto the floor, unwrapping myself from the sheet that had pulled loose from the mattress.

I had left the phone number for the hospital on my nightstand next to the clock—which strangely to me displayed 4:14. I listened and heard quiet, the afternoon stupor having fallen over bird and beast. No doubt my barnyard critters were snoozing under the trees in the warmth of the day. I berated myself for not setting an alarm. How could I have slept that many hours?

I picked up the phone receiver and punched in the number. After connecting to the switchboard, I learned Jeremy had been moved out of ICU and was in a private room. The operator asked if I wanted to ring his room, but I requested to speak to the doctor, or to a nurse on his floor, so I could find out his status. I put the speakerphone on while she had me wait, and I changed out of my sweaty clothes into clean ones. A nurse came on the line and told me Jeremy was stable and resting, and that I could come over anytime to see him.

I doubted I'd be back home soon, so threw a couple of flakes of hay out into the pasture and filled the dogs' bowls with food. I startled Buster and Angel when I opened the door on my way out. They lifted sleepy heads long enough to assess I was leaving and that a walk would not be in their upcoming agenda. A couple of tail thumps later they were back asleep.

I drove much slower this time to the hospital. I kept thinking I needed to call someone, other people, and tell them what happened. I did leave a message with one of the employees at the feed store, instructing Daniel to cover things for a few days. But whenever serious things had cropped up in the past, my first impulse was to reach my mother, and then my brothers. We had always kept a tight network of communication, and now I was set adrift, directionless. I realized that apart from Anne I didn't have any other close friends I confided in and leaned on. My family for all these years had been that strong tower, my rock and my refuge for any emergency. Without that support, I was like a chair wobbling on three legs.

I turned on the radio and heard Genesis singing "Invisible Touch." Wanting to drown out my inner dialogue, which consisted of nine parts guilt to one part self-deprecation, I turned up the volume. The lyrics screamed out at me with a personal message. "She seems to have an invisible touch . . . she reaches in and grabs right hold of your heart . . ." I thought of the recent meltdown at Chernobyl, and how a radioactive core could overheat and explode. The images on TV had been shocking—an entire building gone, devastation for miles around. But the worst part of it was the radioactive particles that carried on the air, contaminating and killing over a stretch of miles and, inevitably, years. The explosion may have taken only moments, but the repercussions were exponential. I remember the announcer saying the fallout was four hundred times greater than the bomb dropped on Hiroshima, and that light radioactive rain fell as far away as Ireland.

The chorus of the song blared at me, stabbing my gut with its pertinent observation: "She seems to have an invisible touch . . . she takes control and slowly tears you apart . . ."

I pushed away the macabre image of people's skin melting off their bodies, then wondered just how far and wide the fallout from my mother's actions would carry. Would my brothers ever speak to me again? Would I be allowed to see my nieces and nephew, watch them grow up? Like nuclear contamination, I envisioned the soil of our lives poisoned so thoroughly that the idea something healthy could someday grow again seemed fatuous. The far-flung effects of her rage were only beginning to manifest—of that I was sure. Would there be any safe haven for us? I didn't allow myself to think that Jeremy would walk away from me, not now, not at this crisis, but I made myself face that possibility. I prayed it wouldn't happen. We needed to cling to each other for safety and support. Or else we'd fall.

Ashes, ashes, we all fall down.

I wiped the tears from my cheeks as I parked and headed into the hospital. Out of habit, I made for the stairwell, having learned Jeremy was now on the second floor. I checked the room numbers as I headed down the hallway, reminiscent of my recent jaunt down a different hospital corridor only weeks ago—visiting Raff at Hillcrest. The two experiences overlapped and merged in my mind as I added the image of my mother traversing a similar hospital hallway twenty-five years ago to sit by my father's bedside.

Had she done that—kept vigil over him as he took his last breaths? Would he have wanted her there? Would she have cried, seeing him wasted and emaciated, her handsome husband ravaged by cancer? I couldn't answer those questions, not anymore. I wondered if Ed Hutchinson had visited my father in the hospital, which got me wondering about Julie's insistent phone message. At some point I had to call her, although her urgencies surely paled in comparison to mine. But I couldn't help wondering what else she had to say, what startling revelation she would present to me.

Jeremy was propped up in his bed with fewer accoutrements attached to his various body parts than before. A blush of color had returned to his face, and that set my heart at ease. His eyes were closed. Sunlight shone through the cracks in the blinds and spilled onto the floor like proverbial rays of hope. I studied a plastic tube that came out from under the sheet and fed into a machine.

"They cut hole in my side and crammed that thing into my lung."

Jeremy's voice startled me with its lucidity. I turned and he grimaced.

"Are you in a lot of pain? Can I do something to help?"

He shifted slightly and gritted his teeth. "You don't want to know how much I hurt." He patted the bed next to his leg. "Sit."

I carefully positioned myself next to him and put my hand on his. I hesitated to touch any part of his body, unsure where all the injuries were. I clamped down on the ache starting in my heart, for as much as Jeremy's face displayed remorse over what he'd done, guilt berated me in spades. I had driven him to this—by letting disaster strike our lives. I needed Jeremy to know I would unequivocally stand by him. I would do anything for him, move anywhere, make the appropriate sacrifices. If it meant leaving the state and all my animals behind, so be it.

I had rehearsed my speech of dedication in the car, but seeing him in such straits caused all my words to flee. I wanted nothing more than to bury my face in his chest and wrap my arms around him, but I knew it would be quite some time before I could touch him again with such abandon—physically or emotionally.

"Lisa . . ." Jeremy's strained voice shook me from my reverie. I didn't realize I had started crying again. "Everything will be okay . . . we'll help each other."

A fluttery sigh escaped my chest. I needed to hear those words. The fear that Jeremy would send me away had hung over my head like a sword of doom. I exhaled in relief, but that only amped up my crying. Jeremy's fingers glided across my cheeks, wiping tears away. When I looked at him, tears welled up in his eyes too.

"Oh hon, I'm so sorry for what I've done to you . . . for so many things . . . but I love you so much, and I need you. You know that, don't you?" His words, whispers like caressing fingers, like curling smoke, enwrapped me in that quiet room.

I nodded. Jeremy stared at the ceiling. "When I first woke and realized I was in the hospital . . . that I was hurt, it hit me. All the arguing, the fights. She was trying to break us apart . . . divide and conquer. I could see it so clearly, how we fell for her ploy. But nothing will make me stop loving you, Lis. And I know we will get through this. Maybe this is a good thing, a way to start over . . ."

I rested my hand on his cheek. "Look, I don't care about anything—the house, my animals, the truck. I just want you to get well and get back on your feet. Let's just get that far for now, okay? We don't need to tackle anything else."

I turned at the sound of footsteps. A nurse came in, with a brusque manner and efficiency written all over her face. "Time for your breathing tests."

Jeremy grunted and his mood darkened. "They need to see if my lung has inflated to capacity. You should probably go. If they have to readjust that tube again, you don't want to hear me scream. Last time, they had to peel me off the ceiling."

"Oh," I said, looking up. "So that's why there are claw marks up there."

A chuckle escaped his lips, followed by a frown. "Ouch, don't make jokes. It hurts to laugh."

"Okay." I gave his hand a squeeze and stood. Another two nurses came in, maneuvering around me. I could tell from their expressions that it was time for me to leave. Relief coursed through my veins. Jeremy was in good hands; he'd recover and be out in a week or so. There wasn't much I could do for him until they released him to go home. Then we could talk and develop a game plan.

I gave him a kiss on his cheek and he stroked my hair. His eyes were full of love and reassurance. Despite the weightiness of all we were going through, his gaze buoyed me like a cork floating over turbulent waves. It felt as if that treacherous storm had begun to pass through and the winds were abating. Maybe not, and maybe a bigger storm was coming. But I had hope, and knowing that Jeremy was determined to hold onto me, we could survive. We might get spit out and shipwrecked on some foreign shore, but we would land intact and together.

My mother underestimated the power of love, I thought, as I walked out to my car. I realized, in a burst of clarity, that was her fatal error. Of all her weapons of manipulation and deceit, she couldn't fathom what it would take to destroy something as simple and pure as love, because it was the one "enemy" she didn't understand. You can't fight something you don't understand.

For the first time in my life, I felt pity for the woman who had raised me. I saw her lashing out at everyone around her because they all had something she couldn't grasp, couldn't take by force. She just didn't get it. Yet, why was she this way? She wasn't the parent who had spent years in foster homes, tossed around like trash, her self-esteem crushed. Was her incapacity to love a genetic flaw? She'd had two stable parents who raised her and sent her to college. My mother never spoke much about her parents, but her words were never unkind. She told us they had died in a car accident when I was ten years old. I grunted. Maybe they weren't dead at all—except in my mother's imagination. I pictured them sequestered and neglected in some smelly, depressing nursing home, wondering why their daughter never visited them.

As I stood on the sidewalk outside the hospital, the cool evening air wafting through my hair, my mind locked on to that day I found my mother crying. Why did my mind gravitate to that moment in time? Something urgent tugged at me. I had witnessed anguish in that solitary instance of her vulnerability, as she her spouted how I had ruined her life, chased away all the men in her life, destroyed her chances for love. No wonder she wanted to ruin mine. Fair's fair, right?

Another memory came unbidden. I was at Heidi's house. Her mother taught me guitar—folk songs and pop tunes. I was in my Joni Mitchell phase, yearning to play like her, and Bess gave me weekly lessons. Heidi was a year younger than I, and she had an older brother who was in high school—a moody, creepy guy who, I now guessed, must have been on drugs whenever I saw him. I couldn't recall his name, but I remembered his glassy red-eyed stare and the way he looked at me—

I sucked in a breath and a rush of recollection stormed my thoughts. I grasped at the bench nearby and lowered down to sit.

How had I forgotten this episode during eighth grade? Fear tingled every nerve, as if I were awakening after a long slumber.

I saw Heidi taking me aside. Where? Her bedroom, the kitchen? Her face was distraught; she looked terrified, but needed to tell me something. I listened in horror to the things pouring out of her mouth, filthy things her brother had been doing to her in the bathroom. How he'd lock the door and take off her clothes, zip down his pants.

I held my breath as her words replayed in my mind, along with all the scary pictures that formed as she detailed one torture after another, doled out by a sex-craved maniacal brother who used her brutally for his pleasure.

At fourteen, I'd had plenty of ideas about sex. But her confession blasted apart my safe and alluring concepts of intimacy. I had no idea a man could do such things to a girl, would dare force such things upon her. I cringed as I replayed those images in my mind. Heidi had been too afraid to tell her mother, so in the middle of my guitar lesson, unable to barricade the agonizing images, I blurted out to Bess the things Heidi had confided in me. For the life of me, I couldn't remember if I told her mother on my own initiative or if Heidi had asked me to intercede. But Bess's face went pale as I spoke—that much I recall—and yet, she calmly told me she'd look into the matter, and then continued on with our lesson.

How in the world had she sat there, listening to the disgusting details I poured out to her? Did she doubt me? Had Heidi often lied to her mother, or showed a tendency to exaggerate? Maybe she was mad at her brother, and decided this was a way to get revenge—making up all that stuff. At the time, I didn't consider she could have been lying; her fear and distress seemed so real. But as I sat on that bench in front of the hospital, I wondered, having recently learned the hard lesson that truth was often a matter of interpretation.

It was shortly after that guitar lesson that I had pushed open my mother's bedroom door and found Elliott Blass naked by the window—exposed to me—and caught my mother's distressed face, not unlike Heidi's had been at the telling of her story. No wonder my reaction had been amplified and caustic.

My jaw dropped, remembering. Pieces joined together, missing pieces I had long misplaced. One memory triggered another, and another, and I found myself confronting my mother in the kitchen later that morning, long after Elliott had dressed in a rush and hurried out.

My mother, preparing sandwiches for lunch. Me, standing there, confusing emotions railing at me, images tumbling, so frightful, I needed to exorcize them from my brain. All the minute features of that kitchen—the orange-and-brown-square design of the linoleum floor, the varnished scalloped-edged pine cabinets, the pale-yellow tile countertops—they came to me in vivid color and immediacy.

My mouth opened and I spoke. Words tumbled out, accusing words that stabbed out of fear and misunderstanding. It hadn't been my intent to ruin my mother's chances at love. My sentences were barraged by those terrible pictures of sex, of that dark side of intimacy I had been exposed to at Heidi's house. I heard Heidi's brother threaten me in a growling voice, the following week at my guitar lesson, while waiting for my mom to pick me up. He had me pinned against the side of the house, out of sight of the driveway, angry eyes piercing mine, out of earshot from anyone who could help me. *You're asking for it. And you're going to get it. You'll pay for what you did.* I squeezed my eyes shut, willing him to leave me alone, but knowing he would never stop hunting me. Not until he did to me what he did to his sister.

A car honked in the hospital parking lot and I jumped involuntarily to my feet. My entire body shook as if someone had grabbed me with both hands and dangled me over a precipice. I drew quick shallow breaths and sweat poured down my forehead. What in the world was happening to me?

I stumbled to my car, unlocked it, and nearly threw myself into the front seat. I locked the door and sat there, unmoving. My mother had wondered why I suddenly wanted to quit my guitar lessons. I gave her some lame excuse, but she didn't press the issue. I never saw Heidi's brother again, although for months, I expected him to sneak into my bedroom at night, or waylay me on the way to or from school. I took to carrying Raff's Swiss army knife, which

I pilfered from his drawer. At night, I kept the knife under my pillow for nearly a year.

I suddenly realized what I had said to my mother in the kitchen that morning, what later led her to cry out her heart—that one and only time I ever saw her cry.

Whether out of confused fear, a jealous attempt to win back my mother's attention, or a primal need to protect my mother from impending danger I thought she was ignorant of, I spilled out a false story of how Elliott Blass had confronted me in the bathroom, naked, aroused.

I sat in my car and shook my head so hard that it hurt. I wanted to shake out the images so they would melt in the air, never to haunt me. But the shaking did nothing to stop the memory of my fabricated confession of encountering Elliott in that confined space and his doing unmentionable sexual things to me. Pictures formed: His hand turning the lock on the doorknob, arms grabbing at my shirt and ripping it open, hot breath traveling across my neck while a rough hand reached down my pants. Images I kept locked away, categorized as authentic, but when put under the microscope of distance and time, proved false upon scrutiny.

I didn't remember how my mother reacted to my outburst because, as soon as the words came out of my mouth, I turned and ran from the room. Was I ashamed—or terrified my mother would know I had lied, and punish me? What on earth had I done?

I tried to imagine the resultant conversation my mother must have had with her fiancé, a man my mother had yearned to marry. Did she confront him with my accusation, or did she silently break up with him, making some weak excuse? I thought back to my mother's tears and her blaming me for ruining her chances at love. My heart fluttered as I realized that her anger toward me didn't have anything to do with her thinking I had lied to her. She surely believed me; my emotions had been too genuine to dismiss.

Having heard my claim of abuse at the hands of her boyfriend, my mother never once made any attempt to comfort me. No words of concern or empathy. Instead of a victim, I was the perpetrator. If I hadn't told her, she wouldn't have had to break up with him. It was all my fault—for speaking up and spoiling everything. My confession had ruined her plans.

I hunched over the steering wheel and cried in great shudders. As horrible as my mother had been, wishing she could have married Elliott in blissful ignorance, my pain stemmed from something altogether different—and, to me, much more reprehensible.

I had lied and consequently ruined my mother's life. I had manipulated her for my own end, to suit my own purposes, however perplexing and naive. I was no different than she. I was my mother's child. A manipulative liar.

And that realization ripped my heart to shreds.

CHAPTER 20

AT NOON, I GOT OUT of my car and walked around to open the passenger door for Jeremy. Upon seeing him, Buster and Angel descended, barking and wiggling, Angel with the tennis ball crammed in tight jaws, pushing her nose to help me open the door wider.

"Hey, guys, down, back off." I pushed them with my weight, but they wedged between my legs and the car door to give Jeremy a big welcome home. He'd only been gone five days, but surely they smelled the hospital on him. Their eyes showed worry. No doubt those smells reminded them of the vet, and those associated odors triggered memories of pain and fear. Jeremy weaseled his way to standing alongside the car and gave each dog a hearty pat on the head.

"Hey, I missed you too," he reassured them with his voice.

I watched him try to bend down to their level, but pain halted his efforts. He straightened with a grimace and gave me his hand the way an elderly person might when needing assistance crossing the street. The doctor had preferred Jeremy stay another day in the hospital, but didn't voice much objection when my husband told her he'd had enough poking and prodding and needles. With some cautionary advice about limiting his movements and taking his painkillers, she released him into my care.

When I had stood with him at the elevator, my hands on his wheelchair, he had given me a curious glance. Maybe he thought I could handle one short flight down before falling apart. Maybe he chalked up my stepping into the elevator as a demonstration of my loyalty and willingness to sacrifice for him. I knew he studied my face as we exited the elevator but he said nothing. He had spent ten years accommodating my refusal to ride in any elevator, regardless how pressed for time we might have been on various occasions. He viewed it as a kind of handicap and never chided me for it. Surely, my sudden willingness to ride in that elevator with him must have startled him. Someday, I told myself, I would tell him my memories of that locked closet. I would tell him everything I had been doing—all the strange discoveries about my parents and their marriage and my father's affair.

But not now. Now, all I wanted was to create some new memories, ones that would knit us together in a strong enough weave so we could survive the weeks ahead. We had big decisions to make in a short amount of time. I was anxious to talk to Jeremy and start making plans. Start figuring out how to salvage this train wreck and find a place—if there was one—where we could both heal, physically and emotionally. The first step, though, was getting Jeremy into the house and comfortable on the couch. Then, when he felt ready, move him up the stairs and into our bed.

I led him to the front door, holding his arm as he worked his legs up the two steps to the stoop. I swung open the door and ushered him inside while pushing back the dogs. They got the hint and went off wandering the property. I saw Jeremy look over at the counter where the insurance papers were spread out.

"That the paperwork for the truck?" he asked.

I turned him toward the living room. "I've taken care of it. Just have to mail off some forms."

I could see Jeremy's mind turning. How it was his fault the truck was totaled. How we couldn't afford right now to buy another, but he could use my old work truck. Wondering when he'd feel well enough to return to work. Wondering if things were okay at the store, or if the world had disintegrated while he had been lying in the hospital bed with tubes attached to his body.

As I led him to the couch and arranged pillows and blankets for him, I watched him look around the room. A lump grew in my throat, knowing he was mulling over our home and what it meant to us.

"Jer," I said, easing him down onto blankets. "Let's just concentrate on getting you well. Do you want something to eat? I made some soup—"

He gripped my wrist and stopped me. I met his eyes. "When do we have to be out?"

I fidgeted in his grip, then relaxed. I could feel an electric tension in his hand, feel something building. "I'm sure we can take whatever time we need. Even the law requires weeks once an eviction notice is served and—"

"I don't want to drag this into some legal wrangling. Look, I spent days thinking this over in the hospital. We need to make a fast, clean break away from here. I don't want to speak to your mother or her business manager—nothing."

I sat beside him and nodded. "So, what are you thinking? Do you want to move away, I mean, far away, like out of state? I'll go wherever you want, Jer. If I never see my mother again, that's fine with me."

Jeremy scrutinized my face. I hoped he could read the honesty there. "I thought about that—leaving town, getting as far away as possible. But then I realized that's just what your mother would want us to do. Give up, run away, declare her the winner." His eyes bore down on mine. "Your mother wants a continuous war, but I'm not going to give her that satisfaction. I remember someone once said, 'the opposite of love is not hate, it's apathy.' I think the best way to deal with your mother and her . . . behavior is just to walk away from her and ignore her. We can't let her feel she's destroyed us. Because she hasn't, Lis." He let go of my wrist and stroked my face. "All this is about stuff. Things, property, houses, money. Nothing tangible, nothing that matters. You see that, don't you?"

My eyes grew misty. I wanted to say something, but the lump in my throat grew so massive I had trouble breathing. I finally forced some words out as Jeremy stroked my face, moving hair behind my ear. His gentle gestures felt huge to me.

"So . . . what are you thinking? We look for a place to rent. You keep the store and I do my landscaping jobs? Will that work?"

"I think so. I can ask around, ask some of my customers. They have ranches, farms. If we can't find anything around here—"

"I don't want to stay here—in Petaluma," I blurted. "I mean, I don't want to have to drive by our place and see someone else . . ." The lump returned with renewed hardness. I tried to swallow.

"So, Sonoma, Santa Rosa. Maybe somewhere north?"

I thought back to when we had first looked for property. How we had fantasized buying acreage in the Wine Country, growing a small vineyard and making our own wine. The cost for such land was prohibitive, but what struck me was the fresh sense of adventure and excitement we had then—newly married and our lives a blank slate before us. Now we had a full blackboard covered in writing, our hands poised with erasers, about to rub it all away. I keenly felt older than my years.

"Sure," I said. "I guess we'll need to start looking at ads in the paper—get the classifieds for those areas." I sighed, wondering if I was up to this monumental task.

"We'll find something, Lis. I know you're worried about your animals."

"I can find homes for them, I'm sure. It might take some time, but it's doable."

"Let's see what's out there, what we can afford. Maybe we won't have to go down that road."

Jeremy was working hard at sounding positive, but I could see much rippling under the surface of his features. He too was Humpty Dumpty, shattered in pieces, feeling around the ground to find bits of himself, unable to see clearly but hoping his efforts would result in some semblance of wholeness. But once you're broken, you know better than to climb back up on that high wall searching for balance. You will always be broken; the cracks can't be hidden even when they're expertly glued together. I knew that from that moment on I would always see Jeremy like that—patched together.

I stood and walked toward the kitchen. "I'll get you some soup. Do you want to watch a movie?"

The phone jangled as I stepped into the kitchen. My heart clenched and I thought of my mother. Was I going to react like that to every telephone call for the rest of my life?

I ignored the ringing and got the pot of soup out of the fridge. As I set it on the stove and turned on the burner, I heard Julie Hutchinson's voice.

"Hi Lisa, it's me, Julie, again. I'm sorry I've left so many messages. You haven't called me back, and I'm worried that maybe I said something that offended you. I hope not. I really need to see you. I apologize for all this melodrama, but it's very important. I know you'll want to hear me out—it's more about your father. Here's my number . . ."

"Who's that?" Jeremy called out from the living room. I could hear the TV playing low as I poured the hot soup into a bowl. "Aren't you going to answer it?"

I brought Jeremy his soup as the message ended and the machine gave a final beep. A baseball game aired on the screen with the sound low. I looked at Jeremy's pale coloring, listened to his labored breathing.

"Do you need to take your meds with some food? You look a little sweaty."

"Yeah, I probably should. But I don't want anything to put me to sleep. Just painkillers."

"Okay." I walked over to the chair where I'd set my purse and rummaged through to find the right plastic bottle. "You're supposed to take these twice a day. Did you already take some this morning?"

Jeremy shook his head. I dropped two capsules in his hand. "So, who was that?" he said. "She sounded . . . upset or something."

I plopped down in the armchair. "Her name is Julie. Her dad, Ed Hutchinson, was my father's boss thirty years ago at Penwell Corporation. I visited them last week in Mountain View."

Jeremy's face registered surprise. "So, did they tell you much about your dad—anything to help you learn more about his death?" He seemed interested—perhaps eager to grab at any conversation to take his mind off our circumstances.

I let out a long breath and started in on my visit to Ed, the pictures of my father, and the RTGs he helped design. Then I told him about my talk with Julie and how she informed me of the affair between my father and her mother. Jeremy's reaction was similar to what mine had been.

"So, what's the big deal about it? Some short affair before your father died. She obviously is holding back. What do you think's going on?"

"I've been trying to guess. Maybe she has something of my father's. Something valuable. Maybe he gave Shirley Hutchinson something before he died—that belongs to us kids. Although, I'm hoping for something more personal—like letters, love letters, maybe. What if my dad said something in the letters that explained his death wish, or his volunteering for that experiment?"

"Wouldn't she have shown you those letters when she met with you? I can't imagine what could be so serious or revealing that she'd be afraid to tell you. I mean, it's been nearly thirty years, and you say her mother died three years ago, so what does any of it matter?"

"Well, none of it matters now." I leaned over and put my chin in my hands. Jeremy turned off the TV and watched me instead. "The whole reason I tried to find the truth about my dad was so I could help Raff. Bring my family closer together." I snorted in anger. "Fat lot of good that did."

"Lis, you're not at fault here." He gestured loosely to our home, meaning our situation. "You didn't do anything wrong—"

"You weren't there when I threw the name Shirley Hutchinson at my mother. When I accused her 'happy' marriage of being a sham, that I had a letter from my father that revealed how miserable he was with her. No one makes Ruth Sitteroff look bad—no one." My words rattled in my throat as they came out. I felt as small as a worm.

Jeremy shook his head and opened his arms to me. "Come here."

I slid from my chair to the couch and eased against his chest, careful not to put any pressure on his ribs. Through my tears, I asked, "Is this okay; am I hurting you?"

Jeremy pressed his face into my hair and mumbled. "It's more than okay. It's perfect."

As crazy and paradoxical as it seemed to my logical mind, Jeremy was right. Sitting with him, injured and hurting, about to lose our house, my family turned against me, it felt exactly that—perfect.

At Jeremy's urging, I called Julie back and invited her to visit us. Without hesitation, she asked for directions and said she was on her way. I relayed this to Jeremy and his eyebrows raised. I doubted he was up to having company, but his curiosity was piqued, and he probed me about the radioactive generators Ed Hutchinson had mentioned.

"There's nothing here," he said, flipping closed the magazine Ed had given me—the one with the photo of my father standing by the SNAP generator. "At least nothing that tells how the thing is built, and how it really works—other than generate low levels of radiation through radioactive decay." He set the magazine on the coffee table and studied me. "Is it weird—seeing a photo of your father, looking happy and . . . accomplished? Just what did this Ed guy say about your dad? Did he confirm the depression, the death wish?" Jeremy spoke the last words in a mocking tone, and I knew he was implying the whole death-wish theory was my mother's cover-up. I still wasn't sure.

"I'm thinking the library should have more information. Maybe something in the encyclopedia, right? Or some science journals?" I searched my brain, trying to remember what else Ed had said about the RTGs. All I could come up with was plutonium with a half-life of eighty-seven years, and that you couldn't get sick from just looking at one—you had to inhale or ingest the radioactive material to get sick. But, thinking about Ed's manner made me wonder whether he had told me the truth—or had he purposely omitted telling me something about these generators? It seemed too coincidental that my father died of leukemia—something often caused by radiation exposure—while he was working on a project involving radiation. I suddenly wished I hadn't told Julie to come over. My feet were ready to run out the door and tackle the card catalog at the downtown library once more.

"I think I'll go research this tomorrow," I said. "See what else I can find out. If that's okay with you." I chided myself for pursuing this apparent dead end. I had more important things to focus on—finding a place to rent, organizing our bills, and assessing our financial situation. Helping Jeremy recover. Yet, this whole scenario compelled me, pulled me into its larger scope. A realization crept over me, like an invading march of ants across my skin. This wasn't just about how my father died, and determining if he suffered depression. This was all about perception and defining truth.

Until now, perhaps like most people, I had thought truth a constant—something that would exist even if the universe disappeared. Universals. Facts. But, in the midst of this noble search, my own perception of truth had shattered—regarding the constancy and loyalty of family. If that intrinsic truth could not stand up to disturbance, then what could?

What if you dig to the root of a matter, to get to that rock-bottom truth, only to find you're standing in a deep, empty hole? Always my mind returned to T. S. Eliot and "The Love-Song of J. Alfred Prufrock": *"And would it have been worth it, after all . . . after the sunsets and the dooryards and the sprinkled streets, after the novels, after the teacups, after the skirts that trail along the floor . . . Would it have been worth while if one, settling a pillow or throwing off a shawl, and turning toward the window, should say: 'That is not it at all. That is not what I meant, at all.' "* I realized then that my need for answers did not revolve around decoding my father's death, but more about finding a reliable way for me to perceive my world—something I now desperately needed to thrash and hack my way through the dense foliage blocking my sight.

"The library? Sure." Jeremy turned his attention back to the Dodger game. I could tell he was having trouble concentrating. His face had lost so much luster—the skin pale and dull from medication and trauma. Some new creases aged him, but he still looked handsome. His was the kind of face that would hold up to the years chiseling away at his features. A two-day's growth of a beard made him appear rugged, reminding me of his childhood in Montana, and how he had hunted and fished with his father in the backcountry. I'd never slept in a tent—not even in a crowded, tourist-ridden campground, let alone wandered over miles of grizzly-bear-infested wilderness. While growing up, I thought having a house in the Marin foothills was the very definition of "country." And our "homestead" in Petaluma was even more rural. I had a sudden urge to sleep outside, under the stars with Jeremy—at least one time before we lost our home. How could I say I really knew this place without such an experience?

A restless energy came over me, waiting for Julie, waiting to hear her next important revelation. On a whim, I pulled out bowls and measuring cups and got busy making blueberry muffins. I went out to the berry patch and scrounged enough ripe berries to suit my purpose. Another month the blackberries would be ready to pick—

I stopped in midthought, realizing I probably wouldn't be here long enough to make my famous blackberry cobbler from this tangled patch I had kept in check these ten years. Making cobbler was a yearly tradition for me. Homemade vanilla ice cream, the cobbler warm out of the oven. I worked back tears filling my eyes. There were plenty of blackberry bushes in Marin and Sonoma counties. Plenty of places to pick them. I could—would—still make cobbler, I told myself. Regardless of where I lived.

Julie must have sped on 101, because, by the time my second batch of muffins came out of the oven, I heard the doorbell. I glanced over at Jeremy on the couch, who had fallen asleep with his chin tucked into his chest, then opened the door and signaled Julie with a finger to my lips. I whispered, "My husband's asleep on the couch." I stepped out onto the porch and eased the door shut behind me. "He just got out of the hospital; he needs his rest." I didn't have the energy to concoct some story about why my husband would be asleep on a couch in the middle of a workday.

"Hospital? Is he all right?" I could tell Julie was asking out of politeness; she seemed brimming over with words she wanted to dump on me.

"Had a little car incident. But he's recovering."

"Oh. Well, that's good news, at least."

The porch felt crowded with the two of us standing there and the dogs pressing up to see who their new visitor was. Thankfully, Julie seemed to like dogs and gave them the attention they required before they chased after a flock of blackbirds chattering on the split-rail fence. "Let's go around the back—on the deck. We can talk there."

Julie followed me around the side of the house, dressed in what I assumed were her work clothes—a stunning pantsuit and low heels strapped around her ankles, which made walking on the grass a little difficult. Her silk blouse—a deep burgundy this time—brought out the rouge in her cheeks. Again, I was taken aback by her elegant beauty. It made me want to see photos of her mother, Shirley Hutchinson, the aspiring model.

We sat on the patio chairs and I put in my hands in my lap, waiting. I didn't feel like making small talk; I wanted to tell her to cut to the chase, as they'd say in those old British TV shows. Spill the beans. 'Fess up. Tiredness sat heavy on me, like a too-thick wool blanket on a balmy night. Maybe after Julie left, I would take a nap, join Jeremy on the couch, with the summer sun baking through the living room windows. A luxurious thought. Whatever stupor I felt, though, was quickly dispelled by Julie's shocking pronouncement.

"Lisa, your brother—Neal . . ." I noticed she clenched her hands as she spoke. "He's your half-brother."

Maybe my face betrayed my confusion, because Julie repeated herself, more slowly. "He has a different father. My father. Neal is my brother—too," she added. She pinched her lips together and waited, watching me process this information. Which didn't want to be processed.

I looked into her face and saw Neal's eyes staring at me, confirming her words. I flashed on the photo of young Ed Hutchinson in the Penwell brochure, now understanding why his face had stricken me with familiarity. The spitting-image of Neal, with darker hair, the eyebrows a little thinner, but the same jaw line and lips; even their stature matched.

My mind reeled with this information but it didn't make any sense. "Wait, I thought you said my *father* and your *mother* had an affair. I don't get this."

Julie exhaled and a gush of words followed. "Lisa, I know this sounds crazy, but it's true. And I should have told you everything when we met. But . . . anyway, my mother didn't know about the baby, about the pregnancy, I mean. When she and your dad got together, had that affair, it was in retaliation."

"Retaliation." The word came off my tongue sounding foreign. I couldn't place the word with a picture.

"You know, to get back at Ed—for sleeping with your mother. Ruth."

"Your father slept with my mother? First? Before Nathan and Shirley ran off to San Diego—or whatever they did."

"Yes. Lisa, Nathan found out your mother was pregnant, and . . . according to my mother, he knew it wasn't his. He and your mother hadn't . . . well, let's say they had been sleeping in separate beds for a while, and so when Ruth turned up pregnant, all hell broke loose."

Neal—Ed's child? I pieced together Julie's words, trying to get a fix on a scene that would play out the way she implied. "So, what you're saying is my dad discovers Ed and Ruth are sleeping together. Ruth gets pregnant—with Neal." I'm trying to figure in the dates. Julie is two or three when Nathan has the affair with Shirley, Neal is born nine months before my father dies. A year earlier—give or take a month—my dad takes off with Shirley and moves out of the house. The numbers fuzzed in my head. And then it struck me—my mother knew Neal was Ed's child—how could she not? And never told any of us the truth. Never told Neal. A gasp stuck in my throat.

"Wait, so, does your father know—that Neal is his?"

Julie waved her hand in the air, dismissing the thought. "No. All this time. You can see why I feel so burdened. Right before my mom died, she told me how Nathan had suddenly come on to her one night—at a company dinner. He was drunk and distraught. Your mother wasn't there, but it's obvious why. If Nathan had learned of her affair—through the discovery of her pregnancy—would she dare show her face?"

I tried to keep up with Julie's words. "So, he made a pass at your mother, and she grabbed her chance—to get back at Ed for what he'd done?"

"Basically. My mother left with your dad, never went home. Who knows where they went. Maybe they stayed in a hotel until they rented an apartment. But, all that time—with your dad sick and Ruth pregnant, my mother never knew. Never knew Neal was Ed's—not until your dad was dying and in the hospital, where he confessed it to her."

I shook my head as if the motion might help dislodge the blockage in my brain. I tried to picture Ed with my mother, picture Ed as Neal's father. The images wouldn't come. Ed's lecherous expression was all I could see, and it disgusted me.

I turned at the sound of the French doors opening onto the deck. I nearly jumped out of my skin; I didn't realize how wound up I was, listening to Julie talk. Jeremy, drowsy and red-eyed, leaned out. "What's going on?" he asked me.

I gestured him over. "You should hear this. It will blow your mind." I added, "Do you need some help?"

He stepped with deliberation and shook his head. "I'm okay. So, you must be Julie. I'm Jeremy." He offered his hand when he got close enough, then dropped into the chair beside me. The sunlight seemed to hurt his eyes, and he turned his chair to avoid the glare. Julie shook his hand and let me catch him up.

"Get this—Julie is Neal's half-sister. Julie's dad slept with my mother right before my dad died." I turned to Julie. "Are you sure? I mean, maybe your mother—"

"She knew. Your dad told her—told my mother—that Ed was Neal's father. That he was sorry—that he had the affair with her to get back at Ruth, that's why he couldn't go home, couldn't live with Ruth knowing she carried, she had . . ." Julie loosed a long breath and I noticed her hands trembled in her lap.

"Wow," was all Jeremy said—the man of few words. I turned and looked at him. "That's—shocking." He pursed his lips and narrowed his brows. I could just imagine him pondering how he could use this information as ammunition against my mother. My mental wheels couldn't turn that quickly.

"Neal has no clue," I said.

"No," Julie said. "When you and I last talked, I gathered none of you kids were told anything about this. I was so startled to find you at my dad's house, asking questions. I thought you had found out, and that's why you went to him, to confront him—"

"And you never have?" I asked, incredulous. "You've known for three years that you had a half brother somewhere, that your dad had a son he didn't know about—and you haven't told him?"

Julie sighed. "My mother made me promise I'd never tell."

"What on earth for?" Jeremy asked, looking paler than ever. "Some kind of power trip for her?"

Julie's voice tightened. "You don't know my father. And my mother wasn't like that. She wanted to protect Neal—"

Jeremy snorted and then laughed. "Right. Leaving poor little Neal in the clutches of Ruth Sitteroff was the way to go. Maybe if your stupid brother—" He looked first at Julie, then at me, "had been raised by his real father, he wouldn't have turned out to be such a loser, such a mama's boy."

Julie shook her head. "Believe me—no matter how bad a parent you might think Ruth is, my father is way worse. He's abusive and mean, selfish and heartless—"

Jeremy smirked. "Sounds like Ed and Ruth would have made a perfect match. Why didn't they just marry and raise the whole brood of you together?"

"Because," Julie said almost unemotionally, "my dad had no vested interest in Ruth Sitteroff. He slept with any woman he could drag into bed. Who knows how many brothers and sisters I have floating around out there? Neal's just the only one I know of for sure."

"Well," Jeremy added, his voice full with cynicism, "maybe Ruth slept around too. Maybe Neal isn't your father's son—maybe he's someone else's altogether."

Julie looked at me. "No, your dad told my mother from his hospital bed that Ed was Neal's father. He knew that for certain. He made Ruth tell him who she'd been sleeping with."

"But, what if she lied?" I asked. "What if she blurted out the first name that came to mind—or a name she knew would upset my father."

Jeremy narrowed his eyes and looked Julie over. "No, she's right. Julie, you like just like Neal. Cut your hair, add a little red to it—put on some jeans and a polo shirt—"

"You could prove it with a blood test . . ." I offered.

Julie shook her head. "I believe my mother. She believed what Nathan told her. And maybe he believed what Ruth told him."

"That's a lot of believing going around—from people not in the habit of telling the truth," Jeremy said with a grunt. He lifted himself carefully from the chair. "I need some water—and it's too hot out here." He wiggled his hand in the air as if summing up all he had heard with that trite gesture. "The drama continues . . ."

We watched Jeremy go back in the house, and I wondered what he thought of Julie's bombshell. Not that it changed anything—or offered leverage in my current dilemma. Or did it?

What would Neal do when he found out he'd been lied to for twenty-seven years? That he had a father all this time and was never told? That was surely something worth pondering. Would he turn on my mother, switch camps? Was it worth even telling him right now? Maybe I would keep it my little secret—a secret weapon to use at just the right time.

Julie stopped that line of thinking with her next words. "Lisa, would you arrange a way for me to meet Neal?"

I glanced into the house and saw Jeremy watching us. My heart felt weighted with lead. "To be honest, I don't know. We're in the middle of . . . a family crisis right now. Like World War III. I'm not even speaking to Neal—or my mother or Raff. The timing is . . . not great."

Julie nodded but I could tell she was disappointed. She'd been waiting three years, anxiously anticipating this moment—to meet the brother she never knew—her only sibling. I could see how she'd want badly to connect.

But, why not? I toyed with the idea. Who was I to challenge fate? The timing seemed divinely appointed. I shook my head. I still couldn't adjust to the concept of Ed Hutchinson sleeping with my mother—and Ed being Neal's father. What must my father have felt—looking at his wife, seeing her belly grow with new life, and knowing the child wasn't his? No wonder he moved out. No wonder he retaliated. Maybe he had been faithful to her all those years, faithfully tolerating his miserable marriage. And then he learned his wife was bonking his boss. And got pregnant, as an added bonus. Did he feel humiliated, a cuckold, a failure? There he was, trying to support his family, trying to be a good husband and father, and then he gets slapped in the face with this affair that Ruth had tried to hide from him. Maybe Ruth considered a back-door abortion but chickened out. Too many women died back then, from dirty instruments and careless hacks who botched abortions. No doubt Ruth put on the appearance of a happy mother, glowing with joy over the impending birth, chatting with her neighbors over the fence about baby names. Unbelievable.

We used to make jokes about Neal—Raff and I—because Neal looked different with his lighter hair and freckles, his disinterest in math and preference for sports. We even teased our mother about the milkman, insinuating how Neal looked more like him, and how Neal wasn't really our brother, that he had been left on the doorstep in a basket with a note pinned to his blanket. My mother would laugh along with us. A longstanding family Sitteroff joke.

Some joke. The joke was on us kids. Particularly on Neal.

I could just picture Neal's face when he learned the truth. And Raff's too. Suddenly, I was eager to indulge Julie's wish to meet Neal. I told her I would arrange a visit.

CHAPTER 21

I PUNCHED IN THE PHONE number, knowing my mother would be at her office. Maybe Neal would be napping on her chintz couch and would answer. The answering machine picked up and I promptly hung up. What kind of message could I leave? I turned to Julie, who hovered at a polite distance from me in my kitchen.

"Why don't you leave a message? Neal doesn't know you—you could just say you have some important information for him. Don't give your last name—because if my mother hears this message, she will put it together in a heartbeat." Julie nodded and waited for me to redial. When the machine beeped, Julie started talking, but was interrupted when the line was answered.

"Hey, this is Neal. Who is this?"

Without hesitation or shame, I pressed the speaker phone. I gestured for Julie to continue. Her voice quavered a bit as she spoke, but I felt that would only enhance Neal's curiosity. Anyone could hear the need in her voice. And Neal was a sucker for any female asking to see him. She introduced herself only by "Julie," saying she wanted to see him to talk about their families. She did a good job holding back.

"What about our families?" he asked. Even over the speaker phone, I could tell Neal wasn't fishing for information. He was outright flirting—without a clue who Julie was or what she looked like.

"I'm sorry to be so mysterious, but I can't discuss it on the phone. Could we meet somewhere—like a coffee shop, some place public?"

Neal paused. "Now? Okay, well, where are you?"

Julie shot me a nervous glance and I shook my head, hoping she'd make up something.

"Well, I'm in Marin County. That's where you live, right?—I could tell by the area code when I dialed."

"Hey, how did you get my number, anyway?" Neal's tone turned cautious.

"I'll tell you everything when I see you." I scribbled on a piece of notepaper and turned it to Julie to read. She nodded. "How about . . . Barrone's Café—in San Rafael? I could be there in, say, forty minutes?"

Neal grew quiet, but before I could scribble anything else, Julie spoke again. "Neal, I won't take up your time. I'll be easy to spot: I'm tall, long blonde hair, thirty . . ."

The word *blonde* did it. I nearly rolled my eyes at Neal's predictable response and shift in voice.

"Okay, I'll be there. Barrone's Café at about four o'clock. I guess I should tell you what I look like—"

"I already know. I'll watch for you." Julie quickly hung up and looked at me. "Maybe I shouldn't have said that."

"Naw, saying you know what he looks like probably intrigued him. His curiosity will spur him on."

Julie's expression grew intense as a cloud of worry passed over. "Lisa, please come with me—"

"I don't think so . . ."

"Really, you should. I don't think he'll believe anything I say."

"He may not. But once he tells our mother, it will be apparent you spoke the truth." I could just picture Neal confronting our mother. Not a pretty picture, but something I would love to witness—from a very safe distance.

Jeremy called out from his spot on the living room couch. "Go, Lisa. You shouldn't miss this—a once-in-a-million opportunity to watch your brother go into shock. And it will give you the chance to confront Neal without your mother standing on his shoulders."

"Please," Julie added.

The thought of facing Neal brought an ache to my gut. Seeing him would require rallying up strength and courage I just didn't have right then.

"If he sees me with Julie, he might turn and walk out," I said.

Jeremy's reply was quick. "Then wait until he meets her and he's sitting down. He won't up and bolt at that point. Not after seeing Julie."

I knew what he meant, even if Julie didn't. One look at her would set my brother's mouth drooling and numb his brain. He'd be too flustered to make a hasty retreat, needing to make a good impression on her. I tried to imagine the worst that could happen. Neal would scream at me, make an embarrassing scene. But, even that wasn't likely. Neal prided himself on his cool, suave demeanor. He wouldn't dare behave that way in public. Maybe he'd hate me even more—so what? Maybe our mother would deny it when he told her, and blame me for concocting such an outrageous story.

But, Neal had been there, listening when I threw out the name Shirley Hutchinson. He'd witnessed the horror on our mother's face. Maybe he questioned her after I left. I wonder what she told him—if anything.

Surely, not the truth.

Anything but.

We took separate cars so Julie wouldn't have to drive me back to northern Marin—and so that I could make a hasty getaway should things turn ugly. Julie followed me into a parking lot two blocks from the café, then after wishing her good luck, I watched her walk down the street and into Barrone's. I had spotted Neal's Honda parked across from the entrance, so I knew he was already inside—no doubt with a table facing the door so he could watch for her.

I'd give them five minutes—I hoped that would be enough time to get things rocking. My stomach was a bundle of nerves. Julie wanted so much to connect with Neal, to form a bond with her only sibling. Yet, the timing of this encounter seemed so inauspicious. How could it not become tainted by all the family drama and hostility? And what point would it serve for me to go inside and no doubt spoil the joyousness of this occasion?

No, Jeremy had been wrong to urge me to go. And Julie could manage without me. Neal would either believe her story or not. What did that matter to me? What Neal did with her information was up to him. My gloating in some way over this bit of revelation would only spark Neal's anger, which he might direct at Julie.

Maybe all this reasoning was my way of chickening out. Regardless, I sat in my car and waited, trusting that Julie would give me a full report when she was done talking. I was stunned, then, when I saw her storm out only minutes after she entered—with Neal fast on her heels.

I slunk in my seat, but my attempt at invisibility didn't work. Julie headed straight for my car. Neal nearly tripped over his feet when he spotted me, his perturbed face reflecting anger and smugness, but not surprise. Julie's distraught expression tugged at my heart. Clearly, Neal hadn't believed a word of her story. My own anger propelled me out of my car. I felt embarrassed for her, for having such a jerk for a brother. I could hardly imagine what he had said to her when she told him she was his sister. And what kind of scene he might have made in the coffee shop.

"So, what's this all about, Lis?"

Neal strode toward me as I planted my feet on the parking lot. I glanced around, wondering if the few people walking along Fourth Street would soon be privy to a loud argument. I lectured myself with stern warnings. This was not about me, or about my need to win or retaliate. Julie deserved some vindication. At very least, some respect. I took a deep breath and let it out as Julie came alongside me. I caught a glance of her face; she was holding back tears.

Neal didn't give me a chance to speak. "I *knew* you'd be behind this ruse. Just how stupid do you think I am?" He positioned himself a few feet away. At least he made an effort to lower his voice; his words came out through clenched teeth.

He pointed at Julie. "Is she an actress? Must be. Did you tell her to cry too? How much did you pay her to put on this little performance?"

Julie crumpled next to me. I leaned in and measured out my words. "You are such an idiot, Neal. Julie Hutchinson *is* your sister. Why in the world would I make this up—"

"Why? Isn't it obvious? You just can't stand it that Mom has the upper hand, that she's finally making you to pay her back for all the money she's lavished on you over the years. You have some nerve—"

"And you are going to hate yourself tomorrow, when you realize the truth. Julie's been trying for three years to find you, to find her *only brother*. She was so excited to meet you and you . . . treat her like this!"

Neal reacted as if I had slapped him. Perhaps he thought I'd cave in and confess my deceit. My words befuddled him.

I turned to Julie, ignoring Neal. "Julie, I'm so sorry. Really sorry. This is just bad timing, that's all. Maybe later, some future time, when things calm down in my family—"

Julie laid her hand on my arm; I felt her fingers tremble. Pain oozed from her eyes. "That's okay." Her voice barely came out above a whisper. "I . . . I'll call you later."

I could tell she wanted to say more, but tears worked their way down her cheeks. She quickly wiped them with her sleeve and lowered her head to avoid further eye contact. I felt terrible for her. Neal stood in silence as we both watched Julie hurry to her car and get in without looking back.

I glared at Neal with such incredulity that his jaw dropped open. My eyes dared him to say a word, one word, any word. I couldn't recall ever pinning him that way, not ever, in all our years growing up. Maybe my fury frightened him.

In a flash, I wondered what had happened to the sweet little brother I grew up with. The pliant, easygoing boy who would tromp off on adventures with me through the neighborhood, play catch with me in the park, ride bikes with me down steep hills, waving our arms in the air as we balanced on our pedals. How many times had I led him, holding his little hand in mine, given him a hug when he was frightened by bad dreams or when kids picked on him at school? I had been his champion and mentor when he was young. And consoled him through his teenage years when Raff was away at college, when he scored low on a test or when a girl he liked spurned him.

This creature that stood before me was some warped concoction of my mother's, some byproduct of years of lies and poison infiltrating Neal's heart and mind. Radiation seeping into the brain and vital organs, mutating cells and DNA and turning an innocent into a puppet on strings. My anger morphed into pity. Neal, the most impressionable of us three children, was soft clay under my mother's hands. How many years had she spent molding him to her whim, calculating ways to turn him into her lackey, siphoning away his will, his dreams, the vision of his future? Here he was, living with her, drifting from job to job, unmoored to his life. I realized in that instant that all her grumblings over Neal—her worry and disappointment over his lack of direction, lack of a steady girlfriend, lack of sufficient income—were part of her act. She had him right where she wanted him, completely dependent upon her and—more importantly—devoted with the passion of a religious fanatic. How had I never seen this?

I stared at Neal as if seeing him for the first time.

There were so many things I wanted to say, but the words withered away. Outrage grew in my heart over the little brother who had been so manipulated. Whose life had been stolen away without his noticing. He was a changeling; some troll had come in the night and whisked Neal off and replaced him with a block of ice, the story I remember from the Maurice Sendak picture book *Outside Over There*. Changelings could be exposed by dangling them over a fire, but what could I do to expose this heinous crime of my mother's? It was too late to leave an inverted coat or an open set of scissors next to the bed to protect him. If my memory was correct, the troll who stole the changeling would slowly drain the life from the child until it died or became an empty shell, a chimera, an unrealized dream that never came to fruition.

One last look at Neal's face validated the truth of my suspicion and filled my heart with a tremendous sense of sadness. Attempting speech would be a waste of time.

I got in my car, backed away from my brother, and drove through downtown San Rafael on autopilot. My mind grew oddly quiet on the drive home. Whatever anger and outrage I radiated vanished as if sucked away into a vortex. At that moment, I could not summon any feelings at all.

A strange ennui engulfed me. I just wanted to get home and curl up next to Jeremy on the couch, watch some corny old movie, and eat popcorn. I needed quiet, unruffled calm, for a few days at least.

Was that too much to ask for?

CHAPTER 22

JEREMY RETURNED TO WORK THE following week, and I spent most of my days looking through ads in various newspapers and checking out possible rentals. There didn't seem to be any places suitable for all our animals—at least, not a place we could afford. We kicked around the idea of defaulting on our construction loan, but knew our credit would be ruined. That was something we could tackle with the lawyer later—figuring out a way to force the transfer over to the new owner of the property—Harv Blake. I thought back to the way my mother had finagled a loan for us—one that hadn't required either her name on it or the attachment of the property, so pleased to help us stand on our own feet. Clearly, even then, she had made sure to keep her distance, so that if things ever fell apart, her finances wouldn't be involved.

I hadn't heard from her or Raff since Jeremy's accident; neither had I heard from Neal—although, it was not as if I expected to. Their corporate silence was just what I anticipated. I toyed with the idea of calling Julie, to apologize for that fiasco in San Rafael, but figured she would contact me—if ever she desired to do so again. She knew Neal's name—he was listed in the phone book. She could pursue him if she dared.

Jeremy had exhausted his list of customers who had rural property. Although he didn't find anyone with a rental, he did receive a couple of offers to board our animals, should that prove necessary. I had put off my trip to the city library, wanting to find us a place to move to first, but after perusing all the For Rent ads in three newspapers, I gave up my search for the moment and sped off in my car to the city. Sitting around waiting for a miracle just made me edgy, so the thought of going into denial for a few hours appealed to me. We had ads running in the papers and posted on bulletin boards. Our "eviction" date was looming two weeks ahead. We needed to make a decision soon, but it would have to wait one more day.

Thankfully, Jeremy was healing quickly, without any real residual pain or permanent damage. Because our truck had been paid off, the insurance company sent us a check that allowed us to buy a fairly new vehicle for Jeremy, and he settled on a five-year-old Ford F-350 the color of his eyes. He seemed content with his purchase and back in the swing of work. Immersing himself in the affairs of running the feed store settled him into routine and lifted his spirits. I noticed, in fact, a sort of lightheartedness, as if a huge burden had been lifted off his shoulders. No doubt, removing Ruth Sitteroff from the equation of our lives made that difference. Like an algebra problem: solve for *x* and get your answer. Replace *x* with the correct number and everything balances. We had replaced the weight of my mother's judgment with the breath of freedom. As much as I still hurt inside, I too felt relief.

I had my mother to thank, I supposed. As I drove over the Golden Gate bridge and looked out at the sailboats slicing through the white-capped waves in the bay, I thought how strange it was that, in the midst of this horrible family war, Jeremy and I had found refuge in each other in a way we hadn't in years. We rediscovered our love for each other in a fashion that surprised me. It wasn't as if we had rallied together to fight my mother, joining forces and finding consolation in a shared mission. It felt more like we'd been set free from a long prison confinement, the bars formerly keeping us at finger's reach now removed so that we could fully touch and hold one another—not just physically but emotionally as well.

While Jeremy's injuries healed, we slept nestled in each other's arms. But as soon as he felt able, he reached out to me as we slid under the covers and reexplored my body with a passion I hadn't seen in many years. With my miscarriages hanging over us, and Jeremy's awareness of my worries over not getting pregnant—and wanting to get pregnant— our lovemaking the past three years had been stifled and burdensome. So much was implicit in our joining, so much expected beyond the simple desire to please each other. That desire to please had lost out in my greater need to reproduce.

I had forgotten what it was like to touch my husband and elicit joy from the mere act of running my hands over his skin. I reacquainted myself with all the lines and textures of his body, and he did the same with me. Something that seemed so simple, so natural, had gotten enmeshed and confused, and rather than need to untangle it all, we surprisingly found ourselves completely unfettered and free to feel again. Sufficient in itself was our lovemaking, which turned playful and easy, much to my astonishment.

Even as I walked into the library and down the stairs to the reference section, my face flushed hot, recalling last night's amorous play. It seemed so incongruous to our external crisis—this joyous calm, this feeling of safety in the midst of a raging storm. But I knew its fragility—our fragility. I cherished these intimate moments and did not take them for granted. They were an unexpected gift, one I was determined to treasure.

After nearly an hour, I found two scientific periodicals with articles on radiothermoelectric generators—RTGs. One focused primarily on the future for such generators, briefly touching on their present use, mostly in Russian lighthouses as a source of low-level electrical output for the beacon. The other periodical was just what I'd been looking for—a physics slant that went into great detail about the construction of the generator and its housing. And the risk of danger. Due to the recent Challenger disaster, the Galileo mission, scheduled to launch that year, had been postponed, and the article about the spacecraft contained a section on some of the components aboard, including the RTG.

I perused the information that detailed what Ed Hutchinson had told me. The use of RTGs as power sources on spacecraft seemed extensive. The SNAP generators had been aboard the Pioneer, Voyager, and Apollo missions, which would involve the designs my father had worked on. The RTG was considered simple by the standards of nuclear technology, with the main component a sturdy container of radioactive material, which served as the fuel. Thermocouples were placed in the walls of the container, with the outer end of each thermocouple connected to something called a heat sink. The radioactive decay of the fuel produced heat that flowed through the thermocouples to the heat sink, generating electricity in the process.

I skimmed the bit on how thermocouples converted the heat into electrical energy and read the passage on radioactivity. I got a quick lesson on radioisotopes and learned that the half-life of the material needed to be short enough so that it decayed sufficiently quickly to generate a usable amount of heat. The need for a quick decay in the safest manner limited the number of possible isotopes, with plutonium 238, sometimes written as ^{238}PU, as the best choice. This was the radioactive material used in the SNAPs my father designed and that were constructed by the Penwell Corporation while he worked there.

Plutonium 238 had a half-life of 87.7 years and emitted low gamma and neutron radiation levels. Many of the Russian lighthouses used a cheaper isotope—strontium 90—which was more dangerous and resulted in numerous accidents and even fatalities when some abandoned lighthouses had been broken into by scavengers. I couldn't find any accounts stating those exposed developed leukemia, but it made me wonder if radiation poisoning led to leukemia.

The subhead "How Safe Are They?" caught my eye. Here's what I read: "RTGs may pose a minimal risk of radioactive contamination. If the container holding the fuel leaks, the radioactive material may contaminate the environment. For spacecraft, the main concern is that if an accident were to occur during launch or a subsequent passage of a spacecraft close to Earth, harmful material could be released into the atmosphere. . . . A consequence of the shorter half-life is that plutonium 238 is about 275 times more radioactive than plutonium 239, which is used in nuclear weapons and reactors. The alpha radiation emitted by either isotope will not penetrate the skin, but it can irradiate internal organs if plutonium is inhaled or ingested. Particularly at risk is the skeleton, the surface of which is likely to absorb the isotope, and the liver, where the isotope will collect and become concentrated."

I seemed to recall Ed telling me that—that the radiation would have to be inhaled or ingested to cause damage. So, if my father had volunteered for that experiment—either knowing it was dangerous, or assuming it wasn't but turned out to be—he may have inhaled or ingested some of the radiation. That is, assuming the experiment had anything to do with the SNAPs. Maybe it involved something altogether different. I was back to *and, or* and *not.*

I sighed and put down the magazine. Without knowing more than I did—which was practically nothing—I couldn't draw any conclusions. My mind kept returning to something my mother had said that day at lunch. She had run into someone, my father's best friend—what was his name? Dave Lerner. Supposedly, he had told her that others had contracted leukemia from exposure during that experiment. Of course, she could have made that up, and I knew it was more than likely a lie—to cover up the line of reasoning that would lead to my finding out about her affair with Ed Hutchinson. But, what if she had spoken the truth? What if she actually had run into Lerner and he'd said just that? That was a possibility.

I pulled out the magazine Ed had given me from my carry bag and flipped through the photos. Dave Lerner had a round full face, sported a goatee—at least he had twenty-five years ago—and wore thick wire-rimmed glasses. I studied his features, guessing him close to my father's age at that time. Would he still work at Penwell? If retired, would the company be able to give me information on his whereabouts the way they had with Ed Hutchinson?

I crossed the room and found the pay phone in the hallway. After scrounging around for quarters at the bottom of my purse, I made the call to Los Angeles and asked my questions. I was informed that Dave Lerner quit working at Penwell in 1978 and they had no current forwarding information on him. His last known address placed him in Seattle, working at a private engineering firm. I wrote down the name of the firm and thanked the person for their help. My subsequent call to Maher Engineering rang through with no answer. I glanced at my watch; maybe they closed for lunch. I would try later.

On my way home, I thought long and hard about the things my uncle had told me about my father. He hadn't seen any indication that my father was bipolar or depressed in any extraordinary way. Sam knew that my parents' miserable marriage had been taking its toll on my father, but not for a minute felt Nathan Sitteroff would scheme to end his life.

But then I thought about Jeremy, and how my mother had pushed him over the edge. Never would I have guessed Jeremy would deliberately drive his truck off a road. Never. Jeremy was as stable and even-keeled as anyone I'd ever known. So, if someone like Jeremy could unravel and not only consider suicide but go through with the attempt, why would my father be any different? Maybe we all had our threshold and when pushed across that line, we fall. My thoughts leaned more and more to this rationale as truth—not the excuse that my father suffered from "bad blood" and had a death wish. Not that because he discovered the truth of his past he willed himself to die, swept uncontrollably to a destiny he couldn't prevent—the way Raff felt about outliving our father. That line of melodrama smacked of my mother's imagination. So, where did this all leave me?

My father had either developed leukemia by sheer bad luck or he had somehow been exposed to radiation. The timing of his death—in relation to learning of my mother's pregnancy with Neal and the sordid affairs—swayed me over to the argument for radiation exposure. Which brought me back to the two doors blocked by the guards. One door opened to the scenario of my father attempting to escape shame and fury by rushing headlong into danger, uncaring of the consequences. The other door opened to my father falling victim to an accident—an experiment gone wrong—never intending to put himself in harm's way, only wishing to distance himself from my mother.

All this led me to the one possible lead I had—which involved finding Dave Lerner. I could perhaps go through the Penwell brochure and try to find some others who had worked with my father. And, if I failed to find Lerner, that would be my plan B. However, for now I would focus on this task, hoping my father's best friend would be able to shed more than just information on the supposed accident. Maybe he could tell me about my father's emotional state, his personality, his dreams and regrets. I longed to hear more, to piece together a clearer picture of Nathan Sitteroff.

When I got home, I checked on all my animals. With a heavy heart, I realized I harbored a fool's hope—thinking I'd find a place that would house this menagerie. After playing with Sassy's triplets—laughing at the way they bounced and twisted in the air, full of delight and unencumbered by the cares of the world—I called the classifieds for the Sonoma and Marin papers and placed ads looking for good homes for my assorted charges. I rang Jeremy at work and he agreed to put a card on the bulletin board and offered to ask his customers too. "Are you sure you want to do this, Lis?" he'd asked. "We might still find a way to board them, so you could visit them."

"I'd rather see them farmed out to loving homes. It would alleviate a lot of stress—knowing they were all adopted somewhere."

"Okay. As long as you're sure. But, what about Buster and Angel? You don't want to get rid of them too, do you?"

I heard a hitch in Jeremy's voice. I knew he loved those mutts as much as I did. And those dogs would be heartbroken if we gave them away. I was willing to give up everything I loved and had worked hard for, but somehow the thought of losing those two mutts was unbearable.

"They're the only family we have. They stay."

Jeremy chuckled and the warmth traveled through the phone. "Okay. Hey, I gotta run. See you after work." He paused as if listening for something. "You okay? You want to go out for pizza or something? See a movie?"

"No, I'm all right. I'd rather just hang at the house with you, if that's okay."

He lowered his voice. "Sure. We could get really comfortable on the couch—a warm blanket, glass of wine, some romantic music . . ."

"Okay, I get the picture." I found my face heating up again, like a teenager asked out on a first date by the cute guy on the football team. "Love you," I said, my heart heavy and light at the same time.

"Same here. I mean, love you too."

I held the phone in my hand a moment after Jeremy hung up. A rush of gratitude filled me and a sense of peace. How could I feel so peaceful with my world crumbling? It made no sense. Then I thought of my mother and the hostility that had seeped through her voice when I confronted her about Shirley Hutchinson. I shook my head in a sudden realization. I'd had no idea at the time what I was saying. Obviously, my mother must have thought I had discovered the truth about Neal's paternity, when in actuality I was just implying I knew about my father's affair. No wonder she'd nearly had apoplexy.

I conjured Neal's irate expression and the way he had yelled at me in the parking lot in San Rafael, embarrassing Julie and flinging accusations. That was all it took to wrench my gut in a knot. Suddenly, the idea of moving to Montana or some other faraway place sounded ideal. What would I do if I accidentally ran into my mother while out grocery shopping? Or bumped into Neal at a gas station? Not that encounters like that were likely; the Bay Area was a huge place and I lived plenty far enough away from them. But, just knowing they were "out there" and that I had to drive through their neighborhood and possibly pass them on the freeway gave me a sense of claustrophobia. Maybe Jeremy had the courage to put on a brave face, a face that couldn't care less—*"to prepare a face to meet the faces that you meet,"* as Eliot nicely stated—but I didn't think I had it in me. My inclination at that moment was to hide or run. I didn't feel at all brave. Would I ever?

I fished a piece of paper out of my pants pocket and dialed Maher Engineering in Seattle. After three rings, a woman answered.

I asked her if Dave Lerner worked there and, to my surprise, he still did. Although he was traveling on business, she said she would forward my message to him when he called in, probably later that day, or perhaps tomorrow. My heart pounded in excitement. I told her it was urgent and gave my name, and specifically told her to say I was Nathan Sitteroff's daughter. She assured me she'd let him know.

That bit of news lightened my mood. I went to the kitchen and pulled out ingredients for spaghetti sauce. Ground beef, green peppers, zucchini, eggplant, a big yellow onion, mushrooms. Jeremy loved my pasta concoctions. I checked the pantry and found a nice bottle of Napa Valley merlot. I felt a bit celebratory. Even though I incurred the wrath of my family, which sat as a constant dull pain in my gut, Jeremy was back home—unhurt and comfortable in my arms. Wasn't that a fair trade-off? How many years had Jeremy complained about my mother and put up with my defending her? I knew his current state of mind had little to do with winning me over to his side and feeling vindicated. Although, he had every right to say "I told you so." Somehow, he'd seen through my mother's ruse and lies, seen her true motives. Why had I been so blind? Even Anne had pointed it out so matter-of-factly to me. Did I just want to believe everyone was good and kind-hearted? Was I that naïve?

The phone rang, startling me out of my musings. I nearly dropped the wooden spoon into the frying pan. I waited for the machine to answer, but when I heard Julie's voice, I picked up.

"Hey," I said. "I wasn't sure you'd ever call me again. I'm so sorry about—"

Julie interrupted me. "That's okay. Listen. I have something to tell you . . . and to ask of you, if you'd at least think about it."

I held my breath. I knew she was going to ask me to call Neal for her. *No way*, I thought. She wants a relationship with her brother, she can figure it out. I just couldn't take another round of bashing.

"Julie, I'd really like to help—"

"I spoke to Neal." Julie let the words soak in. My heart pounded a little harder in my chest.

"What happened?"

She cleared her throat and I heard a thickness in her voice, heavy with emotion. "It was a bit weird. When he answered, he got quiet. Just let me talk. I bungled through trying to explain the story—how my dad had that affair with your mom and she got pregnant. How my mother ended up moving in with your father before he died. All of that. He just listened and let me spill it all out. I don't know whether he believe what I said or not. He didn't ask any questions. Except one."

I waited, then asked. "What did he say?"

"He asked if I would take him to meet his father."

I nearly dropped the phone. A dozen scenarios played through my mind—possible conversations Neal might have had with our mother. *Conversations* was the wrong word, no doubt. More like screaming, ranting arguments. I couldn't picture my mother calming confessing to having had an affair with Ed Hutchinson and, oh, just forgetting to tell Neal he had a father living in California all these years. There was no way Ruth Sitteroff would have admitted the truth. So, what had really happened? Did Neal just awaken with sudden realization that our mother was lying to him? What could have swayed Neal to this course?

The only thing that came to my mind was Neal's deep-seated need for a father. A need so intense that it would rise to the surface through any layer of lies to get air. No doubt, after the shock of Julie's revelation at the coffee shop, the idea had festered in Neal's heart. How could it not? For twenty-six years Neal had believed he was fatherless, a lifetime spent watching his friends play ball with their fathers, and feeling the absence keenly. And now he had learned that a man, who lived not even two hours away, was his real father. Had been, this whole time. It had to irk him.

Julie spoke again. "I told him Ed has no idea. That I only found out three years ago myself. That your mother never told Ed Neal was his son."

"How did he react to that?"

"Same. Just got very quiet."

"So, what are you going to do? Take Neal to see Ed? What if Ed denies it all? Have you thought of that possibility? Or maybe the shock of meeting Neal would kill him—in his state."

"Well, that's the other thing I needed to tell you. Lisa," she said, forcing the words through a closed-up throat. "My dad is dying. A hospice nurse is caring for him now. He may as well hear the truth before it's too late. He'll be dead in a week or so anyway. So, it's now or never."

Julie grew quiet. The smell of burnt onions brought my attention to the stove, where my pan of vegetables looked a bit charred. I turned off the flame and knew what Julie wanted to ask me before she even said it.

"I'm meeting Neal at my father's house tomorrow morning. Nine a.m. Neal would like you to be there."

CHAPTER 23

AS I STOOD WATCHING NEAL get out of my mother's Mercedes, I couldn't think of an appropriate word to describe how I felt. Saying I was uncomfortable was a gross understatement, and *terrified* would have nailed it closer on the head. But once I caught Neal's expression, my jangled nerves calmed instantly.

Neal looked more than distraught. Broken, battered. Like his whole world had disintegrated before his eyes. Emerging from under all those years of thickly applied veneer was a sensitive, hurt little boy. That boy now peeked through the cracks in the veneer; what stood before me was the brother I remembered from my childhood—the boy that would hold my hand tightly against the fearful mysteries of life, confident I would protect him. I knew without a doubt he had fought with our mother—and lost. But, I also knew something Neal probably didn't. That whatever battle he felt he'd lost against my mother only proved him the victor and my mother the loser. Again. Part of me wanted to know every gory detail of their fight, but another part would opt to cover my ears and tune it all out.

Before I could delve into thoughts about Neal's living situation—would he be forced to move out? Would he want to?

Where would he go?—Julie drove up and parked behind my car. Neal awkwardly stop midstride down the walkway, halfway to where I stood on the front stoop. He spun around and watched Julie get out of her car and approach us, looking a lot like a deer caught in someone's headlights.

I decided to be gracious and made the first move. I walked over to him and gave him a hug. He wrapped his arms around me, hesitantly at first, then released into a nearly crushing embrace that scrunched my lungs and made it hard to breath. Even so, the intimacy felt so good, so long in coming, and a sob erupted from my crushed chest. I needed this—this connection with someone in my family, needed to feel that not all the cords had been severed. I didn't have a clue what this portended for the dynamics of our relationship—Neal's and mine, or that of our entire family.

I was so tired of lines drawn and sides taken. Tired of forced loyalties and unspoken expectations. I wanted to be free, released from this cage of obligations. Why couldn't we be honest, speak the truth, tell what was in our hearts without fatal judgment? Why were relationships so complicated? Why so many lies, hidden agendas?

Neal released me and wiped his eyes. He had a hard time looking directly at me. He mumbled something about being sorry but I waved him off and turned to Julie, who stood a few feet away.

Neal turned to her. "Julie. I'm sorry for the other day. I didn't know . . ." He fumbled with words, trying to string them into sentences, but Julie rested her hand on his arm and tipped her head in sympathy.

"Don't sweat it. Listen. This is plain uncomfortable for all of us. But, you need to prepare yourself for worse. First of all, like I said . . ." She turned to Neal and studied him. He was nicely dressed, clean-shaven, hair played down. Rather businesslike. "I have no clue how he'll react. Probably with anger. Probably deny it. But, he's very weak and I doubt he'll put up much of a fuss. Maybe he'll even laugh it off as a joke. Who knows? Just . . . don't expect much, okay?"

I could only imagine how nervous Neal felt, a storm of emotion. Here, about to meet his real father for the first and possibly the last time, no doubt Julie having told him what kind of man Ed Hutchinson was, so who knew how that made Neal feel? Was it worse to have an unknown father or to have one who proved to be a bastard? Where did that leave you?

The question made me think about my dad and how he'd searched for his real father, no doubt with high expectations and hope. Yet, reuniting with his father and seeing what a disgusting individual he was had sent my dad reeling into despair and exacerbated his sense of unworthiness. I no longer believed that discovery had caused him to develop leukemia, but no doubt it had broken his heart. At least Neal hadn't spent a lifetime wondering and searching and waiting for his heroic father to magically appear one day on his doorstep with a Hershey bar in his hand. So, in some way, maybe it was good that Neal only now had learned the truth.

Would Ed Hutchinson have wanted anything to do with Neal, had my mother told him she was pregnant with his child? Would it have changed anything? Would Neal have been spurned and ignored, making him feel as unworthy as our father felt? Or would that truth at least have centered him, explained why he was different from his siblings, setting him apart in some way? I was back to the essential question the conundrum posed: Was learning the truth what set you free—regardless of its import? Nevertheless, being a bastard son in a family could hardly have made Neal feel special.

I pushed all these thoughts from my mind as Julie opened the door. A middle-aged Oriental woman in pale loose clothing came around the corner into the hallway and greeted us. She narrowed her eyes a little and spoke in a hushed tone.

"He's in his den. But, best if you didn't stay long. He's having trouble breathing." She gestured and stepped out of the way so we could pass. I'm not sure what Julie had told this woman, but I doubt it was much. Neal followed behind me, all of us silent, our footsteps on the wood floor sounding loud and ominous. An aroma of coffee wafted on the stuffy air. I fought the urge to open some windows.

Ed Hutchinson sat in his leather padded chair in the dim light emanating from the ceiling fixture with a crocheted shawl around his shoulders. He wore a mask over his face, breathing oxygen, no doubt, from the tank at his side. A pallor extended from his face down his neck, and his forehead beaded with sweat even though the room was cool. In his ratty cotton bathrobe and slippers, with a day's growth of hair on his face, he looked a mess. Much worse than the last time I'd seen him—only a few weeks ago?

As we entered the room, he caught a glance of me behind Julie. He pulled down his mask and immediately broke out in a deep, raspy cough that made me cringe.

"Hey, good to see you, gorgeous. Nice of you to come back. Lisa, right?"

I nodded, not sure of what to say. "I'm sorry you're not feeling better. I know you're not up to company . . ."

He calmed his coughing and stuck the mask on his face, eager to suck in the oxygen it offered. He waved us over and his eyes lit on Neal. A quick study of his face brought him to the conclusion that he was my brother.

"So . . . which one is this? Your younger brother, right?" He spoke through the mask and the words sounded as if they came from underwater. I noticed he hadn't acknowledged Julie at all. She retreated with her back against the wall paneling, quiet, waiting. I thought she'd do all the talking, but it looked as if she was bowing out of that job. I wondered what emotions were running through her, knowing she'd never felt much affection for her father. Knowing Neal would probably be disappointed. Maybe feeling sorry that she couldn't have had a more loving father herself. Maybe, in that way, we were all orphans in that room.What followed was surreal. It was as though I were watching a movie on a level with *Gone with the Wind*, the camera close up on my brother's face as he drank in Ed's features, as he introduced himself and the words tumbled out. My eyes riveted on Neal's shaky hand as he extended it to Ed, and hours seemed to pass before Ed reluctantly reached out in kind, and grasped Neal's hand with the desperation of a man sinking beneath waves and flailing for rescue.

I backed away, feeling excluded from the moment, and joined Julie at the wall. Tears obstructed my vision and I couldn't hear much. To my surprise, Ed listened, wide-eyed, with almost rapt attention as Neal spoke. Absent were the anger and disbelief I had expected. Was Ed all that surprised, or had he somehow known or suspected Neal was his? I couldn't tell. His previously cocky, teasing manner fell from his features like a mask to the floor, and what remained was a visage vulnerable and pained.

I could almost see Ed flip through the years, as if thumbing through pages in a book, trying to find a particular passage, one suddenly important and desperately needed. His puffy eyes glowed with infused memory as he no doubt drew up moments trapped in past years somewhere lodged deep in his mind, cobwebbed and buried under piles of inconsequential life experiences. Images of my mother in his arms, in his bed. Images of my angry father perhaps?

Had Nathan Sitteroff confronted Ed Hutchinson—at work, on a dark street corner? How had my father gone to work at all—facing his boss with this toxic knowledge? Had my father almost spit out the words, the accusing truth of Neal's parentage, only to suck them back in and keep them hidden? Why—to use as a weapon, as leverage for some later time? I tried to put myself in my father's shoes: hurt, angry, betrayed, guilty, ashamed. All those emotions roiling as he looked at Ed's face. Those nine long months, as my mother's belly grew with life, my father looked on—albeit at a distance, from what Julie had told me—and knew Ed was the father. The question that plagued me was, why hadn't my father thrown this fact in Ed Hutchinson's face?

And then it made perfect sense in some odd way. My father hadn't wanted to give Ed any more power over his life and our family than he'd already wielded. And, opening that door would have only led to a path of shame and embarrassment for all of us. Had my father, rather than burdening us with disgrace, decided to carry it all upon himself? Was this some ultimate sacrifice—his carrying this secret to his deathbed, until he could no longer keep it inside, blurting it out to Shirley Hutchinson in his eleventh hour, his only friend and confidant left in the world?

Ed's violent coughing shook me. Neal rested a tentative hand on Ed's shoulder, but the hospice nurse came rushing into the room and gently pushed my brother aside. She helped reposition the oxygen mask over Ed's tear-streaked face, although that did little to ease his distress. I feared that our visit and Neal's startling revelation had worked Ed into a hazardous state. Julie's look said we should leave. Neal's face had written all over it a sense of lost time and a desperation to gather up those lost moments, the way someone might break a strand of pearls and rush about trying to find each one before they rolled into the floor vents.

Over the din of Ed's hacking, the nurse spoke up. "Visit is over. You leave now, okay?"

I nodded and moved toward the doorway. Neal raised his hand.

"I'm staying." His eyes pleaded with the nurse, who studied him for a moment.

"Long as you stay out of the way," she said.

Neal backed up a few steps and let her fuss with Ed. I met Neal's eyes and understood. Maybe Ed would recover enough to talk with him longer. Maybe not. Neal wasn't going to miss this chance, his perhaps last chance, to get to know his father.

I walked out with Julie, the fresh summer air smelling of damp mowed grass hitting me the moment I opened the front door. Sprinklers on neighboring yards flung water over lawns and the sun shone so brightly I had to pull out my sunglasses and put them on to stop squinting. The brilliance of the day contrasted in more than one way to the dimness of Ed's den we had just left behind.

I felt as if I had been thrust into light, coming out of a long gloomy tunnel, one dank and claustrophobic, only to emerge into a vast open space of clean, pure air. I'm sure my feelings had everything to do with Neal's unexpected humility and the refreshing awareness that one door to enlightenment had opened—for him, at least. A door Neal hadn't even known he'd faced, locked and tucked away in some unobtrusive corner of a forgotten room for twenty-five years. A door only four people had known about—and two of them now dead—my father and Shirley Hutchinson. Julie could have kept this knowledge locked away in her heart and none would have been the wiser.

Wiser. I wondered at that expression.

How wise is it to be burdened with a truth like this? I thought of all the thousands of adopted children, not unlike my father, who spend years searching for their birth mother, dredging up pain and anger, hurting adoptive parents in the process. Just how *wise* is such a search for truth? How many of those children actually found their mothers, and upon finding them, were glad with the results? I would venture to guess that most—if they didn't come to a frustrating dead end, having wasted valuable time and resources in their search—met up with a parent who had given them away for the most obvious reason: they didn't want a child. Maybe some lucky few uncovered a mother brimming with remorse and joy at reuniting with their long-lost child. But, more likely than not, their sudden appearance into the life of a woman who had spent years trying to forget the past only stirred up bad feelings. Shame, perhaps, at the heart of many, for whatever reason. For a careless pregnancy, for an immature attitude of irresponsibility?

Who wanted to be reminded of a painful mistake, perhaps finally forgotten, only to be rudely reminded?

So, as I sat on the curb next to Julie, who stared blankly out at the street full of her own ruminations, I put myself on the inquisition stand. What right *did* I have to go digging up the past, looking for a father's story that might only cause pain? Had my mother been right all along? Would the "bad" column outweigh the "good" column? Would Neal's painful discovery of his true father be weighty enough to offset the tremendous boulder of destruction I had laid on the scales? Not only had my family been essentially torn apart by my search for truth, but I may have made life even harder for Raff, rather than help alleviate his pain. Creating this tsunami of a disturbance in our family might be the force that would cause Raff's downfall. Is it possible that, in some cases, truth is better off left unexplored? And, did that mean you were living a lie, and not just in denial?

We seem to believe truth is paramount, and that a quest for truth is the noblest of aspirations. But, maybe *that's* the lie. Maybe living in denial is often the smart and healthy thing to do.

Let sleeping dogs *lie*.

I grunted. Seemed there was more than one way to take that saying.

A half hour passed before Neal came out the front door. He looked exhausted and drained. I know he wanted to say something to me, but I could tell his brain was processing his newfound understanding of his place in the universe. With a slight wave to both of us, distracted and unfocused, he got into his car and drove slowly down the street.

A sigh sipped out of my body, almost like a ghost or entity of its own making. I felt it hovering incriminatingly in the air, like Scrooge's ghost of Christmas future, silently gesturing with a hand to show me the hurtful results of my many life choices. *Come*, it seemed to say to me. *See the carnage of your search for truth. See what happened when the guard stepped aside and opened the door to enlightenment.*

And then, as in Dickens's tale, I pleaded with the spirit. *"Please tell me I can change these things, that they are not set in stone."* I wondered if T. S. Eliot was right when he said there was *time for a hundred indecisions and visions and revisions, all before the taking of toast and tea.* Only time would tell if my actions were foolhardy and reckless.

I felt a sudden urgency, as if I had no time to waste. Today was Tuesday August 4. In two days, Raff would turn thirty-four, a birthday he had made a vow to miss. What was Raff thinking at this moment? Had Neal told him anything about Ed Hutchinson?

I had to know. I had to weasel my way in to see my older brother and, if necessary, face the Jabberwock with him—whether he wanted me to or not.

How? I had no idea.

CHAPTER 24

AFTER I PUSHED MY WAY through the dogs into the kitchen, I noticed a note by the phone from Jeremy. "Dave Lerner called back. Here's his number." I recognized the Seattle area code. Lerner must have called before eight. I had left at seven to head out to Ed Hutchinson's house, and Jeremy usually made it to the feed store by eight thirty.

I put down my purse and walked to the cupboard. My emotions had all drained out after such an intense morning, leaving me strangely empty and desensitized. I heated up a cup of water and made some mint tea, then realized I was starving. I composed some questions in my mind for Dave Lerner as I fried a couple of eggs and listened to the spattering as they cooked, the sound mingling with the songbirds raising a ruckus outside my open window. Summer seemed to concentrate so many smells into one—a rich aroma of earth and growing things. The roses, now responding to the late morning's warmth, released subtle fragrances that permeated the air.

This would be the prominent scent in my memory—years from now, when I thought back to our time in this house we had built. Old roses in bloom, bursting with fragrance as if they couldn't contain their potency within their fragile petal walls.

I clamped down on my heart as it tried to lead me to sadness, to the reminder that my days here were numbered. I told myself that wherever we moved to, I would plant roses first thing, close to whatever window faced south. Last night, someone had called asking to see Shayla, my lame Arab. The woman sounded kindhearted and eager to foster my mare. She even said she might take a goat or two. The thought of a good home for Shayla warmed my heart. Surely, I could visit her from time to time. And maybe, one day, when Jeremy and I figured out our future, we'd get some more animals. It was inevitable.

I stuffed eggs in my mouth while I punched in Dave Lerner's number. His secretary answered.

"Mr. Lerner wanted me to tell you he is en route to San Francisco on a consulting job. He should be . . . landing shortly. He very much wants to meet with you and will call to arrange a time."

"Did he say anything else? Any other message?"

"Only that he hoped you would make the time to see him."

Would I ever! I thanked her and hung up, glad I would get to speak to Lerner in person and not just over the phone. Now I would find the key—the key that would open the door to all my answers. Lerner would know if my father had gone to San Diego. If he had participated in a dangerous experiment. He could tell me if he'd actually spoken to my mother years back and said the things she claimed he had.

I didn't care about catching my mother in yet another lie; I just wanted the truth. Maybe Lerner could shed invaluable light on my father's state of mind at the time. Had Nathan Sitteroff confided all to his best friend? Did men do that in 1960? I thought how hesitant my father had sounded in his letter to my uncle, barely opening up his heart and letting his pain flow out. Would he have been more forthcoming with Dave Lerner, a man he saw and worked with daily?

Knowing I would be moving out of my house in short weeks made me hesitate as I threw open the back deck doors and picked up my clippers. I'd thought to do some weeding in the perennial beds, but why bother? Instead, I kept one ear listening for the phone while I cut stalks of roses to put in vases. By the time I was done, I had nearly denuded all the shrubs, leaving few buds left to bloom. But my arms overflowed with old roses, their fragrance so potent I could taste rose in my mouth. I laid the bundle next to the sink and trimmed leaves and stems, then arranged them in vases.

The phone rang and I was almost disappointed when I heard Jeremy's voice. But, his enthusiasm perked me up as he told me of a beautiful property he'd found for rent on the east side of Sebastopol, off the Bodega Highway. He didn't want to give me any details but said we could go look at it this evening, after he got off work. I agreed and we hung up. Sebastopol was only about a half hour north, not that far for Jeremy to commute. And it was in the opposite direction of where my family lived, so that had appeal. Already, I could feel resistance building in my heart, knowing that nothing we'd find could compare to this place. I doubted we'd ever have a home so beautiful again. Yet, we still had years ahead of us. The thought of starting over, of a new beginning for me and Jeremy, softened my anxiety. That's what we needed. This would be good for us, I reminded myself. Everything here on this property carried a taint on it now. Tainted by my mother's cruelty.

I placed the vases throughout the house, splashing color into every room, every corner, filling the house with the smell of beauty, a scent strong enough to mask the permeating pain, disappointment, and outraged that seeped from the walls as potent as the stench of a fleabag motel room.

As I worked on extricating my heart from my beloved home, the phone rang again. My heart pounded as I heard an unfamiliar male voice on the line.

"This is Dave Lerner. Is this Lisa Sitteroff?" Lerner's voice carried emotion across the line, a soft, pressing voice. Eager, yet hesitant.

"I'm Lisa. I'm so glad you called. Are you in San Francisco?"

"I am." He hesitated. "I was so startled to hear from you—and you sound so grown up. I mean, of course you would be, but the last time I saw you, you were just a little kid." He cleared his throat. "My secretary said you'd been trying to reach me. That you had something important to talk about."

All the carefully worded sentences I had composed in my head disintegrated. But Lerner's voice was filled with kindness and an eagerness to talk, which encouraged me to continue.

"Well," I began, "I've been doing some research into my father's death . . . and uncovering some not-so-pleasant things about my family. . ." That familiar feeling grew in my throat, making it hard for words to come out.

Lerner filled in the awkward moment. "I can understand. You want to know what happened, your dad's death—what caused it. That's only natural."

"I heard you were close to my father. I just thought maybe you had seen him before he died, talked to him—"

"Lisa, your dad and I were very close. And yes, he did confide in me, about many things. He was a great guy and watching him die was . . . unbearable." I sensed Lerner starting to choke up as well. My mind flashed on a documentary I had seen recently, interviews with World War II vets, reflecting on their experiences in the war some forty years ago, still breaking down and shedding tears from the memories of their painful losses in battle, reliving those horrific moments when their friends took on fire and fell at their sides. I supposed that pressing Lerner to share his memories would be like that, but my need for answers outweighed my concern for his discomfort.

"Do you have time to meet me—for lunch or even just coffee? What is your schedule like?" I asked.

Lerner let out a sigh and seemed to pull himself back from the past. "I'd love to see you, Lisa. It's been so many years since your dad died, yet . . . in some ways it feels like yesterday. And I've kept a lot bottled up inside. Things I never talked about. Things . . . I promised your dad . . ."

My heart sped up. "Dave, I need you to tell me what you know, what he said. And I just can't do this over the phone."

"Okay, sure. I agree. I'm booked up for the afternoon. I have to go to Napa. Got a car picking me up in about ten minutes to drive me there. Where is that in relation to you?"

"Actually, pretty close. Not even an hour from where I live."

"That's great. Okay. If you don't mind driving over, I'll call you when I'm done for the day. I'd be delighted to take you out to dinner. I have to fly back to Seattle in the morning. Can you do that?"

"Sure. I'll let my husband know. We're supposed to go look at some property, but I think he'll understand. I don't want to miss this opportunity to talk with you."

Lerner gave me his hotel information and local phone number as my heart raced. After I hung up, I called Jeremy at the store and explained the situation. He picked up on my excitement, and I think he would have tagged along with me had I asked. But he was concerned about viewing that rental property and expressed his worry that someone else might snatch it out from under him if he put off the appointment to see it. If the place held promise, he could take me there tomorrow for a follow-up visit. With that agreed, we told each other "I love you" and Jeremy rang off to help some customers.

I had about five hours to kill and felt at a loss what to do. My heart wasn't into tackling chores, my usual routine of keeping up the property—weeding, mowing, pruning. And I kept mulling over in my mind what I would say to Dave, which made my excitement grow. I felt on the verge of finding out the real truth about my father's death. The guard was about to fling open that door to enlightenment and reveal all. I still clung to the scant hope that there was one universal truth, one clear-cut explanation that would dispel all the murkiness and intrigue enveloping Nathan Sitteroff's demise.

Lerner had sounded so burdened. What could he possibly know that he'd been keeping inside all these years? He'd promised my dad to keep something secret. Was it just the knowledge that Nathan Sitteroff's marriage was a sham—or did it involve something to do with his contracting leukemia—and how that had happened? Maybe it was the truth of Neal's parentage. I wished I could speed up time, and of course, that only made the afternoon drag by as I took Shayla and the dogs for a long walk in the oak-studded hills, the grass dry and crackly under my hiking boots.

As I walked, I thought about Neal and wondered what he must be feeling. Wondered what was transpiring at my mother's house. Surely, things there had to be tense, perhaps volatile. I thought about calling Neal and offering him to come stay with us but threw that idea out as fast as it came. Jeremy, although back to work, was still recovering from his accident, and he needed things quiet—at least that was my rationale. Plus, he and Neal had never been comfortable together, with Neal picking up on Jeremy's unspoken disapproval of my brother's "useless" lifestyle. I know Jeremy would be compassionate and give Neal some room, but I didn't want to aggravate my present marital relationship, which was better than it had been in many years. Neal could always stay at a motel, if it came to that.

I really needed to see Neal. We had things to discuss, but knew it would have to be in his time, when he was ready. Part of me wanted to get to him before my mother did.

Far be it from me to underestimate the long reach of her arm of guilt. Neal had been under her thumb for so many years; she obviously knew how to push his buttons in a heartbeat. What would she say to him, to turn him against me again, to make it look like whatever crisis they were facing had to be my doing? Would he fall for her ruses as before, or had this new revelation of Ruth Sitteroff's betrayal—his first personal betrayal at her hand—severed his trust in her for all time? Our mother had lied to him for twenty-seven years. Had withheld vital information about his identity, and why? All for the sake of family unity—and more likely, for protecting her image on all fronts. What reasonable excuse could she possibly give him for hiding this truth from him? Surely, that had to create some roadblock in Neal's heart.

I had this sudden spark of thought—that maybe my mother had found a way to kill my father—to prevent him from revealing the truth and ruining her life. I knew it was beyond absurd! But, how convenient that my father had died shortly after learning Neal wasn't his. Hadn't he contracted this fatal disease shortly after Ruth's admittance to the truth? A truth she would have hidden even from him, had it not been conclusive. Julie had said my father knew Neal wasn't his because he and my mother hadn't been sleeping together.

My mind jumped to the next outrageous thought—envisioning my mother trying to lure my father to bed after weeks—or months—of abstinence. Knowing she was pregnant and needing to cover her tracks. My mind skipped to Ann Boleyn and how she'd tried to convince her brother to impregnate her, to cover her miscarriage to King Henry, knowing that if her husband found out she'd lost the child, she'd be banished. Unfortunately, though, it was her plan B that got her and her brother beheaded—even without their following through on her insane idea.

I thought back to Shakespeare. Had my father suspected some deceit, an act characteristic of Lady Macbeth? *"Foul whisperings are abroad. Unnatural deeds do breed unnatural troubles; infected minds to their deaf pillows will discharge their secrets."* My mother had committed "an unnatural deed," taking her secret pregnancy to her pillows. What would she have tried? Seduction, trickery? I imagined her doubling the vodka in his evening drink, cornering him in the bedroom, the shower. Using sappy words to make him think she was sorry, that all their problems were her fault, begging for forgiveness? I could just picture this playing out, and my father refusing to fall for her sudden change of heart. Seeing through her manipulation. Being disgusted by her fawning. Knowing she had an ulterior motive for her inconsistent behavior. Suspicion festering.

The idea of murder was outrageous—I knew that. My imagination was galloping off in the distance, a horse without a rider, a rider without a head. And surely, if Dave Lerner had even suspected my mother had caused my father harm, he would have gone to the police, right? Or maybe my father had no evidence, only a hunch. And just how would Ruth Sitteroff have inflicted leukemia on him? I shook all these ludicrous thoughts away and glanced at my watch. After returning a hot and sweaty horse to the pasture, I took a quick shower and changed—getting out just in time to answer Dave Lerner's phone call.

The moment I entered the lobby of the hotel, I recognized Dave Lerner standing by the concierge counter, even despite his bald head. He still wore a goatee and the thick-rimmed glasses I'd seen in the Penwell brochure. He stood a little taller than I and had a fairly substantial beer gut that hung over his nicely pressed slacks. I knew he had no reference for recognizing me, but he caught my eye and saw me walking toward him, extending both his hands to me as I drew close.

"Lisa." He pumped my hands and studied my face. "You sure look a lot like your dad. Wow."

I felt my face flush a little as we walked over to two overstuffed chairs in a corner of the lobby near an open-air bar. I sat next to him, our knees nearly touching. "Thanks for meeting me, Mr. Lerner . . ."

"Just call me Dave."

"Okay. I . . . don't really know where to start."

"Do you want a drink? Glass of wine, a Coke?" Without waiting for my response, he caught the eye of one of the waiters and signaled him over. I ordered a glass of Napa Valley merlot, thinking it was just what I needed. Maybe a whole bottle would be even better. My hands were clammy and my heart raced.

"Well, first," he said, "why don't you tell me how your family is doing. Your brothers, your mom?" I sensed more than polite questioning. Perhaps the last thing he knew, as my father lay dying, was that my mother was pregnant with another man's child. Would he have known any of what was to follow?

I fumbled with a place to start. "My older brother, Raff, is bipolar. He's struggling with depression, and it's not pretty."

Dave's face fell but he waited for me to continue. "To be honest, things are bad on the home front. I mean, I'm married and have a wonderful husband—Jeremy. But, my mother and I—well, we're estranged at the moment. I started researching my past, trying to figure out why my father died . . . I was hoping that maybe learning what happened might help Raff with his depression. Instead, it caused more trouble . . . well, things are pretty ugly right now."

Dave nodded, listening hard, listening in-between the lines. "So . . . what have you learned so far?"

I felt no compunction to hold anything back. Why should I have? I didn't know Dave Lerner, and the more I told him, the better he'd be able to fill in my blanks. "I know my younger brother, Neal, is Ed Hutchinson's son—not my father's—"

Dave's eyes widened and he let out a big exhale. "How in the world did you find that out?" I knew instantly that Dave was privy to that secret. Perhaps it was one of the "secrets" he'd though he would have to dump on my head.

"Long story. I searched out Ed, went to see him. He's dying of lung cancer. I met his daughter, Julie. She told me. Apparently, her mother, Shirley, and my father had had an affair."

"Right. Wow, sorry to hear about Ed."

I sensed he said those words because they were the appropriate response, but I didn't get the feeling Dave Lerner was at all torn up over the news. And so far, what I'd said to Dave was nothing he hadn't known. He urged me to go on.

"I only just learned last week about Neal. And Neal met Ed—this morning—for the first time."

"Wow," was all Dave said.

I sighed. "It was pretty intense. And I don't know if the two of them talked much after I left. Ed is almost too sick to speak. But, it was certainly a shock for Ed to meet Neal and to realize he had a son, after all this time—"

Dave straightened in his chair, his eyes wide with surprise. "So, he didn't know about Neal? Not until today? All these years . . ." He shook his head, processing this information.

"My mother kept this under wraps. And Shirley didn't tell her daughter until three years ago, right before she died. Julie had been carrying this fact around, trying to find her only brother, and then I showed up on her father's doorstep. Her mother had only told her the name Nathan. She didn't know his last name, or that he'd been a Penwell employee."

"And that must have been a shock for her as well." Dave scrunched his eyebrows, remembering. "I didn't know Shirley Hutchinson. Only by sight at a company event here or there. Ed kept her on a pretty tight leash. But then, she left him, divorced him, got custody of their daughter."

"But you knew about my dad's affair with her, right?"

"Yeah. I did. Your dad wasn't proud of it. Felt a lot of guilt over the whole thing. But, personally, I think it was what he needed. Some consolation in his last months. Someone to care for him, help him through the rough spots."

"And what about San Diego? My mother said she had run into you years after my father died and you told her others had contracted leukemia too."

Dave's jaw dropped open. "Others? What others?"

"You know, from volunteering for that experiment. I just need to know—was it really dangerous? Had Penwell recruited employees to volunteer? Or had something gone wrong there that exposed people to radiation? That's what my mother told me."

Dave shook his head, his mouth still hanging open. "I haven't a clue what you're talking about. And I never saw your mother after the funeral."

"Really?" I sat back in my chair and took a deep breath and mulled his words. "So . . . I don't get it. Did my dad go to San Diego?"

"He did. There was some research opportunity down there. That's why he went. After he found out your mother was pregnant, he signed up for the research team—a two- or three-month stint. It gave him some breathing room away from your mother. But, an experiment? Something dangerous? Why would Penwell be involved in something like that? We were engineers, scientists—not guinea pigs."

"Ed Hutchinson seemed to think my dad had volunteered for that experiment too. Although, he didn't recall anything about it."

"Maybe a story he and your mother invented."

"Well, if so, why?"

"Maybe to . . . well, frankly, I don't know. Maybe your mother wanted a reason for your dad's illness. So, she assumed he had been exposed to radiation . . . down there."

A change in Dave's voice made me look deeper into his face. A rush of emotion overcame his features and he closed his mouth, thinking. I stared at him, wanting him to keep talking. The waiter brought our glasses of wine and I sipped mine while Dave signed the bar tab. Dave watched the waiter walk away, and then looked keenly into my face.

"After he came back from San Diego, he was a changed man. He had been to see you kids, and that broke his heart. You have to know, Lisa, that he loved you kids so much. He had wanted to make his marriage work, but . . . he just couldn't stay. He came home to Ruth's growing pregnancy—something that glared at him in judgment. Ruth wanted your dad to go along with the lie—that the baby was his—but it broke his heart. Even after Neal was born, even knowing Neal wasn't his, he still loved that baby. Loved all of you. Your dad had a heart of gold. One of the most . . . honorable and gentle men I've ever known. It killed me to see him so unhappy, so hopeless.

"He went into a spiral, into a deep depression. He showed up to work each day, and I tried hard to cheer him up, but the closer Ruth's due date approached, the more distraught he grew. And he started drinking too. I tried to get him to take time off. He had already moved out of the house, was living in an apartment in Hollywood with Shirley Hutchinson. And when Ruth went into labor, he dutifully went to the hospital and paced the floor, playing the role everyone had expected of him, faking his joy when the nurse came out with the good news of a son. Handing out cigars at work, fielding all the handshakes and congratulations, all the while under the eyes of his boss, Ed Hutchinson, the father of 'his' child. It ate at him, piece by piece."

Dave stopped and tilted his head. "So, from what you told me, Ed didn't have a clue. All that time, your dad working in his office, dealing day in and out with Ed, knowing he was looking at the father of his wife's new baby and Ed didn't have a clue." He paused. "You'd think Ed might have suspected. I mean, wouldn't he have been able to do the math? Even guess there was a possibility he was the father? I never saw him act differently—but, come to think of it, maybe he did."

Dave finished off his glass of wine and got the waiter's attention. I knew I had to drive back home, but one more glass was called for. Dave ordered another round and I waited for him to continue talking. My mind whirled with all these images of my father at work, facing Ed Hutchinson, knowing Ed was the father of his newborn child. What a drama!

"I was just thinking," Dave said," that Ed did seem to treat your dad differently after Neal was born. Maybe he did know and just kept it inside."

"I don't think so. I saw his face this morning, when Neal told him. He was beyond shock."

"Or maybe he had forgotten." Then Dave shrugged. That wasn't something you'd easily forget—that you had a bastard son who was now being raised by your coworker. "Okay, so let's say Ed really didn't know. Maybe your mother reassured him, told him she was sure the baby was Nathan's. Let him off the hook. Protecting her reputation and all that. Their affair had been short. It wasn't like your mother and he had anything going. Ed slept around—with more than one employee's wife," he said with some cynicism. "But, that's another story for another time."

Dave's thoughts ran along the lines of mine—that Ruth would have kept her secret forever—and wished she could have kept it from my father as well.

"You said Ed treated my father differently after Neal was born. How do you mean?"

"It wasn't anything blatant. But at Penwell we all met together many times during a day, your dad and I working on some problem and Ed checking in with us. So, I was often in the room when Ed would face your dad. There was something there. Obviously, your dad was feeling some pretty intense emotion. And it was getting in the way of his concentration. Ed would have words with him about the quality of his work, his deadlines getting behind, stuff like that. Which got your father upset, compounding the tension.

"But, I sensed something else. Not just Ed being annoyed with your father. Ed, for the most part, was a fairly understanding, easygoing guy for a boss. Never clamped down hard with deadline threats or criticizing his team. We had a fairly small department—the engineers and mathematicians. We all got along; it wasn't a competitive environment at all. So, Ed's treatment of your dad was . . . out of place. That's why I wondered if he suspected the baby was his. Maybe Ed had always wanted a son. Or maybe Ed resented your dad out of guilt."

"I don't know," I said. "Maybe more like he was furious at my father for sleeping with his wife—although it didn't seem to count that Ed had slept with Ruth. Julie said her dad was jealous and possessive of Shirley. Maybe my dad living with Shirley was a slap in his face each day, reminding him he'd lost his own wife, and reminding him it was his fault for having had the affair with Ruth, which triggered it."

I thought over all these possibilities as I finished the second glass of wine. "I really don't think he had a clue about Neal. And from what Julie tells me about her father, he probably couldn't have cared less that he had fathered a child. Julie even thinks there could be other kids out there, from Ed's many affairs. She painted him as completely uncaring, and a lousy, abusive father and husband. So, I'm thinking it's something else."

Dave nodded. "Yeah, maybe. But, you're probably right. It was more like Ed to be furious that Nathan had whisked Shirley away from him. Male conquest and all that. We'll never know, I guess." He upended his glass of wine. I got the feeling Dave was more a beer drinker from the way he plowed through those two glasses of merlot. "You are staying to have dinner with me, right? They have a pretty decent restaurant here, or so I'm told."

"Sure, I'd planned to."

"Are you hungry?"

I nodded. "But I know you have more to tell me. And, I have to be honest—I've been digging for weeks now to get to the bottom of all this. It's cost me a lot—emotionally, even financially. I keep thinking I'll never really know the truth . . ."

"Well," Dave said, standing and gesturing at the restaurant I could see through double glass doors, "I often say truth is a matter of perspective. Sometimes it's completely subjective, sometimes not. But truth is always subject to interpretation, regardless. Like Einstein proved—it's all relative. You may think you're standing still, looking out a window at another train that appears to be stationary, only to find you are both racing along at the same speed, and it only *looks* like you're standing still."

I got up and followed Dave into the plushly decorated restaurant, reflecting on Dave's words, which neatly echoed my own observations about truth. *The truth is relative.* Funny, I thought. Maybe among relatives the truth was especially relative.

Some quiet music played from hidden speakers. We wove through tables, the restaurant about half full, and sat at a booth in a far, secluded corner, with windows all around. Outside the window, a Japanese garden looked serene in the evening twilight, featuring a small waterfall emptying into a koi pond. We barely spoke as we looked over the menus, then ordered. With that business done with, Dave laid a hand on mine, a simple, uncomplicated gesture of friendship.

"I remember one day your father didn't show up for work. I knew he'd been sick lately, weak, his face pale. He said he'd gotten the flu and was getting over it. This was about, oh, three months after he'd returned from San Diego. I called his apartment, to see how he was, but no one answered. For some reason I panicked. Something told me your dad was in trouble—I don't know why or how. I clocked out and left work and raced over to Hollywood. I'd been to his apartment a few times since he moved out." He paused while our waiter returned with warm bread and dipping oil. I realized I'd been holding my breath, and let it out. Dave continued.

"I found him unconscious on the kitchen floor. Shirley was out somewhere and the door had been left unlocked, so when no one answered, I just went in—something I wouldn't normally do. But, seeing him there, lying on the linoleum . . . I called for an ambulance and waited. Then I drove over to the hospital, where they got him on fluids and started a battery of tests. At first they thought it was anemia, but when the blood tests came back and they saw his white cell count, the doctors realized he had leukemia." Dave looked through the window at the garden and took a deep breath.

"After that, he was in and out of the hospital . . . until, near the end, he was admitted and he stayed there until . . . it was over. I often sat by his bedside and kept him company. Sometimes we talked, but he eventually got so bad he just rambled. Dwelt on pieces of memories that floated into his mind, things I couldn't understand."

"Did my mother ever visit him? Did she bring us kids?"

Dave looked back at me and I could tell he wanted to give me some consolation, but his eyes were apologetic. "I only know of one time, near the end. I had just arrived as your mother was leaving. I waited by the stairwell because I didn't want her to see me and feel she had to be friendly, make small talk. She had you and your older brother in tow. I imagine she'd left the baby with a sitter. I'll never forget your brother's distraught face . . ."

"Raff. He recently told me how he'd seen Dad in the hospital before he died." I recalled Raff's bitter words—the curse, he called it. How our father had told him he was now the man of the house. Maybe this was the same instance Dave was speaking about. "The memory of that last conversation with our father had upset him a lot."

"Sure, I can imagine. And your dad was very upset she had brought you kids. He didn't want you to see him sick like that. He had told her to stay away, so as she was heading out, he yelled at her, told her never to come back. I can only guess what message that sent to your brother, hearing that. It must have broken his little heart."

Dave suddenly grew quiet, then a change came over his features, a hardening, as if resisting things aching to pour out. "Right before your dad died—maybe a week, maybe less—I arrived at the hospital and headed up the stairs to your dad's room. He was now in a private room, more or less in hospice care at this hospital. I was down the hall when I heard your dad talking. He was terribly upset, nearly hysterical. I hurried to go in to him, then stopped in my tracks. Ed Hutchinson was in there, with him. That completely surprised me. I thought, what's he doing here? I didn't want to intrude, so stood back . . ." He took a deep breath and composed himself, as emotion was starting to get the better of him. "I couldn't make out their conversation. And then, Ed stormed out, and I scooted around the corner so he wouldn't see me. I went in to your father . . . and heard something I've never forgotten to this day. Not a word of it. Like it was branded on my heart.

"Lisa, what I'm about to tell you I've told no one. Nobody in these, what, twenty-five years. I'll try to explain it as best as I can, but there's one thing you need to think about. Your dad was very sick. Often delusional. They had him on experimental treatments, chemo, radiation. It wasn't like today. Leukemia was a mystery. Well, it still is now, in many ways. But, back then, they were trying all kinds of treatments and dosages. Sometimes your father was so drugged he was nearly incoherent, ranting, mumbling about strange things I couldn't make sense of. So, I had to piece together much of what he told me."

He paused, then met my eyes with another apologetic expression. "So, you'll just have to come to your own conclusions, okay?"

I reached for my water glass and took a long sip. Although the room was air conditioned, I felt sweaty in anticipation. As Dave spoke, I listened carefully. Then, I closed my eyes and let the scene unfold as his words entered my ears and painted a picture of what transpired twenty-five years ago. I could only imagine . . .

CHAPTER 25

DAVE LERNER PRESSES AGAINST THE cool pale yellow hospital corridor wall as Ed Hutchinson storms out of Nathan's private room, wondering what might have transpired between the two men. He glances down the hallway and waits until his boss gets into the elevator and the doors close before he takes a hesitant step toward Nathan. The thick drapes are drawn and only filtered light delineates the surroundings. Nathan is sitting up in bed, pillows propped, an IV dripping into his arm, machines whirring on both sides. His face is flushed; surely, he is worked up and angry, and filled with frantic energy as he tussles with the sheet covering him. In a fit of frustration, he pulls the sheet loose from its bindings on the sides of the bed and throws it over his feet, unaware of Dave standing just inside the door entry.

Dave clears his throat and Nathan looks up. Nathan opens his mouth to yell, but then, in the haze of the room and through the haze in his mind, he recognizes his friend and throws his head back on the pillows in anguish.

"I can't take this sheet on me. It's like a dead weight, makes my skin crawl . . ."

"Here," Dave says, rushing over to help, "I'll get it." Dave removes the entangled sheet and tosses it over the nearby chair. Nathan is in a pale blue hospital gown that barely reaches his knees. Dave notices how pale Nathan's skin is, and how thin his legs are. He looks away, wanting to give Nathan some dignity, but Nathan doesn't seem to notice.

Nathan exhales. His face is beaded with sweat, blotchy and pasty; the illness racking his body has worked its way into his eyes, making them look diseased. Dave has never been this close to someone so near to death and feels torn between helplessness and agony. He can almost feel his own blood poisoned, and wonders what Nathan must be sensing—his body now awash with cancer, his own blood cells on attack, as if he himself were the enemy. He knows Nathan is fighting a losing battle and wonders if his best friend has come to terms with his impending death or is still in denial. So many hours he's sat by Nathan's bedside, but never once have they spoken directly about his disease.

Dave reaches for the cup of water and adjusts the straw. "Here, drink. You're so worked up, you need to calm down."

Nathan mutters something but it's garbled. Dave leans closer to hear better. Something about Ed and the nerve of him coming here.

"What was that all about—Hutchinson visiting you here? He's upset you." Dave knows all about the tense dynamics between Nathan and their boss. Would Ed stoop so low as to come to Nathan's deathbed and chew him out for sleeping with his wife? Or had they argued about something else? Dave realizes he shouldn't have asked; it will only get Nathan worked up again.

Nathan's breath is shallow and his words come out in shreds. "He came, you know . . . to the apartment . . . some time ago. Looking for Shirley . . . barged in. Said he followed me home, from work . . . grabbed her arm and tried to pull her out the door . . ."

Nathan tries to chuckle, but the effort flushes his face and starts him sucking air. ". . . as if he could force her to go back to him. Even swung at me . . . but I backed away. Never said anything to him after . . . let it pass." Nathan's voice rises in pitch; he strains to sit upright. Dave reaches over to help him, but Nathan starts to thrash.

"Whoa, let me help you, buddy. You really should—"

Dave dodges Nathan's arms and inches away. Nathan keeps talking, the words coming faster and more tangled. "He can't take it? What . . . it's doing to me? How could he? I could kill him . . . kill him . . ."

"Why? What's he done?"

Nathan breaks out into a sob and tears force their way out his eyes. "My fault . . . oh, so wrong . . . I thought . . . thought I could just . . . just close my eyes and make it all go away. I'm . . . so ashamed . . ."

Dave carefully rests an arm around Nathan's shoulders while his friend cries, letting loose a flood of tears Dave has never seen. Maybe, Dave thinks, this is good, his crying. Letting it all out. Maybe Nathan hasn't cried at all. Maybe it's hitting him now—the realization that he will soon die, leave his three children fatherless. Dave can't even fathom that kind of heartache. But . . . shame? What is he ashamed of? Leaving his family?

"Why?" Dave asks as Nathan's tears slow down. "Why do you feel ashamed? This isn't your fault—this disease, your illness—"

In a sudden flash, Nathan grabs Dave's arm in a fierce grip. Even though Nathan's hand is shaking, his fingernails dig into Dave's skin. "It is! It is my fault! All my fault . . . I caused this . . ."

"Caused what?" Dave is thinking about the affair. How Nathan had run off with Shirley, and how that brought about Ed's fury. But, what did that have to do with his leukemia?

Nathan interrupts Dave's thoughts with more ranting. "Leaving Ruth . . . abandoning my children . . . thought by running I could hide, be safe . . . But, I couldn't . . . he did this to me . . . God . . ."

Nathan starts weeping again. Dave ponders his dying friend's words. Maybe Nate is thinking God is punishing him for his choices. Nathan had more than once mentioned this line of reasoning before. Dave doesn't know what Nathan believes about God, but he knows that when you're close to death, you can't help but question and wonder if someone is up there.

So, maybe he is blaming God for all this. For taking him away from his children, all because he walked out on them. As if God was saying, "You want out, I'll give you 'out.' " That's the only thing Dave can think of as he tries to piece it all together and find something consoling to say.

"If there is a God," Dave says softly, "He can't be like that. Wanting to cause suffering. Punishing good people with deadly diseases . . ."

Nathan thrashes some more, this time knocking over his water cup. "Not him! Not God!"

Dave sits on the chair beside the bed as Nathan drops his head back on the pillows. He wishes he could think of something to say, anything to help ease Nathan's agitation. He sits quietly while Nathan continues to mutter, kicking his legs in little motions that reminds Dave of a small boy working himself up to a temper tantrum.

Dave is tired, weary. He hasn't had breakfast and his stomach rumbles. The stringent smells of the hospital irritate his nose. He wants to cheer up the room, turn on a light, the TV, something to distract Nathan away from his mood, but knows it would be counterproductive. This is something Nathan needs to get out. Maybe no one else comes to visit him—except Shirley. Nathan probably holds back from exploding at her. Chivalrous to the last. But he can speak freely with his best pal, let out the frustration and anger. That's okay.

Dave thinks he should encourage Nathan to keep talking, but maybe Nathan is done. Dave looks at his friend, whose eyes are squeezed shut, his mouth tight in a line, tension rippling across his features. Maybe, Dave thinks, he should buzz the nurse, have them give Nathan something to knock him out. He's at a loss what to do, what would be best for his friend.

Nathan's eyes open and he stares at Dave vacantly. The room is quiet while Dave waits, ponders on the things Nathan has said, none of it making sense.

"Simple . . . really. The casing only forty centimeters long . . . easy to dismantle with the right tool . . ."

Dave leans closer. What in the world is Nathan talking about? As his friend goes on about dimensions and weight, Dave's eyes widen. "The SNAP 3. That's what you're talking about, right?"

Nathan nods excitedly. "Not hard to get one . . . in storage, security . . . no problem getting through security . . . press the right sequence of numbers . . ."

A chill runs through Dave's heart and he stops breathing. What on earth is Nathan going on about? He realizes his friend is describing how to take apart the housing on the SNAP 3 and remove the components—a housing he helped design.

Dave's heart races. Is this something Nathan has done, or is this just another example of Nathan's cancer-ridden brain wandering off on tangents? Yet, as Dave looks deeply into Nathan's eyes, he sees a strong focus and concentration, unlike other times when Nathan would just blabber. This comes forcefully as a memory, in Dave's opinion, and he does not like what he is hearing or where he thinks all this is leading.

Nathan startles Dave by suddenly laughing. Dave looks on in shock as Nathan's laughter brings tears to his eyes. Soon, he is laughing and crying. In between sobs, he forces out more words.

"Simple, see? . . . no one would know . . . late at night . . . strap the fuel cell under . . . desk . . . close proximity . . . radiation leak . . . brilliant, actually . . ."

Dave tries to get Nathan to look at him "What? What did you do? Why?"

Nathan is still laughing; tears soak his hospital gown just below the neck. Dave reaches for a washcloth and wipes Nathan's face. Nathan grips Dave's wrist again, this time softly, his hand shaking uncontrollably. "After . . . switched offices . . . had the desk sent to the city dump . . . no one would know . . . no one . . ."

Nathan sits up in bed and turns toward the window; it takes some effort. He gestures to the drapes. "Please, open . . ."

Dave spreads the fabric apart slowly, allowing time for the bright winter light to spill into the room. Nathan squints but a smile comes over his face. "They say . . . confession is good for the soul . . . forgiveness . . . I tried. Can't forgive myself . . . Easy to forgive others, but never yourself."

At his point, Dave is in a panic. It's pretty clear what Nathan has just confessed to, but it's unbelievable! How could Nathan do such a thing, something so calculated and self-destructive? All because his wife gave birth to another man's baby? Was that it? Was Nathan so distraught that he felt he could no longer go on living, and did the only thing he could think of to end his life?

Why this way? If you wanted to die, there were quicker methods—pills, a gun, jumping off a bridge. But, expose yourself to a large dose of radiation that would only stretch out your pain and suffering? Or, was that the point? Nathan feeling his shame merits suffering? This is insane! Dave thinks. Bizarre and insane!

Nathan stares out the window, then turns to Dave, who is stunned by the sudden calm on his friend's face. "I told him I forgave him. For all the rotten things he did . . . doesn't matter anymore, does it?" Nathan chuckles again. "Didn't want to hear that . . . forgiven . . ."

"You mean Ed, right?"

Nathan nods, his eyes closing. "I'm tired. I think . . . you should leave . . . But, promise me. Promise not to tell anyone. Not Ruth, not Ed, Shirley, no one . . . promise!"

"Of course, Nate. I promise. Won't tell anyone. Ever."

"Okay . . ." Nathan shakes his hand toward the door and soon his breathing deepens and his face relaxes. The morning's events have all but drained away Nathan's last bit of strength.

Dave pauses for a moment and studies his friend's face—unaware that this is the last time he will ever see it. His mind is spinning with this sudden understanding of the source of Nathan's leukemia. Disbelief, puzzlement, confusion. All these things flit through Dave's brain as he tries to picture Nathan sneaking one night into the SNAP storage area of the warehouse, the building where the prototypes and other components are safely stored. Wouldn't someone notice a fuel cell missing? Or had Nathan closed up the housing, leaving no one the wiser? Maybe months, even years might go by before someone realized the part was missing. The SNAP might be halfway around the world at that point.

As Dave walks toward the elevator, he thinks of all the hours Nathan had spent behind his closed office door, secluding himself, always working intently on a project, wanting to be left alone. At the time, Dave had just thought it was Nathan's way of avoiding Ed Hutchinson, hunched over his desk, working on formulas. And that when, months later, Nathan suddenly switched offices, thinking it was because the third floor was scheduled for painting and refurbishing. Dave never gave it a thought when Nathan moved down to his floor, leaving behind all his furniture, just doing what management told him to do. How had Nathan arranged that?

Dave takes one look back down the hallway before stepping into the elevator. How can Nathan expect him to keep this a secret, not tell a soul what he had just revealed to him? Shouldn't someone be told? The doctors? His employer? And then, Dave realizes it's too late.

Too late to save Nathan, too late for this information to help him in any way, except maybe hurt those who love him. No, Dave concludes, Nathan made him promise and he would honor that promise. He would leave Nathan to his shame and pain, let those feelings die with him in the grave where they could not hurt anyone else.

He is glad no one gets on the elevator with him as he travels down to the lobby. It's just too painful for anyone to see a grown man cry.

My heart hurt, listening to Dave tell his story. I thought I would have mountains of questions, but I didn't. In fact, I couldn't think of anything at all to say. I was beyond stunned. All this time my mother had sworn that my father'd had a death wish, willed himself to die. And it was true! In some skewed way, her reasoning was sound—my father believed he had bad blood, so gave himself a blood disease. This, then was the deed without a name my father had done—a deed I now could name. Maybe, deep down, Nathan Sitteroff never felt worthy of life. Maybe he had suffered from depression like my brother, and like his sister, who had killed herself. But the details were shocking—and so outrageous. Who would ever believe it? Did I?

We finished our dinner, even though I don't remembering tasting any of it. Dave looked exhausted from the telling and so we spoke of other things, a variety of topics, staying far away from heavy subjects that weighed on our hearts. After dessert and coffee, I thanked Dave profusely for taking the time to see me and revealing to me what he knew. I could tell he felt both burdened and relieved. He had finally told someone about my father's confession. And yet, how did that make matters better?

I thought of my conundrum and how learning the truth was supposed to set me free. Shouldn't it? I didn't feel free at all; rather, a weight had been dumped on my shoulders. I thought I'd be weightless, flying, no longer encumbered by the burden of uncertainty. How could I ever tell Raff what Dave had revealed to me? It would only make him hate our father even more.

I tried to determine how it made *me* feel. Did I feel betrayed? Abandoned? Could I justify what my father had done? How had Raff put it?—my father had chickened out. Couldn't face life, so abandoned his kids, leaving Raff to assume the mantle of man of the house. No wonder Raff resented him. But, did I resent him?

At that moment, I couldn't say. I only knew I felt weary and sad, thinking about my father going through with his mad plan to expose himself to radiation. Why couldn't he have just divorced my mother and gotten on with his life? Sure, divorce wasn't all that common, but—kill yourself? Wasn't that a bit drastic? Did it all come back around to my father having a death wish? Feeling unworthy of all life had to offer? I had come full circle, stopping in the very spot in which I had started. Had I learned anything, anything at all?

"Lisa, I know this is all hard to process," Dave said as he walked me to my car in the lighted parking lot of the hotel. "But, you need to remember what I told you earlier. I could only piece together what your father said. Who knows how much of it was truth and how much was delusion? Maybe your father made it all up, his imagination coming up with a crazy answer to explain his disease. I couldn't find any proof. I tried to learn where they had dumped the desk, tried to research into the missing fuel cell, but I couldn't do much without raising suspicion and alarm. Stealing something like that is more than a felony—it's a breach of top security. If I had said anything, I could have been implicated, lost my job, even been arrested. So, who knows if your father was telling the truth, or if he was fantasizing? Without proof, there are only his words . . . and my interpretation of them. He was simmering in shame, and guilt. Those feelings can make a person say things they don't mean, admit to things they haven't done."

We stopped at my car and he placed a hand on my shoulder. "Maybe all or part of what he said was true; maybe none of it. You have to allow that possibility."

The irony, once more, slapped me in the face. And, or, or not. An appropriate epitaph for my father's tombstone, the theme of his life, the focus of his intellect. Boolean algebra. What had lured my father into that field? Was it some subconscious awareness that the math mirrored his existence? It seemed his whole life was one strange, insoluble conundrum.

I knew at that moment I would have to acquiesce to that explanation, without ever having the deep satisfaction of knowing the truth, of tasting the albatross and realizing without a doubt that I was indeed free.

CHAPTER 26

JEREMY'S ENTHUSIASM GREW EXPONENTIALLY THE closer we got to the rental house in Sebastopol. I had worried that he would find fault with anything listed for rent, as nothing could compare to the haven we had built for ourselves. But, he seemed genuinely thrilled with this house. I wondered, as I lowered the truck window and let in the refreshing early morning air, if he was more excited with the idea of finally severing ties with my mother than with moving.

We had talked late into the night, Jeremy wanting to hear everything Dave Lerner had said and offering theories of his own. He felt the whole idea that my father had enacted such a melodramatic suicide smacked of fantasy; that no reasonable, logical man would devise such a painful and tragic way to die. Men are efficient and practical, he'd told me. Or maybe a man who was a hopeless romantic might possibly *think* of such madness. But a scientist looking for a way out of his marriage? Jeremy blew it all off, disbelieving the whole idea.

I tried to convince him it made sense, and that Lerner had no reason to make it all up. I conceded that my father may have confused the issue a bit with all that talk about God and forgiveness, but what other conclusion could I come to? It was Occam's razor—the most logical explanation would be the true one. Certainly, my father didn't magically give himself leukemia; there had to be an external source. Jeremy opted for coincidence—that my father just happened to get sick; maybe all the stress compounded his susceptibility, made his system tired and weak. Maybe his flu or anemia had opened the way for leukemia. The coincidence theory didn't sit well with me. Yet, I knew Jeremy's argument made sense—that a man like my father might have taken an overdose of pills or jumped off a bridge had he truly been suicidal. But strapping a radioactive fuel cell under your desk so you would die a slow, agonizing death?—that was something out of a Shakespeare tragedy. Which made my mind leap to my uncle's words—how my father had love drama and acted in plays throughout his teen years. Maybe my father did have a penchant for the melodramatic. And dying in this manner would have fit the bill.

Jeremy turned off the Bodega highway onto a narrow but recently paved lane, a community-maintained road, Jeremy explained. About a half mile farther down sat houses nestled under some oaks and conifers. Jeremy turned into the last driveway on the right and pulled up to a dark-wood-sided two-story house. I expected to see something old and farmlike, but this place had been recently built, perhaps five or ten years old, more of a modern-style architecture with a large round window over the front door and a small balcony facing the front. Two nicely landscaped flower beds flanked the walkway, and what caught my eye were the numerous rose bushes blooming under what appeared to be the kitchen window, facing the sunny south side of the property. Jeremy caught me looking at the roses and smiled. He knew that would score some points.

The houses on either side were set back about fifty feet but secluded by tall escallonia and Oregon grape shrubs, giving the place an ambience of privacy. Jeremy dialed the combination on the realtor lock, removed the key, then ushered me inside the rental. Tall ceilings, white walls trimmed with pine molding and wainscoting, and beautiful oak floors met my eyes as I stepped down into a large sunken living room.

"And how much does this cost a month?" I asked, knowing my eyes were wide and impressed.

"Turns out the owner is a longtime customer at the store. I recognized him last night when he met me here to show me around. He's giving us a deal—one year lease . . . and check this out . . ." Without showing me around the house, he went straight for the sliding door that led to a small deck. The yard appeared small until I followed Jeremy through a latched gate in the wooden fence. "How's this?"

My breath caught in my throat. "No way . . ."

Jeremy chuckled at my response, standing quietly to take it all in. At least an acre of pasture stretched out before me, enclosed with nice Keystone fencing and housing a small barn *and* a horse paddock for two. Behind the pasture a thick grove of firs blocked any further view, but I could tell no one lived in back of this property.

"There's a gate in the far corner of the fence. Do you see it? Leads to a trail that connects to BLM land. Thousands of acres you can ride over." He smiled at me, his eyes dancing with joy. I think what pleased him most is knowing I could bring some of my animals with me. My heart melted in awe. Even without having seen the rest of the house, I knew it was perfect. I felt as if God were comforting me by providing this peaceful place for Jeremy and me to start over, and to heal from all the recent hurts.

"There's only one catch," he said, narrowing his eyes and putting on a serious face. My heart thumped hard. I didn't want anything to spoil this dream that seemed to be materializing before my eyes. Jeremy opened the gate into the pasture and whistled. "There are a couple of out-of-shape, feisty babies that need some discipline and attention. Think you can handle them?"

"Babies . . .?"

Before I could say more, I heard a horse nicker and then two flashes of brown and black came bounding across the short fescue grass from behind the barn. The bay was a mare, maybe two or three, with a beautiful conformation and full of energy. The darker one was a gelding, maybe the same age, with a white blaze on his nose. Both horses trotted right up to us and started snuffling our pockets, looking for treats.

"The owner has no other place to keep these two, and when he heard how much you loved animals . . . well, I kinda promised you'd work them. He says they need a lot of training. They're too young to ride, but might be fun company for you." Jeremy shrugged, but he knew quite well he'd won me over with these two beauties. "Oh, and he said if we really liked them, he'd sell them to us for a good price. No pressure or anything. You know, just in case you get unduly attached. You did say you wanted us to start riding together—"

"You'd have to wait a couple of years for these two to be able to carry your weight." I stroked the horses and rubbed behind their ears. They lapped up the attention, then when they were sure I didn't have any hidden treats, nipped at each other and ran off.

"Well, what's two years?" Jeremy asked. "The time will fly by."

I wrapped my arms around him and breathed in the smell of summer. Trees, grass, sage—a mingling aroma with a hint of roses. In the morning light, the air practically glowed. "It's perfect, really. I can't believe this is a rental."

"Reynolds built it for his daughter and son-in-law a few years ago. Then the kids had to move away for work and he didn't want to sell it, hoping they'd come back at some point. But he's assured me we can stay here as long as we like. We can even sign a three-year lease, if you want to."

Jeremy took me through the rest of the house. It was a bit smaller than ours, but had a big garage and a large bathroom with a walk-in shower. I took it all in as Jeremy showed me around, talking about the hot water heater capacity and the sprinkler system and things I really didn't need to know about, but he seemed pleased to rattle off all the details. He sounded like a realtor showing a property.

The moment we arrived home, he called Mr. Reynolds and told him we'd take the house. We could move in anytime, he said, which shook me with the realization I would have to pack and take down curtains, peel the pieces of myself off the walls and empty out closets, only to fill another house with all our stuff. The idea seemed daunting. But I could take my animals with me—although I decided to let Shayla go to the interested woman. That would make the most sense, since I knew Shayla would pick on those two horses, wanting to be the boss of the pasture. She needed someone who could devote time and attention to her, which I seemed to lack these days. I felt comforted knowing I could still foster my remaining critters, unless others responded to my ads and wanted to provide homes for them. The less animals I had to take care of, the more time I could focus on our marriage and rebuilding our lives.

It struck me in that moment that I *would* survive this betrayal of my mother's—that it might actually be possible. Sadness and hurt instantly welled up, as if someone had switched on a fountain of pain in my heart. How many years would it take to get over my hurt? Would I ever? But, what was I really losing? Criticism, harsh judgment, the constant feeling of failure and guilt? Those were all burdens. What I was really missing was the love, support, and gentleness I had never received from my mother in the first place. I'd only thought I had those things because I was told I did. The emptiness that hollowed out my stomach was not so much from this recent loss but the excavating of an empty place that had been hidden deep inside me my entire life. Maybe now that this cavern had been exposed and uncovered, I could fill it with something else—like self-esteem, confidence, a sense of worthiness and purpose. All things that were never present because the place into which they fit had been sealed off.

"A couple of guys at work said they'd come over and help us move. We'll just rent a big U-haul and make a couple of trips. Should take a day at most."

"I guess I need to start packing . . ."

Jeremy gathered me in his arms and studied my face. "Are you okay with this, really? I want you to be happy. I know this is hard, all this work we put into our home, the gardens, the pond, years of work . . ."

"It's okay, really. I love the rental; it's perfect. I'll be happy anywhere, as long as you're there with me."

Jeremy laughed. "Yeah, me and a few goats and ducks and dogs."

Jeremy walked over to the fridge and got out a decanter of orange juice. "Well, I should get to the store. I can grab a muffin on the way. And you . . . I guess we'll need to get boxes and start packing."

"I can do that." I got out two glasses, and as Jeremy poured, I noticed the red light blinking on the answering machine. Someone must have called while we were out, but it was barely eight o'clock. I wondered who would have called so early.

Raff's tired and raspy voice came out the small speaker. Even Jeremy stopped in his tracks, halfway to the table. Before I could think through why Raff would be calling me so early, his words, short and pointed, struck me like a knife in my heart.

"Lisa . . . I just wanted to say . . . well, say good-bye." There was a long pause and Jeremy caught my eye, his expression full of alarm. I thought Raff had ended his message, but then his voice came out, barely a whisper, choked-up words full of pain.

"So, good-bye, Lisa. Know I will always love you. I'm so sorry . . . sorry . . ."

With a click, the line went dead, and the silent, pulsing red light on the machine stopped blinking.

CHAPTER 27

"JUST IGNORE IT, LISA. IT'S melodrama. The more we pay attention to Raff's histrionics, the more he sinks down. He is the actor on a stage, and wants us to join him, playing these roles that the doctors say . . ."

I heard Kendra's words, but they sounded like gibberish. As I held the receiver to my ear, tapping my foot impatiently, I wanted to scream. Her mollifying and unperturbed tone reminded me of a hypnotist trying to put her patient under suggestion. Her patient: meaning me, and I wasn't buying that. Kendra knew the statistics—bipolar patients usually made good on their threats—at some point. If Raff was talking suicide again, then why wasn't anyone paying attention? The suicide success rate for manic-depressives was off the charts. My anger grew along with my fear.

I couldn't bear to listen any longer and interrupted her oratory. "Where is he? Do you know?"

"He left for work early today. He should be at the office."

"Have you called to see if he's really there?"

I could almost hear her shrug and it made me want to kick the wall. I would accomplish nothing by lecturing her, and it would only waste precious time.

"Never mind," I said a bit curtly. "I'll find out." *And if I get around to it, I'll let you know—as if you really cared.*

Before Kendra could even say good-bye, I hung up and dialed Raff's work number. I looked at the time—8:44. Raff's ninth-floor office, in a posh section of the downtown financial district, was in a well-secured building. Entrance required keys for the elevators from the underground parking lot, and security maintained cameras and guards throughout. When Raff failed to answer his phone, I was at a loss how to reach the security office for his building. I only knew the address and the company name. Maybe I could call one of the actual bank branches and get a phone number. But as I considered I the time it would take to try to get a hold of someone to locate the right number, I knew the effort would be futile. They probably woudn't have these phone numbers for the corporate office.

I called Information and they gave me some general numbers for the corporation. No one answered as I waited impatiently for nine o'clock to roll around, thinking at any moment someone would arrive, would pick up the phone. But after numerous attempts, I grew too frantic. Alarms went off inside me and I grabbed my purse and ran out to my car. I told myself I was being stupid, that Raff was probably there, brooding or just staring at a wall. Or maybe he hadn't even gone to his office. I might drive all the way to the city, hassle with finding a parking space, and tromp up the stairs—only to find his office vacant.

Where would he go? I racked my brain as I drove a bit over the speed limit, on autopilot heading for San Francisco. Fog draped the freeway and the visibility was poor, so the traffic dragged as I climbed the hill out of Sausalito to the Golden Gate Bridge. Mist condensed on my windshield and I ran the wipers, letting the gloomy day add to the misery I felt in my heart.

I let my mind wander back to our childhood, trying to remember Raff before things got bad. Memories surged like a tide, washing in images of us playing board games and building forts in the backyard and riding bikes in circles in the cul-de-sacs with Kyle and Anne. Raff studying thick books on strange topics, reciting all the time—poetry, facts, trivia, snatches of dialogue from plays,

Kentucky Derby winners and their jockeys, the names of all the presidents in order and the terms they served, the capitals of every state and every country. I could hear Raff talking in a voice not unlike my uncle Samuel's, measured, confident, soft.

Hard as I tried, I couldn't remember any girls he dated or had a crush on in high school. He'd been fairly shy; all that bluster and bravado only served to cover his insecurity around girls. I knew he'd met Kendra at college during one of his manic periods, those months earmarked by unexpected overconfidence and flagrant risk-taking. The few times I had witnessed Raff in the height of a manic phase of his illness, I was shocked and hardly recognized him as my brother. Kendra's words then made sense to me—his acting and melodrama. Life became a huge stage upon which he starred, and everyone around him became a pawn for his reckless imagination. Maybe after so many years of enduring Raff's roller-coaster emotions, Kendra had refused to take part in those "productions" any longer.

But I couldn't brush off Raff's ominous tone and enigmatic farewell as mere acting. Maybe bipolar people often threatened suicide to get attention, or to emote. Maybe, as perhaps Kendra saw it, Raff was the proverbial boy who cried wolf. Yet, at some point the wolf *did* come, and when no one believed him, he got eaten alive. Sure, it was the boy's fault, for broadcasting so many false alarms, but did he deserve to be eaten because of that?

I only had to drive a few blocks past Raff's office before I found a paying lot that still had empty spaces. I took the ticket the machine spit out and found a spot, then hurried along the sidewalk, pulling my coat tightly around my neck. The fog soaked my face with moisture as I ran—as if the city was collectively weeping—and I wiped my eyes with my sleeve as I pounded the sidewalk, weaving among the crowds of people heading for work.

I arrived breathing hard at the security counter in the ornately tiled lobby. One of the two uniformed men asked my business and I explained my need to find my brother. An emergency, I told them. I showed my ID while the other guard attempted to buzz Raff's phone. They had no record of him coming in, but Raff wouldn't have come through the front door; he always parked below and took the elevator straight to his floor.

"I'm sorry; he's not answering—if he's there."

"May I please go up and check on him?" I wondered if these men knew about Raff's previous episode of attempting to squeeze out the window. If they did, they showed no concern.

"We can't let you go unauthorized—"

"I know that. Can one of you escort me up there? Look, he's got . . . emotional problems. And it's his birthday and he gets depressed. I'm worried about him."

One of the guards came around the counter and gestured me to follow him to the elevator. Unexpectedly, my heart started thumping hard as the elevator doors opened. My face flushed and nausea hit me like a punch to the gut. I shut my eyes and walked into the elevator car, willing my breathing to slow, counting to ten silently, trusting the elevator to speed to Raff's floor. Ten seconds; I could do this. Fear welled up, irrational and insistent. Hadn't I already worked this conundrum through and mastered it? Obviously not.

As the car rose floor by floor, I clenched my jaw and my fists, telling myself my fear was illusive. It hit me as I nearly jumped off the elevator at the ninth floor that this was what Raff probably told himself every day, all day long—*my fear is irrational. I can just will it away. I can do this on my own power. I don't need drugs or chemicals or therapy.* The mind was a mystery; we want it to respond to our logic, to listen to us, to obey our commands. But as weird as the expression sounded, our minds had a "mind" of their own.

I had set out to help Raff, to solve a conundrum that I thought would take away his pain, but after all my digging and uncovering clues, I had failed. My father had suffered from depression, in some form or another—maybe he wasn't bipolar or couldn't be neatly labeled by the medical community, but he did want to die. For whatever reason, he had found it more logical to turn his back on his three children—three innocents who depended on him and whom he loved—and kill himself.

And now, twenty-six years later, his own son wanted to kill himself—and leave behind three children who dearly loved him. It made no sense, no sense at all. Raff was a victim of his mind, trapped in some crazy repetitive time loop that demanded he replay history. Would Kevin, his son, continue the pattern, helpless to control his destiny in the same manner of his father and grandfather before him? The thought sent shivers up my spine.

Frustration and failure saturated my very being. I had nothing to offer Raff—no magic words, no answers, no vorpal sword he could use to fight the Jabberwock. What in the world was I even doing there? I would probably make matters worse, like one of Job's would-be comforters who sat beside him and only gave him grief.

No answers, no comfort, no help.

But, I had to try. I had this crazy hope that deep in his heart he really didn't want this role. That he was just waiting for someone to take his hand and lead him off the stage and out the wings of the theatre housing this lousy play. That he was so tired out from all his fighting that he was ready for rescue.

After a minute or two of knocking, the guard reached in his pocket for a key ring. He found the key he wanted and inserted it the lock, and as the door clicked open, my heart leaped into my throat.

The guard, opening the door . . .

All this time I had focused on finding the door to enlightenment, but seeing it played out now in these unnerving circumstances gave me pause. Did I really want to see what was behind that door? My search for truth thus far had come at a price—as if along with the unearthed truth came a proportionate measure of pain.

The guard began to open the door.

"Go away!" Raff yelled in a hoarse, frantic voice from somewhere in his office. The guard stopped, with the door mostly closed, and looked at me, his eyes questioning my intent. I waved him off with what I'd hoped was a look of confidence. *I can take care of this; don't worry.* Yeah, right. I wondered for a split second if I should tell him to call for help, get backup or something. Was I overreacting? I thought of Raff's tone on the answering machine, sounding as if he'd already checked out ages ago. The only thing I had to offer Raff was my love and a listening ear, even if they proved impotent weapons against his consuming darkness. What else could I do? I couldn't turn my back on him and wait it out, pretend his pain would go away. I had to accept the fact that maybe his pain would never go away.

The guard retreated a few steps and waited, no doubt to make sure I had the situation under control. I noticed a walkie-talkie in a holder clipped to his belt. He could summon help in a flash, which gave me a little reassurance. I pushed open Raff's door slowly and noticed the room was semi dark with the lights out and blinds shut.Raff seemed to be resting his forehead on his desk, and his hair—badly in need of a cut—flung over his face, so I couldn't see him.

He strung out his words with bitterness. "I. Said. Go. Away!"

I took a few hesitant steps into the office. Raff didn't move, not a tremble or flinch. I wondered what medication he was on, if any, and what it was doing to him. "It's me. Lisa," I said as gently as I could, as if my words had weight and could knock him over with the slightest force.

Raff kept his head buried. "What do you want?"

"Just . . . checking on you. I haven't seen you in a while . . ."

Something like a harsh laugh burst out of him. "Yeah, right. No one wants to see old gloomy Eeyore. 'It's my birthday . . .' " Raff imitated Eeyore from the Winnie-the-Pooh cartoons in that low, gravelly voice. " 'And nobody cares. No balloons, no song and dance, no presents . . .' "

Raff lifted his face and the pain shone so stark and exposed that he almost looked physically wounded, as if someone had struck him. I drew in a breath and came a little closer. Then I caught a glimpse of something that rested on his desk, directly under his chin.

Fear shot through me as I recognized the out-of-place object he loosely held in his right hand.

How in the world had Raff gotten a gun!

My body seized up. I fought the urge to lunge at him and wrest it from his grip. But he saw my mind working and grasped the weapon tighter, warning me off with his piercing stare. Neither of us needed to say a thing—the gun shouted out its own story, and I didn't like a word of it.

Intense lassitude fell down on my shoulders, pressing me with heaviness, like gravity I couldn't hold up under. My knees buckled and I dropped to the Berber carpeting and found it hard to breathe. Raff's unemotional face showed empty eyes—eyes that reminded me of Jeremy's in that moment when he'd walked out of the house and said, "that's it; I'm outta here." I wanted to find words—words that could help, words that could heal, but I realized they were vaporous and insubstantial. What were words anyway? Sounds? Noises? They held no power—not power against pain like this. Like trying to topple a Grizzly with a spitball. I burned with self-recrimination. Words were all I had, and I could think of nothing to say, nothing at all.

Raff looked down at the gun and swiveled it a little, first one way, then another. I couldn't take my eyes off it. I considered running back out and alerting the guard—if he was even still there—but it would only take Raff a few seconds to lift the gun and blow off his own head in the interim.

My muscles started to shake over my entire body, as if I had a chill. My teeth chattered although the room was comfortably heated.

"Just go, Lisa. It's too late. You can't save me." He cleared his throat and added in a mutter, "No one can." He was like a man sinking under waves and knowing help would be too late in coming.

"Oh, Raff . . ." I knew if I suggested anything, it would tick him off, like pulling a pin from a grenade. His slow, barely perceptible movements belied the hair-trigger nervousness I sensed in the way he fondled the gun. The moment stretched, and every second, marked by the beat of my heart, felt like the last second on earth. Time had run out, the last grain of sand had slipped noiselessly through the hourglass. Somewhere chained in the fortress of my skewed brain I heard the Wicked Witch of the West cackle, just another minion of the Grim Reaper.

"I have seen the eternal Footman hold my coat, and snicker, and, in short, I was afraid . . ."

"Dad never made it this far . . . never saw his thirty-fourth birthday. He died a week earlier." Raff's face drew in and grew in intensity, as if he were gathering memories and balling them up, making them small and concentrated—potent plutonium that he could chew and spit out—or choke on.

"You know, it's ironic that the most vivid memory I have of Dad was the day he walked out on us. Of all days." He paused, his eyes loosely staring at the gun, as if mesmerized by it.

I breathed shallowly, not wanting to make a sound, but had trouble hearing Raff's muttering through the clamor of my pulse thumping in my ears.

"You weren't there," he said. "I don't know where you were . . . maybe in bed, asleep,"

He snorted and shook his head, slow motion, eyes glued to the gun. I sat maybe three feet from his desk and calculated how long it would take for me to leap up and reach it. But my limbs were still weighted by extra gravity, so I listened to Raff talk, trying hard to hear what he was really saying.

"I was eight years old. Just a little older than Kevin. I was standing in the hall, in my pajamas . . ." Raff sucked in a sudden breath as if he hadn't breathed in a few minutes and was surfacing for air. His sudden movement startled me and set my heart racing even harder. I tried to calm myself, to not appear menacing in any way. Raff raised his eyes and caught mine in a net. I went limp and refrained from struggling.

"I'm listening," I said.

He cocked his head, remembering. "He seemed so tall, you know. It was late at night—at least late to me. I had already gone to bed, but I heard them arguing and got up. Neal was crying—I remember that. Mom was in her nightgown and she was holding him in her arms and he kept crying and wouldn't stop. I was thinking, 'Daddy's home!' for some reason. He hadn't been home much. I missed him, missed him so much."

Raff shook his head, going deeper. His fingers tapped on the gun, his pointer resting on the trigger. I made myself tear my gaze away from the gun and focus on Raff. I could hear voices in the hall. What if the phone rang? What if someone came in? I knew I had to be ready to leap at that weapon should anything distract Raff at all. But voices and footsteps diminished, then faded. Raff never noticed. He sat up a little straighter and scowled.

"I wanted to cry out to him: 'Why have you been gone so much? Don't you love me? Don't you want to play with me, read me bedtime stories?' He moved to the door, then put on his coat and hat. I wanted him to run over and hug me, to tell me how much he loved me . . . instead . . ." Raff choked up and his face flushed deep red.

"I came and stood next to Mom and clung to her nightgown. I realized Dad wasn't staying; he was leaving again. And this time he had a suitcase. I thought, well, maybe he's taking another trip. He has to work. Mom says he goes away on trips because his work is important. He builds airplanes and spaceships and he's very smart."

Raff's voice changed as he spoke. He was lost in memory and was eight years old again. His eyes shone with intensity as his words came out faster and more heated.

"Do you know what he did? Do you?" I shook my head as Raff grew more agitated.

"Daddy, I cried, why are you leaving? Don't leave me. Don't!" Raff yelled but his voice was small and far away. 'You have to stay here. You can't leave!' I ran over to him, blocked the door, grabbed his coat and yanked on it, trying to pull him into the room, away from the door, but he didn't budge. He . . . he didn't even look at me, just . . . pried my fingers off him, like I was *vermin.*"

I instantly flashed back to Raff's words in the hospital. Kafka. Gregor Samson waking up and discovering he'd turned into vermin overnight. Repulsive and loathed by his family, having to hide in his room so no one would see his vile appearance. Raff was that vermin.

Raff's eyes snapped to mine, like magnets that, when brought close together, are unable to resist and lock together with sudden force. "And he said . . . 'I don't want him. I don't want anything to do with him. Or you!"

He pointed our father's accusatory finger at me, and then his voice broke into a million sharp pieces and sobs gushed out, a dam of anger and hurt flooded across his desk, across the room, striking me hard.

In that moment of time, a moment that stretched and hovered, I understood. Enlightenment flooded me as if someone had turned on a spotlight. As if the guard had flung open that door he'd been guarding. I could almost hear that heavenly host singing at the top of their lungs in the glorious light of truth.

Heedless of the gun and Raff's ire, I stood and walked over to the desk and took his free hand in mine, ignoring the weapon in his other hand, a weapon that paled in comparison to the more deadly weapon Raff mistakenly pointed at his heart. The one he wielded in his memory had the fire power of a nuclear bomb. I pictured it as an RTG, leaking radiation and contaminating all within its confines. Raff, like our father, had been dying of toxic contamination.

But it was a mistake. It was all a grave mistake.

"Raff, he wasn't talking about you. He was talking about Neal."

My brother lifted his head slightly from the table. Tears had soaked his hair and it hung in a soggy mass over his eyes. He looked like a confused eight-year-old, desperately needing answers.

I had his attention, so I kept talking. "You thought he meant you. 'I don't want him,' he said. He meant Neal. Dad left because he couldn't stand it that Neal wasn't his son. Raff, Mom had an affair with Dad's boss, Ed Hutchinson. Neal is Ed's son, not Dad's. That's what he meant. He couldn't live in our house, looking at Neal, knowing that baby wasn't his."

I was blabbering, thinking I made no sense, that Raff wouldn't understand, wouldn't believe me. I knew he had no clue. Our mother hadn't told him a word, and Neal hadn't seen or talked with Raff in a few weeks. But something shifted in Raff's gaze, a focus that brought him back from that distant place he had been wandering lost in.

"What?" This time his voice was an adult's. The boy was gone.

"Dad tried to stay home as long as he could. But he couldn't take it any longer. He had gone to San Diego for a research project, came back and Mom was pregnant. He knew the baby wasn't his.

They hadn't been sleeping together, Raff. Dad moved in with another woman. He left because . . . he couldn't look at Neal, day in and day out, knowing his boss—the man he faced every day—had gotten his wife pregnant. Don't you see?"

Tears streamed down Raff's eyes. I hoped that rather than tears of pain they were tears that could wash away all the lies and misconceptions Raff had suffered throughout his entire lifetime. I hoped some of this truth had power beyond mere sounds and noises, but I couldn't tell. I squeezed Raff's hand and he squeezed back.

"I talked to his best friend a few days ago. He said Dad loved you more than anything. It was Mom he couldn't stand. She betrayed him, lied to him. Drove him into depression. He had to get out. But he never stopped loving us. Loving you, Raff."

I paused, letting my weightless blanket of words settle down upon him, coat him, and wrap him with new understanding. He sniffled and swallowed, then looked at me. Something had shifted. I couldn't tell what, but his shoulders lifted and his head straightened.

I sighed and gave him a smile that I hoped would somehow convey how much I loved him. The love that poured out of me was so thick and potent I imagined it coating him like a second blanket, encasing and protecting him against all the waves of hurt beating up against the shores of his sanity. He was on an island, so very far away, and I could see him, so small, so alone. I waved and caught his eye. After a moment, he lifted his hand and waved back.

He saw me. I cleared my throat.

"A man walks into a nondescript restaurant tucked away in an alley. It's taken him years to find such a place, and he's now old and broke, having spent every penny on his search . . ."

Raff's eyes brightened with recognition. "The conundrum . . ."

I continued. "His agitation is palpable. He orders albatross—broiled. With trembling hands, he picks up his fork and knife and slices off a piece of the seared white flesh. The juices drip onto his plate as he brings the morsel to his mouth. The aroma nauseates him as he squeezes his eyes shut and bites down."

A shudder escaped Raff's chest—one that seemed to have been locked inside for twenty-five years. He wiped his face with his expensive white shirtsleeve and loosened his grip on the gun. I kept speaking, looking only at Raff.

Now I saw the desperation of a man yearning for a lifeline. He was ready, more than ready, for rescue. He had been waiting for someone, anyone, to hand him his vorpal sword so he could kill the Jabberwock. Now I realized Raff had thought the Jabberwork was our father, but he had been mistaken. The beast with the fiery red eyes that waffled through the tulgey wood was a fabrication, a chimera, a phantasm of misunderstanding. It had no substance. It could be easily vanquished.

I then looked past my brother, and the words came out of my mouth of their own volition.

"The man's weathered face relaxes. He sighs, sets the knife and fork on the starched linen tablecloth, and places a hand over his heart, as if to calm its beating. He smiles at the waiter, who bows politely and attends to the other diners. Relief washes in absolution. He raises his eyes to heaven and whispers, but no one hears him . . ."

I waited, and, right on cue, Raff opened his mouth and whispered in agreement with the man in the restaurant, the man who had spent his life searching for the answer, searching for the door to enlightenment.

"Thank God, I'm free."

As the words tumbled out, Raff spilled into my arms, his elbow knocking the gun to the floor. He pressed his head against my head and wept, running his fingers through my hair in a mindless manner, the way our mother used to stroke my head on that rare occasion when I'd be in bed with a fever.

I let Raff hold me there, and his touch no longer felt like the desperate grasp of a man sinking under the waves. It felt liberating and weightless—like soaring, like flying.

Like freedom.

CHAPTER 28

"HERE, I PICKED UP MORE at the store," Jeremy said, kicking open the front door with his shoe. Flattened cardboard boxes tumbled onto the floor as he failed to notice the neat stack of boxes I had positioned to take out to the truck.

"Oops, sorry," I said, "Guess that wasn't the smartest place to put those."

He scooted my stack over with his foot and surveyed the living room, where I sat pulling books off the bookshelf and loading them into more boxes.

"Looks funny. The room so empty. It looks bigger without all our stuff."

We had already moved most of the furniture—the couches, tables, beds, appliances—and they were fitting nicely in the rental.

"Do you want some lunch? I have sandwiches in the ice chest that I brought back from the new place."

"Yeah, I'm starved." Jeremy carried an armload of boxes into the kitchen and set them on the counter. Yesterday—Sunday—he had brought over four big guys from the feed store—employees who spend much of their day hauling, loading, unloading, and stacking hay, straw, and fifty-pound bags of feed. Just the right kind of muscle for moving refrigerators and unwieldy mattresses. We treated the guys to pizza—four extra-larges with the works, and they polished off three gallons of lemonade. It almost felt like a festive occasion, and we got everything moved faster than we'd hoped.

But, today, Jeremy seemed out of sorts, pensive, irritable. He had been so cheerful and positive these past weeks, trying to buoy me up, no doubt still feeling guilty for his little tumble over the highway railing. Neither of us had mentioned the accident after Jeremy got out of the hospital. I wanted to forget it ever happened, but I knew it ate at Jeremy's gut. He had never fallen apart like that before, and he took pride in being strong and capable. Surely, this black mark on his soul was costing him psychically. Yet, what could I say to him, to reassure him? I could only hope that, in time, he would forgive himself and chalk it up to being human.

"You think your brother will show?" he asked from the kitchen.

"He said two o'clock. Why wouldn't he?"

Jeremy came into the living room and plopped on the floor next to me. He picked up a large photography book I had set aside (because it didn't quite fit in the box I was presently packing), and flipped through the pages of estuary birds while chewing his sandwich.

"Just . . . well, I can't see Neal offering to help us pack. He never lifts a finger to help anyone."

"Oh, give him a chance. Maybe he's trying to change." I reached for the packing tape and sealed my box. I still had two more long shelves full of books to go. "Maybe he just wants some company. It's gotta be weird for him. My mother forced him to sell his house, then kicked him out of hers. Two nice houses and now he's in a small studio apartment in San Rafael, staring at the freeway. Takes some adjusting."

Jeremy only grunted and stuffed the crusts in his mouth. He taped together a box and started loading it with books, working beside me in silence. I would have put on some music, but we already moved the stereo and records to the new house. And my tape Walkman needed batteries—which were packed somewhere . . .

"So, have you talked at all about things? What he and his *father* said to each other? And, how it all came down with your mother? That's a story I'd like to hear."

I picked up animosity in Jeremy's voice. Maybe this move was starting to hit him. Now that the rooms were emptying—like our lives draining out of the place we loved so much—the stark reality of our circumstance stared us down. There was no denying that tearing up roots caused pain; my heart hurt every time I took a box out to the truck. These things, our things, belonged here. So much of what we'd bought over the years we had picked out to sit in a special spot. Every shrub and tree on the property had been planted in a specific place, to add color or shape to the landscaping.

I wouldn't get to look out my windows to my pasture or to the pond, but I coated all those regrets with gratitude. Gratitude for having Jeremy back in my life, gratitude for a beautiful new home to live in. Gratitude for our health, our work, for peace and simplicity. I never realized how entangled and complicated my mother had made our lives. So many demands, unspoken expectations, pressures. We had been more slaves than family. Jeremy always called over to fix something, tolerating my mother's way of ordering him around. Me, always cleaning up after her, running errands for her, taking care of family get-togethers—things I gladly did, acts of love that were never appreciated, only expected as dutiful behavior.

Jeremy got up and went over to the front door. He opened it and stood there a moment, listening and looking down the road.

"What?" I asked. "Someone here?"

"A light blue BMW, just running their engine, parked about halfway down our driveway . . ."

Before I could say anything, Jeremy was marching down the front steps toward the car. I didn't know anyone who owned a car like that. I pulled on my sneakers and trotted after him, and the dogs followed after me, running over from the barn. No one ever came down our driveway, aside from an occasional delivery truck. Maybe it was one of Jeremy's employees, although the car was a bit pricey for a feed store grunt.

"Hey, wait up," I yelled, but Jeremy ignored me, intent on questioning the inhabitants of the vehicle. Just as he came alongside the car, two doors opened, and a man and woman, nicely dressed, maybe fortyish, got out. I whistled to the dogs and called them to my side so they wouldn't accost the visitors. The woman, who had her hair pulled back in an austere bun and was a little overly made up, entwined her arm around the man's and seemed to be taking in the property with a pleased expression on her face.

The man extended a hand to Jeremy, who shook it, although I could tell Jeremy would rather have not. "I'm Bill Fisher. This is Wendy." The woman only nodded and offered a polite smile.

"Are you lost?" Jeremy asked. "What address are you trying to find?"

The man hesitated. Jeremy's tall stature overshadowed his barely six-foot-tall frame, and Jeremy's strong manner did not set him at ease.

"Uh, Mr. Blake gave us this address . . . you're Mr. Bolton, right?"

It only took a few seconds to piece together the situation. I watched Jeremy's stance change into a protective, almost antagonistic, position. "What do you want?"

The man looked at the woman, then back to Jeremy. "We were told we could drop by, take a look at the house . . ."

"No, you can't." Color rose to Jeremy's cheeks and his words came out tight and threatening. I held onto the dogs' collars, and almost wished I had one for Jeremy, to yank him back.

Jeremy mumbled. "I can't believe this . . ." He turned to me. "They can't even wait until we move out. They have to start sending people over, just to shove it in our faces."

He stared at the man, maybe hoping to discourage any thoughts of moving into our house. "Just . . . go. Get out of here. And tell Mr. Blake he does not have permission to send anyone over here. We have until the fifteenth, so I don't want to see you or anyone else drive up for a looky-loo. Got that?"

Clearly, these people weren't expecting such a cold reception. Harv Blake should have known better than to send potential renters unannounced. What was he thinking? That we'd invite them in for tea? Jeremy had to be right—this was Blake's way of rubbing our noses in our mess. And I had no doubt he'd been prompted by my mother to do so.

As Jeremy stormed to the barn, I shrugged apologetically and watched the couple get in their car and back down the driveway. Buster and Angel escorted them to the county road. By the time I looked over at Jeremy, he had disappeared. I ran over to the barn and found him sitting on the edge of the hay palette, his face buried in his hands.

He started to talk, and I leaned my head closer to hear him as he spoke through his hands.

"You know what I wish I could do? Take a baseball bat and smash all the windows and doors. Even torch the place." He looked up at me and his eyes were both fire and ice. "Why should anyone get to live here? We put in all the work; we built everything, planted everything . . . ten years, thousands of hours. And what do we get out it? What! Nothing. Not one damn thing we can call our own . . ."

I laid my hand on his shoulder but couldn't think of anything to say. The truth of his words, their raw honesty, set off my own pain, and I tried hard not to cry. I listened to my husband sob, knowing tears were streaming down his face, knowing he didn't want me to see him like this but unable to control the tears. I thought of consoling phrases—that we had each other, that we'd buy our own house someday, but Jeremy already knew these things. It still didn't assuage any of the pain.

After some time, Jeremy wiped his face and blew his nose, using a tissue he found in his pocket. He took a deep breath and looked around the barn, taking it in. The dogs came running in, frisky and exuberant, a sharp contrast to the mood we shared. "I think . . . I'll take the dogs for a long walk. I just need to blow this off, clear my head. Do you mind if I bow out from visiting with Neal? I don't think I can deal with making friendly talk right now."

"Sure. No problem."

He stood and we walked back to the house together. The dogs, having heard the "w" word, pranced around Jeremy, pushing their noses into his legs as if spurring him to move faster.

Jeremy laced up his hiking boots and gave me a perfunctory kiss on the cheek. I ruffled his hair and reassured him with my eyes that we'd be okay. He tried to muster a smile.

"I'll keep packing," I said as he headed around the side of the house for the hills. "Everything will be okay," I added quietly, tears pooling once more in my eyes.

Neal drove up as I loaded the last box in the pickup's bed. I still had the den and the bathrooms to finish, but I didn't need Neal's help, although it had been kind of him to offer.

"Hey," I said as he got out of his Datsun, noting he was no longer borrowing our mother's Mercedes, "perfect timing. I need a break and there're some beers with our names on them in the ice chest."

Neal gave me a hug. "Sounds good. Looks like you're making progress."

"Most of it's done. We moved all the furniture yesterday, so we're down to the small things. And then we'll transport animals."

Neal followed me into the house as I went for the ice chest and pulled out two cans of beer. "Wow, this place is empty." His voice softened. "This must be horrible for you guys, having to move out. I'm really sorry—"

"Hey, it's not your fault. It's mine. We should have never let Mom buy this place. Jeremy warned me . . . but I didn't listen. Now we're paying the price."

"Well," Neal said, looking seriously into my eyes, "none of us saw this coming. And it's wrong." He snorted. "A lot of things wrong."

"Yeah. Welcome to my world."

We went out to the back deck and sat on the blanket I had spread out. With the temperature hovering in the nineties, a beer sounded just right. I popped the top of the can and took a long drink.

"Where's Jeremy?"

"Taking the dogs for a hike. He'll be back in a while. You hungry?"

"Just ate a big lunch."

"So," I ventured, "how's your apartment? Do you like it?"

Neal shrugged. "It's fine. I'm not home much. Got a new bartending job. And I'm coaching Little League for the rest of the month."

"That sounds like fun. I remember going to your games when you were little. You always wanted to be the pitcher, but they stuck you in right field."

"Yeah, but I still had fun. I get a kick watching the little guys try to hit the ball and run the bases. I'm helping them with their stance and hand positioning—that kind of stuff."

We sipped our beers and let the moment settle. I knew Neal was gearing up to talk about heavier things, so I waited. Finally, he turned to me and set down his can.

"Julie and I had a long talk the other day. She told me everything . . . about her mom, about our dad's—I mean, Nathan's last months. Man, I don't know if I'm ever going to get used to putting it that way. What's a father anyway? My supposed father died when I was a baby, so I never knew him as a father. And then I learn about Ed—too little too late, I guess. I'm still fatherless, so I wonder, does it all really matter?"

I snorted, couldn't help myself. "It matters that Mom lied to you, to all of us. You could have known your real dad all along. Maybe Ed might not have wanted you in his life, but at least you could have made your own choices—whether to pursue a relationship with him or not."

Neal nodded. "It was surreal, Lisa. Talking to him. Here's this guy, dying, someone I've never met in my life, and yet, in some weird way, he felt familiar. Maybe it was just his face, seeing something in myself there, however slight, or maybe it was more. Just hearing the way he talked, his gestures. Like I could tell we were related, although, from what Julie tells me, he's a real asshole. But, he was nice to me, at least, while we talked. Didn't say much, of course; he wasn't feeling up to it. But, I got the impression he had a lot he wanted to say, things he wished he could share with me, fill me in on stuff—his life, the work he did . . ."

"Makes sense. So much to catch up on, but he'd run out of time. It must have been disappointing—for both of you. Did he—

have any idea he had a son? Or was this completely a surprise to him?"

"He said he had no clue. And he ranted a bit about Shirley, his ex. She had known all along about me, but never said a thing—for over twenty years. I understand why, but, well, in some ways I don't. Why didn't Shirley come find me and tell me? She knew her own daughter had a brother. Wouldn't she have wanted us to connect?"

"You'd think so. But maybe she didn't want to expose you to Ed Hutchinson. You have to remember, Neal, that Ed beat her, and Shirley took Julie away to protect her. She felt Ed might have hurt his own daughter. So, you can see why maybe she kept her secret to herself. For everyone's good. Doesn't make it right, though. But, she may have felt it was the only option."

"Maybe when I was a baby or a vulnerable kid. But, why not find me when I was a teen, when I was older and could have decided for myself?"

"I think Nathan made her promise not to tell. She could have just been honoring his wishes."

"Whatever." Neal shook his head. "I tried to talk to Mom about all this, but she freaked. Yelled at me and told me it was all a lie."

"Really? How in the world does she think that will fly? You know, I had dinner with Dad's best friend last week—Dave Lerner. He knew all about Ed being your father. It's not just something Julie or her mother made up. Other people knew. He said, though, that Nathan loved you as his own, regardless."

I fell quiet, thinking of Raff's words, how our father had screamed at our mother. *"I don't want him, don't want to have anything to do with him."* I understood how my father could and would have said that in a moment of anger. But I believed with all my heart, from what I had learned about Nathan Sitteroff from the people who knew him well, that he would have loved Neal as much as he loved us. *If* he could have found his way to stay alive long enough.

I pulled my hair off my neck and made it into a sloppy ponytail. The heat felt good, baking deep into my bones. "Who knows what would have happened if Nathan hadn't died? Would it have been all hushed up, and Nathan have raised you as his son, matter closed? Or would he have told you the truth at some point, and let you decide what to do with that knowledge? From what I've learned about him, I bet he would have been straight with you. It's anyone's guess."

Neal grunted with a cynical expression on his face. "Mom did admit, though, that he had left her, had an affair with Shirley. Made it look like she was the victim, that dad left her for another woman, abandoning her while she was pregnant. Oh, but, she forgave him. It was the drugs, she said. They gave him too much medication and it made him crazy, irrational. She blamed all his behavior on the treatments he was getting for his leukemia. She said that when he was dying in the hospital, he apologized for hurting her, that he loved her and wished he could take all the hurt back. Wished he'd never left."

"I doubt he said that. He moved in with Shirley Hutchinson months before he got sick. It had nothing to do with the meds making him crazy."

"He did?"

"Yes. When he and Shirley found out about their spouses' affair, they went to San Diego together. Apparently, Dad signed up for a research project there, to get away from Mom. He had just found out she was pregnant and knew it—you, sorry—were Ed's child. He couldn't take it. Couldn't live in the house knowing that . . . having to pretend."

I shut my mouth before I said any more. At this juncture, I didn't want to bring up what Dave had confessed—that my dad killed himself by exposing himself to toxic radiation. At some point I hoped to share this with my brothers, but now was not the time. Neal, especially, had too much to process, and his life was in as much of an upheaval as ours. And Raff—well, maybe there would never be a good time to share this knowledge. Maybe some doors were better kept bolted shut and blocked by a guard.

"I thought he volunteered for some dangerous experiment and that's how he got leukemia. Isn't that what Mom always said?"

"Yeah, well, I've learned recently that you can't believe everything she tells you." Neal matched my smile with his own. "Have you talked to Raff about any of this?"

Neal picked up his beer and finished it off. "I wanted to, and then . . . well, you know. And now that he's back in the hospital . . ."

"In time. At some point he will get better. I know he will. His attitude has changed. He's more hopeful."

Neal looked at me, glad for that reassurance—I could tell. He had always looked up to Raff, despite the eight-year gap in age. I suddenly felt burdened by all the healing that needed to take place in my family. It wasn't just me and Jeremy; Neal had his weight he carried around, and Raff had his—even more burdensome. How had we accumulated so much baggage? I thought of the photograph of our family, the faded black-and-white print of Dad standing next to Raff, and me kneeling beside my mother as she held baby Neal. We all looked so young, so untainted. Although, I knew now that emotions must have rumbled inside my dad as he stood there, posing with Ed Hutchinson's baby. How different things appear on the surface.

Neal came over and wrapped his arms around me. "Lisa," he said, his words breaking up as he spoke, "I'm so sorry I was mean to you. I was under Mom's spell, and all she'd do is complain about you, put you down. And you were just trying to keep everyone happy, make sure we all got along. You were always a good sister to me, and I admired you a lot. You know that, right?"

My heart ached, more from joy than from hurt. "Sure. I know I can be pushy and opinionated sometimes . . ."

"Yeah, well you got that from Mom. And, I guess I got the good looks from my real father. Julie showed me some photos. Ed was a pretty handsome guy, wasn't he?"

I playfully pushed at Neal. "Looks aren't everything. Ed was a jerk too. So, don't take after him in that way. Start treating your girlfriends right."

Neal chuckled, then fell quiet. "Julie invited me to the funeral. Said it would be small, just a few people. But I said I didn't think I should go. It just didn't feel right."

"I understand."

"After seeing me, I think it softened him up a bit. Julie said he broke down after I left. Apologized for being a bad father, for neglecting her all those years . . ."

"Well, that was downright nice of him. I guess a lot of people repent on their death bed. Doesn't really balance out all the years of abuse and neglect, though."

"She felt he was sincere. I'm glad he did it. She's obviously been carrying around a lot of resentment. He's leaving her his house and all his stuff. She said there were some boxes of photos he'd stashed away. Wants me to come over sometime and go through them with her."

"I think that would be nice. Neal, I like Julie. I'm glad you have another sister. And I'm glad she has you. I think you're all that's left of family for her in the world. So, be sure to make up for some lost time and get to know her, spend some time with her. It'll be good for both of you, I think."

"I think so too. Although, I wouldn't wish this insane dysfunctional family on her."

"Right. Just isolate her from the rest of us. You've got enough baggage of your own to dump on her."

"Hey!"

"It's true."

Neal laughed. "Yeah, it is, isn't it?"

We spent two hours talking, catching up on little life details, avoiding the topic of our mother. I realized I hadn't sat and chatted like this with Neal in years. We essentially had to get to know each other all over again, but by the time he left, I knew we were closer than ever. The resentment I had been harboring for him as of late had been flamed by our mother, in those delightful private jabs she loved to make behind backs. Neal wasn't half as bad as I'd conjured him in my head. My heart bloomed with affection for him, my little lost brother, still a bit lost but now finding his way. Now, if only my other brother could follow suit.

As I packed the remaining odds and ends, I thought of Raff facing our father in that hospital room, the air rife with tension and pain. And Dad trying to control his anger and hurt toward our mother as he made an attempt to reach out one last agonizing moment to his son, trying to fit all his love into a few difficult words. How guilt-ridden he must have been! Having walked out on Raff months earlier, perhaps he realized how Raff many times must have stood at the window, looking out expectantly, searching for his daddy's car—exactly how young Nathan Sitteroff had watched for his errant father through those filthy windows of the foster homes in New York.

The parallel of the two scenes, juxtaposed and overlapping, struck me with sadness. Therapists say we repeat our childhood, pass on behaviors to the next generation. Parents who abuse their kids often become abusive themselves. Parents who were abandoned walk out on their kids. Patterns, so engrained and hard to break, repeat themselves. Just as Nathan's father had walked away from his young son, so too Nathan had walked out on Raff. Perhaps it was subconscious; perhaps he had been driven to replay the only script he ever knew—a father making empty promises and never coming home.

Raff had hidden our father's words deep in his heart, in a horrible secret place that festered in pain. *"I don't want anything to do with him."* Our dad had meant Neal, but Raff hadn't known that. He only knew his father was storming out the front door, leaving him behind. I can't even imagine what an eight-year-old boy would have felt, believing his father was leaving because he couldn't stand the sight of him. He thought his father had loved him! Raff could only come to one conclusion—a conclusion our mother never tried to denounce—that he was unlovable and unworthy. This, then, was his Jabberwock—the beast that faced him down with the words emblazoned on his chest: Unlovable. Unworthy. Bad. No wonder Raff wanted to die.

But maybe now, understanding those words hadn't been meant for him, understanding Nathan Sitteroff's anger wasn't directed at his son but at his wife, Raff might find a door to freedom. The guard had put up a strong fight, and the lock had been tricky to open, but there was no denying that Raff's door to enlightenment had swung free. Whether or not the truth would set him free, ultimately, only time would tell. Raff had tasted the albatross and now knew he was irreprehensible. He was not to blame. He had done no wrong.

Hopefully, this truth would work its way into Raff's very soul and lead him to healing.

I looked around at my empty house, at the shambles of my life that, unexpectedly, had also led in some ways to healing. No one said the truth would be painless. But, I was beginning to believe the axiom after all. Truth did set you free—if you were brave enough to face it down and pay the price.

CHAPTER 29

EVEN AFTER A WEEK OF sleeping in our new bedroom in our new house, I still felt as if I were on vacation, in some hotel far away. My mattress and blankets should have anchored me in familiarity, but the night sounds were different. The animals in the pasture were farther away, so I couldn't hear the quiet night noises they made. Crows instead of songbirds lighted in the trees and the raucous cawing jarred me each dawn, like an annoying alarm clock. Still, a peace permeated every room, the way a wind dies down over the surface of a lake and allows the reflections of clouds and birds to mirror back in perfection, without distortion. Being in that house, with Jeremy lying cuddled up next to me, felt just like that. I could see the objects of my life reflected in the mirror. Undistorted, Simple. Smooth as glass.

"You awake?" I asked.

Jeremy's breathing had deepened. He often fell hard asleep after we'd made love at night. No wonder—with hauling things in and out of the feed store all day long, getting up at five most mornings. On occasion, he would even fall asleep midsentence. I'd never known anyone able to drop off to sleep so quickly. It took me an hour or two, always, to unwind my tension, and loosen my thoughts enough to let them drift away on some slack tide. They clung stubbornly to my brain, like barnacles, regardless of how trivial.

"Hmm . . . what?" He stirred and slid an arm across my waist, then lifted an eyelid and looked at me in the room softly illuminated with moonlight. A piece of full moon clipped the corner of the large window, and I could see the lights on the nearby houses twinkle like stars. I let out a contented sigh and stroked Jeremy's hand. He abruptly rolled over and lay partly across me, his face close to mine. His eyes shone with some inner light as he gazed at me.

"You can't fall asleep, can you?" he asked. He began rubbing the side of my head and I moaned in delight. I loved having my head rubbed. A chuckle escaped my mouth as I thought about the goats and how they'd dig hard into my hand, their eyes rolling in ecstasy, whenever I rubbed their heads. "What's so funny?"

"I'm just like Sassy, begging for more."

"Oh, you want more, do you . . ." That was all the invitation Jeremy needed to let his other hand start roaming south. I found his mouth with mine and kissed him, feeling a rush of desire surge through me. After a moment, though, he pulled back and lessened his advances.

"What is it?" I asked. "Something wrong?"

Jeremy shook his head. "I just don't want to lose this . . . feeling. Lisa, I know things had gotten way complicated with us, and now, with this move, and with things changing . . ." He drew in a breath and I laid my head on his chest and let him take his time. Unburdening was a slow process for Jeremy. It took just the right moment, the right mood. It was not something he comfortably managed, but when he had something to say, he had to find a way to get it out or it ate him up.

"I knew you were pregnant—" He stopped when his voice choked up. Instantly, my gut twinged in remembrance.

He started stroking my hair softly, reminding me of how Raff had done the same thing just last week, as he held me in his arms and wept. A sudden memory jolted me—of my father. Was it a memory? I was back in my bedroom with the nursery-rhyme wallpaper, my father singing me a lullaby, and he was stroking my hair, just like this. I pulled my thoughts back to Jeremy and listened.

"Last month. When I . . . moved out. I could tell."

I took his hand off my head and held it. He turned and moved back so he could look at me. His eyes showed guilt.

"What are you saying?" I had never considered it, but surely Jeremy of all people would have spotted the telltale signs of my pregnancy—my moodiness and irritability from the nausea I'd tried to keep from him. I guess I hadn't been very good about hiding the signs. But after all I'd been through, I hadn't wanted him to know, not until—

I stopped my mental rambling. There was a reason Jeremy was admitting this. "Go on."

"Lisa, I know you were hurting. I know how awful it was for you, and I was being selfish. I know that now. Those other times . . . when you lost the baby . . ."

Jeremy suddenly started crying and it jarred me with its unexpectedness. I forced back my own rush of suffering and tried to understand what he was saying.

"I couldn't take it. I had to distance myself, so I wouldn't hurt anymore. Every time you miscarried, I felt such pain—and loss. I know you felt alone and misunderstood, but . . . they were mine too. I wanted us to have a baby so badly, and wanted to see you happy and fulfilled, hold a child in your arms, our child." Jeremy gushed out more tears and trembled as I drew him tighter against me, his heat radiating in the cool of the room.

I was flabbergasted by my own naivety. I'd never thought to consider how Jeremy had felt, and what my pregnancies had meant to him. It was my body, my baby. I never thought in terms of "ours."

"That's really why I moved out . . . because . . . I just knew what was coming. I'm sorry, Lis. I couldn't take it, going through that one more time." He spoke quickly, in an apologetic tone. "And it was wrong of me, so wrong. I was only thinking of myself and needing to distance myself. I had to get away. I was selfish. And cowardly. And I wasn't there for you when you needed me the most."

Before I could sift through the mash of my feelings merging with his, he wiped his eyes and said, "Please forgive me. Will you? I promise I'll never do that again, walk away when you're hurting. I've done it too often, and I can't respect myself anymore."

Without meaning to, I started to cry. "Of course I forgive you! I didn't know. I mean, that you cared so much. I thought you didn't care, because you never said anything, after I miscarried. You'd just be silent, morose. I thought you were glad, that you didn't want a baby, and that I was pressuring you . . ."

"Oh, no! Nothing like that. Lisa, I want us to have kids, but if we can't, that's okay. I brought those adoption brochures because I thought it might give you some hope, that we could have a family—"

"And I thought you got those brochures because you didn't care. Just to mollify me or something."

"No, that's not what I meant. Not at all."

"If one, settling a pillow by her head should say, 'that is not what I meant at all. That is not it, at all.' "

We both grew quiet, leaving me to think about how I had misunderstood Jeremy. I thought I knew him so well, yet, it was as if I didn't know him at all.

I let the lines of Eliot's poem slide through my mind, as it so often seemed to do those days, tagging along on my journey like a cartoon balloon of reminders, like side notes on a manuscript page. *"And would it have been worth it, after all, would it have been worth while, after the sunsets and the dooryards and the sprinkled streets, after the novels, after the teacups, after the skirts that trail along the floor—and this, and so much more? . . . If one, settling a pillow or throwing off a shawl, and turning toward the window, should say: 'That is not it at all, that is not what I meant, at all.' "*

The poet's musing about himself could have been written for me: *"I am an attendant lord, one that will do to swell a progress, start a scene or two . . . deferential, glad to be of use. Politic, cautious, and meticulous, full of high sentence, but a bit obtuse; at times, indeed, almost ridiculous—Almost, at times, the Fool."*

That described me to a T. My role in my family and the way I saw myself, certainly the fool. I had sought to swell a progress, and

I had surely started a scene or two. Always deferring and glad to be of use. All those other characteristics were true as well. Almost as if T. S. Eliot knew me inside out. I had thoughts those traits would well serve me and my family, but they'd all come back to bite me.

Yet, in my headlong foolish rush to find answers for Raff, something good seemed to have come out of the wreckage. More than one thing. I needed to keep reminding myself of that. There was plenty to scavenge from the flotsam and jetsam to build a bigger, better ship to sail the turbulent seas of this life.

Jeremy and I held each other in comfort. "It's so hard, isn't it—to really see another person?" he said. "So easy to misunderstand, even when you've been intimate with them for years. Things aren't always as they seem."

I nodded, my head pressed against his warm, broad chest. I knew Jeremy felt some relief at having let all this out. And I felt deeply moved by his confession.

"Do you know what a conundrum is?" I asked.

Jeremy jerked a little by the strange turn of topic. "You mean a puzzle?"

"It's a word problem. My brothers and I used to tell them when we were teens. Some are pretty simple, but others are complex, took days to solve."

"Give me a for-instance."

"Okay." I thought for a moment. "A man walks into a bar and approaches the counter. He asks the bartender for a glass of water, and then leans in close and whispers something to him. The bartender suddenly pulls a gun out from under the counter and puts it up against the customer's head. The customer gasps and then waits nervously. After a minute he says, 'thanks.' Then the bartender smiles and says, 'no problem.' The customer drinks his glass of water and then leaves the bar."

I waited until Jeremy asked, "So, what's the catch?"

"Well, you have to figure out why the bartender pulled a gun out from under the counter. Why the guy said thanks. Ask me some yes or no questions."

"Okay. Do the men know each other?"

"Nope."

"Uh, is the bartender insane?"

"Nope." I started to smile when I noticed Jeremy's serious expression. He looked exactly the way Raff used to, aiming to find just the right question to get to the answer quickly.

"Did the customer ask him to shoot him?"

"Nope." Jeremy started fidgeting. I started giggling.

"Come on, give me a clue."

"Can't."

"Why not?"

"That's not how it works. You have to solve the conundrum."

Jeremy playfully punched me. "But that's not how real life works. You can't always figure things out. And—" he said, with a poke in my ribs, "there're ways to cheat!"

"Hey, tickling is not allowed. You get black marks on your report card!"

"Just tell me the answer, okay? I have no patience for this kind of thing." Not like Raff, who would mull a problem over for days and never give up, never relinquish ground in defeat. He had a crown to defend and a kingdom to rule. In the end he had always solved every conundrum. Including the only one that really mattered.

"Okay. The guy has the hiccups," I said evenly.

"Hiccups?"

"Yeah. Don't you see? He goes into the bar and asks for a glass of water . . ."

"Then whispers to the bartender that he has the hiccups. So the guy pulls a gun out and scares them out of him!" Jeremy smacks his hand on his head in mock stupidity.

"Right."

"And that's why the customer thanks him and leaves. Man, that is so dumb!"

"Dumb?" I reached over and yanked the pillow out from under his head. "Dumb?" I whacked him one hard on his head. He pushed it away and grabbed me so that I was crushed against his chest.

"Yeah. Dumb."

I chuckled. "Well, you couldn't figure it out, so how dumb was it?"

Jeremy sighed and pulled back to look into my eyes. "It just goes to show that things aren't always as they appear. A person might do or say something, meaning one thing, but someone else will read it all wrong. Maybe that's what your conundrums are all about—showing how we completely misread the circumstances. We make things more complicated, when the answer is often simple."

I snuggled up close and reflected on how much Jeremy had been hurting alongside me while I suffered through my pregnancies and lost those babies. I had been so consumed with my own feelings that I had failed to see him clearly. And he had done the same with me. If we had just been open and brave enough to face the truth, we could have weathered the pain together. Built each other up instead of tearing each other apart. Simply avoided all this misunderstanding.

The answer was always simple, once you figured it out.

CHAPTER 30

NOT EVEN A MONTH AFTER Raff's "episode," I found myself pregnant again. Jeremy and I discussed it and decided right away to detach ourselves from the outcome. We hadn't planned it, and with my batting average it was safe to say I would probably miscarry. Which sent me back into the hell of rampant hormones, nausea, and lethargy. On top of that pile I added my frustration and anger. Why should I have to suffer so unfairly for nothing? Jeremy also hated seeing me miserable and agreed—as he'd watched me lean my head on the toilet in anticipation of another violent heave. If this one didn't "take," we would resort to something we hadn't used in years—birth control. I just couldn't deal with this anymore—though we were both behaving a little better this time—with more honesty and courage.

Jeremy pampered me through the first twelve weeks, then, as I passed the line of demarcation—the fifteenth week, the farthest any of my pregnancies had gone—I dared go to my doctor for a check-up. So far, no bleeding. She asked us if we wanted to hear the heartbeat, but I quickly shook my head. I couldn't allow this pregnancy to dig its claws into me just yet. There was still time for raised hopes to be dashed. We pretended as if nothing had changed in our lives, as my morning sickness subsided and my pants started getting a little tight. Although we didn't make a pact, we had an unspoken understanding: the subject was not to be mentioned. I eased up on my gardening work, although the winter months were always slower. Jeremy avoided saying anything baby-related, but let it slip that I did seem to glow.

Thanksgiving came and went. Neal and Raff had come over for an early celebration the day before. They had still planned to go to our mother's the next day, more out of tradition and attempting to keep some sort of truce going with her. Why, I don't know. I hadn't spoken to my mother since the day I had screamed at her over the pay phone in the hospital, when Jeremy was lying inured and in pain. Neal had apparently had a few "interesting" discussions with our mother after meeting Ed, but he didn't go into much detail. I suspected he wanted to spare me the melodrama and not rile me up, given my tenuous condition and all that.

Frankly, I was glad. Just the mention of my mother sent my blood boiling. As much as I wanted to forgive her and try to understand her, I couldn't get past the hurt. I didn't know how my brothers could face her. Raff especially. I knew he made his appearances at her home out of duty and cowardliness. He'd finally gotten on meds that alleviated his misery, but he felt brittle and weak. Whatever it took to make peace.

I held my tongue. They had to make their own choices. I had made mine. Perhaps one day my mother and I would start over, but at that moment in my life, I hoped I never saw her again. A relationship with Ruth Sitteroff came at too great a price. Just look at the price my father had paid. And Raff, and Jeremy. No thanks.

Jeremy told me he had spoken to the hospital chaplain during his stay at Marin General. As we sat drinking sparkling apple cider and waiting for the ball drop in Times Square on TV, ushering in 1987, he shared his thoughts about my mother—the first time we'd mentioned her in months.

"When I told the chaplain what happened—about how your mother was taking away our home and treating you with such contempt, he said some people were toxic. They acted like a cancer in your life, robbing you of health and strength and injecting only poison. He showed me that passage in the Bible, where Jesus says 'don't throw your pearls before swine or give what is holy to the dogs.' There's more after that verse. It says if you throw your pearls before swine, they will trample those pearls under their feet—and then turn and rip you to shreds. I never knew what that meant until he asked me what I felt was holy in my life. I said, my marriage. My health. My dignity and self-esteem. He said these were holy, and we have every right to cherish and protect these things. Jesus didn't say to roll over and let the swine tear us apart. He said to stay away from them.

"So, no matter how much kindness you showed such people, exposure to them would eventually kill you. The effects could be subtle, barely perceptible, but, over time . . ."

Jeremy's words sank deep into my soul, a penetrating salve of exoneration. And then I thought of my father, sitting at his desk, knowing he had escaped his poisonous marriage only to choose another deadly substance to expose himself to. Day after day, working on his equations, fitting all his problems into his Boolean algebra framework. Every problem solved simply by *and, or, not.* Every problem but the one that had Ruth Sitteroff as a factor. For that one, he couldn't find a solution, not one that balanced on both sides. Not an equal or equitable one.

So, he cheated. He hadn't cheated death, but he had cheated his wife. And cheated us in the process. All because Ruth Sitteroff had first cheated on him.

"So," I said, cuddling up with Jeremy on the couch as the muted countdown to the New Year seeped out of the TV speakers, "you have to cut cancer out, if you can. Before it's too late. Before it spreads. You can try to stop it—radiation, chemo, diet—but if those methods fail, what choice do you have, right?"

"Or maybe, at some point, you could build up a resistance. Lisa, maybe someday you'll want to try reconnecting with your mom, but for now . . ."

I snorted in response. "I can't imagine ever talking to her again. Ever." Jeremy leaned in closer and wrapped the blanket tighter around us. Maybe he was trying to make me feel safe and protected. "She would have to grovel for a very long time before I would let her back into my life. Into our lives. Look what she did to you. I won't give her the chance to stomp on you again."

"People change."

"Rarely."

"But, some do. Maybe your mom will realize what she's done, how much she's hurt all of you—"

"And, why *did* she do that?" My voice raised in pitch and I pulled back to challenge Jeremy. "There's no excuse for her lies and betrayal. She forced us out of our home. She lied to Neal his whole life, not telling him about his real father. And she stood on the sidelines and watched Raff suffer, knowing she could have helped, knowing she could have told him the truth and maybe he wouldn't have suffered so much." I exhaled hard and shook my head. "I've been mulling over this for months. I can't figure it out. Was it out of fear, guilt? Was she just afraid she'd be left alone in the end, abandoned by everyone? Or did she feel so guilty for having that affair and getting pregnant, she couldn't think of anything else but covering up her crime? If so, look at the cost of her lies! It's inexcusable."

"You're right, Lis. It *is* inexcusable. And maybe you'll never know why. Maybe your mother is selfish and heartless by nature. Some people are just rotten through and through and there's nothing you can do about it."

"You just said people can change, feel regret. Now you're saying she can't change."

"I'm saying I don't know. We don't know anyone's true nature. You can only go through life being true to who you are and try to protect your family. Right now, I have a family to protect, and I don't want Ruth Sitteroff getting anywhere near it."

Jeremy placed his hand on my belly and at that moment something amazing happened. I gasped.

"It kicked! The baby kicked!" I immediately clamped my mouth shut. I feared saying something that would jinx my pregnancy, but I couldn't help it. I was so astonished at the feeling inside me, of the life banging on the wall of my abdomen demanding to be acknowledged. I was five months pregnant at that point and we hadn't mentioned the baby, not even once.

Jeremy kept his hand there and waited. I waited. The baby kicked again and Jeremy blurted out a laugh. My doctor had assured us we were pretty much out of the danger zone. A miscarriage at this point would be unlikely. But neither of us felt comforted by the odds. Jeremy must have been thinking along the same lines when he turned to me, love in his eyes, and spoke.

"Lisa, something could go wrong at any time. There's always a chance of that. Not just miscarrying. You can have problems with the delivery, or something could be wrong with the baby. Or your kid could get some terrible disease, or get hit by a car crossing the street—"

"Well, thanks for being so morbid!"

"You know what I mean. Life is dangerous. You have to trust and go with it. Do your best, but you can't worry about everything, expecting disaster at every turn. Otherwise, you'll never enjoy life at all."

"I know. You're right." We let our words dissipate on the air, but our unspoken thoughts filled the space around us just as noisily. Jeremy removed his hand and pulled down my sweater, then bundled me back up in the blanket.

"Well," he said, holding up his glass of cider, "here's to a new year, a new start. It's gotta be a better year than last."

I clinked my glass against his and drank my cider. Then the phone rang.

"Who's that?" Jeremy asked. "It's after midnight." He disengaged himself from the tangle of blankets and went into the kitchen for the phone.

"It's probably Neal," I said. "Wishing us happy New Year. He knew we were staying up. He's over at Julie's going through all those boxes Ed had packed away in the attic."

Jeremy answered the phone and nodded. I heard him wish Neal a happy New Year, then he grew quiet as he listened. I turned and watched his face as he came into the room, then handed me the phone. Just one look at his expression sent my heart fluttering. Had something happened?

I took the phone from him. "Neal, is everything okay?" "Sure. We're going through photos and stuff. And Julie's been packing up Ed's office. Someone's coming to pick up all the furniture on Friday."

"Doesn't sound like a fun way to celebrate New Year's."

"Oh, it's been great. We went out for sushi, and we're working on the second bottle of champagne right now. Julie brought over some photo albums of her and her mother. She was a pretty cute kid—and had just as many freckles as I had."

"So . . . what's up?" I knew he had said something puzzling to Jeremy.

"Well, Julie found something stuffed in the back of one of Ed's desk drawers. It may be nothing, really. She wanted me to call you and tell you."

"What is it?"

Neal paused. I heard Julie in the background, saying something to Neal in an agitated voice.

"It's a sealed envelope, addressed to you," he said. "With the words 'my confession' written under your name."

CHAPTER 31

NEAL HAD TAKEN THE ENVELOPE home with him and said he'd be by in the morning. I knew he wouldn't get to our house until noon, having stayed way into the night at Ed Hutchinson's house, helping Julie and hoping to avoid dodging drunk drivers. Nevertheless, I was so curious about the letter I couldn't sleep at all. Not that I slept much these days—with the baby pushing against my bladder and my needing to go to the bathroom every few hours. Over the phone, I had urged Julie to open the letter and read it to me, but she refused. I suspected it had less to do with being polite and more to do with dread. What in the world could Ed have confessed to before he died? And why address it to me? Whatever wrongs he had done seemed most likely to be pointed in Julie's direction—or Neal's. But, perhaps since he'd already apologized to both of them personally, he felt an urge to spare some apology for me. I didn't expect too much in that "confession." Something along the lines of "I'm sorry I had an affair with your mother and got her pregnant."

At dawn, as I waited for Neal and brewed coffee for Jeremy, still asleep in our bed in the back of the house, I tried to remember what Dave Lerner had told me about Ed visiting my father in the hospital. Maybe Ed had tried to apologize to my father for the affair. Or, maybe Ed had been mean to him, and before he himself died felt some remorse over that. The way Dave had presented it, my father was nearly incoherent and overly emotional. What did Ed think when he saw my father like that—emaciated and dying—so young, leaving behind a family? Did it trigger some guilt, reminding Ed of his mistreatment of Shirley and his disregard for Julie? If it did, he must have discarded it quickly, for, accordingly to Julie, Ed never made an effort to be a father to her, or to make it up to Shirley. To the contrary, it seemed Ed grew more mean, more hardened, more distant.

I could imagine the relief Ed must have felt when my father died. No longer would he have to face my father each day—the man who was living with his wife. Of course, he had no idea how my father felt, looking at the man who had impregnated *his* wife. If only Ed had known then, would it have made a difference? Would my father have divorced my mother? Would Ed have claimed Neal as his own? With all that deceit out in the open, perhaps my father wouldn't have killed himself; no longer would his be a secret burden to carry. Sure, it might have been the scandal of the year, but once the dust settled, why couldn't everyone have gotten on with their lives? Even now, I still didn't get why my father felt he had to die. Why he'd do something so horrific.

I went out to the pasture, wearing a thick coat. Frost coated the grass like a white sheet and my breath came out steamy. Winter rested heavily on the ground, just as I felt heavy with child. Even though a hush draped the landscape, with all life storing energy, moving slowly, an undercurrent of expectancy vibrated in the trees and bushes as I gazed out across the field. Maybe it was just me, but underneath the dormancy I sensed a stirring.

I didn't know how much time passed, but I sat next to the fence and watched the horses graze and the goats chase each other around. I now only had two old goats, a sheep, and four ducks—aside from Reynolds's two horses. I could have given all my animals away, but I had rescued the ducks when they were babies, and they laid eggs that were great for baking and French toast. The woman who had taken Shayla also took Sassy and her kids. It's pretty hard to resist baby pygmy goats and I missed them, but was glad they had a good home. The woman had a day care and no doubt those goats were getting plenty of attention.

I molded my hands around my burgeoning belly. I still couldn't get used to the idea that a life was growing inside me. A person, someone who would have an identity and personality and look like Jeremy and me.

For the first time since I'd gotten pregnant, I let my imagination wonder what this child would look like. Jeremy's gray eyes and thick hair? My narrow shoulders and knobby knees? A boy, a girl? We hadn't even talked about names and I didn't even know what names Jeremy would like. I used to go through names in the baby book, when I was young and hopeful, before the first miscarriage. I had written down a list in order of my favorites, but that list had been torn up and thrown out years ago. I supposed we would just have to make a new list. Although I knew what name I wanted if we had a boy: Nathan.

"There she is," I heard behind me. I turned and Jeremy waved, his jeans and T-shirt on, no coat. A Montana boy through and through—the cold didn't faze him a bit. No doubt he had smelled the coffee and gotten up. Neal came through the gate, arriving earlier than I'd expected. Maybe he hadn't been able to sleep either. With another wave, Jeremy went back into the house. Neal, looking like he'd had little sleep, came over to me.

"What time did you leave Ed's house?" I asked, giving him a hug.

"About five. I dozed off on Ed's couch for a couple of hours and I think Julie was asleep in one of the bedrooms when I snuck out. I didn't want to wake her. Hey, I want to show you these pictures she found."

We walked over to bench situated near the barn. The day was starting to warm and I shed my coat. Birds sang in the trees and the world seemed new, quiet, hushed in awakening. January first, just one other day like any other, only significant because we humans picked this day to mark a new year, the beginning of a new cycle of seasons. Even so, it felt like a turning point, a point on which my past and my future hinged. A point where I had walked through a door and locked it behind me.

Neal sat close to me, with our legs touching. He pulled out a manila envelope from his coat pocket. "Some of these are from Shirley's photo albums, and a few are from a box we found at Ed's. Look at this."

He withdrew a stack of black-and-white photos. They were the old kind of glossy prints, with the white wavy edges, some a little brown with age. I looked at each one. Pictures of Shirley holding baby Julie, of Julie as a toddler, taking first steps, swimming in a pool, dressed in cute bonnets and patterned sun dresses. I studied them, making my way through the stack, then stopped when I saw a photo of Ed and my father standing together, arms thrown over each other's shoulders. My father looked happy; I guessed this was pre-Neal. Other photos of my father at work, at what looked like a company baseball game, and some with Dave Lerner and men I assumed worked at Penwell Corporation.

The last one startled me for a moment, until I realized it was Shirley who had her arms around my father, posing for the camera, the two of them smiling. I couldn't tell where the photo had been taken, but my father's countenance contrasted to the ones I had just looked at. His face was serious, strained, pained. He looked sick.

Neal sat quietly, and when I got to the last photo and set the stack in my lap, he reached deep into the large envelope and pulled out a smaller white one.

"Here." He handed it to me. Ed's writing scrawled in black ink. *To Lisa. My confession.* "I'm going to see what food I can scrounge up for breakfast."

"We've got cereal, and eggs and bread. Help yourself." I took Neal's hand and squeezed it. "Thanks. I'll be back in soon. I already ate, so just make something for yourself, okay?"

I watched Neal walk through the gate and then let out a breath. I thought about my search for truth, my search for my father, a man I never knew. When I started this journey, I'd had no memory of him at all, but as I uncovered details of my father's life, I seemed to have shaken free bits and pieces of him that clung to my mind in some secret eddy of memory. Now I had a clearer picture of

Nathan Sitteroff, and a better understanding of my family and what forces had shaped and maimed us.

An ache grew in my heart. I missed him, this father I never knew. Yet, somehow my body remembered his arms around me—big, strong protective arms. My ears remembered his voice, his singing to me, telling me nursery rhymes and bedtime stories.

Maybe my hormones were acting up, but I started to cry. Sadness filled me to overflowing, thinking about my father and how unhappy he was. How he'd missed out on watching me grow up—my first day at school, learning to ride my bike, graduating high school. All the benchmarks of my life. And Raff's life. I had no idea what it was like to grow up with a father. I felt deficient, deprived, and yes, a bit resentful.

Why? I asked him. *Why couldn't you have stood up to our mother, just divorced her? Even run away and started a new life somewhere else? Why did you have to die?*

I swallowed hard, past the lump in my throat, and wiped my tears with the sleeves of my coat. I ripped open the envelope and unfolded three sheets of paper. The writing was nearly illegible. Wild and emotional, the words splattered the pages in a sort of mad rant. Ed had been dying when he wrote this, and no doubt terrifically emotional. I strained to read his writing, but once I got through the first three lines, I found myself adjusting to his penmanship, and the recognition came faster.

Confused, I reread the first paragraph, making sure I read correctly. The choppy incomplete sentences forced me to fill in blank spaces and make assumptions. One passage on the second page was smeared, almost as if Ed had tried to wipe out the words with his hand. Some sentences were struck out, with heavy black lines that made dents in the paper.

I read slowly and carefully, and as I read I felt my face heat up, as if a furnace under my cheeks had been ignited. My breath hitched and I held it in, fearing to breathe, fearing to move. With effort, I held on. My hands trembled and I nearly dropped the pages before I made it to the last word on the last sheet.

What I read shocked and terrified me. I had no idea if any of what Ed wrote was true. Like my father on his death bed, Ed's words could have been the ravings of a diseased mind, easily explained away.

For, I knew I would not be able to prove or disprove his claims. As I put the pages down gently on the bench next to me, I closed my eyes and pictured the scene. Perhaps everything he confessed to was true. Or maybe only part of it had happened, and the rest was the product of his guilt-ridden mind. Or maybe it was all a lie.

And, or, or not.

Ed Hutchinson lifts his eyes from the papers on his desk. He watches as his coworker, that wife-stealer, walks out the door of the adjacent office, his coat over his arm and his hat in his hand. Ed glances up at the clock above the window. A few minutes after five. Some of the engineers have already left; others are working late. Ed tries to look relaxed as he gathers his things and heads out to the parking lot, but his hands are shaky. He avoids meeting anyone's eyes and gives a slight wave, mumbling good-by to those he passes as he strides straight down the hall to the large heavy double doors.

Brisk fall air greets him as he exits the three-story building and heads toward his car. He doesn't lift his eyes, but he knows where Nathan Sitteroff parked. He hears the brown Buick start up as he gets into his Cadillac and turns the key. With a surreptitious glance, he checks the rearview mirror and follows the Buick with his eyes as it leaves the lot and turns right, into the street.

Ed feels his rage grow exponentially with each minute passing as he drives in traffic, following the Buick a few car lengths behind. The traffic is heavy, and Ed finds it easy to keep Nathan's car in view, although his anger is urging him to punch his way through. He has no choice but to go with the flow of the cars around him, but eventually he sees Nathan's right turn signal flicker and the Buick going over the off ramp at North Gower Street heading south.

Ed hastily pulls over to a curb as Nathan parks the Buick in a street space. Ed watches as his coworker enters a light blue stucco building. It's in a busy commercial part of town, and as he looks up, he notices floors of rundown apartments above all the small businesses. A blue-collar part of town.

Ed seethes. This is what Shirley has given up her spacious, expensive south-of-the-boulevard home for? Trash litters the streets. Ed spots a wino sprawled against a lamppost. Hispanics and Asians everywhere; few whites in sight. Bile rises to his throat in disgust. No way is he going to let his wife stay here. She should be home, with him. She's his wife, dammit!

Ed storms out of his car and into the building. Once inside, he scans the names on the bank of mail slots lining the wall. Sitteroff. 2-D. He hurries to the back stairs and takes the steps three at a time, then makes his way down the hall until he gets to the apartment he is looking for. When he pounds on the door, Nathan answers, throwing the door open. His face shows surprise.

"What are you doing here?" Nathan asks, his voice far from polite. "You followed me." It's an observation, not a question.

"Where's Shirley? I'm taking her home."

Nathan shakes his head and laughs, which makes Ed fume even more. How dare he laugh at him? "Home? You mean brothel, right? Where you bring all your female conquests to your bed. Now why in the world would Shirley want to go there?"

Ed doesn't move a muscle, and Nathan blocks the doorway. Nathan is a little taller, but Ed is stronger. He can beat the crap out of Nathan; he doesn't doubt it.

"Who's here?" Shirley calls from the back room. The bedroom, no doubt. The thought flames Ed's anger hotter.

"And where's my daughter? Is she in this flea trap with you or at some spic's day care?"

Shirley clearly hears Ed's booming voice. She comes partway into the living room and her eyes show shock at his presence. She instinctively backs up and nearly bumps into the wall. "Just go away, Ed. Don't cause any trouble."

"Trouble?" Ed raises a fist. "I'll show you trouble. You're coming home with me. Now! And where's the kid?"

"She's taking a nap. And you're going to wake her—and get all the neighbors coming out their doors—if you don't lower your voice." Shirley speaks in hushed tones, as if hoping to get Ed to quiet down. It has the opposite effect on him.

He yells, so the whole world can hear him. "I don't give a damn if anyone hears me! You belong home. You belong with me. How can you stand to live in this rat trap? This crap in the ass-end of Hollywood. What's gotten into you?"

Ed starts to push his way past Nathan, but Nathan stops him with his hand. Ed feels strength and determination behind the action. He pauses.

"Listen," Nathan says, "Shirley is staying with me. She's not your property. And you wouldn't have lost her if you'd treated her right. You're a bully—and unfaithful to her. She deserves better."

Ed slaps Nathan's hand away and stares him down. "Yeah, like you're any better? You walked out on your wife—and three kids! Your wife's at home with a new baby, but do you care? How faithful is that?"

Nathan grabs Ed's arm and tries to push him back, but Ed swings and his fist clips Nathan's jaw. As Nathan reacts, letting go to cradle his chin, Ed storms past him and yanks on Shirley's arm, pulling her forcibly toward the door.

"Stop it, Ed!" Shirley starts hitting him with her free hand, on the head, slapping his face, pounding his chest, but he won't let go. "I can't leave the baby!"

Ed's focus is on the door. He doesn't plan to stop his momentum. "Let your boyfriend here take care of her. He's a father; he'll know what to do."

Shirley is shrieking by now, and neighbors are coming out into the hallway or peeking out partially open doors to see what all the commotion is about. Shirley catches the eye of one neighbor and yells to her, "Call the police! Help!"

When Ed hears that, he lets go. Nathan has an arm raised in challenge, but Shirley is between the two men. She reaches over to Nathan and pulls down his arm. Ed hears Julie wailing from a back room. All the noise has woken her up. Great. He hadn't wanted to make this big a scene. All he wanted was to get his wife and take her home.

He feels defeat rush at him as he realizes this is not going to play out the way he planned. He strides over to Shirley and slaps her hard across her face. She cries out and falls to the ground. "Oh, get up and stop whining! You always make everything into a production. Like you're auditioning for a commercial or something."

Nathan puts his arms around Shirley and cradles her, protecting her. Ed fumes even more. Seeing her in his arms is the last straw.

"I'll kill you, Sitteroff. You take your hands off my wife. You have no right to touch her—she's mine."

"And you had no right to touch my wife, either. Did you? But you went ahead and slept with her. How is that all right?" Nathan's eyes are daggers.

Ed can't think of anything to say in response. But Nathan's argument doesn't mollify him; to the contrary, it sets loose such rage that Ed can't help himself. He takes another swing at Nathan, this time connecting squarely in the stomach. Nathan's groans and doubles over. Shirley wraps her arms around him, pulling him back away from Ed.

"Get out!" she screams. "Right now. The police are coming and they'll arrest you. You want that? You want a criminal record? All those times you beat me, I never said a word, never reported you. But, I swear to you, Ed Hutchinson, you lay one more hand on me, or on Nathan, and I'll find a way to get you thrown in jail. And how will that look at Penwell? Maybe you'll lose your job. No one will respect you or look up to you anymore. The happy-go-lucky, swinging, party boy Ed Hutchinson will just be another loser out on the street. So, scram!"

Ed throws Nathan a sour, condescending look. "What a wimp. Won't even be a man and fight. No wonder your wife went looking elsewhere for a real man. Someone who could satisfy her—"

"Why, you!" Nathan starts to lunge for Ed, but Shirley holds him back long enough to allow Ed to turn and storm down the hall. Ed is aware of eyes on him, but what does he care? He doesn't know anyone in this part of town, and he sure couldn't care less what they think of him. Maybe they'll treat his wife differently now—knowing she's living in sin with another man. He hopes he ruined her day.

Fury lifts and speeds Ed to his car, then surges through him as he races back to Burbank. The last thing he wants to do is go home, to his empty, lonely house. He can't abide the thought of walking through the corridors and rooms, no one there to cook and clean for him but his Mexican maid, who can't speak a word of English. What he wants is noise, distraction, the companionship of a warm body, someone who doesn't know him or his name, who will not pass judgment on him or tell him how to act or what to say.

His thoughts keep slipping to the vision of Shirley in Nathan's arms. Despite his disgust, he allows himself to picture them together in bed, naked, intimate. His rage keeps churning, like lava rising, about to erupt.

He gets off at the Burbank exit and turns in at a bar he frequents. He's only a half mile from Penwell. He knows he can find what he's looking for here. He's gone home many a night with a girl from this place, and they weren't cheap and overly made up like the whores he hated to stoop for when desperate. He made good money—his clothes attested to his status. He held a prominent job in the aerospace industry, Why, he helped build spacecraft that would one day go to the moon, and maybe even Mars. That always impressed them. Throw a few bills around at a bar, buy a girl a few drinks—he knew how to win them over. Sometimes they were so impressed they didn't even want his money. They just wanted him.

Ed straightens his tie and puts on his sport jacket. He looks in the rearview mirror, adjusting it so he can see his face. He smoothes his hair and then gets out to accomplish his twofold goal—get sloshed and get laid.

But as the night progresses, Ed finds that the more he drinks, the more keen his pain. He'd hoped to drown out his anger at Nathan and Shirley but the alcohol only exacerbates it. With each passing hour, he grows more furious, more desperate. The two women he approached turned him down, and none of the regulars are here. Sexual tension floods his limbs and he needs release. In a haze, he keeps drinking, hoping he'll pass into oblivion, or something will shake loose. Something has to give. He can't keep up this level of tension much longer.

Nathan! He fixes his ire on this man who has stolen his wife, has makes him look like a fool. And Shirley. After all he'd done for her, given her. The money he lavished on her, gifts, clothes, a car, a beautiful house. And this is the thanks he gets? He could kill them both—and he should. He should drive back over to that dump and strangle the both of them. But, what about Julie? He thinks about his little girl. He never wanted to have kids, but Shirley had insisted, begged. He figured having a kid would keep her home, out of trouble. Get her away from those leering photographers and male models who ogled her and lusted after her. That was the only way he could pry his wife from her ambitions. But now that she has a kid, what good is it? It sure didn't stop his wife from jumping into another man's bed, did it? She just dragged the kid along with her—a witness to her mother's infidelity. Shirley was just another whore. All women turned out to be whores, didn't they? Just like his mother, who had left his father for another man when Ed was ten. They all deserved to be punished.

But what better way to punish Shirley than to take away the man who protected and adored her?

The idea grows as the evening wears on and the alcohol slowly wears off. At closing, the bartender ushers Ed out into the parking lot and the crisp night air sobers him somewhat. Now his anger smolders like a hot coal, radiating in his gut, burning, burning. He pictures his body full of radioactive plutonium as he looks down the dimly lit Magnolia Avenue empty of cars, a lonely street in the November night.

Suddenly, he has the perfect solution to his problem. It is magnificent. Mean, vindictive, and yet somehow poignant in its scope. The irony strikes him in a funny way and makes him laugh. Why should he burn inside? Why not Nathan? He should be the one who suffers.

Without a second thought, almost mindlessly and void of emotion, Ed drives over to the Penwell facility. He parks in the back. Security is minimal, for this is just a warehouse, where prototypes for the engineering projects are stored. Ed is very familiar with this place. He knows exactly where he is going and what he plans to do. His palms get sweaty with the thought of pulling off this crime. He's no criminal, but he knows he won't be able to come up with any good excuse if he is stopped and questioned. He can always claim he is drunk and doesn't know what he's doing. He's sure had enough scotch tonight to validate that story. So, he proceeds in confidence.

He walks to the single metal door on the side of one building. He punches a security code into the pad and opens the door. Might as well look and act as if he's drunk and not snooping around. If any guards are around, they'll find him soon enough. He switches on lights and marches down the hall, but no one comes over; there's no one in the building. Just my luck, Ed thinks, whistling a little, his anger now morphing into glee. Every nerve in his body tingles as he opens the door to a room at the end of the corridor. And then, at one more door, he punches in another code, then pauses. The green light gives him the go-ahead. This is his moment of decision. He can turn around and just go home, forget this.

But, he's come too far. And he knows now there is no other way. Justice needs to be served, and he can't think of a better way to serve it.

With precision and efficiency, with a clear and determined mind, he opens drawers and gathers tools, then sets to work. He disassembles the aluminum outer shell of the SNAP 3 standing over in the corner. They had brought this one over for the photo, for the brochure. And they had posed right there, he and Nathan, and the other members of the team. Ed looks across the room, recalling the photographer's bright flashes and Ed smiling, standing next to Nathan, both of them smiling, and knowing they hated each other's guts. Ed knew the module would be taken back to Distribution. But, no one would know. They'd find out later, when it would be chalked up to a mystery—or someone's mistake.

Ed muses over possible scenarios as he deftly works the screws and removes the assembly. He thinks how he will tell Ruth Sitteroff something that will remove any suspicion. Like how that research project Nathan went on in San Diego was really a top-secret experiment. Something Nate volunteered for, and ended up exposing him to radiation. That would work. If she tried to investigate, she'd hit a wall and assume it was covered up. Any official denial of the "experiment" would look suspicious. Ed snickers at the thought of Ruth making phone calls and getting no answers.

He takes the iridium casing off and lifts out the high-strength graphite blocks that hold the fuel cell. This he doesn't take apart, because he knows the risk. Instead, he finds a box and places it inside, then carefully closes up the RTG. Satisfied it looks untampered with, he pockets three tools, then puts the rest away, closes drawers, turns off lights, and leaves the room, making sure it locks behind him. In the next room, in the closet, he pulls out a contamination suit his size. It's lightweight but bulky. This he places in the box, then heads out.

No one is at the office building—not at three a.m. No security is needed here, when the only things of value are the intellects of Penwell employee geniuses. Hard to steal those, Ed thinks, then laughs at the image of some alien spaceship coming to earth and sucking intelligence from scientists' minds. Just like those sci-fi movies they show in the cinema.

As Ed enters Nathan's small office, he pauses. He thinks how his coworkers would laugh at him if they found out Nathan was living with Shirley. It is bound to get out sometime. Sure, while those two were in San Diego, that was a different story. But, here! He thought once they got back, he'd be able to knock some sense into his wife. Didn't she feel guilty for breaking up Nathan's marriage? How could they both blame him for their affair? This has to stop. It does! Shirley was right. He could lose his job, lose everything he worked hard for, lose his reputation. He is not going to let that happen. He will not let some insignificant, arrogant mathematician ruin his life.

Whatever hesitation Ed feels now vanishes. His anger, renewed and flaring like someone blowing on hot coals, squelches his last vestige of conscience. He closes the office door and dons the suit. He makes sure all the seals are tight and pulls a mask over his face. He knows there's very little chance any of the radiation can hurt him with such short exposure time, but he's taking no chances. He's almost giddy, picturing Nathan sitting at his desk, completely unaware of the danger he is in, unaware that his life, which has poisoned Ed's, is soon to be poisoned too. He plots how he will bury Nathan with work, work he must do alone and not with others. Work that will require long hours behind his desk.

Ed works quickly. Uses a tool to separate the two halves of the graphite blocks, revealing the core. Ed studies this innocuous-looking cylinder. It weighs heavily in his gloved hand. Funny, he thinks. It gives no indication of its danger. It looks simple and unimportant. Ed reaches into the box and pulls out a strip of insulation strapping. He gets the snippers out of the box, and the hammer and nails, then crawls under the large desk. It's deep enough that Nathan could scoot his chair all the way under and still not hit the fuel cell. Ed places it up against the edge of the desk at the far back, underneath where it will never be detected. He holds it in place with one hand while he hammers the strips across the cell, latching it onto the wood.

He wiggles it, then smiles, satisfied. It's perfect.

Ed leaves the room, then puts the suit and tools back in the box. He drives home, careful to follow the speed limit as his heart thumps wildly in his chest. He finds a dumpster in an alley behind a Laundromat and tosses in the suit and tools and graphite blocks. He knows the third floor of his office building is scheduled for renovation in two months. Ed will make sure the desk gets taken to the dump when Nathan gets temporarily moved out of his office.

A wave of joy flows over him, lightening his mood considerably. He walks into his big empty house, but tonight it doesn't feel oppressive and lonely. For the first time in many nights it actually feels good to be home. At some point Shirley will come back to him. It is inevitable. With no one to care for her and support her, she'll have no choice.

Ed smiles and pours himself a drink. She will be desperate, and remorseful. She'll probably beg him to take her back. She will have nowhere else to go.

He downs his scotch in one large gulp and nods, pleased with his decision.

He'll take her back. Oh, yes, he will. And he will make her pay.

CHAPTER 32

I WALKED TO THE HOUSE, numb, reeling. When I stepped inside, Jeremy rushed over. My face must have alerted him somehow.

"Hon, are you all right? Are you sick?" I knew he feared for the baby; that worry floated below the surface of both our minds every waking moment.

"I'm fine, Jer. Just a little shook up. This letter . . ."

I stuffed the envelope back into my pocket. Neal, sitting in a chair reading the newspaper, studied me. "What did it say? Do you want me to read it?"

I thought of all the explaining I'd have to do if he read Ed's insane confession. "Maybe later. It would only confuse you. Let's talk another time, okay?"

"Okay." He shrugged and went back to reading, but I knew his curiosity was elevated. He would just have to be patient. I knew now I'd have to tell him everything, and Raff needed to know too. Someday. But right at that moment, I was overcome with exhaustion and a bit overwhelmed.

"Hey, I made some fresh-squeezed OJ. Sit down and let me get you a glass." Jeremy helped me over to the couch and went and fetched my drink. I didn't realize how shaky I was until I took the glass out of his hand. "Anne called. Wanted to wish you a happy New Year. Asked if you planned to meet her on Wednesday. She seemed fired up to get back in shape—her New Year's resolution."

I chuckled. "She does that every year. I'll call her in a while."

Neal dropped the newspaper onto the coffee table, having read the sports section thoroughly. "Well, I gotta get back. Planning to watch the Rose Bowl game on my TV. Got some friends bringing pizza." He came over and kissed my cheek. "Take good care of that little squirt in there. Uncle Neal's going to teach him how to throw a baseball when he's big enough."

I gave Neal a sideways glance. "He?"

Neal shrugged. "Or she. I recall you had a pretty good arm yourself."

"Don't forget it."

Neal laughed and waved me off.

Jeremy walked Neal to the door and showed him out. I drank my juice, still shook up, trying to wrap my mind around the implications of Ed's letter. Had my father truly been murdered? Is that what he had tried to tell Dave Lerner in the hospital? *"So easy to forgive others, but so hard to forgive myself . . . it was all my fault."* Maybe he meant Ed's murdering him was all his fault, that he had provoked Ed, pushed him over the edge. That made sense.

I pulled out the envelope from my pocket and reread the first paragraph.

"Lisa, I am so sorry for the pain I caused you, all of you. I didn't know about Neal. I swear, if I had known, I would have never done what I did. I was angry, so angry. I was out of my mind. I can only hope and pray you will forgive me. Your father did. He forgave me. I didn't want his forgiveness. I yelled at him. I wanted him to curse me, damn me to hell. But he didn't. I told him what I'd done, but he forgave me anyway. I don't understand, not at all. Why didn't he tell me about Neal? Why? I have lived with this horrible guilt all these years. And it has eaten away at me, little by little, like poison in my blood. I am glad I am dying. I can't take it any longer."

A great sigh broke loose from inside me. I had come to the end of my father's story; I had navigated this convoluted maze and now where did that leave me? What had compelled me, those months ago, to uncover the clues to his death? Some crazy notion that I could help Raff? Where had that come from?

Perhaps my buried memories of my father, a man who had imprinted his goodness and love on my heart so long ago, had nudged me toward truth. Toward a need to vindicate him somehow, clear his name of the false labels slapped upon him: cowardly, suicidal, heartless. I had supposed that if I searched for him, searched hard, I could find him. And I had. At least, I believed I had.

It struck me that I had no idea where my father was buried. In Los Angeles somewhere? Or would his family have buried him in New York? I made a mental note to call my uncle Samuel and ask. I was long overdue to pay my respects. Although, my father seemed more buried in my heart than in some cemetery plot.

Jeremy came into the living room and sat beside me. He looked out the window at the winter morning, at the garden that lay dormant, the rose bushes cut back, leafless, stunted. I gazed at the alders across the street, their spindly bare arms outstretched to the heavens. They seemed to be yearning for spring.

"What a beautiful day," he said, stroking my hair. "A new year. Full of promise."

He looked down at my belly and smiled at the life growing inside me. I felt strangely sad and joyous at the same time. And although I felt heavy with my pregnancy, heavy with anticipation and, admittedly, a little fear and worry over what the future held, something lifted off my heart. Some burden, a reprieve of sorts.

For years I had carried around my own poisonous guilt—for my failings as a dutiful daughter, my inability to make my mother happy, my lack as a wife. Even guilt over my miscarriages, as if I had done something wrong, so that I didn't deserve to have children. And now, after having found my father, Nathan Sitteroff, these self-recriminations were dissolving. I felt light, as if flying.

I looked at Jeremy, the only man I had ever loved, oh so loved, and my heart soared like a helium-filled balloon escaping into the heavens. I thought of the man in the restaurant—the man who had spent the better part of his life looking for answers. Looking for truth.

I'm free, he said.
I mouthed the words along with him.

C. S. LAKIN

WRITES NOVELS IN NUMEROUS genres, focusing mostly on contemporary psychological mysteries and allegorical fantasy. Her novel *Someone to Blame* (contemporary fiction) won the 2009 Zondervan First Novel competition 2009 (published October 2010). Lakin's *Gates of Heaven* fantasy series for adults (AMG-Living Ink Publishers) features original full-length fairy tales in traditional style. Already in print are the first books in the series, *The Wolf of Tebron. The Map across Time*, *The Land of Darkness,* and *The Unraveling of Wentwater*, with two more to follow. In addition to her mysteries and fantasy series, she has also written the first book in a Young Adult sci-fi adventure series: *Time Sniffers.* Her contemporary mystery *Innocent Little Crimes*, now published by Imajin Books, made the top one hundred finalists in the 2009 Amazon Breakout Novel Award contest, earning her a Publisher's Weekly review which stated her book was "a page-turning thrill-ride that will have readers holding their breaths the whole way through."

Lakin currently works as a freelance copyeditor and writing mentor, specializing in helping authors prepare their books for publication. She is a member of numerous writers' and editors' groups. She edits for individuals, small publishing companies, and literary agents, and teaches workshops and does critiques at writers' conferences, and occasionally guest blogs on writing sites. She has a blog featuring weekly in-depth writing instruction and tips on publishing and thriving as an author (**www.livewritethrive.com**) and she specializes in manuscript critiques (see **www.CritiqueMyManuscript.com**).

Lakin lives in Santa Cruz, CA, with her husband Lee, a gigantic lab named Coaltrane, and three persnickety cats. You can connect with her on twitter: @cslakin and @livewritethrive. Or visit her author page on Facebook: **www.facebook.com/C.S.Lakin.Author**.

Don't miss these other novels of drama and suspense by C. S. Lakin:

INTENDED FOR HARM

AT THE HEIGHT OF THE Vietnam War in 1971, Jake Abrams is desperate to leave his oppressive home in Colorado and begin a new life in college in LA, but his dreams are waylaid when he meets Leah, an antiwar protester who pushes him into marriage and family. Jake tries to juggle school, his job, and raising four children, but Leah turns to drugs and drinking, and finally runs off with her rock band, leaving Jake reeling.

When he falls for Rachel and marries her, his children rebel. And when Joseph, their love child is born, Jake makes the same fatal mistake his own father did--he shows favoritism to this divinely gifted boy who has the power of healing. After Rachel dies in childbirth, bringing Ben into the world, Jake turns his back on God and buried himself in denial. His children are wild weeds, and as they grow, the older sons' resentment of Joseph's gifts fester until they can take it no longer. The family hides a dark secret of murder, which Joey threatens to spill out of righteous indignation and fear of God, and the only way to stop him is to kill him. The intend harm for him, but God has other plans for Joseph, and in a divinely orchestrated twist, years later Joseph confronts his brothers, who do not recognize him. True to the Bible story this is patterned after, Joseph is reunited with his estranged brothers, and Jake finally welcomes his long-lost son back into his arms, which brings closure and healing to his hurting family.

***INTENDED FOR HARM** is available at all online retailers as an ebook.*

A THIN FILM OF LIES

THE STORY TELLS OF A homicide detective, Fran Anders, whose next case throws her into the lives of Mike and Alisa Jepson, a couple whose marriage is disintegrating fast. When leads coming into the precinct point at Mike Jepson as guilty of murder, Fran watches the damage wrought on this couple, yet is unable to ignore the incriminating evidence. When Mike ends up arrested and in jail, Alisa takes comfort in a friend—Dee Dee—who moves in with her but soon becomes her worst nightmare. Mike hires a PI who uncovers clues to who is setting Mike up, but Alisa is caught in a trap before Mike can protect her. Although Fran reaches out to Alisa during her crisis of faith, she is unable to stop events from barreling toward a crash. Yet, despite the tragedies to follow, Fran sees how God has used the Jepsons' trials and pain to bring Alisa back into His arms, with hope that Mike might follow suit.

Fran is a dedicated, no-frills cop who takes her job seriously but with a wry sense of humor. She suffers from the unbearable heat, from unrelenting allergies, but does not suffer fools. As much as she wants to please her superiors, she knows her true boss is—God—and she answers first and foremost to his leading, which sometimes takes her beyond the call of duty, often to the ire of those around her. A middle-aged, divorced, single parent with two teens, Fran hopes someday to find a great man and remarry, but she's not holding her breath. Right now, she just wants to be a good cop and mother, and use her faith to help those she encounters in her line of work learn there's someone "up there" who truly cares for them.

A THIN FILM OF LIES *is available at all online retailers as an ebook.*